40
hours

Kathrin Lange

LUME BOOKS

LUME BOOKS

First published in 2021 by Lume Books
30 Great Guildford Street,
Borough, SE1 0HS

ISBN 978-1-83901-446-8

Typeset using Atomik ePublisher from Easypress Technologies

www.lumebooks.co.uk

PROLOGUE

Darkness. Enveloping him like a blanket, winding around his body, his waist, arms and legs. He can practically feel it against his bare skin.

Bare skin?

The idea seems to be toying with his very sanity. Why is he naked? The question cuts through the murkiness in his mind, prompting further questions. His arms. Why can't he move them? And why do the muscles on his sides tremble when he tries to raise his arms? Something is pressing against the soles of his feet. Something rough, like unseasoned wood. Fine splinters pierce his flesh.

He feels no pain.

The quivering of his muscles, the pricks in his skin – vague impressions, at best. Every sensation is two-dimensional, like shadow figures on a wall.

He stops his futile struggles and, instead, concentrates on his eyelids. He is sure they are open, but the darkness doesn't clear. He squeezes his eyes shut. And reopens them. His lashes are stuck together, but he manages to pry them apart. The darkness hasn't vanished, but a faint light is now shimmering within it. A light at the end of the tunnel, a blurred gray rectangle.

Where am I?

The question floats to the surface of his mind, yet immediately plummets back into the depths of his confusion.

He blinks. Once. Something is pricking his eyes. He blinks again, his eyes feeling like stones sinking deeper into their sockets. He blinks a third time and realizes that the gray rectangle in front of him is an open door. His sense of balance returns, but what he feels now contradicts everything he expected. He is regaining consciousness, isn't he? Then why isn't he *lying down* like normal? He is vertical and has no idea why.

So he waits.

His skull feels as if it has been stuffed with cotton, but his other senses are slowly emerging. A continual beeping. A regular rhythm. He raises his head, which had lolled forward onto his chest. And all at once, the pain strikes.

At first, dull and distant. An unrelenting burning in his hands and feet, agony unlike anything he has ever experienced.

A shiver shoots through his body. A sob catches in his throat as he finally grasps what has happened. He blinks again, shuts his eyes as tightly as possible. Tears them open again. And then it all becomes clear: In front of him, a wall. Gray tiles, evidently very old. The open door. Pale light streams in, but he cannot see past it.

He turns to the right, gazes down his outstretched arm. Sees something red but has no idea what it might be. Then he catches sight of his hand. Twisted, jutting into the air, a claw, every muscle tensed.

His trembling intensifies.

He looks in the other direction. The same horrific sight: an outstretched arm, the red thing, which he now vaguely recognizes as a rope encircling his upper arm. The contorted fingers, and in the middle of his palm – an iron-gray jewel. No! His mind wants to scream, but he resists.

He jerks his head back, banging his skull against something hard. He glances down. His body is stretched out like his arms. His first impression was not mistaken - he is in fact almost naked with only a cloth wrapped around his waist, nothing more. Goosebumps cover his bare chest, as red rivulets trickle down it and bright spots dance before his eyes. Is he hallucinating? And then he notices something else.

Fascinated, his gaze comes to rest on a third iron-gray object: the one protruding from his feet.

A nerve-wracking beeping fills his ears. An IV drip is suspended close to his face, its tube tickling his cheek. And now he realizes what the beeping is: a cardiac monitor. If he twists his head around as far as possible, he can see it. The bright spots on his chest! They aren't hallucinations. They are electrodes recording his heart functions.

He leans his head back against the wood.

And the all-important realization finally dawns on him, dissipating his confusion. The gray objects are nails.

He opens his mouth.

And laughs.

PART ONE
HOUR 1 TO HOUR 14

Father, forgive them,
for they know not what they do.
(Luke 23:34)

CHAPTER 1

Faris Iskander's eyes were burning. For some months now, he had been unable to shake his leaden weariness. Months in which he had only slept a few hours each night. Months in which, whenever he finally managed to fall asleep, he would wake up with a panicked scream from the same recurring nightmare.

The desperate weeping of a child. Fire, closing around him …

He rubbed the bridge of his nose with his thumb and index finger. He had been standing at the bedroom window for ages with a mug in his hand, staring out into the gloomy night, which was now gradually giving way to an equally dismal morning. An old Metallica CD was playing in the background. Faris had turned the volume down out of consideration for the other tenants, but he could still hear James Hetfield singing *Ride the Lightning*. He had the song on repeat. He closed his eyes but reopened them right away, because his eyelids felt like sandpaper. The sun wouldn't rise for another hour. Besides briefs and t-shirt, the only thing he wore was the leather strap Laura had bought him on their vacation in Egypt. He never took it off. The Arabic characters branded into it – *Laura and Faris* – were barely legible at this point, which seemed to him an appropriate analogy for their relationship. Laura had left him, a good two years ago now. Even the explosion which had nearly blown Faris to pieces hadn't inspired her to return.

Flash before my eyes, sang Hetfield. *Now it's time to die.*

It had been stiflingly hot in the city over the past few days, almost like the height of summer, but a thunderstorm had hit Berlin the night before, and the temperature had dropped noticeably. So much so that Faris had closed the window during the night because he felt cold. He could see his reflection in the windowpane. His face a pale oval, floating ghostlike in the darkness, framed by longish black hair. His shirt's V-neck revealed part of the dark red burn scar that stretched across his chest and right bicep. He couldn't take his eyes off it. As dawn broke, his silhouette faded. He sighed and once again became aware of the cup in his hands. With a weary smile, he toasted himself, put the mug to his lips, and drained it.

The bitter liquid seared his throat, and he grimaced.

The protagonist in the Metallica song woke up from his nightmare, and Faris envied him. He remembered the box on the top shelf of his wardrobe where he normally kept his gun. He exhaled deeply through his nose. The box was empty at the moment, as Faris had recently been suspended from duty as an officer of the State Office of Criminal Investigations.

Pull yourself together, he admonished himself. There was nothing worse than people who wallowed in self-pity. Yet he wasn't immune to it, in the small hours of the morning. That was when the memories crept up to torture him, and the pictures and sounds he had been carrying inside for ten months refused to leave him in peace.

The child crying. A wave of fire rolling towards him. Then blood and corpses. Soft moaning. Heart-rending screams …

Faris shut his eyes and rubbed his forehead. He had gotten lost in his thoughts again. Now, it was completely light outside, and Metallica was still playing in the background. Three floors below him the Berliners had long since begun their day's work – he would gladly have joined them.

He gazed into the empty cup and sighed, then turned away from the window and walked out of the bedroom. He crossed the tiny corridor without glancing into the mirror on the wardrobe. He knew, without looking, that his eyes had the burning expression of a crashing junkie. In the long term, lack of sleep was worse than anything dropped cold turkey. He walked over to the kitchen counter and picked up the

4

glass carafe to pour himself a refill. The coffee had been stewing on the hotplate for hours and now tasted like sludge. Whatever! At least it was hot.

As Faris took another sip, a chirping noise interrupted his thoughts. For a moment, he had no idea where it was coming from, but as it grew louder, he recognized the sound. It was the new phone he had bought the day before.

Faris cast a disgruntled glance at the coffee maker before switching it off, setting the mug down, and going in search of his phone. It wasn't in his leather jacket or in the jeans he had carelessly dropped onto the bedroom chair the night before. He finally discovered it underneath the Haruki Murakami novel he had left open on the bedside table. He fished the phone out and stared sullenly at the flashing blue display. *Private Number*, it said. After spending two hours yesterday trying to understand all the unnecessary functions of the device, he had lost all interest in entering his few contacts, but even if he had, it wouldn't have been of any use to him now. The caller had blocked their own number.

After stepping back to the bedroom window and casting a glance at his barely-recognizable reflection, he took the call.

"Iskander."

"*As-samu alaikum*, Faris." The voice was electronically distorted to a deep bass.

The blood in Faris's veins froze.

CHAPTER 2

As-samu alaikum.

It had been ten months since Faris had last heard these words, and he was immediately catapulted into the past. He was no longer in his bedroom, but in the foyer of the Klersch Museum. The blue lights from a battalion of squad cars were flashing across the walls beside him. His stomach felt as though it had been turned inside out, and the headset which his colleagues from the Forensic Science Institute – FSI for short – had given him was pressed against his ear. In front of him, on the other side of the richly ornamented double doors, behind which the kidnapper had barricaded himself with his hostages, a child was crying. It was the soft, hopeless noise made by someone who knew they were going to die.

"One question, Faris." Faris heard desperation resonating in the voice of the hostage-taker. "A dark-skinned man, a belt, ten kilos of explosives. What do you get when you combine these?"

In a vain attempt to keep his acute fear under control, Faris clenched his right hand into a fist. He had to sound calm, he knew that much. He slowly ran his tongue across his lips.

"Let's talk," he said. "I was born in Alexandria. I'm a Muslim, like you …"

But the hostage-taker interrupted him mid-sentence. "Wrong answer." The sound of the voice made something in Faris's chest tremble.

"Listen …" he shouted. But it was too late.

"*As-samu alaikum*, Faris Iskander," the hostage-taker said.

A second later, the door exploded in a rain of splintering wood as a wave of fire rolled towards Faris and engulfed him …

The memory of the detonation and the merciless pain that followed caused Faris to gasp for breath, standing there in his bedroom.

The caller on the other end of the line laughed, the distortion of his voice causing it to sound like a rattle. "You remember!"

Faris's heart raced. He closed his eyes, took a deep breath. "Listen," he began, shivering as he realized that this had been the last word he uttered to the bomber last year.

"Tsk, tsk," was the caller's disparaging reply. "You should've learned something by now."

Faris gritted his teeth. "Who are you?"

There was a slight pause before the caller replied. "You have no idea?"

The explosion in the museum … Faris saw himself flying through the air, slamming into the wall … He had been too seriously injured to get back up, but before he lost consciousness, he had stared through the opening where the door stood shortly before. Smoke blocked his view, and as the members of the special task force stormed the hall, his strength evaporated. He lost consciousness. The last thing he saw was a dismembered finger with red nail polish, lying directly in front of him on the blackened tiles and pointing at him as if in accusation.

Faris cleared his throat. *Keep calm.* This unknown caller couldn't be the bomber from back then. That was impossible!

"Our FSI guys swore that no one could survive an explosion like that," he murmured. Ben Schneider, one of the FSI experts, had put it more colorfully: "That blew the bastard sky high."

The man laughed again.

Faris swallowed hard. "What do you want?"

"Check your inbox!"

Faris pressed his lips together and tapped his phone's small screen. He opened his email app, and his inbox appeared. There was a single message in it. Faris opened it. No message, just an attachment. Faris clicked on it.

A film began to play.

The first three or four seconds of the footage were blurred. Nothing but a few gray and black splotches, and a little green and blue. Heavy breathing could be heard, a noise reminiscent of suppressed sobbing, then incomprehensible mumbling. In the next moment, the image sharpened.

And Faris froze.

He could see a man lying with outstretched arms on a cross-shaped beam construction. The picture zoomed in on his pale face, which was covered in blood that streamed from under a crown of thorns. His eyes were unnaturally widened in horror. The camera panned down the body of the man, on whose chest light-colored circles could now be seen. They seemed totally out of place at first glance, but on closer inspection, Faris realized they were electrodes.

The picture zoomed out again.

Another man appeared in the frame, but although the first man could clearly be seen, this one had his back to the camera. The hood of his sweatshirt was pulled down over his forehead, completely hiding his face. He was holding a long nail and a heavy hammer.

Faris drew his breath in sharply through his teeth. Powerless, he watched the man with the hood kneel down next to the other one. How he set the tip of the nail in the center of the victim's palm.

And raised the hammer.

The blow was powerful, driving the nail through flesh and bone, and deep into the wooden beam below.

Faris watched it in petrified horror.

The victim threw his head to one side, but didn't cry out, simply moaning softly. Blood gushed from the wound, looking almost black.

"Shit!" mumbled Faris.

The hooded figure then nailed the other hand down. When he turned to his victim's feet, he began to tremble, however. This time his blow wasn't precise enough to drive the nail all the way through the feet and into the wood. The man had to take another swing. The crucified man moaned again as the nail was driven through his feet.

Breathing heavily, the man set the hammer aside. For several seconds, he remained kneeling. Finally, he picked up two red ropes, which were carefully coiled beside the cross. He wrapped one around each of his victim's upper arms and tied it off. He then attached an array of cables to the electrodes on the crucified man's chest and connected these to a small box, which he clamped to the man's loincloth. Only then did he get awkwardly to his feet. He stepped to one side and disappeared from the picture. A regular, rapid beeping began, and Faris guessed that a cardiac monitor had been switched on.

A heavy chain rattled.

The cross started to rise. The camera zoomed in on the victim's face, and Faris couldn't take his gaze from the man's eyes. Something new was mixing with the horror in them – a kind of blankness, suggesting the influence of drugs. This was probably why he hadn't yelled out in pain. The picture zoomed out again to show the entire scene. When the cross had almost reached its vertical position and gravity began to pull on the man's body, he threw back his head and let out a scream. The beeping of the cardiac monitor quickened. Faris's stomach lurched.

For a moment, the camera continued to display the picture of the crucified man, then the screen went blank. The film was over.

Faris stared at the small screen. With his free hand, he brushed his hair back from his sweaty forehead.

He slowly lifted the phone back to his ear.

"Did you watch the video?" came the caller's voice.

"Yes."

"Good," said the man on the other end of the line. "Trust me, it's genuine."

Faris didn't reply.

The caller gave a derisive snort. "The man on the cross is in my power. And now I want you to do the following. Go to the Bismarckstraße subway station. Now."

Faris clenched his fingers around the phone. "And then?"

"I'll tell you the rest when you get there. Oh, and Faris … If you notify your colleagues or anyone else, I'll know."

9

Faris remained silent. The line was quiet for a moment. Then the caller laughed again. "Feeling stubborn, Faris? Remember the explosion in the museum …"

The back of Faris's neck began to tingle.

"No one else at this point," the unknown caller insisted.

At this point?

Faris's mind stumbled over the words, but he had no time to think about them because the caller now hissed: "Bismarckstraße subway station. You've got five minutes!"

Without another word, he hung up.

Alexander

"EVIL IS THE PRICE OF FREEDOM," said the voice from the light.

Alexander let the hammer fall and blinked. He wanted to take a step forward, wanted to see what the figure hiding behind the glaring aureole in front of him looked like. But the voice had forbidden it. "DO NOT LOOK AT ME!"

And Alexander obeyed.

Instead of staring into the light, he now looked up at the crucified man. Something warm tickled his face, and he wiped his forehead.

"YES," said the voice. "IT IS FINISHED."

Trembling, Alexander took a deep breath. His gaze rested on the man on the cross. "It's not right," he murmured. His heavy heart was hammering so hard he felt sick.

"EVERYTHING IS AS IT SHOULD BE," the voice countered. "TRUST ME!"

Alexander choked, but then he nodded. His tears blinded him, and he could feel them running down his cheeks. They felt cold. Cold like the stone in his chest.

The crucified man was looking at him. Alexander could see the pain in the familiar eyes.

"HE WILL NOT SUFFER," the voice from the light had assured him. "I WILL SEE TO THAT."

But was it right? Alexander groaned under the attack of nausea that swept over him. A delicate sound reverberated in his head. A rhythmic, penetrating beeping. He hunched forwards.

"YOU MUST BE STRONG!" the voice commanded.

He straightened up. "Yes," he whispered. "I want to be!"

"THEN GO NOW. CLEAN YOURSELF! YOU ARE FILTHY!"

He obeyed, leaving the tiled room, which contained nothing except the cross, the man upon it, the bright light. And his own horror. He stood in front of one of the sinks, which were mounted in a row on the wall beneath the now dull mirrors. The light illuminated him from behind, and he could clearly see that the voice was right. Blood was splattered across his face, speckling his pale skin as if a painter had splashed him with a large brush full of paint.

The red cried out his guilt to heaven.

Alexander turned on the faucet with a trembling hand and washed himself thoroughly, as the voice in the light had commanded. When he looked up again, he finally knew that everything was good now.

For a moment, he looked himself in the eye.

"I have crucified my father," he whispered.

And then threw up in the sink.

CHAPTER 3

God in Heaven! I really am too old for stuff like this!

Sister Xaveria of the Order of the Merciful Sisters of St. Charles Borromeo felt sick. *It's your own fault!* she chided herself. She was almost eighty years old, so why in the world had she agreed to go on this trip to Berlin? Why was she sitting here in this stuffy, over-filled subway instead of where she belonged – in her convent? She was trying to conceal her nausea as best she could, but her companion, Sister Bernadette, seemed to have noticed anyway.

"Are you feeling alright?" the almost-forty-years-younger nun asked, leaning forward to peer more closely into Xaveria's face. "Your nose looks a little pinched!"

Xaveria could see her reflection in the other woman's eyes. She smiled ruefully.

"It's just the air down here," she offered as a placating explanation. "As soon as we're back above ground, I'm sure I'll feel better right away."

In silence, she asked God to forgive this white lie. It wasn't the subway's stuffy air, rank with fumes and the stench of oil, that had upset Xaveria's stomach. It was the excitement. The exhilaration of leaving her cloister in Trier for the first time in twelve years. And not just to leave it, but to go on such a thrilling trip as this.

She would get to see the Pope tomorrow!

If that wasn't reason enough to have butterflies in her stomach, then nothing in the world could move her anymore, Xaveria thought.

Sister Bernadette nodded as she threw what had to be the hundredth glance at the subway map the thoughtful hotel receptionist had given her.

"We have to get out at the next station," she said. "We're meeting the others there, and then we'll have to change to the U2."

Sister Bernadette's face was unusually splotchy, and Xaveria realized that the younger nun was also nervous. They had planned to attend one of the numerous morning services being held today across the city between eight and nine. They wanted to head to the Olympic Park afterward and take in a few sights. They would enjoy a nice day in Berlin, like perfectly ordinary tourists.

The subway train shuddered before coming to a jolting stop in the middle of the inky black tunnel. Xaveria found herself staring at a section of graffiti, a serpentine shape she couldn't decipher. The train car's internal lights had ripped the image out of its usual darkness, and Xaveria suddenly wondered who would descend into the murky depths of the Berlin subway system to decorate its walls.

Other riders were obviously entertaining more dismal thoughts. "Hopefully, not a bomb threat," a young man beside Xaveria remarked. "Otherwise we'll be sitting here for a while." But before she could respond to this, they started moving again.

The young man looked relieved.

Sister Bernadette reached for the finger-thick glow stick she had bought from a souvenir seller and planned to wave in the air at the papal Mass tomorrow. It was hanging around her neck from a rainbow-colored band, and she was playing with it nervously.

Xaveria reached for her hand and held it firmly.

"When we get back home, I'm never leaving the convent again as long as I live!" she declared.

Sister Bernadette remained respectfully silent.

Xaveria patted the back of the younger nun's hand one more time before releasing it. "I mean, the Pope! What else will be left for an old nun like me to experience?"

Sister Bernadette laughed. "Listen to you talk! You'll end up outliving half the convent, considering how fit you are."

Xaveria was about to tell her about how badly her back ached after spending two nights in that horribly soft hotel bed, but she decided not to. She would keep that to herself. Except for her father confessor, she hadn't told anyone about the heart arrhythmia that had started up a couple of weeks ago.

Because that wasn't important.

In his unending wisdom, God would decide when to call her to Himself. The only thing Xaveria had ardently asked Him for was to survive the next day and a half. Tomorrow, in the stadium, she would try to snag a seat in the front row. Maybe she would even be able to shake the Pope's hand at the end of the service. After that, she would confidently and happily meet her maker at whatever point He deemed best.

She caught herself smiling at the thought of this.

The train slowed down and entered one of Berlin's vast number of subterranean stations.

"We're here." Sister Bernadette stood up from her uncomfortable plastic seat and craned her neck. "There are the kids and Father Wagner."

She pointed out the window at the platform where a group of twelve teens and a man in a black suit and clerical collar stood waiting for them. A white sign hung above their heads.

Bismarckstraße was written on it in black letters.

The Bismarckstraße subway station had three separate entrances. Faris reached the one across from the Commerzbank and paused to catch his breath as he studied the clock. Relieved, he determined that he had reached his destination in the stipulated time frame. The five minutes weren't up yet. He ignored the glass elevator waiting at ground level and hurried down the staircase that took him to the first station level. Down here, the air was still stuffy from the heat of the previous days, and the pervasive, repulsive stench of the subway system engulfed Faris. He came to a stop next to a kiosk selling coffee and croissants. On his way over, he had considered calling his colleagues at the state police, but then abandoned the idea. At this point, it seemed too risky. For as long as he didn't know what the guy on the other end of the line was planning and whether the video he had sent him was real or not, he should play it safe and assume that somewhere out there a crazy fanatic had a man under his control. It was better to err on the side of caution and do what the man demanded.

As Faris stood in the subway station, wondering what to do next, the phone in the pocket of his hoodie started to go off. He pulled it out and answered.

"What now?" he asked, forcibly slowing his ragged gasps.

He was out of breath from running, and adrenaline was still tingling in his veins. He could feel the tension throughout his body, the prickling sensation of the hunt. He had missed that for the past ten months, but this was the first time he had realized the extent of that feeling.

"Out of breath?" the distorted voice of the caller asked derisively.

Faris decided not to respond. "What next?"

Just a few meters away, two uniformed colleagues from the federal police strolled past. They were chatting, and Faris thought about subtly attracting their attention.

"Don't even think about it! If you give them any kind of signal, there will be consequences!"

A convulsion shot through Faris's shoulders. He spun around, scanning the walls and ceiling. He came to a stop when he caught sight of a camera, the lens of which pointed directly at him.

"Yes," he heard the caller say. "I can see you, my dear. Say 'cheese'!"

Faris clenched his jaw. The officers walked past him, only three steps away. Faris caught a few words of their conversation; they were apparently chatting about the church conference currently taking place in Berlin. One of the officers glanced at Faris, and he was aware of being scrutinized a little longer and more intensely than the other travelers. He was used to that. Although his Egyptian ancestors had carried Berber blood in their veins, which gave his skin a lighter tone, his Arabic heritage was easily recognizable from his dark brown eyes, black hair, and distinctive nose. What wasn't written on his face were the facts that he had moved to Germany as a small child and was a

German citizen. Nor could anyone know about his position as an officer in a special police squad – at least, his position when he wasn't under suspicion.

"Go down the escalator," the caller ordered. "To the platform for the trains to Ruhleben."

In order to reach that particular platform, Faris had to descend one more level, cross the platform for the 7 Line, and then take the escalator back up again.

"What if I refuse?" he asked.

"You really want to take that risk? I'm sure you remember what happened the last time you failed." The stranger hesitated, then added: "*Boom!*"

Faris shut his eyes to the horror. He fleetingly thought he could hear the explosion in the museum, believed he was once again surrounded by searing fire. It wasn't easy to shake himself out of the memory that swept over him. He moved stiffly toward the escalator. A man in a suit, carrying a briefcase, caught him and roughly shoved past. Faris hardly heard his hastily murmured apology.

"Good!" the man on the phone remarked, as Faris went further underground.

He wound his way through the crowd on the lower platform and took the escalator back to the upper level. Once there, his eyes fell on a concrete wall which had previously been painted with a garish jungle scene. Now, it was decorated with a cartoonish depiction of a church choir. The pale violet tones chosen for the new painting's design clashed sharply with the yellowish-green color of the rest of the station.

Dozens of people were standing on the platform, waiting for the next train to pull in. All sorts of civil servants on their way to work, and at least an equal number of church conference attendees, who stood out in their rainbow-colored scarves.

Faris's attention was drawn to two women in their early thirties. They stood close together and looked uneasy. The reason for this seemed to be five young men who had apparently been out drinking all night. They were leaning against a grim-looking poster for a death metal festival and kept staring at the women a little too attentively. Faris registered the five men's baseball caps, their low-slung pants and, above all, the fact that all of them had their hands hidden in their pockets.

Before Faris could figure out what the guys were up to, several people on the opposite platform began to sing a hymn. *Jesus Christ, my sure defense*, Faris heard. He couldn't make out any other lyrics, since at this point the caller spoke up again.

"Did you know," the distorted voice said absently, "that this isn't the first ecumenical church conference? There have already been two others, one of which was also in Berlin. But this one is something special, isn't it? For the first time, Catholics and Lutherans will be allowed to take communion together. That's amazing, Faris, don't you think?"

"If you say so." Faris's eyes fell on one of the rainbow-colored conference posters that had been plastered around Berlin for weeks. He had memorized the Bible verse on them by now, as had every other Berliner who had mastered the art of reading.

"That poster," the caller exclaimed, indicating that he could still see Faris. "Don't you think the motto is a little awkward?"

Faris forced himself to nod. He tried to search for the camera as inconspicuously as possible and discovered it to his right, inside a niche below the edge of the ceiling. It was mounted right next to an old station clock, with a face that glowed bluish-white. It was an ordinary surveillance camera, like the dozens of others located around Berlin's subway stations. Faris felt his jaw tense again.

The bastard had hacked into the municipal transportation system.

"Read it!" the man ordered.

"What?" Faris mumbled in confusion. He had been momentarily distracted.

"The poster. Read it out loud! Now!"

Faris's hand tightened around the phone, but he once again obeyed. In a flat voice, he read: "*Speaking the Word of God Boldly.*"

A young woman in business dress, who had also arrived on the platform, stared at him skeptically. However, when she saw that he was on the phone, she relaxed and smiled at him. One of her incisors was a little crooked. *What a brave new world*, Faris thought. *No one worries anymore, when they hear someone babbling.* He gazed at the woman for a moment, wondering how he could unobtrusively convince her, and all the other passengers, to leave the station.

"Don't waste your time on her!" the caller ordered. "She's not important. Do you know which Bible verse this motto is based on?"

Faris tried to relax his muscles. "I'm Muslim."

"Oh, I know that, my dear! And I also know that you're only Muslim on paper." A subdued chuckle crackled through the phone. Due to the electronic distortion, it sounded like the buzzing of an insect. A very aggressive insect. "I'll tell you. The quote comes from the book of Acts. Chapter four, verse thirty-one to be precise. *And they were all filled with the Holy Spirit and spoke the word of God boldly.* I assume you have no idea how this verse starts, either."

Faris never got to answer, because at that moment, laughter rolled toward him, and a group of people were carried up to the platform on the elevator for Line 7. He saw two nuns in light-blue habits, a man in a clerical collar, and about a dozen teenagers. They all seemed to be in high spirits. They were chattering and laughing as they walked so close to Faris that he had to move to give them room. One of the nuns – who had to be at least eighty – a woman with very pale eyes, studied him briefly and then gave him a friendly smile. Her younger companion was wearing around her neck one of those cheap glow sticks that had been for sale everywhere over the past few days. Faris nodded at the two nuns and shifted his focus back to his conversation.

"No," he murmured. "I don't."

As he said this, the leader of the baseball cap gang, a young man in a white sleeveless shirt sporting a tiger tattoo on the bulging muscles of his right bicep, zeroed in on the priest. He immediately pushed off from the tiled wall and took a step forward.

Faris watched him.

"Shit!" he heard the caller exclaim.

"Good morning, Father," Tiger Boy said with a grin, as he assumed a provocative stance in front of the priest. "Heading off to play with more little kids, are you?"

Two of his buddies trailed him, while the other two remained where they were.

The priest decided not to react to the challenge. He said something to the older nun, who retreated a short distance.

Tiger Boy's face darkened. It was obvious he didn't like being ignored. Faris gritted his teeth. If he didn't intervene, things might quickly get out of hand. Without weighing the pros and cons of what he was doing, Faris stuck his phone in his hoodie pocket and moved forward.

"Hey!" he called, drawing Tiger Boy's attention away and to himself.

Out of the corner of his eye, he noticed the two guys who had been reluctant to join Tiger Boy set themselves in motion. Faris pointed in their direction and shook his head rapidly. The two of them stopped in their tracks and the other passengers increased the distance between themselves and the small group.

Tiger Boy stared fixedly at Faris. "What do you want, *kaffer*?"

Faris forced a smile as he brushed off the insult. "If you get out of here right now," he amiably declared, "there won't be any trouble."

Tiger Boy threw back his head and burst out laughing. Faris suddenly remembered the caller on his phone, but he didn't have time to care about him at the moment. "Get out of here!" he ordered. "Leave these people alone."

"Who do you think you are?" The young man advanced a step.

Faris didn't move. He slowly slid his right shoulder a little forward, seeking to stabilize his stance.

Two of the gang members planted themselves on either side of their leader, while the other two nervously shifted their weight from one leg to the other.

"I think we should …" the priest began, but Faris interrupted him with a wave.

"Move back!" he ordered him, without taking his eyes off the gang.

The sounds behind him indicated that the priest was doing as he had asked.

"Come on," he heard the cleric whisper. "We should do as he says." Then steps, moving away.

The volume of the group's conversation made Faris think that they had retreated to the foot of the escalator which led up to Wilmersdorfer Straße. He would have preferred them to leave the station altogether, but at least the remaining passengers were giving them a wide berth. He willed himself to relax, pushing to the back of his mind memories of a very similar situation just a few days earlier.

The gang leader lunged quickly to punch him in the chest, but Faris grabbed his hand, jerking it hard and causing the man to lose his balance. At the same moment, he ducked under the heavily muscled arm and straightened up behind Tiger Boy's back.

"I told you to get out of here!" he hissed in his ear.

Tiger Boy tried to break free, but Faris's grip on him was firm. Without much effort, he twisted the guy's wrist. The young man stood up on his toes with a yelp of pain. The burn scar on Faris's chest began to throb dully, but he was used to that. The pain no longer presented a hurdle.

"Let go of him, *kaffer*!"

The noise of a switchblade opening was loud in the silence that followed this demand. One of the two flanking gang members now took a small step forward.

Faris looked straight into his eyes. "If you don't stop moving," he said quietly, "I will snap your buddy's wrist, as well as his elbow," he snarled provocatively through his teeth. "And yeah, that's extremely painful."

To reinforce his words, he increased the pressure on the wrist just a little. Tiger Boy gave a stifled cry of pain.

The blade was lowered.

"That's good," Faris said. "As soon as you idiots vanish, I'll let him go."

The young men obeyed without any protest. They turned toward the exit and slid past the nuns and teens who fearfully moved as far from them as possible. The priest was the only one who didn't move. He glared darkly at the four guys, and it seemed that at least for this one moment, he wanted to seem bold and daring.

Faris waited until the men had disappeared. As the sound of an approaching train rushed toward him out of the tunnel behind, he pushed Tiger Boy away. The guy spun around, but instead of also taking to his heels, he leaped at Faris. His punch, fueled by extreme frustration, was aimed at his opponent's head.

However, Faris had not merely reckoned on this happening – he had hoped for it. He pivoted deftly, sending his right fist into Tiger Boy's stomach. The young man folded in half. Faris followed this with an uppercut and almost delivered a third blow. In the nick of time, he caught himself and stepped back.

Another punch would have been unnecessary.

Tiger Boy landed on his knees, clutching his stomach with both hands. Blood was gushing from his nose, staining his wife-beater shirt. Woozy, he swayed a little as a warm gust of air, smelling of oil and metal, announced the approaching train.

Faris's hair fluttered. He grabbed Tiger Boy and yanked him roughly to his feet. He then turned him around and shoved him toward the escalator.

"Get lost!" he said, coolly. "Or I'll keep going." Half of his words were swallowed by the sound of the train's brakes.

This time, Tiger Boy had had enough. On unsteady legs, he stumbled toward the escalator.

The train pulled to a stop. The doors opened with a hiss and released people onto the platform. The priest hurried toward Faris with the older of the two nuns in his wake.

"Thank you so very much!" she cried, her pale eyes filled with concern. "Are you hurt?"

Faris rubbed his aching fist and tried to suppress the satisfaction this short fight had catalyzed inside him.

"No." He avoided the nun's efforts to grasp his hands to examine them herself, jerking his head toward the train. "You should get on, or you'll have to wait for the next one."

The priest nodded. "Thank you," he added as well.

With a sweeping gesture, he herded his sheep into a car. "Come along, Sister Xaveria!" he called to the eighty-year-old nun.

She was the last to board, and before she stepped onto the train, she sent Faris a timid, slightly admiring smile.

As he watched the doors slide shut behind her, Faris pulled the phone from his pocket. "Are you still ...?"

"Of course," the caller interrupted him. "That was really impressive, Faris! Especially the moment you got yourself under control and didn't hit him again."

Faris glanced up at the camera, whose black eye seemed to be mocking him. He didn't know what to say, so he didn't reply.

The train pulled out. The draft tousled Faris's hair as the train disappeared into the tunnel, leaving him standing on the platform.

"*Boom*!" the caller said.

The next second, the blast wave from an explosion lifted Faris off his feet and hurled him against the wall.

CHAPTER 4

Alexander

"EVIL IS THE RESULT OF HUMAN FREEDOM."

How much time had passed? Alexander didn't know. He had collapsed at the base of the sink, but now the soft voice was calling him out of the darkness. On quivering knees, he got back to his feet, propped himself up on the dirty porcelain sink, and gazed out into the hallway.

A delicate, splashing sound was echoing in his head again. Something was dripping onto the floor.

Blood. It was trickling out of the crucified man's wounds.

He instantly felt sick again.

"PULL YOURSELF TOGETHER," the voice ordered sternly. But he couldn't manage that. Alexander vomited again, this time missing the sink. Just as it had over the years whenever the whip had met bare skin, his vomit splashed across the old tiles. It felt like his stomach was trying to escape through his throat. His tongue was coated with an acrid taste. His eyes teared up as he stood for the second time.

He felt so unbelievably weak.

"IT'S ALL RIGHT," the voice from the light said. "YOU DON'T NEED TO FEEL ASHAMED."

Actually, he felt a little better. Alexander turned around, trying to gauge his status. Much better, in fact.

"Who are you?" he asked into the light, blinking. The figure within it was still just a blurry outline. "Are you an angel?"

The voice laughed quietly. "MAYBE THAT'S WHAT I AM. A MESSENGER."

The crucified man groaned, and Alexander gave a start. "A messenger of the Lord?" he whispered.

The laughter broke off. The voice said nothing, and Alexander was afraid he might have annoyed the messenger. *The messenger of the Lord.* He felt cold. The light was very bright, but something propelled him toward it. He wanted to see the angel, to touch it.

"STOP WHERE YOU ARE!" the voice said harshly.

Alexander hastily stumbled back to his old place, "O … of course," he stuttered.

It was quiet for a moment.

"YOU ARE FORBIDDEN FROM COMING ANY CLOSER TO THE LIGHT," the angel declared. "REGARDLESS OF WHAT HAPPENS."

Alexander nodded. "What should I do now?" he asked, tentatively. Blinded as he was, he could only make out the vague shape of the angel lifting his arm and pointing at the man on the cross.

"TELL ME ABOUT HIM," the voice ordered Alexander. "TELL ME EVERYTHING."

Faris couldn't breathe.

The explosion's blast wave had hurled him back against the tiled station wall, and everything around him had briefly gone black. As he regained full consciousness, sound was the first sense to return. Through the ringing in his ears, he could hear a child sobbing, but in the next second, he realized that he was mistaken. The crying wasn't coming from a child but from an elderly woman not far from him. She was covering her mouth with both hands, staring at the chaos through wide eyes. Someone was screaming loudly in anguish. A man close by kept babbling, "Oh God! Oh God! Oh God!" He seemed to be uttering this through a mouthful of cotton, as blood welled out of his mouth and nose.

Faris turned over, coughing. The impact had knocked all the air out of his lungs. His burn scar hurt, but this was the old, ordinary pain, nothing new or more intense. This time, the fire surge hadn't reached him, just the blast wave. He propped himself against the wall and tried to get his bearings.

"Have mercy, Lord!" screeched the woman close to him. Faris's ears rang shrilly.

He lurched to his feet, his head clanging like a giant bronze gong. He shook it a little to try to clear the haze that was collecting before his eyes. A figure swayed toward him. A woman in a red dress.

She was saying something to him, but he couldn't understand it. Her voice also sounded muffled and distant.

The fog finally cleared. The clanging in Faris's skull subsided, and only the ringing in his ears remained. However, it, too, was abating, so that he could now understand the woman.

"What did you do?" she screamed.

He coughed one last time, spitting out soot and ash. He then straightened up to his full height. "What are you talking about?" He still felt breathless.

"You blew up the train!" the woman shrieked.

Faris couldn't wrap his mind around this. His gaze fell on the phone that the explosion had blown a good distance away from him. He glanced at the camera which had been sheltered from the blast wave by its niche. The black camera lens stared apathetically at Faris. He ignored the woman's screams and filtered out all the other sounds around him as he concentrated completely on his phone. The screen was glowing through the dust that was slowly starting to settle over everything. To Faris, the distance to the device seemed further than to the moon, but he managed to stumble over to it, lean over, and pick it up.

"*And after they prayed,*" he heard the distorted voice of the caller, "*the place where they were meeting was shaken.* That is the first part of the verse we were talking about earlier, Faris. Isn't that marvelous? So very ironic!" A quiet chuckle was half lost in the ringing in Faris's ear.

The hairs on the back of Faris's neck rose. "You bastard!" he gurgled.

He thought about the group of teens who had boarded the train along with the nuns and the priest, but this image was overlaid by another picture that appeared in his mind. *A severed finger with red nail polish.* With his free hand, Faris ran his fingers through his hair, pressing down on his skull as if he could save it from imploding. As he did this, he discovered that he was bleeding from a head wound. He stared for a moment at the blood on his fingertips before wiping them quickly on his jeans.

"You blew up that train!" he stammered into the phone. "Why?"

The woman in the red dress was still beside him. "You!" she yelled. She tried to grab Faris's arm, but he yanked it from her grasp. Out of the corner of his eye, he caught sight of two men in suits who were staring at him and whispering to each other.

The caller laughed once more. "How ironic, Faris!" he said sarcastically. "They think you set off the bomb, and do you know why? Because you look Arabic, that's the one and only reason."

Faris tried to shake off the woman by moving a few steps away. A man was lying there, stretched out on the floor. A young girl was kneeling next to him, pressing her hands on the bloody something that had once been his abdomen.

"Papa!" she sobbed over and over.

Faris pointed at the two of them. "Help them!" he ordered the woman in the red dress. "Call for an ambulance."

That worked. The woman left his side.

Faris turned his back on her and the man with his daughter.

"Why did you blow up the train?" he yelled into his phone.

The blood from his wound was trickling into his eyebrows, and he wiped it away with the back of his hand.

The two suits were still whispering with each other.

"They think they can read who you are from your face," the caller sniggered. He was then quiet for a moment before continuing: "Do you remember the video I sent you?"

"The crucifixion?" Faris took a deep breath. He might finally learn what all this was about. "Of course! Why?"

"Somewhere out there, Faris, in your lovely Berlin, a man is hanging on a cross. Your task is to find him. As long as his heart keeps beating, all's well. However, if it stops before you find him … Well, as the Bible verse says: *the place where they were meeting was shaken.* I think you know what I mean." He paused.

Faris struggled for clarity in the midst of his confusion. "But his heart could stop beating any moment," he whispered, his voice tinged with horror.

The stranger disagreed: "No, it won't, and do you know why I'm so sure about this?"

Faris shook his head. The muscles in his neck felt as if they were made of wire. "No."

"Because God is on my side, Faris. As I hammered the man on the cross, I put myself into *His* hands. Do you know what divine judgment entails?"

Faris nodded.

"You let God decide," the caller explained, nonetheless. "If *He* agrees that my effort is just – and I'm firmly convinced that He will – *He* will make sure that the crucified man survives for the next forty hours. Forty hours from right now, Faris. Do you understand?" He sounded more than amused now; he sounded enthusiastic. "Oh! And to answer your question, I blew up the train to show that I'm serious about this."

As he was speaking, Faris pressed the balls of his thumbs against his wound to stop the bleeding and lowered his arms. He simply couldn't believe what he was hearing.

"Why?" he whispered, glancing at his watch. It was a few minutes after eight.

"Maybe I want to be a beacon for others. Who knows? By the way, starting right now, my instructions about not talking to your colleagues are null and void. You are welcome to bring SURV on board." He hesitated, then added: "Find the man on the cross within the next forty hours. Or *as-samu alaikum.*"

The prolonged beep on the phone indicated that the connection had been broken. In Faris's ear, it sounded like a scream.

"*As-samu alaikum,*" he croaked.

This was a corruption of the traditional Arabic greeting. It didn't mean *peace be with you*. It meant *death be with you*. Faris had no time to mull over the meaning of these words, because at this juncture, the two suits screwed up their courage and stepped toward him resolutely.

"Hey, you!" one of them called.

He was taller than Faris and at least thirty kilos heavier. He had clenched his hands into fists and was holding them in front of his massive body like a prize boxer.

Faris lowered his phone. "What?"

"Don't move!" The second man now took a step closer. He looked slight compared to the other man, but he also looked wildly determined. The eyes that met Faris's were filled with loathing.

Faris had made no move to leave, but now wasn't the time to point out this detail to the two would-be heroes. He wanted to say something, but the slim man didn't let him get a word in. "I said, don't move!" His voice cracked.

And before Faris realized what was happening, he jumped forward and grabbed his arm.

Faris took a step back. "What are you …?"

"Shut the fuck up!" the man growled.

His grip was firm. As Faris tried to jerk away, he realized the muscles in his right shoulder were no longer following orders. Something must have gotten pulled in the explosion. Nonetheless, he was still able to free his arm from the man's grasp.

"You blew up the train," the skinny one yelled.

Faris sidestepped the one built like a boxer, but the man refused to give up. "You son of a bitch!" he wheezed, as he pulled his arm back.

Faris blocked his punch. "You're making a m …"

His shoulder protested, and his head was swimming with the after-effects of the explosion. He saw the next blow coming, but couldn't avoid it quickly enough. He was hit in the neck and then, immediately, in the mouth. As his lip split, he could taste blood.

"Listen!" he cried. "I'm a poli …."

"He's the bomber!" he heard the skinny guy shout. "I saw the whole thing. He was holding his phone and set the bomb off with it."

While all this was going on, a group of onlookers had been gathering to watch, and the mood of the crowd was growing blatantly aggressive. To Faris, the people with their pale, dusty faces, burning eyes and slumped postures looked like zombies.

"Probably ISIS," someone mumbled.

Faris's ears were roaring. He focused on the boxer, but he sensed a movement behind his back. He was about to spin around, but it was too late. Arms tightened forcefully around his chest. He tried to slip free, but in vain.

"Damn it!" he cursed. "You're making a mistake! I'm a policeman!"

"Terrorist!" a shrill voice screeched. It belonged to the woman in the red dress who was still kneeling beside the injured man. He could see the hate in her eyes.

He once again tried to break out of the arms locked around him, but then he gave up. He allowed the boxer to step close to him and grab his upper arm, while the man who had caught him from behind took hold of the other one. With legs apart, Faris stood there, surrounded by all the ghostly figures with their hate-filled gazes, feeling as if he were trapped in Dante's *Inferno*. A kick in the back of his knees almost knocked him to the floor. He fought to keep his balance.

"Bastard!" the boxer hissed in his ear.

At this moment, several uniformed officers stormed down the half-buried stairs.

"Police!" one of them called.

He stopped on the next-to-last step and took in the scene. His experienced eye picked out Faris as the focal point of the turmoil. He gave the others a terse order, then reached for the holster at his side and unsnapped it. After taking care of that, he descended the last two steps and headed for the mob.

"What are you doing here?" he asked.

The woman in the red dress took over as spokesperson. "What are we doing?" she cried. Faris could hardly bear her shrill, plaintive voice. "We caught the bomber, that's what we've done." She pointed at Faris, and with an icy knot in his stomach, he realized that her fingernails were long and red. "That's him!"

The mob started moving, clearing space for the officer who was instantly in front of Faris.

"Jochen." Faris lowered his head in relief. He had known Sergeant Jochen Baumgarten since his time at the police academy.

"Faris?" Baumgarten's eyes widened in astonishment.

Faris simply nodded. Out of self-respect, he once again tried to twist free from the two men, but to no avail. The hands wrapped around his arms were like vises.

"What are you doing here? I thought you were sus ..." Baumgarten broke off. "Let him go!" he ordered abruptly. "This man is a police officer."

The fingers finally loosened a little.

"Are you serious?" It was the slim man who spoke. He looked uncertainly back and forth between Faris and Baumgarten. His shirt collar was drenched with blood that had seeped from a cut on his neck. The fabric was sticking to his dusty skin.

"Hurry up!" Baumgarten bellowed.

The next moment, Faris was free.

"Thank you." Faris took his colleague's proffered hand and shook it. His shoulder protested with a dull pain.

"What are you doing here?" Baumgarten repeated once more.

Faris thought about the caller and the phone that he must have stuck in his pocket at some point, prior to the confrontation with these self-appointed guardians of the law. He swiftly felt for it. "I ..." he was reluctant to speak openly in front of the onlookers. "I'm a witness, just like the rest of them."

The woman in the red dress refused to meet his eyes, as did the boxer, but the skinny man wasn't backing down. The man's face revealed a mixture of relief, shame and doubt.

Baumgarten pointed at Faris's bleeding lip. "I assume these two heroes gave you that, right?" The officer recognized a punch-inflicted wound when he saw one.

Faris wiped the blood off his lip with his thumb, studied it, and nodded.

"Do you want to file a complaint?" Baumgarten asked. A typical question for him. For many years, he had cultivated an attitude of "us cops versus the rest of the world".

Faris looked at the boxer. This time, the man didn't avoid his gaze. His chin jutted out stubbornly, like a child caught doing something naughty.

"No," Faris said quietly. "They were just trying to do the right thing."

The boxer now lowered his eyes.

Faris swallowed down a sigh. He looked Arab, and there was nothing to be done about that. If he had been in these two men's shoes, he might have suspected him, too.

CHAPTER 5

"God, you look like shit!"

Sitting on the remnant of a concrete pillar, Faris lifted his head at the sound of the deep voice. A man, around the age of fifty with a slight paunch and thinning hair, was standing behind the paramedic tending his lacerations. The man's eyes reflected the horror everyone was feeling, at the chaos that reigned in the completely demolished subway station.

"Hi, Paul." Faris inhaled through his teeth. The paramedic had just sprayed something onto his forehead that burned like hell. "It's nice to see you, too."

The man was Paul Sievers, Faris's partner at SURV, the Special Unit for Religious Violence. Paul grinned, but Faris had known him long enough to know when he was just pretending. The suffering around them touched him deeply.

Faris's gaze traversed the rubble, coming to a stop on the disfigured body of a woman in business clothes. Try as he might, he couldn't tell if this was the woman with the slanted tooth who had smiled at him earlier. The paramedics had hung a tarp in front of the man with the stomach wound and his sobbing daughter. A short distance away, a man was screaming long and loud for someone named Hilde. Everywhere he looked, Faris now saw his colleagues. They were helping the first responders with the victims, interviewing the witnesses, and spreading comfort as best they could.

Faris wanted to lower his head, but the paramedic wasn't done bandaging his wound yet.

"Please stay still," he said.

Exhausted, Faris obeyed. "Why are you here?" he asked Paul. "I thought you were on vacation. Weren't you supposed to go to the Baltic with Christa?" That was what Paul had told him the last time they had spoken on the phone.

Paul had shoved his hands into his back pockets, and now he shrugged. "There was a lot to deal with in the office because of the church conference, so we postponed our trip for a few days." He glanced around. "It looks like that was a good call."

Faris followed his partner's gaze. Things were escalating behind the suspended tarp. "Papa?" shrieked the girl, but nobody seemed to be paying attention to her. "Out of the way!" Faris heard the paramedic shout, followed by the familiar sound of a defibrillator. The girl began to whimper.

Faris gritted his teeth. His paramedic finished dressing the wound. "That's it." He leaned over the opened case sitting at his feet, pulled off his gloves, and tossed them inside. "You should go to the hospital for a complete examination," he advised his patient before walking off. "You might have a concussion."

A uniformed police officer, whom Faris only knew by sight, approached them. "Can you walk?" he asked as he watched the paramedic move away.

Faris nodded.

"Then please leave the station. Report up on ground level to officers who are taking state …" he broke off as Paul turned toward him. "Hey!" he exclaimed in recognition.

Paul nodded at him. "Faris is one of us, Fred."

The officer turned back to him. "A fellow officer as witness?" he asked with a certain degree of satisfaction. "Great! I bet we'll get more useful information from you than we are getting from the civilians."

"Islamists?" an older woman moaned as she was led past them. She stared malevolently at Faris. "Wretched monsters!"

Faris shook his head. The caller's distorted voice echoed through his head again, followed by the museum bomber's last words.

Wrong answer!

"This wasn't an Islamist attack," he said, instantly wondering how he knew this with certainty. After all, he had no idea who they were dealing with. The caller had distorted his voice, so Faris couldn't tell anything about him.

Paul looked at him quizzically. "Let's go up to street level."

The first members of the forensics team were arriving. In their white suits, they looked like astronauts, and Faris and Paul gave them a wide berth to avoid getting under foot. On their way up to the surface, Paul paused in front of a small flower shop: "What *exactly* happened?"

"A bomb. That's all I know. It must've been on the train that entered the tunnel right before the explosion." Faris recalled the elderly nun with the pale eyes, the group of teens that had been with her. He felt a hard knot form in his chest as his heart clenched up.

"Why are you here? You never take the subway," Paul asked, insistently. The stairway up to the exit was short, and the gray light made the dust in the air shimmer.

Faris pulled his battered phone out of his jacket pocket and held it up. "I was sent here."

Paul furrowed his forehead, perplexed.

"This morning, I got a phone call. A distorted voice dropped a bunch of hints and ordered me to come here."

"Ordered?" Paul cocked an eyebrow. "How?"

They reached the surface. Practically all of Wilmersdorfer Straße was blocked by police vehicles and ambulances that were parked all over the sidewalks and road. Flashing lights sent twitching reflections onto the surrounding buildings, and more and more vehicles were arriving with blaring sirens. People were running around all over the place. Even up here, the paramedics were tending to the wounded. Faris watched as a zinc casket vanished through the door of a hearse. Dozens of officers were standing close together, speaking with witnesses or discussing what to do next.

And on the edge of the chaos lurked the inescapable news vans from the local television and radio stations. The first cameras were already running.

Faris pulled Paul between the ambulances. "There's a chance it's the guy from the Klersch Museum." His voice sounded husky.

Paul's eyes widened. "The museum bomber? That's ridiculous. He blew himself up in that explosion." His eyes fell on a man in a navy-blue suit standing off to the side of the action. He was talking to several other suits, obviously politicians. A dark look flitted across his face, but he turned back to Faris. "Honestly, partner. There's no way it could be the culprit from back then."

Two paramedics emerged at the top of the stairs, carrying a stretcher. The body upon it was completely covered with a white sheet. The two men hesitated and looked around, as if lost.

The hairs on Faris's arms stood on end. "*As-samu alaikum,*" he whispered. "Those were the words the person who called me used in greeting."

"Shit!" Paul blurted out.

Faris gulped and nodded in agreement. Like a gentle breeze blowing past his ear, he heard the child weeping. "*As-samu alaikum.*" He had to clear his throat.

Paul recognized the extent of his concern. "What now?"

"The caller gave me a message." Faris watched the two paramedics who simply decided to set their stretcher down between the ambulances. "He said that this bomb wouldn't be the last."

The dark hood of another hearse rounded the corner.

Faris reached into his pocket. "And there's one other thing that you're not going to like," he said grimly, reaching for his phone.

Alexander

"I don't know what to say," Alexander whispered.

"YOU DO," the voice of the messenger countered. "TELL ME HOW EVERYTHING STARTED."

And, strangely enough, Alexander knew what the messenger meant. "It began on a Sunday at my grandma's," he murmured. He

35

remembered. "Christmas. It was Christmas, at my grandma's."

And then he began his story.

Grandma has made rouladen, and Alexander has found a piece of tough meat on his plate. The longer he sits hunched over it, poking at it, the more it looks like the carcass of a small animal. The dark sauce resembles dried blood, and although he dutifully chews and chews on it, he can't swallow down the next bite.

He honestly tries, but when he gets close to forcing the chunk of meat down his narrow throat, he gags. He almost spits the chewed meat onto the white tablecloth. Grandma comes to his rescue at the last second, holding her hand flat underneath his chin to catch the disgusting remnants.

"That's all you can manage?" she asks, sounding friendly and concerned. Alexander's eyes dart over to his father, but he is deep in a conversation with his grandpa, so Alexander nods uneasily.

With that, Grandma picks up his plate. "You don't need to finish it," she says with a smile. "When I was your age, I didn't like rouladen, either." She stands up and starts to clear the table. All the others are done with the meal by this point. "Just wait a second. It's time for dessert. You'd like some, right?"

Alexander is so happy, which is why he forgets to glance in his father's direction. As he turns his head, he notices that Father is watching him. He swallows hard, but his father's face doesn't reveal any displeasure. Alexander thinks he is safe.

Sitting next to him, Mother is drawing little eights in the starched white tablecloth with a fork handle. She refuses to make eye contact with either him or Father ...

Alexander broke off.

"It feels horrible to think about all this," he sniffled. "I felt so betrayed by Mother!"

"YOU MUST FORGIVE HER," the angel said. "SHE'S YOUR MOTHER."

Alexander nodded before resuming his story …

A few minutes later, Grandma returns with the dessert. Vanilla ice cream with hot cherries, his favorite!

Delighted, he gazes at the plate sitting in front of him. He can hardly wait for the others to get their servings so that he can start eating. His stomach growls loudly, since he hasn't eaten much until now. He reaches for his spoon and submerges it into the mixture of red sauce and slightly melted ice cream. The first spoonful is halfway to his mouth, when Father's strident voice cuts through the air.

"Stop!"

He doesn't speak loudly, but Alexander freezes instantly. As his spoon jolts to a stop, a little of the red sauce drips onto the tablecloth, leaving a fat spot.

Father's eyes are fixed on him, and he feels as if he is being examined by an x-ray machine. "You didn't honor Grandma's meal," Father declares. "Which commandment did you break?"

"Werner, please!" Grandma's voice is pleading. The look he gives her is cold, and she falls silent.

Tears pool in Alexander's eyes as he realizes that the ice cream is now completely unreachable. Right in front of him, the delicacy melts into a pool of redness rimmed with white cream.

"Which commandment?" his father repeats, mercilessly.

Mother doesn't move.

Alexander glances at his grandma for support, but she too no longer seems capable of standing up to Father. She is staring awkwardly at her own plate. Alexander's eyes threaten to well over.

"Don't cry!" Father demands. "Which commandment?"

He forces himself to swallow. It feels like he is about to choke on Grandma's dried animal meat. "The fourth one," he finally whispers.

"And what does it say?"

"Honor your father and mother, that your days may be long in the land …"

37

Alexander sniffed. The memories from that day broke over him like a storm. He could still feel the spasm that cramped his small body as the first little part of his heart transformed from warm flesh to cold stone.

"KEEP GOING," the angel commanded.

And he obeyed.

He has obviously recited the commandment correctly, since for a brief moment his father's gaze softens. For a fleeting second, Alexander hopes that he will still be allowed to eat his ice cream, but that hope is in vain.

Father leans forward, reaches for his plate, and pulls it to the center of the table. "You won't be having dessert," he declares. "While the rest of us eat, you will consider what the words you just uttered mean."

Alexander's eyes search for those of his mother and grandma, but neither of them meet his gaze. Only Grandpa stares furiously at Father, but when the latter shoots him a warning look, he lowers his head as well. Alexander watches as his mother's spoon sinks into the ice cream and lifts it to her mouth. She swallows with difficulty.

Alexander stopped.

The voice of the messenger in the light was very soft and friendly. "THAT IS GOOD. THAT WAS A GOOD START. THANK YOU!"

"The disappointment made me feel sick," Alexander continued. The tears he was struggling to keep back tasted bitter in his throat. "That was the first time I felt …" He paused.

"THAT WAS THE FIRST DAY YOUR FATHER FELT THE BURDEN OF HIS OWN SINS," the messenger explained.

Alexander wasn't sure, but he thought he could hear fury in the other voice.

CHAPTER 6

"This was just a warning?" Paul's eyes widened as he heard what the caller had said.

"The only reason the train exploded was to show us that he's serious," Faris confirmed. Every fiber of his being was taut. "There's obviously another bomb somewhere, and if this really was just a warning, I guess that the second one will be significantly larger." He swiped through his phone's files until he found the email with the video. "He sent me this." He turned the phone so that Paul could see the film. Faris watched as his partner's face moved from horror to increasing bewilderment as the gruesome events played themselves out on the screen.

By the time the video ended, Paul looked completely baffled. "I don't get it," he mumbled.

"I don't, either. I don't know much more than you do. All I have is what the guy told me." Faris cleared his throat before continuing. "This man here," he tapped his phone. "He's somewhere here in Berlin, and he's hooked up to a heart monitor."

Paul waited for him to say more, but Faris could already see recognition dawning in his eyes. Paul was a seasoned policeman, and in their work together at SURV, they had seen some of the most bizarre, horrifying things.

"If that man on the cross dies ..." Faris didn't need to finish the sentence.

Paul fell back a step. "Oh, God!"

Faris nodded slowly.

Paul needed a moment to gather his thoughts, but eventually straightened his shoulders. His eyes swept the area, coming to rest once more on the tall man in the dark blue suit he had noticed earlier. The man's name was Martin Andersen. Faris knew that Andersen was the head of State Police 5, the department that handled state security matters. The investigation into this bombing fell under his purview, and he was here on site to gain a sense of what had happened.

At that moment, Andersen's conversation came to an end. He exchanged a few final words with the local politicians beside him, then discovered Faris and Paul. He walked over to the two of them and held out his hand to Faris.

"Detective Iskander, isn't it?" He was a carefully coiffed, clean-shaven man with penetrating blue eyes and narrow fingers with seemingly manicured nails. "Someone was just telling me that you witnessed this attack." He studied Faris's dust-covered body from head to shoes.

Faris nodded, choosing to keep to himself the fact that currently, he wasn't *actually* a detective. "This morning, I got a phone call that prompted me to come to this location." He ignored Andersen's questioning eyes. There would be time for details later on. He left out the story of the altercation with the gang members and gave a brief summary of how the train had exploded.

Andersen's jaw tightened. "You're saying that you received a call that *prompted* you to come here. What does that mean?"

"The caller sent me something that you should see."

Before he could play the video, one of the politicians Andersen had been speaking with joined them.

"Marvin?" The man's face was gray. Faris had seen him somewhere before, perhaps on TV. The man was probably from one of the senate departments.

Andersen turned toward him.

"The Senator of the Interior is on his way." The man rubbed his eyes as if he could wipe away what all he had already seen.

Andersen nodded and then turned back to Faris. "Did the caller provide any clues that could help us classify what happened here? Islamist terrorists? Radical right-wingers?" Since the NSU case, which had initially been dubbed the *Döner Murders* and later turned out to be one of the biggest cases of right-wing capital offenses in the history of the BRD, the state police always considered the possibility of neo-Nazi terrorists.

Faris shrugged. His head and shoulders still hurt, and the persistent ringing in his ears hadn't subsided. "You really need to see the video."

"Marvin – the Senator of the Interior," the man from the senate urged.

Andersen looked thoughtful. "I'll be right there." However, he didn't immediately follow the man to the dark limousine that had just come to a stop at the end of a long row of rescue vehicles. Instead, Andersen turned back to Faris. "I have to go justify myself to the Senator. Arrange for a ride to Tempelhof so you can answer more questions about this unknown assailant." Tempelhof was the internal nickname for the building on Tempelhofer Damm that held the offices of Department 5. "I'll watch your video later. Show it …"

Faris raised his hand to interrupt Andersen. "If it's all the same to you, I'd like to join my colleagues on Keithstraße and start working on the investigation." Keithstraße was the location of State Police 1, the department in charge of personal crimes under whose auspices SURV fell.

"What makes you think this is an SURV case?" Andersen asked.

During the interruption caused by the man from the senate, Faris had forwarded the video to the point that showed the man nailed to the cross. He now held his phone out to Andersen. "This is what I received right before the explosion."

Andersen's expression was inscrutable. He glanced up silently, watching as the Senator of the Interior climbed out of the limousine where he was instantly engulfed by a crowd of people. "Understood," he decided. "You seem to be right. This really does look like an SURV case. Go ahead and go! I'll follow as soon as I can."

Jenny woke up because someone out in the hallway was shouting, "Dieter!"

She remained lying where she was without moving – on her side, one hand under her face, the other behind her on her back. This was how she often slept, ever since the pediatrician had advised her, six years ago, against sleeping on her stomach. The guy out in the hallway yelled "Dieter!" again.

Jenny hollered: "Dieter, get out there, or I'll drag you out myself!" She then glanced up.

The underside of another mattress was hanging above her head. A sagging metal frame composed of numerous iron rings, intertwined like the mesh of a chainmail shirt Jenny had seen several months ago in Rothenburg. When she and her best friend Pia had arrived at the youth hostel the day before yesterday, all that had still been available was this bunk bed. The two girls had argued for a while about who would sleep in the upper bunk, but Pia won out in the end.

"Dieter, don't be an asshole!" The voice rang out a third time. "Just get out here!"

Jenny held back a grin. Besides the dozens of church conference attendees, the hostel was currently lodging quite a few young men who were obviously going to some rock festival. Most of them were wearing ripped jeans and leather jackets. At supper last night, Jenny had caught sight of one guy with long, pitch black hair, whose biceps and neck were covered with tattoos. He had smiled at her over the salad bar, and for some reason, Jenny thought he looked sweet. Perhaps she would run into him again today.

She sat up with a yawn. Thanks to their other four roommates, who had stayed up chatting until way past midnight, she hadn't slept well. Two of them had transitioned to snoring so loudly that it had almost been comical. Fortunately, the four graces had dragged themselves out of bed before six this morning and were long gone. Jenny and Pia had taken grateful advantage of the opportunity to snatch a little more sleep.

Jenny now reached for her watch, which she had cautiously stashed underneath her pillow; the result of being a long-time veteran of hostel stays. She rubbed the sleep from her eyes and peered at the time. Eight twenty-five. Perfect!

She swung her feet contentedly out of bed.

"Dieter!" The voice in the corridor shouted again. This time, it sounded farther away and muffled as if it had rounded several corners.

"Dieter, Dieter," Pia mumbled sleepily from the upper bunk. "Hopefully, nothing bad's happened to you."

Jenny grinned. "He might be lying dead in the Landwehrkanal." Yesterday, she and Pia had visited a Rosa Luxemburg exhibition, and afterward, the two of them had discussed the labor leader's death for some time.

The bed springs above Jenny creaked, and Pia's tousled blonde head appeared over the edge. "Sleep okay?"

Jenny yawned again. "After the bears left the forest, yes." She stretched. "A little short, but that's alright." They had a full day ahead of them. They wanted to attend two Bible studies, a worship service at the Gedächtniskirche, and a few other events.

Jenny's thoughts drifted back to the long-haired guy from last night. Why in the world hadn't she introduced herself?

Standing up, she walked over to the window and stretched again. The sky looked gray. It was too bad really, since apparently, until yesterday, it had been fairly warm and sunny here. "The good Lord could've sent us better weather, especially considering that his two great church bodies are reuniting for these few days."

Pia's hand slid out from under the covers. "Watch your mouth!" she warned, mimicking her mother's tone of voice. "That's blasphemy you be saying!"

With a grin, Jenny stuck out her tongue. She thought back to the long campaign she had waged to get permission to travel to Berlin on her own with Pia. In the end, the only reason her parents had agreed was because the church conference was their destination – and above all, because she promised that they would attend the papal Mass. Jenny once again felt slightly guilty about the arguments they had had. After taking off her yellow pajamas, she stuffed them into her backpack, and slipped into her jeans and a sweater. It looked cool outside.

But all that didn't matter, did it? She was here. In Berlin. Together with Pia. She would see the Pope. She pulled on her sneakers, then slid her arms into the denim jacket her father had bought her for the trip. Something that felt like a finger poked her into her side, and she rummaged around in her pocket for it. It was the glow stick she had bought, right after her arrival, from a souvenir shop. She wanted to use it tomorrow during the massive concluding service. She repositioned it in her pocket so that it was more comfortable and wouldn't bother her. Her thoughts then turned to the nice guy with the tattoos.

Would he be at supper again tonight?

She swore that she would speak to him this time.

Shortly before nine-thirty, Faris found himself back in the so-called War Room, the large office on the upper floor of the State Police building on Keithstraße.

This was the headquarters for Department 119, which hadn't existed until a few years ago. At that time, the city had witnessed a series of brutal honor killings. In their aftermath, the head of the state criminal division had managed to pry funding for a new murder division from the Senator of the Interior. And, since this commission was always summoned whenever a crime had any connection with religion, it had been unofficially dubbed SURV: the Special Unit for Religious Violence.

"Andersen doesn't know anything about your suspension. You know that, right?" asked Paul, who had driven Faris over to the office.

Faris was sitting at the desk that had been his until recently; before the explosion and, more importantly, before his suspension. The desk pad was still the same, the one he had brought from home. It was some old paper thing he had received as an advertising gift from an auto shop. Besides that, not much else remained from his earlier time here. His old coffee cup had been replaced by some expensive-looking, matte black vessel. In place of his photo of Anisah, his sister, now stood a stylish plexiglass cube containing snapshots of various attractive young people.

Faris folded his hands on top of the desktop as he stared blankly ahead. In the room's silence, the ringing in his ears sounded even worse. "Let's just keep it that way for the time being," he suggested. He thought about the phone in his pocket. The caller had had some particular reason for calling him, of all people, and he wanted to find out what it was.

"Where are the others?" he asked.

The SURV team was composed of seven permanent investigators and a contact person at the forensics institute. Of these eight staff members, at least half should have been on duty, but the War Room was deserted except for Faris and Paul.

"A briefing," Paul surmised. "I bet they're being filled in on what has happened."

Faris forced himself to breathe deeply. His shoulder throbbed from the collision with the subway station wall. Standing up, he walked over to the sink in the corner of the room. He leaned heavily against the sink edge and stared into the mirror. His eyes were reddened, and his skin was unnaturally pale from the fine concrete dust that had settled, like a veil, across his entire body. His black hair had a gray shimmer to it, which made him look like an old, hunched man. And this was exactly the way he felt.

He turned on the water and held his hands under the cold stream. All of a sudden, a wave of memories washed over him. He heard a child weeping. Scenes he had witnessed stood out sharply in his mind – not as vague and threatening as those that came at night in his nightmares, but garish and painful, like a fresh wound. He saw a finger with a red polished nail but didn't know if it belonged to the dead woman in the museum or the woman in the red dress. He then envisioned the subway train vanishing into the dark gullet of the tunnel. Fire spewed from it and enveloped him. He could smell burning flesh. His own flesh. Voices and screams echoed through his skull. He heard the girl over and over again, sobbing *Papa!* He heard the shrill accusing words of the woman.

What did you do?

He sluggishly splashed water onto his face and ran his damp hands through his hair. Dust and pieces of concrete fluttered down, landing with a faint clattering sound in the sink. Glancing past his lower arm, his gaze fell upon the dark blue carpet. From the door to his seat and from there to where he was now standing, a trail of light gray footprints were visible. His footprints.

He shook his head. "What did you do?" he murmured.

Seeming to sense that Faris needed a little time to pull himself together, Paul had busied himself with the task of getting the coffee machine to work. He now turned around. "What did you say?"

Faris realized that he must have uttered the words out loud. He straightened up. "What did you do?" he repeated. "A woman at the scene asked me that. The people thought I was the bomber." He moved his shoulder, trying to interpret the pain. Just a bruise. He couldn't shake the image of the injured man with the abdominal injury, the horrified, bewildered look on the daughter's face. He shut his eyes and inhaled as much air as he could.

His old chest wound twinged with pain, and he had to cough. In the distance, he heard the door open, and when he opened his eyes again and turned around, a young man he didn't know was standing in the room. Dressed like a civilian, he was slender and darkly tanned. His legs were clad in designer jeans, and his shirt was adorned with a discreet logo on the left-hand side of the chest.

Paul nodded at him. "Faris, this is Marc Sommer."

Faris knew that Marc was new to SURV. He held a degree in psychology, and within the group of case analysts who had completed their police training over the past three years, he was considered one of the best. However, Faris also knew that Paul hoped that Faris would soon return to the team, and this had resulted in tension between him and Marc.

Faris smiled at Marc, who looked relieved. He had very light, watery-blue eyes. "Hello, Faris," he said in greeting as he extended his hand. "It's nice to finally meet you." His eyes darted over to the desk with the black cup and the plexiglass cube. Both things fit so well with Marc's appearance that Faris knew instantly who had received his desk. Clenching his jaw, Faris gazed at his own damp hands. After cutting off the faucet, he reached for a paper towel and dried his hands before taking Marc's hand. "Hello, Marc." He turned back to Paul. "I looked Arabic, and that was more than enough reason for their assumptions." His thoughts wandered back to the museum bomber, and for a moment, he didn't move as his mind weighed the various possibilities.

Could the caller have been the attacker from back then? Could he actually have survived the devastating explosion?

Faris sighed. Looking into the mirror, he saw that his hair was still gray. His efforts to clean it had only resulted in short strands sticking out jaggedly in all directions. He smoothed them flat before returning to the desk and settling heavily into the chair. If it bothered Marc that he was claiming his old seat, his younger colleague didn't let it show.

"You're thinking about the museum bomber, aren't you?" Paul asked, cautiously.

Faris didn't reply. There was no reason to. He and his partner had always understood each other without saying a word, and it was a good feeling that over the past ten months, none of that had changed.

Marc seemed to sense that there was some kind of exchange between his two colleagues that he wasn't in on. He cleared his throat awkwardly as he crossed his arms. "The museum bomber? What does he have to do with this?"

The ringing in Faris's ears grew louder and muffled Paul's attempt to bring the new guy up to speed on the caller and the video.

"Faris?" Paul's voice startled him.

Faris blinked. A glance at the clock above the door revealed that several minutes had lapsed. Paul's face was expressionless. "Everything alright?" he asked.

"Yeah." Faris nodded.

"You two are wondering if the caller was the same man who blew up the Klersch Museum?" Marc picked up the plexiglass cube and turned it over in his hands. "Didn't the explosion destabilize the building so much that they had to tear it down? And the death count was high, right?"

"Yes," Paul confirmed somberly.

"Seventy-five." Faris declared, his voice sounding rough. The explosives unit had run all sorts of analyses, and in their final report, Faris recalled that they had documented seventy-five bodies. But had they been able to definitively identify any of the body parts they had located as belonging to the attacker? He couldn't remember and would have to check.

"My knowledge about what happened is fairly general," Marc admitted.

Paul searched Faris's gaze, waiting on his mute permission before starting his account. "The whole thing started as a run-of-the-mill hostage situation. Faris just happened to be in the area when a call came in that a man had entered the museum and taken seventy-four people hostage. Faris was the first one on the scene, and he was able to get the man to talk about himself. He learned that the hostage-taker was Syrian. He had married a German woman, but they were divorced. He had assembled a bomb belt after his wife denied him visitation rights with their child. After abducting his son, he took the child to the museum in order to demand his parental access."

Paul's eyes never left Faris as he spoke. Faris felt as if he were being stretched on the rack.

A man with dark skin, a belt, ten kilos of explosives. What would that lead to?

"Let's talk," he had said to the man. "I was born in Alexandria. I'm a Muslim like you …"

And then the bomb on the other side of the door went off, sending the hostage-taker, his son, and seventy-three other people to their deaths.

All because he, Faris, had made a mistake and completely misinterpreted the situation. More than that – because he had jumped on the same bandwagon as every other crappy racist out there. An Arab? Of course, he had to be an Islamist fundamentalist. Faris hadn't wasted even one second questioning his assumptions about the man's motive.

His stomach rebelled as he thought about the bodies, about the red-painted fingernail.

He rubbed his forehead and ran his fingers through his hair.

"You couldn't have done anything." Paul's voice roared in his ear.

Faris began to shake his head but froze mid-movement. "Let it go," he murmured. He knew Paul's opinion on this matter, just as Paul knew his.

"God, Faris!" he heard his partner curse. "You still act as if *you* were the one who pushed the button, not that bastard!"

Faris didn't reply. What could he say, anyway?

"After the explosion, you were put on sick leave for a while," Marc said, a few moments later. "But you're recovered now, aren't you?"

Faris moved the arm that had been seriously injured in the explosion. The burn scar across his bicep tightened. He could guess the next question, and he wasn't wrong.

"Why aren't you back at work yet?"

It was very quiet in the room for several seconds. Faris then replied: "I was supposed to come back to work about three weeks ago, but I ..." he paused.

"Screwed things up." Paul ended the sentence for him.

Faris snorted grimly at this construction of things. His thoughts turned to a Saturday evening, three and half weeks ago. After nine months of struggling with his rehab regimen and dragging himself out of the hole that the explosion had blasted him into, he had gone out for the first time that evening. At a bar near the zoo, he had crossed paths with a skinhead idiot wearing jump boots, who had planted himself in front of Faris and defiantly called him a "dirty Arab bomber". In light of the museum attack and especially of his own self-recriminations, this accusation tripped a switch inside Faris. The next thing he remembered, he was kneeling on top of the guy and punching away at him.

It had taken three other bar patrons to drag him off, and he was very fortunate that they reacted so quickly. Otherwise, he probably would have beaten the skinhead to death instead of just pounding him to a pulp. Of course, they immediately suspended him from the SURV squad, and now all he could do was hope that the hearing he would soon be attending would go in his favor. Maybe – and this was the hope that was keeping him from going off the deep end – they would show some sympathy for his meltdown due to his trauma and let him work again.

He was about to say something when the door opened, and an energetic woman with dyed red hair rushed into the room.

"Faris? Are you alright?" Her voice sounded excited and very concerned. She came to a stop in front of him, her large eyes resembling those of a startled owl. "I heard what happened."

Faris forced himself to nod. "Thanks, Gitta. I'm okay."

"Thank God!"

Gitta Müller was the SURV administrative assistant, a secretary with special responsibilities and – as she liked to call herself in flights of irony – the unit "mother". As she gazed at him, Faris had to smile, and he was suddenly painfully aware of how much he had missed her over the past ten months. Gitta always wore voluminous garments in shades of lilac, orange and red, which she complemented with a huge array of necklaces, bracelets and rings. As she leaned down to plant a kiss on his cheek, she clattered and clanked like a junk collector. She smelled like a mixture of patchouli and orange, and Faris was reminded of the incense sticks his sister Anisah had enjoyed burning as a teenager.

Gitta scrutinized Faris from top to bottom, as her hands fluttered through the air. "Lightning does strike twice sometimes," she mumbled. She looked as if she could hardly believe what had happened.

He slowly shook his head. "It wasn't a coincidence, Gitta," he corrected her, thinking about the unknown caller.

Gitta's darting eyes froze for a moment, fixed upon him. "I know." Reaching out, she patted Faris's cheek.

"I'm alright, Gitta," Faris assured her once more.

She nodded. "Of course!" She then recalled something. "Oh! I just wanted to let you know that the briefing is over. Tromsdorff is rounding up the entire team. Shannon will be here any minute. Ben, too. Andersen also called to say that you should start without him."

Gitta stopped to think, and as always happened whenever she did this intensely, she froze completely. She finally blinked herself back into action. "I'm so relieved that nothing happened to you, Faris." And with those words, she hurried off to her tiny office, which was located at the front of the War Room, sandwiched between the sloping roof and the elevator shaft. With its glass walls, it resembled a terrarium for exotic animals.

The door fell shut behind her, and despite the panes of glass, it felt to Faris as if Gitta had taken all the color in the room away with her.

CHAPTER 7

There was no time left for reflection since, right after Gitta's exit, the door swung open again, and Superintendent Robert Tromsdorff strode in. He was the head investigator on the SURV team and the original founder of the squad. Tromsdorff had successfully brought together some of the most skilled state police investigators, along with psychologists and scientists, to create a powerful team. Their strength was in the area of operational case analysis, which people commonly referred to as "profiling". Originally, SURV had been authorized due to increasingly violent activity within the Muslim milieu. However, it had quickly become clear that there were more than enough *other* radical religious groups out there to keep them busy. They had handled cases involving fundamentalist Christians, as well as murder investigations in Orthodox Jewish and sectarian communities.

As he reached the center of the room, Tromsdorff came to a stop and stared at Faris. "Great Scott!" he exclaimed. He was an athletic, well-conditioned man who was in the habit of combining sports coats with t-shirts, which made him look a little like Sonny Crockett from the old TV series, *Miami Vice*. However, he was anything but a daredevil, but was rather one of the most competent and level-headed Department 1 team leaders. Faris owed him a lot, since Tromsdorff had promoted him and convinced him to dedicate his skills to SURV – a decision that Faris had never regretted.

Without even a glance at Paul or Marc, Tromsdorff strode over to

Faris. He silently took in Faris's split lip and forehead laceration. After doing that, he looked straight into his eyes. "How are you doing?"

"So far, so good," Faris replied.

"Did they check you out for a concussion?"

"Yes," Faris lied, feeling Paul's disapproving eyes on him.

At that moment, two other people walked into the room. One of them was a woman, who looked strong, compact and extremely athletic. She wore her blonde hair cut super short, and her face was sprinkled with freckles. Her long legs were clad in tight jeans, over which she wore two well-coordinated sleeveless tops, and her arms were as muscular as a man's. This was Shannon Starck.

"Doing alright, Faris?" Shannon had an American accent, since until recently she had lived in the US, where she had studied organizational sociology and psychology. She had written her dissertation about radical evangelical sects. Tromsdorff had met her at a conference in Seattle, and when he learned that she had dual German–US citizenship, thanks to her German father, he had convinced her to pursue her career at the German State Police. On their team, she was the specialist for Christian fundamentalism.

Faris smiled at her. "Yeah. Thanks for asking, Shannon."

"Shit," she exclaimed. "When they told us that you were there when the bomb went off on the subway, I thought they were kidding." She strode over to her desk, which was covered with all sorts of odds and ends. Picking up a tennis ball, she began to squeeze it in one hand as she nonchalantly leaned back in her chair and watched as the second newcomer greeted Faris.

Ben Schneider was a slightly overweight, completely colorless man. Everything about him seemed washed out, from his sand-colored pants to his faded sweatshirt to his strangely yellowish hair. There was a single exception to this rule: his eyes. They were an amazing shade of sparkling blue. *Lapis lazuli blue*, Faris thought, just as he did every time he encountered Ben.

"You're a real hero, you know that?" Ben's tone was reverential and ironic at the same time. He functioned as the go-between who linked the FCI specialists with SURV personnel, and Faris knew no one who was as hard to figure out as this forensic technician. None of the profiling tricks Faris had learned over the years ever worked on Ben.

Ben didn't give Faris the opportunity to respond. Instead, he immediately plugged the laptop he was carrying into a projector. Faris wasn't surprised by this, since the technician was well-known for adopting unusual behaviors when he was working on a case. Faris often thought that this was linked to his sphynx-like character.

"So, here are the facts." Tromsdorff leaned against the so-called case table; a long, plain, metal table that ran down the center of the room. Two whiteboards were mounted in the corner, and this area served as their ops base. This was where they discussed – and solved – most of their cases.

"As you all know already, this morning, at the Bismarckstraße Subway Station, a bomb went off. According to what we know right now, at least twenty-seven people, including several children, lost their lives down there. The state security division is looking into the possibility that this was a terrorist attack, but we have reason to believe that we might have a religiously motivated attack on our hands. If so, the case falls within our jurisdiction." He looked at Faris. "For those of you who are wondering why Faris is here and not at the hospital where he belongs, in my opinion ... Faris, it would be best for you to explain."

Faris gazed at his colleagues' tense faces. Taking a deep breath, he decided to stand up to give his explanation. He pushed himself upright, ignored the light dizziness that washed over him, and started to speak.

"As you all know, I saw what happened at the subway station. That was due to a phone call I received this morning." Pulling the phone out of his pocket, he held it up and explained once more how the caller had ordered him to go to the Bismarckstraße station. As he spoke, Gitta emerged from her glass box to listen and Ben wrapped up his setup efforts. His laptop now sat open on the case table, and the projector was running, beaming an empty white rectangle onto the wall.

Faris handed his phone to him. The IT specialist connected it to his computer as Faris described the video that the unknown caller had sent him.

With a remote, Ben lowered a screen from the ceiling. He then bent over his keyboard and tapped in a command. The desktop interface appeared on the screen, followed by a black window. Without taking his eyes away from it, Faris reached for his chair and sat back down. The familiar sounds of the video began; the heavy breathing and the stifled moaning. The blurry colors came into view, and finally, the image sharpened.

Faris, who knew the video all too well by now, concentrated on his colleagues' faces as they watched it for the first time. Tromsdorff flinched as the hammer rushed downward. The color drained from Marc's face. Gitta's eyes grew huge, and her bracelets clinked as she covered her mouth with her hands. Shannon very attentively followed every movement on the screen, and it was obvious that she was already formulating her initial thoughts about what she was seeing.

The video continued to play. The muffled groans of the crucified man, the fury of the hammer blows, the rattling of the chain, and the anguished scream of the victim as the cross was set upright – all of this echoed through the horrified silence of the individuals gathered around the table.

The video finally ended. For a heartbeat, they sat there as if turned to stone.

"Well." Faris spoke into the oppressive silence, shattering the others' torpor.

"Okay," Tromsdorff groaned. "This is definitely an SURV matter. Can we assume that no special effects were used?"

Ben pursed his lips. He played the video forwards and backwards several times. "I'll have to analyze it more closely, but at first glance, I have to admit that it looks damned real."

Tromsdorff nodded, as if his own opinion had just been confirmed. His lanky body resembled an electrified spring. He had pushed up his jacket sleeves, and Faris could see the tendons in his arms.

"But what does this video have to do with the explosion?" Gitta asked.

"The explosion on the subway was just the opening act," Faris explained. "The caller claimed that the man he nailed to the cross is wired to another bomb. The moment the heart of the man on the cross stops beating, the bomb will go off."

"Oh God!" Gitta exclaimed. She leaned against the doorframe, looking as white as a sheet.

Tromsdorff cast her a concerned glance. "Do we have any clues that could lead us to the second bomb?"

Faris shook his head. "I'm not sure. Eventually, we'll get something from what he said, but I haven't reconstructed that in detail yet. He quoted the church conference motto."

"*Speaking the Word of God Boldly*," Gitta interjected.

Ben and Paul nodded. Marc dropped into a visitor's chair, looking distracted. Faris had only just met him, but he assumed that the young analyst was already working on his own theories. Tromsdorff wouldn't have brought him onto the team if he didn't work that way.

"Right. And the caller told me where the quote came from," Faris continued. "Somewhere in the Bible, but I can't recall the exact verse. When the bomb went off, he quoted another part of the passage, and I can remember that just fine. *And after they prayed, the place where they were meeting was shaken.*" The force of the Bible verse broke over Faris like the blast wave had done earlier. Balling his hands, he pressed his fists against his temples. He then pulled himself back together. He could recall every single word that had been said to him except for the Bible verse, every breath the man had drawn on the other end of the line, every sound in the background. Later, he would add all these details to the case file, but everyone here in the room was seasoned enough at profiling to know that often the first unconscious impressions held the secret to solving a case. This was why Faris repeated what had been said to him, word for word: "Somewhere out there, Faris, in your lovely Berlin, a man is hanging on a cross. Your task is to find him. As long as his heart keeps beating, all's well. However, if it stops before you locate him, then … Well, as the Bible verse says, *the place where they were meeting was shaken.* I think you know what I mean."

As Faris was talking, Ben turned to face a different computer and typed something on its keyboard. He had obviously been looking up the Bible passage, because he spoke up as soon as Faris was done. "The Acts of the Apostles." Everyone looked at him. "Chapter four, verse thirty-one. *After they prayed, the place where they were meeting was shaken. And they were all filled with the Holy Spirit and spoke the word of God boldly.*"

"The place where they were meeting," Shannon repeated quietly. "He's given us a clue about where the bomb is located."

Gitta sighed. "That could be anywhere in Berlin. The church conference is in full swing." She was right. More than five thousand separate events were planned, all across the city. Over a quarter of a million visitors were expected to attend.

Tromsdorff cleared his throat. "We'll get to that shortly." He then turned to face Faris. "Do you have any idea why the caller chose to call you, of all people?"

"I'm not sure. But he claimed to be the Klersch Museum bomber." Faris quickly filled his colleagues in on the Arabic quote and its meaning.

"*As-samu alaikum.*" Tromsdorff nodded. "I remember that."

"Peace be with you?" Marc scratched his head. "Why does that …?"

"*As-samu alaikum* doesn't mean *peace be with you,*" Faris interrupted. "*Peace be with you* translates as *as-salamu alaikum.* On the other hand, *as-samu alaikum* has one syllable less, did you hear that? It is an insult. Loosely translated, it means *death be with you.*"

"Oh." Marc looked shocked. With a self-effacing gesture, he brushed the hair from his forehead. "I didn't know that." That fact was obviously embarrassing to him. Like so many times before, Faris was amazed at this kind of self-consciousness, which struck him as typically German.

"You couldn't have known," he said. "Like I said, these were the final words the museum bomber said to me."

"Hmmm." Tromsdorff rested his chin on his hand. "And if I recall rightly, we never gave that information to the media."

During this discussion, Gitta had returned to her glass box. For the past year, the State Police had been using a new computer system, called DigA A, which could save and organize case reports, including the sound recording and crime scene photos that were gathered over the course of an investigation. This was why Gitta could sit comfortably at her desk and call up all the materials related to the museum case – which was what she was doing right now.

Returning to the group with her laptop, she declared: "At first glance, here is what I know." She started reading her screen. "There were seventy-five fatalities. And the forensics team was able to positively identify some of the body parts as coming from the bomber." She studied Faris. "There's no way your caller could have been the man from the museum, Faris."

Faris rubbed his eyes. He had already suspected this was the case. "And yet, that's who he's pretending to be. Why?"

"Maybe it's just a trick," Paul theorized aloud. "A trick to get you to immediately go to the subway station."

Faris shrugged. "It's possible. Or the guy is somehow connected with the museum case."

"How?" Marc asked.

Helpless silence spread throughout the War Room. They wouldn't get anywhere like this!

"Can you get anything off of Faris's cell phone?" Tromsdorff asked, turning to Ben. "Find some kind of clue about the caller, that is?"

Ben reached reluctantly for the battered device sitting on the table. "The call came from an unlisted number. In order to get the relevant data from the service provider, we need a court order. The same goes for the sender of the email with the video attachment. We will need to contact the email provider and hope that the guy was stupid enough to register the account with his actual name and address."

"You can't believe he did, though." Faris shook his head decisively. "The man hacked into the Bismarckstraße camera system. He isn't stupid!"

"The subway cameras ..." Tromsdorff rubbed his chin. "The security officers are already working on that. Perhaps we'll get lucky, and our culprit was noticed by someone on the subway staff."

Ben gazed thoughtfully at Faris's phone, as if the dusty device could reveal more to him. "You don't have to be on site to tap into the camera feed for the subway. Hackers do that kind of thing every day from their couches." He walked over to the two whiteboards and picked up one of the fat dry erase markers before making the first note on their board:

culprit = hacker?

"That could be one explanation as to how he knew the Arabic phrase," Ben continued. "He could've hacked into the DigA A."

"Great," Tromsdorff remarked. His disgruntled expression revealed that the idea of somebody hacking into their internal data bank system did nothing to brighten his mood. "Notify your colleagues in IT, Ben. They need to check on this. And then contact the service providers! The order is just a formality. You can get started right away."

After clicking the lid on the marker, Ben set it down before sitting back at his computer and starting to type. A beep indicated that he had sent a short inter-office email, presumably to the IT team that managed the internal networks. He then reached for his phone and punched in a speed dial number. After waiting a moment, he said: "Carla, it's me. We need to trace an email message and a phone number. The court order should get here shortly." He listened for a second. "Yes, I put the information on the server for you. Please put a rush on this. It's really important!" He hung up without saying goodbye. "That will take a while."

"Okay." Tromsdorff stared thoughtfully at the screen. "Let's follow our normal protocol for this. Video analysis, criminal profile. You know what to do, folks!"

"The video might provide some clues about where the cross and the victim are located," Shannon suggested.

Ben typed several things on his trackpad, and behind him, a shot of the crucified man appeared. His head sunk onto his chest, blood from the wounds made by the crown of thorns was running down his face, throat and chest. His fingers curled rigidly into the air. If it weren't for the electrodes and the transparent tube leading from the IV drip down the man's throat, the scene would have looked like a hyper-realistic religious painting.

Faris studied the image closely. Except for the man and the cross, all there was to see was a gray wall. He couldn't have even said if the wall were made of concrete or covered in old wallpaper. The background was simply too blurry. "We won't get anything from it," he predicted.

Marc raised his hand but didn't wait for anyone to let him jump in. "Do we have any idea how much time we have until the next bomb is supposed to go off? I mean, how long can the man on the cross be expected to survive this torture?"

Having played with her tennis ball throughout the conversation, Shannon now deposited it back into the chaos on her desk and stood up. "A crucifixion," she explained, sounding a little like a professor in a lecture hall, "entails massive physical trauma, along with significant blood loss – at least, if you take into consideration the flogging and the crown of thorns. Our culprit seems to have foreseen this blood loss, as far as I can tell, presumably it's why he's supplied his victim with the IV drip."

"What does that mean?" Tromsdorff interjected.

Shannon took a deep breath. "That means that he is planning to keep his victim alive for a while. However, the blood loss isn't the biggest problem when it comes to a crucifixion. It's the rigidity." She walked over to the screen and pointed at the man's outstretched arms, using a pen she had picked up on her way over. "The stretched arms and the fixed vertical position will eventually interfere with the victim's breathing, and in the end, he will suffocate."

"Have there been any studies of how long it can take, until …" Faris decided not to finish his question.

Shannon looked at him seriously. "Yes, there have been. If the shock and blood loss don't kill them right off the bat, a victim can survive for hours, even days." She pointed at a spot next to the victim's hips. "That is a seat board, on which the man can support himself whenever he has a hard time breathing. In ancient times, it was a way to prolong a victim's suffering."

"Good Lord!" Faris heard Gitta murmur. "That's brutal!"

"No," Faris suddenly exclaimed, and the others stared at him in amazement. He didn't explain to Gitta that he wasn't contradicting her, rather Shannon. "Our victim won't live for days. He won't survive more than forty hours."

"How do you know that?" Paul asked, confused. The others were also gazing at him in bewilderment.

Faris recollected the rest of the caller's exact words. "I remember that the stranger emphasized several times that we only have forty hours to find the man …"

CHAPTER 8

Alexander

The figure inside the aureole moved. Although much time had passed, during which Alexander had alternated between sitting on the floor beneath the cross and pacing up and down like a caged animal, he still couldn't make out anything more than a human-like shadow within the blinding light.

"WE MUST WAIT," the voice had said, after which it fell silent for a long time. Alexander believed he could feel the fury emanating from the light. The more he thought about it, the more convinced he was that this figure was an angel from the Lord.

Didn't the Bible say that the sight of them caused fear and trembling?

The man on the cross groaned, and Alexander glanced up at him. Why was it so difficult for him to call that man his father?

The rhythmic beeping was making his head hurt.

Finally, the angel spoke again.

"I WOULD LIKE YOU TO TELL ME WHAT HAPPENED AFTER THAT CHRISTMAS SUNDAY," he said.

Alexander swallowed. He didn't want to remember. The memory hurt, and he wished to forget about it forever. But the angel was unrelenting.

"SPEAK!" he ordered.

And Alexander obeyed.

After that Christmas Day, nothing in particular happens for a long time. Father reads in his Bible. He prays a lot and talks constantly about God. At some point, Alexander notices that his father has stopped eating much, if anything, at mealtimes. He only gnaws on a piece of lettuce, takes a sip of water. And wastes away. Shockingly fast.

Then one day, when Alexander asks him if he is sick, a smile spreads across his face.

"Not anymore," he replies.

But Alexander doesn't understand.

"I was sick," his father explains to him. "Here, inside." He places his hand over his heart. "Sick from the sin that dwells inside here. But now that is over."

"How can it be over when you still look so bad?" Alexander asks. His father's skin looks gray and wrinkly, like that of a very old man. His pants flap around his bony hips.

"The body isn't important," his father tells him. "Everything depends on the spirit. The spirit is the only thing that matters. The soul. Did you know that Jesus Christ spent forty days fasting so that he could escape the devil's temptations?"

Forty days! That seems like such a long time to Alexander, and he wonders when his father stopped eating. He doesn't know.

"The devil is ever-present," his father explains. "He tries to ruin us, every day, every second."

Alexander thinks about this. "I'm not sure," he mumbles.

His father grabs his arms and stares wildly into his eyes. "Have you harbored any bad thoughts recently? Perhaps about me or about one of your friends?"

Alexander hesitates.

"When you pray, do you sincerely speak to God from a full heart?" Father's voice is now becoming more forceful. His eyes are darting back and forth rapidly.

Alexander feels spellbound. He swallows.

"Have you had any unchaste dreams? Have you envied anyone

63

their worldly goods?" The questions fire from Father's mouth with increasing speed, like bullets shooting up Alexander's mind and smashing it to pieces.

"Have you cursed? Insulted your mother? Did you …" Father shakes him. His breathing is growing labored, and yet the questions continue to rain down heavily on Alexander.

Did you …

Have you …

"Yes!" Alexander finally shouts. *"Yes! Yes!"* Tears roll out from under his eyelids and down his cheeks. A deep, despairing sob works its way up from his chest. Father lets him go, but the sob now reaches his throat, and it shakes him just as much as his father had shaken him beforehand.

"Yes," he whispers as his shoulders slump. *"I did all of those things."* He feels miserable, overflowing with filth and garbage to the point of feeling disgusted with himself. A powerful, uncontrollable twitching takes possession of his body. It has to be the devil who has him in its clutches!

"You don't need to cry." Father's voice is suddenly very gentle.

In amazement, Alexander gazes at his face. A smile spreads across his father's features, as something other-worldly beams out from him.

"God will forgive your sins, if you honestly and candidly repent of them."

"How can I do that?" Alexander whispers. Yes, he has yelled at his mother, but isn't that just the way things are? And yes, he has secretly read dirty magazines under his covers and jerked off. But how can he repent of something that feels so good?

He tries, but isn't successful. *"I'm a bad person,"* he whispers in despair. His eyes are burning.

"No, you aren't!" His father now grabs him again, forcing him to look up. *"You only have to do what I'm doing."*

"What should I do? Fast, like you?"

His father doesn't reply. Instead, he starts to recite a Bible verse: *"And immediately the Sprit driveth him into the wilderness. And he was there in the wilderness forty days, tempted of Satan; and was with the wild beasts; and the angels ministered unto him." Father takes a breath before continuing in a monotone ...*

With stinging eyes, Alexander stared into the garish light.

The angel of the Lord stood inside it, very calm. "TEMPTED OF SATAN," he repeated quietly. And then he started laughing in a way that made Alexander's hair stand on end.

"Did I say something wrong?" he asked anxiously.

"YOU?" the angel asked. "NO! HOW COULD YOU POSSIBLY THINK THAT?"

Alexander didn't answer. He felt little, insignificant and stupid in the presence of this bright, blinding light. Just as he had always felt stupid in Father's presence. Stupid and ignorant. Filled by the desire to be led.

"Tell me what I should do," he begged.

The angel laughed once more. This time it sounded sad. Weren't the angels of the Lord full of mourning? Alexander tried to recall the old stories his grandma had told him, but he failed. He was confused. His heart pounded.

"CONTINUE YOUR STORY," the angel finally told him. "YOU STARTED TO FAST. AND THEN?"

And Alexander remembered.

His mother doesn't notice right away because he is very careful. At first, he simply eats a little less, leaving the meat on his plate and then finally the potatoes too. However, she inevitably notices, eventually. Her eyes filled with concern, Mother watches him eat one evening.

"Are you sick?" she asks, sending Father a dark look. She has long had suspicions about what is happening.

Alexander shakes his head tentatively. Lying is a sin; Father has taught him.

A deep wrinkle appears between Mother's eyebrows. "Werner?" Her voice is chilly.

His father doesn't move.

"What is going on with the boy?" Mother's voice is now trembling, incredulous. "You're making him fast too, aren't you?" Her eyes are huge, and Alexander can see himself reflected in her pupils.

"Are you making the boy fast with you?" Mother shouts.

Father shakes his head. "Not me. The Lord."

At that, Mother springs to her feet, her napkin landing on the kitchen table. "The boy's only twelve!" she shrieks. "He's still growing! Tell him this minute that he has to stop this nonsense!"

But Father shakes his head again. "The devil is lurking everywhere," he says softly. "We have to keep him at bay!"

With this, the mask of fury on Mother's face collapses into a thousand little folds. All of a sudden, she looks gray. Gray and empty. "You beast!" she utters tonelessly. "Stop this insanity, or Alexander and I will leave you immediately."

Father doesn't answer, just stares mutely into her eyes. For a long moment, they gaze at each other, and then Mother spins around and strides furiously out of the kitchen …

Alexander fell silent as he shakily took a breath. The garish light was blinding him, and he covered his eyes with his hands.

"IT'S ALRIGHT," the angel consoled him. "IT'S ALMOST OVER. JUST TELL ME WHAT HAPPENED AFTER THAT."

Without raising his eyes, Alexander murmured: "She was gone the next day." Even now, today, it was hard for him to believe this. "She just abandoned me. She left me behind with …" He hesitated as he lowered his hands and gestured at the man on the cross. "With him."

"SHE DIDN'T ABANDON YOU," the angel contradicted him. Was Alexander hearing correctly? Was the angel's voice shaking now? "LISTEN TO YOUR HEART. YOU KNOW THAT SHE DIDN'T WANT TO ABANDON YOU."

Alexander didn't want to hear his words, didn't want to think about where they were driving him. He covered his ears. "No!" he shouted. "No!"

"WHAT DO YOU THINK?" the angel asked.

Alexander refused to say. Tears trickled out from beneath his lowered lids. He shook his head vigorously. All of a sudden, he was twelve again, and sobs were wracking his body. "She's gone, just gone! And she isn't coming back. And Papa and I are standing in the garden."

"IN THE GARDEN," the angel repeated.

"In the garden." Alexander opened his eyes, staring directly and unblinkingly into the harsh light until his head started to ache. The pain drove the horror into his heart. "We have dug a hole and filled it in again. The flower bed now looks very fresh."

"Forty hours." Paul tilted his head to consider this. "It's possible that he meant to give us a clue about what he is planning. Do you know when these forty hours were supposed to start?" he asked Faris.

"With his call. That was at three minutes past eight."

Standing up, Paul walked over to the whiteboard on which Ben had already made the first note. He picked up the marker and drew a quick perpendicular line on the board. "Let's assume that this is Zero Hour." Starting from the line, he drew a long horizontal line at the end of which he wrote a fat 40. He ran a quick mental calculation. "The forty hours will be over … tomorrow, around midnight."

"Shit!" This curse was from Shannon.

Faris scanned the row of his colleagues. The tension in the room had suddenly spiked. He could feel that clearly.

"Tomorrow night," Shannon continued. "The concluding service begins at eleven o'clock pm in the Olympic Stadium. By midnight, it will be in full swing."

The Olympic Stadium! Faris closed his eyes. Of course, he had read about this special service. It had been announced as a Service of Lights and promised to be truly remarkable. His neighbor had recently explained to him what would make this event so special: During this service, the first papal-sanctioned ecumenical Holy Eucharist in the Christian world would be held. Despite five hundred years of the Catholic Church refusing to grant communion to Protestants, and several decades of denying that the collective Protestant faith community had a right to call itself the Church, an about-face had taken place in recent months. The reason for this had been the unexpected death of the previous Pope, in a plane crash over the Atlantic. At barely sixty years old, his Ukrainian successor qualified as a very young Pope. Immediately after his selection, he set a course toward ecumenical dialogue. And, at least for the time being, the imminent communion service represented the achievement of this process.

"Fucking shit!" Ben cursed. Not one person in the room contradicted or admonished him.

Still standing at the whiteboard, Paul took a step to the side and started the first of the case lists. *Motive?* he wrote at the top, before glancing around the room.

"To prevent the communion service," Gitta conjectured. It was the first thing that had shot through all their minds.

Paul jotted it down. "That would suggest that our culprit is a militant Christian," he murmured as he wrote.

"Umm …" Ben wanted to jump in, but Faris was quicker.

"But would Christian fundamentalists set up something like this?" He motioned at the image of the crucified man. "I mean, in my opinion, this looks more like someone's *mocking* the Christian faith, doesn't it?"

Leaning back in his chair, Ben crossed his arms.

Shannon shook her head. After her lecture on the physical effects of crucifixion, she had returned to her desk, where she was kneading her tennis ball again. "In Indonesia, there are fanatics who have themselves nailed to crosses every year at Easter, a spiritual experience of sorts. You're thinking about this from a Muslim perspective, Faris. For a Christian, a representation of a crucifixion isn't blasphemy. It's different to what mockery of the Prophet would be for Muslims." Bending over her desk, she scribbled something on a notepad sitting in front of her. "I'll check to see if there are any local sects that go in for crucifixions. Maybe there's a connection with groups that oppose the ecumenical service."

Paul pointed at Shannon with his marker. "We should also keep a look out for theatrical groups, especially passion play groups."

"Good." Tromsdorff looked satisfied. "Anything else?"

Ben opened his mouth to say something, but at that moment, he noticed something on his laptop screen. He bent forward to study it at closer range. Tromsdorff waited to see if he wanted to join their conversation, but the technician was now absorbed in what was on his computer.

Paul stared at the picture of the crucified man projected onto the wall. "Why such a complicated staging?" he asked the group.

The others looked at him.

He scratched his neck. "I mean ... A basic timer would suffice for him to achieve his goal. A simple countdown. Why the crucifixion? Why forty hours?" His eyes skimmed across his colleagues' faces, but nobody could answer his question.

"Shit," Ben suddenly mumbled.

Faris studied him with curiosity, but at that moment, the door swung open, and Marvin Andersen walked in. "Hello, everyone."

"We're just developing the first profile of the caller," Tromsdorff informed him. "And this much we can say – we think he's planning to attack the papal service tomorrow night." He succinctly filled Andersen in on their earlier discussions.

Andersen listened attentively before pulling out his phone and dialing. "Kevin, the Olympic Stadium. Raise the level to Priority 1." He hung up and then waved at Paul. "Continue!" he urged him.

After politely waiting a few seconds to see if Andersen wanted to sit down – which he gave no signs of doing – Paul repeated the question that he had asked a few moments before. "Why such a complicated staging?"

Tromsdorff was the first to formulate a theory. "He seems to want to settle an account of some sort."

"That's possible." Faris nodded. The same idea had occurred to him. "The crucifixion is a code. He wants to tell us something."

He thought back to the caller's words to him after the subway explosion. "When I asked why he was doing this, he mentioned divine judgment. And a beacon."

Tromsdorff was still leaning on the case table. His t-shirt shimmered starkly white. "Remember the exact words!" he ordered.

Faris closed his eyes. The man's distorted voice began to whisper inside his head, and Faris quoted him. "I asked him why. And he said, 'Maybe I want to be a beacon for others.' The whole time he sounded as though he was about to burst out laughing. And then he said, 'Find the man on the cross, Faris… Or *as-samu alaikum*.'"

"That phrase," Paul resumed his commentary. "Could it help us at all?"

"No!" Ben interjected.

Tromsdorff's eyebrows rose. "How can you be so sure, Ben?"

"Because the bastard actually *did* hack into DigA A, just as we suspected. Our IT team has just sent me an email about that. They hadn't even noticed it before now. The guy's really good. And I'm afraid that he knows every detail of the museum case."

Ben leaned back and crossed his arms behind his head. He was furious, as everyone could see. He had been personally involved with development of the firewall for the digital file archive. Faris suspected that he felt this attack on their server as a personal affront. "Can IT figure out where the attack originated?" he asked.

Ben shook his head. "They're trying, but they probably won't be able to determine that conclusively before the forty hours are up." He wrinkled his nose and snorted. "Did I mention that the guy's *really* good?" Reluctant admiration had crept into his voice. "And there's one more thing." He pointed at the image of the crucified man.

He let several seconds lapse before continuing. "He isn't alone."

CHAPTER 9

Alexander

The light emanating from the angel hurt his eyes. He hesitated, but then he tried once more to move toward it, even though the angel had forbidden him to do that.

To his astonishment, he wasn't told to move back. The light enveloped him, bright and warm. His skin almost prickled a little, just like it had under the strong spotlights they had used for the nativity plays in the church. What … What if this wasn't some kind of spiritual light?

Alexander held out his hand.

What if the light didn't contain a messenger from God, but merely a person? Hadn't he thought he recognized a human silhouette? A silhouette without wings?

Disgusted by himself, he shook his head at his own thoughts and rubbed his temples. Always these terrible thoughts he could never shake! Why was it always harder for him to believe than it was for his father?

He retreated from the light that beamed from one of the corners beside the door. Instantly, he felt an urge to flee from this low-ceilinged, tiled room, but in order to do that, he would have to walk straight toward the light. And although he already had, to a certain extent, the idea of doing *this* felt impossible. Trembling, he withdrew even more, to the farthest corner.

"Why can't I be like you, Papa?" he asked.

But the crucified man didn't reply.

Alexander lifted his chin. "Angel?"

Nobody answered him.

"What do you mean, the culprit isn't alone?" Faris asked. "How do you know that?"

Instead of answering, Ben started the video again. "Watch," he urged his colleagues.

Faris squinted, but he still couldn't see what Ben meant. Shannon was the first one who realized what was going on.

"The zoom function, right?"

And before Ben could even nod, Faris saw what she meant. The camera was obviously mounted on a tripod, at least it wasn't wobbling. But it was deliberately zooming in on certain details in the scene – on the crucified man's face, on his hands as the nails were being driven into them. Somebody must have operated the camera as the man in the hood swung the hammer.

They didn't have just one culprit to track down, but two.

For a while, no one spoke. Paul silently picked up the marker again, writing *Two culprits???* on the case wall. He considered what he had written for a moment, then erased the three question marks.

"Alright then." Tromsdorff pushed himself away from the case table and began to restlessly pace the room. "Let's try to expand our profile. At least one of the culprits is smart and organized. He's capable of planning and implementing something like this. He's capable of hacking into the DigA A system. We need to assume that he is very deliberate in whatever he decides to do."

Shannon cleared her throat. "Can we assume that the caller is Arabic?"

Tromsdorff now took Paul's spot at the whiteboard. Next to Paul's list of motives, he started a new list that he titled *Culprits?*

Underneath this word, he quickly jotted down the following list: *militant Christian fundamentalists, fanatic single Christian culprit,* and *Arab ethnicity.*

He was still writing the final word on the list, when the door opened, and a woman entered the War Room.

Faris suppressed a groan.

The woman was slender and fairly short. Her black hair was cut into a severe bob, the edges of which looked razor sharp. The ends of her hair brushed gently against her cheeks as she approached the group. Her eyes were discreetly shadowed in gray and silver, but her lips were colored with bright red lipstick. The color on her nails matched that lipstick, and Faris fleetingly saw the severed finger once more. He blinked the image away and concentrated on what was going on around him right now.

The woman was Dr. Anke Geiger, the supervisor and executive director of Department 1. As such, she was Andersen's equal, and she was also Robert Tromsdorff's direct supervisor. The boss of all of them.

There wasn't a person in the room who could stand her.

"Please don't let me interrupt," she said. "It'll be like I'm not even here." After sitting down on one of the unoccupied chairs, she crossed her legs and tugged down the edge of her dark gray skirt. Her calves looked strong and sinewy, as if they were the result of an extreme running regimen.

Tromsdorff shifted his shoulders uncomfortably, before pointing at the last of the points on his list. "We were just wondering if we might be dealing with an Arab perpetrator."

"Does that mean that we have an Islamist attack on our hands?" Dr. Geiger asked.

"No," Faris told her.

She raised one of her perfectly plucked eyebrows. "No? And what makes you so sure of that?" She studied him defiantly, and just like every other time he had anything to do with her, he had the unpleasant feeling that she didn't trust him. The way she treated him – coolly and suspiciously – had frequently made him wonder the cause behind the latent Islamophobia that emanated from her.

He opened his mouth, but at that moment, Geiger's eyes narrowed to slits. "What are you actually doing here?" she inquired frostily. "If I remember rightly, you've been suspended, Mr. Iskander."

"He was at the subway station when the bomb went off, Anke,"

Tromsdorff stepped in to explain. Wrinkles had appeared at the corners of his mouth, and he looked exhausted. This was the effect that Geiger had on him, every single time they interacted. She had this effect on numerous people.

"Really?" She coldly examined Faris, who felt as if he was under a scalpel. "How did that happen?"

"Anke," Andersen now cut in. "Don't you think we should leave these good people to their work?"

She wanted to say something but reconsidered. "Fine," she said. "Continue." This was visibly hard for her to concede. "But please tell me first, Mr. Iskander, why you're so certain that this has nothing to do with an Islamist attack."

Faris took a deep breath. "I'm not totally certain," he clarified calmly. "All I meant to say is that it would be extremely unusual for an Islamist attacker to use Christian symbolism."

Out of the corner of his eye, he saw Andersen nod. "He's right," the Department 5 director said to Geiger.

She didn't seem happy about this.

Faris tried to hold back his budding anger. "The caller …"

"Which caller?" Geiger interrupted.

Faris saw Ben roll his eyes behind her back. He gulped down a frustrated curse.

Unlike her predecessor, who had authorized SURV's creation, Geiger believed that the special unit was superfluous. Just like everyone else in the room, Faris knew that she was always on the lookout for reasons to shut down SURV and to transfer its responsibilities to the state security division. She was a huge fan of the United States' War against Terrorism, and Faris recalled a sharp argument between Geiger and Tromsdorff about the line that divided military operations and crime prevention – and about the controversial National Defense Authorization Act the US President had signed several years earlier. To date, Tromsdorff had always succeeded at parrying Geiger's attacks against SURV, thanks to his tactical cleverness and his willingness to make use of his contacts in the highest echelons of the police hierarchy.

He now informed her, in minimal words, of the calls that Faris had received. He also explained the content of the video and the conclusions that they had already reached.

"Can anyone in this room confirm Mr. Iskander's statements?" Geiger asked.

Andersen stared at her with bewilderment. "What do you mean?"

"I'm just wondering if anyone else has spoken with this mysterious caller."

"No," Tromsdorff replied. "Why …"

"So, all we have is Mr. Iskander's claim …."

"*Detective* Iskander," Paul interrupted.

Her head whipped around, and her eyes bore into his momentarily. "As I was saying, all we have is *Mr.* Iskander's statement," she repeated, placing emphasis on the word *Mr.*, "that there even *was* a caller."

"What are you trying to say?" Faris exclaimed. He jumped to his feet but quickly sat back down, feeling dizzy.

"Yes, Anke, what?" Tromsdorff now intervened. His face was somber, and Faris could see that he was disgusted by his supervisor's behavior. Time was ticking away on them, and instead of focusing on the case, they had to deal with this woman's prejudices.

"Robert," she sighed, as if speaking to an obtuse child. "I'm about to walk into a press conference because a bomb just went off on the Berlin subway. According to your theories, there is a direct threat to the church conference. What do you think people are going to say when it gets out that we're letting a …" she broke off.

Muslim, Faris thought, but Dr. Geiger wasn't dumb enough to reveal her true feelings. She reconsidered her word choice and continued, "… *suspended officer* work on the investigation?"

Faris closed his eyes. She had played her trump card, and she knew it.

"Have you told your colleagues everything you know?" she asked Faris.

He nodded reluctantly, only then opening his eyes again. "But I haven't officially added my information to the case file."

"Fine. Then I want you to repeat it one more time and then leave the premises. You are suspended, and you haven't lost anything by your involvement in this case as a witness."

Faris searched Tromsdorff's face, reading regret there. He had to give his supervisor credit for making one last attempt: "Faris is my best investigator, Anke, and we need him here! You could lift his suspension. You can't send him away!"

An arch smile was the only answer Geiger gave him.

"The caller contacted him, specifically," Paul now interjected. "There has to be a reason for that."

This caused Geiger to glance at Faris's phone, which was still sitting on the table next to Ben's laptop. "Is that yours?" she asked Faris.

He nodded grimly. He knew that if he opened his mouth right now, he would shout at her.

"Leave it here!" Geiger ordered.

"What if he calls back?" Ben cut in. "And Faris doesn't pick up?"

The question floated in the middle of the room, and everyone stared at Dr. Geiger expectantly. However, before she could reply, Ben's phone rang. He answered.

"Yes?" He listened for a second. "That's what I thought," he said. Then, immediately, his eyes grew huge. "Say that again!"

He listened intently to what the person on the other end of the line was saying.

"Shit," he cursed. "Thanks, Carla."

He hung up and stared at the phone, as if it had suddenly transformed itself into a snake. "That was Carla," he said, unnecessarily. "It appears that our culprit is using an internet phone service. She was able to trace the call back to a provider in Poland, but that's all. It's a dead end. However, the email with the video ..." He fell silent, gazing at Faris, his eyes pensive.

"Keep talking!" Geiger barked.

"The email with the video the guy sent you, Faris ..." Ben swallowed before continuing. "It came from your own home computer!"

"That's impossible!"

Faris didn't notice that he had jumped to his feet until a wave of dizziness washed over him again, and he had to grab onto the edge of the table. He dropped heavily back into his seat. "That's simply not possible!" he repeated in confusion.

Geiger's eyes bore into his. "I'm truly sorry, Mr. Iskander, but I'm slowly starting to wonder if it isn't perhaps your intent to obstruct the investigation, instead of helping with it."

Shannon and Paul reacted to these words with incredulous laughter.

"I didn't send myself that email!" Faris shouted. "That's …"

But Geiger interrupted him. "Determining that isn't a priority right now. We'll deal with you later. We have a bomber to find!" She glanced toward the door. "Make your statement, and then leave."

Faris tried to catch Tromsdorff's eyes, but at that moment, as he was about to speak, something overcame him. A flashback washed over him, a billow of fire and pain. Unable to fight it, he doubled over and wheezed in agony. The attack vanished as quickly as it had hit, but the brief moment had been enough. Geiger had seen it.

And she understood what had happened. "You're a ticking time bomb, Iskander," she hissed through tight lips.

Tromsdorff cleared his throat. "Perhaps it really would be for the best, Faris," he murmured. "Paul can take your statement."

"No," Geiger disagreed. "I would like someone from the 118 to do it, so we can have a neutral perspective on whatever he has to say."

Faris nodded curtly, although he was struggling to keep himself under control. With her last words, she had indirectly accused the SURV team of being biased. Everyone in the War Room was aware of that. Frosty silence spread throughout the space. Faris stood up. "*I* am *not* your problem," he said as calmly as he could.

He then crossed the room, yanked open the door, and practically dashed down the corridor to the staircase.

"Faris! Wait!" Tromsdorff's words echoed down the hallway after him.

Tromsdorff caught up with him at the lower landing. "Calm down!" he begged. He looked like he had a stomach ulcer. Deep lines ran down from the corners of his mouth.

"*Calm down*?" Faris struggled to keep his volume low. "That incompetent bitch!" He pointed upstairs.

"Faris!" Tromsdorff reached for Faris's arm and looked directly into his eyes.

"I didn't send the message to myself," he said. "You have to …"

"I know. Ben will find the proof, I'm sure of that. And when he has it, I will put her hand to the flame and force her to admit that she is the one hindering our investigation, not you. But for the time being, my hands are tied."

"I can help you, Robert." Fury continued to surge through Faris. Anger because he was about to be kicked out the door, forbidden from helping with this case. He clung to that outrage, as he checked his watch. It was already after noon. They had only thirty-six hours to catch a culprit for whom nothing was beyond the pale. Thirty-six hours! Good Lord!

You are a ticking time bomb, Geiger had claimed.

He tightened his jaw. He'd be damned if he would prove her right! "Okay," he said, after taking a deep breath. "Is there any way that I could still help you?"

"Not officially, but you need to make sure you stay accessible." Tromsdorff glanced around. "Get yourself a new phone and call Paul so that we have your number. We'll see what happens after that. First, though, you need to give your statement to the 118."

The 118 was one of the murder commissions, and like SURV, it was also currently working on the bomb case. In all likelihood, half of the Berlin police force was probably working on the same thing.

Tromsdorff waited until Faris nodded.

"Good," he then said. "I'll try to convince Geiger that we need you on the team."

Faris listened to the blood rushing in his ears. "What if he calls again, Robert, and I don't answer?"

Tromsdorff didn't know what to say to this. "Let's hope that we figure out how to handle it by then."

"If he sets off another bomb in retaliation, she'll have …"

"I know, Faris."

"Good grief, can't you go over her head or something?"

"I can't, and you know that." Above them, on the stairs, they could hear the clatter of high heels. "SURV might be the only department in a position to actually catch this guy. I have to make sure that our team remains operational for this."

Geiger descended the stairs. As she walked past, she sent Faris and Tromsdorff a belligerent look, but she was smart enough not to speak to either of them.

Tromsdorff waited until she was out of earshot. "I will talk to her and try to change her mind," he promised. He looked unhappy as he said this. "Go to the 118 and make your statement."

"Let me stay!" Faris begged, although he knew there was no point in asking.

Tromsdorff shook his head. "Geiger has it in for SURV, you know that as well as I do. If I disregard her direct order, I'll end up sacrificing the whole unit. You know she's just waiting for the opportunity to shut us down."

Faris lowered his head. Tromsdorff was right. The SURV team had to remain intact. There were no alternatives. "Light a fire under Ben so he figures out as fast as possible how the guy managed to send that message from my personal computer."

Tromsdorff nodded wearily. "I will. And you stay available." Tromsdorff patted Faris's arm one last time. "I'm sorry, son. There's nothing else I can do right now."

CHAPTER 10

Faris's statement for the 118 was filmed and immediately added to the DigA A file system, so that all the investigators working on the case in various departments could have access to it. The entire procedure took barely an hour. Faris asked his colleagues if it was wise for them to keep using the digital archive, and they assured him that the IT specialists had found the hole in the firewall and fixed it. Faris thanked them before leaving the building on Keithstraße.

It was a few minutes after one o'clock as he hurried down the staircase in long, frustrated strides. He raced past the guard station and through the double oak doors, out onto the street. A bicycle courier had to swerve wildly around him as he launched himself out onto the sidewalk.

"Watch out!" Faris yelled after him. His frustration was dancing as red dots behind his eyelids.

"I did!" the courier bellowed back of his shoulder. "You aren't face down on the sidewalk, are you?" And with that, he sped off.

Faris took a deep breath, trying to calm down again.

There were several cell phone shops along Kurfürstenstraße, which intersected Keithstraße near Department 1's building.

He picked one at random and asked the young man behind the counter to show him several budget phones with prepaid cards. He ignored the slightly irritated look the man sent him as he registered Faris's dusty, battered appearance and finally chose a device that cost just sixty euros. He paid with his bank card and asked the salesclerk to insert the SIM card and give him a quick overview of the phone's functions. Then he stuck the phone's charger into his jacket pocket, where he had previously kept his regular phone, and left the shop.

The sky had cleared a little while he was inside. Faris dialed Paul's number. When he reached his colleague's voicemail, he left a short message. "It's me! Robert asked me to stay in touch. This is the number where you can reach me in case of emergency." He hung up and deposited the phone in the pocket with the charger.

As he considered what he should do now, he heard someone call his name.

"Iskander!"

Faris turned around and almost groaned aloud when he saw who was hurrying in his direction. "Niklas," he murmured.

The man who came to a stop in front of him, panting, was at least twenty kilos overweight, a reality that he was trying to hide with an untucked red-and-blue checkered lumberjack shirt. He was wearing black biker boots, and a leather jacket with a cocked collar completed the carefully crafted image of the investigative journalist. With a quick visual sweep from top to bottom, he took in Faris's appearance. "Did you get caught in a sandstorm?" he asked with a grin.

Faris gazed down his body. He desperately needed a shower and fresh clothes. With a weary smile and a shake of his head, he met the reporter's eyes.

Niklas had already pulled a digital recorder out of his jacket pocket, but he hadn't turned it on yet. "What happened?" he asked.

Faris had known Niklas Hesse for a long time. They had met during their last year of high school, just before final exams. After that, they had both joined the police department and taken their exams together. However, while Faris had chosen a classic police career track and spent a while doing patrol duty, Hesse had taken a different path. While Faris pursued his career, eventually being tapped by Tromsdorff to join the SURV team, Hesse stayed at the police academy as an instructor. Two years ago, he had finally left the academy, and Faris had lost sight of him. Several months later, though, Hesse had returned to Berlin. He was strangely changed, and instead of working once more for the police, he had left the force and founded an investigative online magazine called *hotnewzz.tv*, which barely made him enough to scrape by, these days. He had never told Faris what he had done for the few months he was away, but after a hard grilling, had admitted that there was a woman involved. Faris assumed that she had broken his heart.

"No comment," was all Faris said.

Hesse just laughed, then glanced toward Keithstraße. After a brief moment of consideration, he said, "Are you back at work now?" He knew about Faris's suspension.

Faris shook his head. "I was there as a witness." Geiger's ouster still infuriated him, but he kept that to himself.

"As a witness?"

Faris nodded. "And you?"

Hesse shrugged. "The subway bombing, of course. I'm on my way to Keithstraße. I thought I might get more information there than at the station. Everything over there is still cordoned off for quite a distance." He tapped his forehead at the corresponding spot to where Faris's bandage sat. "You really took a hit there, didn't you?"

Faris forced himself to smile. "Don't even bother. You won't get anything out of me."

"Come on!" Hesse's eyes suddenly narrowed. "Bismarckstraße! Isn't that pretty close to your apartment?"

Faris didn't reply.

"Of course!" Hesse's eyes once again scanned him from head to feet. "You were down there when the bomb went off, weren't you? That's why there's a bandage on your hard head."

Faris sighed. "There'd be no point if I denied it."

"And?"

"And nothing." Faris turned to go.

But Hesse refused to be shaken. "Come on, bro! You can't ditch me like this."

"Wanna bet?"

This was a little game they had been playing since Hesse's reinvention as a reporter. Hess acted stubborn, and Faris played hard-to-get as long as possible. At the same time, the reporter was one of the few journalists that Faris had ever unofficially passed along information to. He had always been able to trust Niklas. During their friendlier moments, they even shared personal secrets that they didn't tell anyone else. Niklas knew about Faris's psychological problems, and in return, the reporter had shared that he had spent a long time in therapy to work through the time he had spent in an orphanage as a child.

A woman with a stroller walked toward them. She strode with great determination, as if she were charging with a battering ram. Faris and Hesse let her pass between them.

"There were fatalities," the reporter tried again. "I went over there, but your colleagues wouldn't let me go down."

Faris sent him a sideways glance. "Why do you think that was?"

Hesse snorted. "The people have a right to ..."

Faris broke into laughter. His anger at Geiger was slowly dissipating. "Spare me!" he exclaimed. He resumed walking, knowing fully well that Hesse wouldn't let him slip away.

"Dadgummit!" The reporter hurried after him. For several minutes, they marched side by side down Kurfürstenstraße, and because Faris was walking quickly, Hesse soon started to wheeze. "Can't you slow down a little!"

Faris stopped. "You should work out more," he teased.

Hesse was about to respond, but at that moment, Faris's new phone started ringing. It had a shrill, old-fashioned ring tone, the sound of which made Hesse grimace. "What kind of cheap phone is that?" he asked as Faris pulled out the device.

Faris ignored his derision. He answered without even glancing at the screen. "Partner?" It had to be Paul, since he was the only one who had this number.

"I just wanted to let you know I got your message," Paul declared. "Everything okay?"

Faris glanced at Hesse, then turned his back on him. "Yes. Niklas is with me. Just happened to run into him on Kurfürstenstraße."

"Alright. I assume he's right next to you, salivating with curiosity, right?"

Faris turned his head. "Something like that," he confirmed with a smile.

"I can imagine. Now, listen. We'll try to keep you in the loop on things as much as possible, until Tromsdorff manages to bring you back on board. This is where things are. We're still working on the caller and the video. Shannon is looking into the known fundamentalist extremists. Andersen has set up a team that is doing the major footwork for her, and we're getting an officer from the 632 who'll be our go-between with Andersen's guys."

"Good. I assume the guys are really chomping at the bit, right?"

The officers in Department 632 were used, among other things, to ending hostage situations. Most of them had been trained in both psychology and criminology and were always called in when there was a need to convince a hostage-taker to surrender.

Faris could hear a grim smile in Paul's voice, as his partner replied: "They're hoping the guy will break cover soon, so they have something to do."

Faris ran his fingers through his dust-coated hair. "We're all hoping for that."

"We're working on it, partner. Have you remembered anything at all that could help us?"

"I don't have even the slightest notion who the guy could be." Faris shook his head. By this point, Hesse had walked around him and was staring curiously into his face, so Faris turned around once more. "Could you try to convince Tromsdorff to give me access to the DigA A? I'd like to look through some things there." Because of his suspension, he had lost his access to the case files.

"Are you heading home?" Paul asked.

Faris glanced at Niklas Hesse. Of course, he could have gone home and accessed the DigA A archive on his own computer, but his personal device was old and not the fastest thing around. Skimming through the audio and video files on that machine would be a tiresome task. "Not yet," he replied. "Just try to get Tromsdorff to reinstate my access."

Hesse walked around Faris again.

In muffled tones, Paul said something to somebody else in the room, then he was back on the phone. "All uniformed units have just been instructed to keep their eyes out for any places that could hold a cross. Maybe we'll get lucky, and someone will discover something that could lead us to the crucified man before ..." he broke off here.

But Faris knew what he had been about to say.

... before the next bomb goes off.

"Oh, and one more thing," Paul added. "Geiger took a look at your statement, and she asked Ben to take a picture of the crucified man. At this moment, she's sharing it with the press."

"Hmmm." Faris rubbed the bridge of his nose. It was routine procedure to ask the public for clues in missing persons cases. However, in this instance, he wasn't sure if Geiger's decision was wise or not. The caller hadn't explicitly forbidden this course of action, but what did they actually know about what made him tick? They couldn't simply dismiss the possibility that he might snap if he saw the picture of his victim online or discovered it in a newspaper. And yet, Faris forced himself to calm down. Geiger might be somewhat narrow-minded, but she wasn't stupid. She and her staff would have carefully weighed the pros and cons of releasing the picture.

"We're hoping to get some information about the identity of the man. Gitta is going through the old files from the museum case, but so far, we haven't found anything."

"Something might come to me." Faris took a deep sigh. "I'll call as soon as that happens," he murmured.

"Good. I'll talk to Robert about the DigA A." Again, Paul seemed to turn away from his phone. "I'm coming," Faris heard him call out to someone else. "The code monkeys seem to have plugged the hole in the firewall," he informed Faris.

"I know. The guys with the 118 told me about that."

"Good. We'll stay in touch," Paul promised before hanging up.

Faris stood on the sidewalk of Kurfürstenstraße and stared at the phone in his hand. His head and shoulders ached, and for a moment, he lacked the energy to take even one more step.

"Sounds as if they put you out on the street," Hesse remarked.

Faris shrugged. "Looks like it."

Hesse grinned broadly. "Because of that thing with the skinhead asshole? What was his name?" Hesse was one of the few people to whom Faris had told the full story of his fight with the neo-Nazi.

"Rainer Golzer."

"Well, if you ask me, they should've given you a medal for what you did."

Faris just sniffed.

"Fucking skinheads!" Hesse was becoming increasingly agitated. "They should all get punched in the jaw more often!"

Faris didn't react to this. "Do you have a fast computer I could use?"

"Sure. If you'll give me a few bits of information in exchange."

After brief consideration, Faris agreed. "The bomb in the subway. There was an emailed confession." He was elaborating on the truth just a little. "But we can't trace it because the sender is some kind of crappy hacker."

"Hey!" Hesse protested. "There are no such things as *crappy* hackers!"

Faris didn't press this point. "He managed to make it look as if the email came from my PC. This was why Geiger wouldn't even consider letting me work on the case, regardless of my suspension."

"How annoying! But in all seriousness … Doesn't the queen know that these days it's quite easy to send an email from any computer you want?" Faris shrugged, and Hesse continued. "All someone had to do was smuggle a trojan onto your computer, and presto, he could send out any message he wanted."

"Would it be possible for someone to figure out if my computer has a trojan on it?" Faris asked.

"Sure. All I'd need to do is get into your apartment and take a closer look at the machine."

Faris hadn't missed Hesse's transition from the generic *someone* to the specific *I*. A weak sparkle had appeared in the reporter's eyes, the onset of hunting fever. Faris knew all too well what this felt like, and he could feel it start to spread inside him as well.

"Fine," he decided. "If you can help me prove that, I'll give you more details about the case."

CHAPTER 11

They took Hesse's motorcycle to Faris's apartment. The first thing Faris saw when he stepped inside was the mirror in the hallway. He stopped abruptly. He looked like a victim from the collapse of the World Trade Center, completely covered in a fine gray dust. More like a ghost than a living person. As Hesse started up his computer to look for clues to a trojan, Faris took off his jacket and went into his bedroom. He quickly slipped off his pants and t-shirt. In just his underwear, he strode into the bathroom, finished undressing, and took a shower. When this was done, he stood dripping in front of the sink, and turned on the light above it to thoroughly examine himself.

His eyes still had the burning expression of exhaustion and sleep deprivation. The water hadn't been able to wash the dust from all the fine lines in his skin, so he looked older than he actually was. He brushed his longish hair off his forehead before reaching for a towel and drying off. When he was done with this, he looked halfway civilized again.

As he reached for the light switch, ready to turn it off, his eyes fell on the burn scar on his torso. It slanted, dark red, from his hip over his right pec up to his clavicle, and then across his bicep, almost to the shoulder joint. At various spots, the skin puckered in ugly folds, while other patches had an odd, pockmarked pattern to them. People at his rehab program had explained that these were where the synthetic fibers of the fleece shirt he wore that day had seared themselves into his skin.

For a few seconds, Faris stood motionless, incapable of moving, incapable even of lowering his hand which was still holding the light switch. He just stared silently at the wounds the explosion had left on his body and waited for the flashbacks to start. To his relief, they didn't.

He could pull himself together after a few moments.

With a sigh, he flipped off the light and left the bathroom. In his bedroom, he pulled a clean pair of jeans and a t-shirt from his closet and got dressed. His hoodie had suffered too much in the explosion, so he reached for his leather jacket before leaving his bedroom to join Hesse in the living room.

"Well?" Faris asked. "Found anything yet?"

Hesse was perched on the edge of an armchair, balancing Faris's relatively aged laptop on his knees.

"Here's the bastard." He gestured at the screen. "You really do have a trojan on your hard drive."

"A trojan." Faris had only a vague notion of what that was, and Hesse clearly saw that straightaway.

The reporter grinned. "Someone has laid a lovely egg in your nest. Think of it this way. A trojan is a program that can take complete control of a computer. Most of the time, it's dormant, so you don't notice it's there. For example, someone could smuggle one onto your computer via an email attachment, and once it's there, it won't wake up until a certain time and then it will take some kind of action. This one here sent you an email with a video link this morning."

Faris ground his teeth. "Can you tell where the trojan came from?"

Hesse nodded. "Eventually."

"Could Ben do it?" Faris asked.

Hesse shrugged. "Ask him."

Faris went back into the bedroom, lifted his dusty sweatshirt jacket and pulled his new phone out of it. With it and the charger in one hand, he walked back over to Hesse while dialing Paul. When he had him on the line, he asked to speak with Ben. The Forensics Institute specialist sounded grumpy when he picked up.

In a few sentences, Faris explained to him what Hesse had discovered.

"There really is a trojan on my computer. Could you determine where it came from?"

Ben muttered something that sounded like "decompile." Then, "It could take a while," he added.

"How long?"

"Too long for our needs, I'm afraid."

Faris looked at Hesse. "Thanks, Ben," he said and was about to hang up when Ben distinctly cleared his throat. "Yes?" Faris asked.

"I would never ever advise you to do anything illegal," Ben said quietly. "That's obvious, right?"

"Of course!"

"But there are people out there who don't have to follow the rules as much as we do."

"You're talking about Niklas, right?"

Ben murmured something unintelligible. "I have to go now." And with that, he simply hung up.

Faris ended the call too. While sticking his phone and the charger into his leather jacket he asked again, "Could you find out who put that trojan on my computer? Quickly, I mean."

Hesse grinned. "Yeah, but I'll need to make a quick run home. I need a few of my toys to do this." He started to close the laptop but hesitated and shot Faris a questioning glance. "Alright?"

Faris didn't think for long. "Alright," he said. "But I'm coming with you."

At the youth hostel, lunch was served at eleven-thirty, and since Jenny and Pia had missed breakfast that morning, they decided to replace that meal with pasta and meat sauce.

They had just sat down with their plates, when a deep voice with a slightly amused undertone spoke up behind Jenny. "This isn't exactly calorie-friendly eating."

Pia, who was sitting opposite Jenny, looked surprised. Jenny quickly swallowed the bite she had already taken and turned around. Her heart did a somersault when she saw that it was the guy from yesterday.

Today, his tattoos were covered by a long-sleeved t-shirt, the front of which featured a picture of some heavy metal band. With a grin that looked a little sheepish, the young man pointed at the unoccupied chair at Jenny and Pia's table. "May I join you?"

Jenny nodded. "Sure." She felt her cheeks flush and was glad that she had put on a little makeup this morning. Hopefully, her blush wouldn't show up as clearly.

With fascination, she watched him turn the chair around, so that its back faced the table, and then sling one of his long legs over the seat before sitting down. "Not that you need to do that," he said, smiling roguishly.

"Huh?" Pia said. Her fork was floating halfway between her face and the plate.

"Count calories," the guy clarified. "With your figures, you could treat yourselves to a little spaghetti Bolognese, in my opinion."

"That was a compliment," Jenny declared, and she almost started laughing, because at that very moment a fat clump of sauce tumbled off of Pia's fork and splatted onto the table. "A *little*," she chuckled.

The guy grinned back. "I'm Dennis," he said, introducing himself good-naturedly.

Jenny and Pia did the same. "What are you doing here in Berlin?" Pia asked, having already scraped the sauce off the tablecloth and smeared it on the edge of her plate.

"Attending the church convention. What about you?"

Jenny stared at Dennis in disbelief. "For real?"

He laughed again as he fished a roll out of the basket sitting in the middle of the table. "Yes. What's so weird about that?" he asked, as he tore his roll in half.

Jenny shook her head. "Nothing, just …" She suddenly didn't know what to say.

"You don't look like someone who goes to worship services or Bible studies," Pia offered helpfully. "We thought you were here for the music festival."

Jenny envied Pia the self-confidence she radiated as she smiled at

Dennis. She didn't seem even slightly embarrassed. Jenny realized that this annoyed her.

"Really?" Dennis took a bite from his roll and chewed contemplatively. His eyes twinkled with amusement. "What do you need to wear to attend a church conference? An overcoat and orthopedic shoes?" He peered over the edge of the tabletop at Pia's feet, which were clad in modern, knee-high boots with heels.

"Something like that," Pia giggled. "What are you doing today?"

"I thought I would look around Berlin some. This afternoon, there's a lecture on the Sermon on the Mount that I'd like to hear."

"You're serious about that, aren't you?" Jenny now cut in.

Dennis turned to face her, and she felt simultaneously hot and cold. "Of course." He tugged at his t-shirt. The rest of his roll sat abandoned on the table.

"You like the Sermon on the Mount?" Jenny bit her lip. Why did every sentence she managed to squeeze out sound so wooden?

"It's a cool story, don't you think? And you? What are the two of you doing?"

"We went to Museum Island yesterday," Jenny answered hastily. Crap! He had to think she was a total dumbass. She hadn't even answered his question.

But Dennis simply nodded with interest. "And? Was it interesting?"

Jenny gulped as he now stared right at her. His eyes were dark brown, which she had already noted the previous day, but now she noticed that his pupils were ringed with honey brown. Gorgeous eyes. "Yes," she said, as Pia exclaimed, "No!"

"Aha!" Dennis laughed. "It's good that you both agree."

Jenny threw Pia a dark glare. "The Rosa Luxemburg exhibition is good!"

"True," Pia admitted. "But how about we spend the day together and paint Berlin red? We wanted to take a city tour. The Brandenburg Gate, Checkpoint Charlie, all the touristy stuff."

"Sounds tempting." Dennis didn't look at Pia as he said this. His eyes were on Jenny. "What do you think?"

"About what?" Jenny's head was spinning. All of a sudden, she felt terribly warm! And then that question! Things couldn't get any worse at this point!

"About the possibility of my joining you. You haven't said anything about that, and I don't want to be a burden to anyone."

"You aren't." Jenny bit her lip. Why couldn't she show just a little more enthusiasm? After all, Dennis was really nice, and she would be ecstatic if he spent the day with them.

"Honestly?" He looked so intently into her eyes that she couldn't breathe.

"Honestly!" With a jolt, she stood up. She had to get out of here, or she'd pass out. "It would be great if you came along." With those words, she fled the cafeteria. The last thing she heard was Dennis's startled voice.

"What's wrong with her?"

CHAPTER 12

Berlin's lunchtime traffic was always horrible, so Faris decided it would be best for him to leave his car where it was and to ride along with Hesse on his motorcycle.

They always met in bars or restaurants, so Faris hadn't been to Hesse's place since the reporter's return to Berlin. It now occurred to Faris, as they snaked at breakneck speed between the densely packed cars, that he had no idea where Hesse was living these days.

He leaned a little to the side, to ask Hesse this very question. The airstream roared past his ears, as the helmet that Hesse had insisted that he wear pressed uncomfortably against the laceration on his forehead.

Hesse turned his head for just a moment and grinned at Faris before concentrating on the traffic once again. "Just wait. You'll be surprised!"

And Faris actually was.

Hesse left the City Ring Road, taking the Tempelhofer Damm exit. He drove past the Air Lift Memorial and along Columbiadamm Road until they reached the former gate to the old Tempelhof Airport.

"Don't tell me that you live in this huge box?" Faris exclaimed, after Hesse had parked his bike.

The reporter was still grinning.

He led Faris onto the old airport grounds, past buildings still wrapped mutely in the corsets of their ponderous Nazi facades. It had been years since Tempelhof was operational. Back when it was shut down, there had been heated discussions in the city about what to do with the historically significant buildings and the long runways. The Berliners living in the adjacent neighborhoods had quickly taken over the landing strips for use as a recreational park, but even yet today, there were no formal solutions concerning what to do with the huge buildings, which stretched for thousands of meters. Following a campus party at the old airport some years ago – during which programmers, bloggers and inventors from sixty-six countries had gathered – a handful of attendees had stayed behind. Like the European squatters of the mid-eighties, they had simply commandeered the complex and lived there for several years. As far as Faris knew, the police had received orders not all that long ago to break up the illegal commune in the airport building.

He now followed Hesse through one of the smaller sets of double doors, down a short corridor, and up a narrow stairway. After passing through one other door, they found themselves in the middle of the airport's abandoned terminal building.

Faris stood stock-still. "Wow!"

This terminal was tied to one of his earliest childhood memories. He must have been around four. His parents, along with Faris and his older sister Anisah, had just arrived at Tempelhof from Egypt. Faris recalled how he had stared out through the giant glass doors to where a steady, gray rain was falling from an equally gray sky – a rain unlike anything he had ever seen before. And he also still remembered turning around and seeing tears running down his mother's face. It was the first time he had ever seen her cry. Back then, he had wondered how the raindrops outdoors had reached his mother's cheeks.

"Impressive, isn't it?"

Faris gave a start. He had been so wrapped up in the past that he hadn't noticed when Hesse stopped beside him. The luggage carousel was here as well; and the check-in counters, which ran along the long sides of the terminal, were still intact. The squatters had colorfully painted the panes and the walls of the small counter cubicles, so they looked like a collection of little hippie cottages. Two withered yuccas were standing in front of one such "cottage", and the nooks and crannies everywhere were filled with filth, empty bottles, plastic bags, and garbage of all kinds.

"I thought we'd cleared out the commune," Faris murmured.

Hesse gestured possessively across the whole expanse. "You did. I got here after that." He glanced at Faris. "Come on."

They crossed the terminal hall and walked up one of the two staircases that led to where the restaurant had been located on the gable end of the building. Up here, there was a gallery-like collection of offices. A strange smell was floating in the air, a combination of vapors from ancient flooring materials and all the rotting trash. Faris grimaced in disgust.

Hesse led him through the gallery to one of the offices. Unlike the other doors, the one to this office had been carefully fitted with a padlock. The reporter fished out a key, opened the lock, and invited Faris to enter.

"Wow!" Faris exclaimed for the second time as he stepped over the threshold.

The former office was perhaps twenty-five meters square, and its blue carpeting, like the flooring out in the passageway, had clearly seen better days. Every centimeter of the floor area was being used. There were at least a half dozen computers standing around – some sitting on a massive oak table that looked like it had been salvaged from the dump, while others were simply standing on the floor. Thick cables snaked across the floor before vanishing into old cable ducts or into black boxes, the short sides of which held little flashing green and red LEDs. Besides the computers, there was a narrow plank bed that sat against the milk glass panes across from the door, and a small kitchenette that had apparently been left behind by the airport's former food service provider. All in all, the space looked exactly as Faris imagined a computer freak's residence would. As soon as the door closed, you forgot where you were.

Hesse deposited Faris's laptop on the oak table, before pulling out an old desk chair which he kicked towards Faris. "Sit down! I need to start up the computer, and that'll take a moment. I'll make us some tea, and then we can start."

He walked over to the kitchenette, filled a pot with water from a large plastic canister, and submerged an old immersion heater in it.

"The power's still on?" Faris asked in amazement. He ignored the proffered chair and remained standing.

Hesse nodded as he rummaged through one of the cupboards for a tea tin. "I have to be a little creative, but yes. Unfortunately, someone would notice if I kept all the computers running at once, so I have to turn them off from time to time." He spooned the loose-leaf tea into a tarnished tea ball and hung it inside a porcelain teapot decorated with pictures of roses, which looked about as out-of-place here as a Persian carpet would in a homeless shelter.

"Why here?" Faris looked around and felt a hint of irrationality. Previously, Hesse had lived in a small apartment in Charlottenburg, and this change of residence was somehow – bizarre.

"Why do I live here?"

"Yes."

Hesse didn't answer until the water started to boil. He extracted the immersion heater and poured the tea. The scent of cherries filled the room, intensifying Faris's feeling of irrationality. "Well, because I don't have to pay rent. Since your esteemed colleagues evicted the squatters and sealed up the building, I've had it all to myself. Nobody bothers me. Nobody even suspects that I'm in here." He stretched out on his cot and leaned against the milk glass panes. "It's perfect, I'd say."

Faris wrinkled his forehead. He gazed at Hesse inquiringly, but then his eyes fell on a framed photo standing in the midst of all the cables and devices, looking practically as incongruous as the teapot with the roses. He picked it up and studied it. It showed a dark-haired woman with a wide, cheerful smile and dangly gold earrings in the shape of little stars.

"Is this the woman you left Berlin for?" he asked, turning the photo around so Hesse could see it. On the back side of the frame, a price tag from IKEA announced that the item had cost 8.99 euros.

For a long moment, Hesse stared at the photo, and a shadow flitted across his face. "Yes," was all he said.

Since his return to Berlin, Faris had tried a few times to find out more about this woman, but the reporter had refused to talk. Faris had changed the subject every time to spare Hesse any further awkwardness. Although they talked about a lot of different things, women hadn't really been among them, even before now.

"She looks Arabic," Faris said, setting the picture back in its place.

"Hmm," was all he received as an answer.

Faris glanced back over his shoulder through the open door into the huge terminal hall. And all of a sudden – so unexpectedly that Faris almost registered it as pain – the state of mind he had been living in for months now received a name. *Doomsday mood*, he thought. He promptly felt such a profound loneliness that he started to shiver. He suspected that he wouldn't make it here more than a couple of days before wanting to send a bullet through his skull.

Hesse got up from his cot and removed the tea ball from the pot. The aroma of cherries intensified. He then poured the tea into two mugs and handed one of them to Faris. At almost that exact moment, several computers buzzed to announce that they were now booted up.

"So," Hesse declared, "we can get started!" He rubbed his hands together, and suddenly he was back to being the investigative journalist.

Faris cleared his throat. Those few sentences about the unknown young woman in the picture had reminded him of Laura and their screwed-up relationship. He rotated the faded leather bracelet around his wrist and held back a sigh. "Good. You can have the whole story, but you have to promise me that you won't publish it until I give you the green light!"

Hesse rolled his eyes. "Come on, old man, I …"

Faris shook his head determinedly. "No, Niklas. It's really important. Promise me!"

From beneath his disheveled hair, Hesse studied him. "But is it something big? It's about the subway bombing, right?"

Faris recalled his colleagues' theory that the next attack would be at the candlelight Mass, and considered which bits of information he should reveal.

Usually, an event would be canceled, and the population would be warned, whenever evidence indicated that an attack was being planned. However, in this case, such decisions would be postponed until concrete evidence proved when the next attack would occur. Forty hours was a long time, and besides, nobody knew how many bombs the attacker had hidden around the city and which he would detonate if they tried to intervene in his plans.

What they needed more than anything else was information.

"Yes," Faris replied slowly after he had thought through all this. "It's about the bombing in the subway. And we're afraid there will be more."

Hesse's eyes widened. "More attacks? Did he threaten that in his confession letter?"

"Basically, yes. As you already know, my hands are tied. You would help a lot if you could figure out, as quickly as possible, the location from which the man sent the trojan to my computer."

Hesse stared at his hands. "You know that the methods I use won't produce usable results, right? If we actually learn something, you couldn't use it as evidence in court."

Faris nodded.

"And you also know that working this case on your own could cost you your job, don't you?" the reporter continued.

Faris gritted his teeth and nodded again.

The lives of hundreds of Berliners were at stake here. Over sixty thousand people were expected to attend the communion service tomorrow. Sixty thousand! What a nightmare! How could he care about his job, in the face of that? Conversely, if he managed to put a stop to this bastard's game, it would be a price he would pay – not happily, but in good conscience.

"Get started," he commanded curtly.

Hesse rubbed his chin and mouth, then sat down. "Alright. Let's see what we can do."

With that, he rolled his chair over to the old oak table, which ran the length of the room and was covered in papers, electronic devices, and all kinds of technical gadget. The only thing Faris could identify with relative certainty was a mixing console. He knew that Hesse needed it to work up the audio files for his magazine.

A gaudily colored flame symbol adorned the monitor that the reporter now turned to.

Hotnewzz.tv, Faris read. It was the logo from Hesse's website.

Hesse clicked it away and saved some kind of file to a data stick, which he then inserted into Faris's laptop. He typed something into Faris's machine but hesitated before hitting the enter key.

"Uh, are you really sure you want me to do this?"

Faris considered this. "What's the worst that could happen?"

"I need to transfer a program to your computer. If your colleagues analyze it later, they'll find this program and know that you ..." He shrugged, leaving the rest of the sentence hanging in the air.

"Could they trace it back to you?" Faris asked.

Hesse grinned. "No."

This illegal activity wouldn't come back and haunt the reporter. Faris took a deep breath. "Do it."

"You won't give me up, if they grill you?"

"Of course not!"

"I'd tell them that you threatened to beat me up if I didn't do it." The journalist grinned again.

"Just get on with it."

Hesse pressed the enter key, and a loading bar appeared, growing longer as the copying process advanced. After a few seconds, the installation was over. Hesse immediately activated the installed program.

"So," he commented with satisfaction as he leaned backward. "This will take some time."

"How long?" Faris inquired.

"It depends how good your guy is."

"Okay." Faris glanced around. "Until the results come in, could I use your internet access to ..." he broke off when something chimed. Hesse had received an email.

The reporter turned toward his own computer and leaned forward. "Oh," he said. "A message from your family."

Faris stared at him in bewilderment, before looking up at the monitor – where he saw that Hesse had received a notification from the State Police press department. The subject line read: *Important Press Release from the Berlin Police Department.*

Hesse opened the message. "Does anybody recognize this man?" he read aloud. He then clicked on the attached photo, tilted his head, and scrutinized it.

It was the video still that Paul had mentioned before; a snapshot of the crucified man. And obviously, Ben had worked on it before it was sent out to the press. He had chosen a detail that didn't include any part of the cross. With the help of Photoshop, he had erased the blood running down the man's face and the crown of thorns. Only by looking closely could you tell that anything had ever been there.

But Hesse *was* looking closely. "Looks strange," he remarked. "What did they remove from his forehead and cheeks?"

Faris took a couple of deep breaths before supplying a concise summary of the crucifixion, the cardiac monitor, and the fact that a major bomb would go off in Berlin as soon as the victim's heart stopped beating.

Hesse's eyes grew larger with each passing sentence. "What a story!" he exclaimed.

At that moment, Faris felt very dizzy. He had to grab onto the edge of the table to keep from collapsing. For a second, the room grew dark around him.

"What is it?" he heard Hesse ask. He blinked and realized that the reporter was staring at him concernedly. "Are you feeling okay?"

He shook his head, which instantly began to ache dully. "Just a little headache." He let himself sink onto the desk chair that the reporter had offered him earlier.

"Did you get yourself checked out for concussion?" Hesse leaned over to the side and rummaged around in a piece of furniture that looked like an old nightstand. He fished out a blue-and-white carton that he tossed onto Faris's lap. It held painkillers. Faris took two of them and washed them down with the rest of his tea.

As he did this, Hesse started to type on his keyboard again. He clicked through several menus before writing a short caption.

"Do you know this man ?" Faris read. Hesse had shared the press release on his own website, which was what dozens of other online editors were probably doing right now, as well. In an hour and a half at most, the photo would be on the covers of all the newspapers.

The question was how the caller would react to this. He hadn't been in contact again, but the chances were good that he would call back when he saw the photo. And then he would learn that Faris had been excluded from working on the case. Faris swallowed. It was only a matter of time until the next bomb went off in the city. Of that, he was certain.

He suddenly felt unbelievably tired. Pulling out his phone, Faris dialed Paul's number.

"Sievers," the familiar voice of his partner declared on the other end.

"Paul, it's me."

"Faris. Where are you?"

"At Hesse's. He's just given me his Wi-Fi password, so I can access DigA A now. Has Tromsdorff worked that out yet?"

"Reluctantly," Paul said honestly. "He's taking a huge risk, you know." He didn't wait for a response, but immediately gave Faris the password. If he wondered why Faris had gone over to the reporter's place and wasn't at home, he gave no indication of that.

"Any news?" Faris asked. "I mean, other than the fact that the photo of the victim has now been released."

"You've already seen that." Paul sighed. "Andersen's ordered additional units to the Olympic Stadium. They're supposed to help the officers already stationed there to search for explosives. Requests for additional canine units have been sent out to the neighboring states."

"Has the caller been back in touch?"

"Not yet, we ..."

The rest of Paul's sentence got lost in a shout from Hesse: "Woohoo!"

Faris glanced hastily over at the reporter who was staring intently at his screen.

"Sorry about that," Faris said to Paul. "I didn't get your last sentence."

"I was just saying that we aren't sure yet if we should be happy or worried about that," Paul repeated.

"Shit!" Hesse growled at the same time.

"Wait a second, something's going on here." Faris stood up and walked over to the reporter. The first responses to the article that the reporter had just posted were now dribbling in. As so often, Faris was amazed at the speed with which things happened online. And how little sense they often made. As he skimmed the first lines, he saw that most of the comments were unusable.

Ugly guy! wrote one user.

Another responded with: *You think so? He doesn't look like a criminal.*

Nor is he, Faris thought. As he read through the remaining pointless comments, more and more of them appeared at the bottom of the list.

"Have you got anything?" he heard Paul ask.

Faris told him no. "The first responses to the photo of the victim are coming in. They're all trash."

Paul sighed. "We expected that! I'm sure the guys in the phone center have received a lot of nothing too, since the release of the photo. I think I'll head over there to see if they've gotten anything useful."

"How long do you think your program will need to get results?" Faris asked Hesse.

The journalist shrugged. "One hour. Two, three. No idea. Like I said, it depends on how good your guy is." While Faris talked with Paul, Hesse had made a first few attempts at sensationalist headlines.

"Bomber keeps Berlin in suspense," Faris read. "An attack motivated by faith."

Motivated by faith … Faris thought about his SURV colleagues, who were probably brooding over the analysis of the video right now.

He pointed at one of the computers. "May I use this?"

"Sure. The browser's already up and running, have at it." The reporter didn't look up from what he was doing.

Faris sat down and used the code that Paul had given him to log into the DigA A database. He knew the reference number for the Klersch Museum case by heart. He typed it into the pertinent search box. And just like that, he had access to all the reports, photos, and audio files that the investigators had compiled so far.

However, instead of tearing into them immediately, he hesitated.

Something in him protested at the idea of once again combing through all the details he had tried so hard to forget. He stared distractedly at the milk glass panes and let his thoughts drift.

Occasionally, when a case stumped him, he used this technique very deliberately, and occasionally something floated to the surface. A detail, a tiny fragment, that was out of place. A snatch of conversation that constituted a clue. Or just a hunch.

A hunch ...

Faris suddenly had a feeling that the answer to all of their questions wasn't in the old files, but in the words the caller had uttered to him on the phone.

He closed the museum file and opened today's new file instead. He didn't have the reference number for this case memorized, but the DigA A system was organized in such a way that the most heavily accessed files were listed on the right-hand side of the screen. And, since all the police officers in the city of Berlin were currently hunting for the bomber, this file stood at the top of the list.

It had already grown quite large. Faris located the recordings from the phone bank that was in charge of fielding the clues coming in from the general public. He also found the statements from the eyewitnesses of the subway explosion, as well as the first reports from the officers who had begun to interview the relatives of the museum bombing victims. Shannon Starck, his SURV colleague, had already made two entries in which she debated whether the two largest Christian fundamentalist groups in Berlin, God's Word Mission and Christ Freaks, could in any way be connected with the attacks.

Faris quickly skimmed Shannon's texts and the interviews. He then clicked on the audio file that had been generated from his own interrogation. When talking to the other officers, he had tried to quote as accurately as possible the two conversations with the bomber. He now started the recording. His voice sounded odd, and he listened to it as he would to that of a stranger.

At the spot where he heard himself murmur "And then he told me that I should go to the Bismarckstraße Station", he stopped the file. "Do you have something I could write with?" he asked Hesse.

"The second drawer from the bottom." Hesse pointed at the night-stand from which he had pulled the painkillers earlier.

Faris opened the drawer and pulled out a legal pad and one of several orange ballpoint pens, all of which bore the logo for *hotnewzz.tv*. He then began to reconstruct, word for word, his conversations with the bomber a second time.

The first thing he wrote on the tablet was *as-samu alaikum*. He added a question mark and wrote: *the bomber from the Klersch Museum?*

You remember, the caller had said. And: *You should've learned something by now*. Just like the Arabic phrase, this pointed to some kind of connection between the caller and the museum bomber. The SURV team had already dismissed the likelihood that this was one and the same person, but there still had to be some link between the two men. Faris suspected that somehow the motive behind this serial bombing attack was rooted in the old museum case.

The question was simply, how?

In large letters, he wrote on the sheet of paper: *How does this all fit*, ending this note with three question marks.

Thoughtfully, Faris gazed at Hesse's back.

From his apartment, the subway was only just reachable in such a short time frame. This meant that the culprit wasn't merely well-informed about the events from the Klersch Museum attack. He also seemed to know where Faris lived.

How does the culprit know me? Faris wrote on the pad. And underneath it: *Motive?*

Paul and the others had hypothesized that the caller had a score to settle with Faris.

MOTIVE Faris wrote once more in capital letters, before adding *score to settle* beneath it. He then started to gather together the ideas as they came to him.

Klersch bomber.

Relatives of the bombing victims.

He struck out the first line, drew a wavy line under the second. With the pen, he tapped one of his teeth. None of the interview reports contained information that went beyond utter dismay and general ignorance among the museum victims' relatives.

In frustration, Faris stared at the words *score to settle*, and at that moment, an idea came to him.

Besides the bomber himself and the families of the victims, there was one other person who had been connected with the attack at the museum, albeit only indirectly.

Faris looked up. "Golzer," he murmured.

Hesse spun around in surprise. "The skinhead you beat up? What about him?"

"He could have a motive for all this here!" Faris tossed his pen down on the tablet.

"You really think that because you gave him a thrashing and he now feels like a wimp, he's decided to blow up half of Berlin?" Hesse's skepticism was clearly written across his face.

"I lost my temper because he called *me* a bomber." Faris shrugged. "I know it sounds a little far-fetched."

"It does." Hesse peered curiously at Faris's laptop screen.

Faris stood up. A few years ago, the Brandenburg police had investigated the Hells Angels. During that case, they had learned that the motorcycle gang was tightening its links to the neo-Nazi scene. They had also been successful, at around the same time, in preventing several bomb attacks by rocker gangs in Potsdam. Suspecting Golzer of the attack in the subway was, of course, far-fetched, but Faris could no longer tolerate being in this cramped office. A jittery disquiet had settled over him, making it impossible for him to sit still.

"How long do you think this will take?" He gestured at the laptop to indicate what he meant.

Hesse shrugged. "I was just thinking that it'll probably take a while yet."

"Okay." Faris pulled his shoulders back. "I'm going to pay Golzer a visit."

He pulled his phone out of his pocket and grabbed one of Hesse's business cards, which were sitting on the desk. He rapidly keyed Hesse's cell number into his own phone and dialed. As soon as Hesse's phone started playing the theme music from *The Untouchables*, he hung up. "And now you have my new number. Call me as soon as you have something, okay?"

"Uh-huh." Hesse was only half-aware of what Faris was saying. He seemed to be wrapped up in something, and Faris decided to use this to his own advantage.

"May I borrow your motorcycle?"

With one hand, Hesse waved toward the nightstand. "The key is somewhere on the top." He leaned back over his laptop and pressed the enter key twice.

Faris left the journalist to his technical antics. He picked up the key and left the airport terminal the same way he had entered it earlier with Hesse. The oppressive, apocalyptic feeling that he had experienced when crossing through the huge check-in area returned, but he pushed it away. A quick glance at the clock told him that he still had thirty-three hours.

This time, he didn't bother putting on the helmet.

CHAPTER 13

Jenny and Pia arranged to meet Dennis in front of the youth hostel at four o'clock. When the two girls had finished their lunch, Pia wanted to go shopping, and since Jenny didn't know what else to do on her own until their meeting, she decided to go up to their room and read a little. She had brought along the newest thriller from her favorite author.

However, she never made it to the room because she ran into Dennis on the staircase.

"Hey," she mumbled. He was standing two steps above her, so she had to look up at him. "It almost looks like you were waiting for me!" She was a little proud that she had managed to come up with that remark.

He grinned. "Maybe I was."

Her heart skipped a beat. Was he serious about that? She scanned his face for any signs that he was teasing, but she didn't find any. His gaze was open and friendly.

"What are you doing right now?" he asked.

She shrugged. "I was just going to read a little."

"Read?" He uttered that word as if it were something astonishingly indecent.

Jenny felt her face start to grow warm again. "Why not?"

He descended one step, and Jenny instinctively moved down a step as well.

"I won't do anything to you," he promised, moving back up to his original position. "I was just thinking that there was still a little time until our city tour. Would you maybe like to go out for some ice cream with me?"

Jenny's heart once again skipped a beat. The thought that *this can't possibly be true!* shot through her head, and she resisted the urge to glance over her shoulder. Where was the hidden camera? Someone had to be playing a cruel trick on her!

"You're kinda nervous, aren't you?" Dennis asked in a slightly mocking tone.

She shook her head. "Not really." She bit her tongue because that came out much more gruffly than she had intended it to. "I'd love some ice cream," she added hastily.

Dennis grinned. "Then, let's go! I know a nice ice cream shop not too far from here." He started to reach for her hand, but thought better of it and didn't. He simply walked down the stairs close beside her.

A couple of girls, whose highly teased, pitch black hair indicated that they belonged to the rock festival group, stared at Jenny in disbelief. And this was the moment that Jenny realized that she was actually about to go out for ice cream with this cool guy. A big grin threatened to spread across her face. She quickly squeezed her lips together. There was no way she was going to run the risk of looking like the cat that had swallowed the canary!

"You obviously know your way around Berlin," she said, in a bid to jump start their conversation.

He laughed. "No wonder. I live here!"

Jenny glanced at him out of the corner of her eye. "You live in Berlin? Then why are you staying at the hostel?"

They had reached the outside door, and Dennis opened it for Jenny. After the two of them stepped through it and the clamor of the city surrounded them, he answered her question. "I ran into a little trouble with my big brother, who I'm living with these days." He expressed this oddly, as if he didn't get along well with his brother.

"Your big brother?" she probed a little deeper.

"Hmm." Dennis guided them toward the right. "Rainer. He's a major asshole!" He didn't give the impression that he wanted to discuss what had happened, so Jenny decided to change the topic.

"I don't even know your full name," she said.

"Golzer," he replied.

They now reached the small ice cream shop, which had a nostalgic fifties decor. Here, too, Dennis held the door for her, letting her step inside first. "Dennis Golzer."

About thirty minutes later, Faris climbed off Hesse's motorcycle in front of an old, roughly plastered building. He stared at the black-white-and-red flags hanging in all the windows with a mixture of outrage and uneasiness. In the past, this had been a popular restaurant, but now it served as a clubhouse for a group of neo-Nazis. As Faris knew, a shady beer garden was located in the back courtyard, and it would have looked idyllic if its enclosing walls didn't have various Nazi symbols scrawled all over them. A black banner was mounted above the entrance door with its elaborate grill. Printed in Gothic script, the words *Nationalist Resistance Berlin* announced which group resided here.

With an uncomfortable feeling in his stomach, Faris leaned the bike on its kickstand. It was obvious that he had driven right into a dicey situation, but he had no other options. He knew that Rainer Golzer, the neo-Nazi he had beaten to a pulp only four weeks ago, was a member of this club. Faris told himself that this was one way that he could assist in his Keithstraße colleagues' investigation, but if he were honest with himself, he liked the kick he got from being here. A little scuffle with the skinhead would provide a welcome outlet for the chaos that the explosion had set off in his mind.

Wouldn't it?

He took a deep breath and shoved any misgivings he felt into the farthest corner of his mind – where they belonged.

He slowly walked up to the club house. His arrival had apparently not gone unnoticed. The door swung open before he even reached the front steps, and two young men stepped out. Neither was particularly tall, but they were muscular. They wore combat trousers and jump boots, and their arms were crossed over their chests so that Faris couldn't read the words on their black t-shirts. Only one of the two had a shaved head, while the other man had his hair clipped in an old-fashioned crew cut.

Faris recognized the skinhead. Four weeks ago, he had been at the bar when Faris had shattered Golzer's nose and cheekbone. Golzer had called him Michi.

Michi. Faris couldn't help chuckling at the name's innocuousness.

Michi was the first to speak. "What's so funny?" he grumbled. His high-pitched voice suited his name more than his martial appearance did. And something seemed to be off with his eyes. He squinted as if he were nearsighted and only then realized who was standing in front of him. "You're the *kaffer* who beat up Rainer ..."

"Exactly," Faris interrupted him. "I'd like to talk to him." His shoulder muscles tensed involuntarily the moment Michi recognized him. He tried to inconspicuously relax them again.

Michi's expressions transitioned rapidly from confusion to disbelief to sheer scorn. "For real?" He looked at the other guy and gave his head a backward jerk before his comrade spun around and disappeared into the building.

Faris steeled himself for what was coming next and took another step forward. In the beer garden, voices grew louder, and he realized that various club members had gathered back there. He tried to stifle the doomsday feeling that was threatening to overwhelm him here, far from the airport complex.

"Yes," he shot back, raising his hands. "I just want to talk to him for a minute."

From behind Michi, another man stepped outside. Rainer Golzer. In contrast to the other two neo-Nazis, he was wearing simple jeans and a white t-shirt adorned with the letters *NRB* printed in the same script as the banner. The bruises on his face were almost gone, but the fractures in his nose and jaw areas were still quite recognizable. The entire left side of Golzer's face looked slightly dented, but he wore the symbol of his struggle with a certain degree of pride. Faris's cramped shoulders began to ache.

While Michi remained at the top of the stairs, Golzer descended to ground level. "Got tired of living, huh?" His chin was thrust forward belligerently.

Faris shook his head, the adrenaline already pumping. "I just need to ask you a question."

"Have they let you go back to work?" Golzer came to a stop about one stride away from Faris. "That was pretty much a given!" He squinted disdainfully. He had long, dark eyelashes and pale lips. Without his shaved head and the letters *NWB* tattooed over his right ear, he would have been a guy women flocked to.

"I'm not here on official business," Faris explained. "I was just wondering if you had anything to do with the bomb that went off on the subway this morning." The feeling of impending doom in his chest expanded, until it felt like he was staring into a bottomless black chasm. A small group of young men stepped out of the gate to the right of the building and formed an irregular semicircle behind Golzer.

"The bomb?" Golzer chuckled incredulously before turning to his men. "Did all of you hear that? Some camel fucker blew up our subway, and this joker thinks that one of *us* had something to do with it."

His men obviously found nothing funny in this theory, since instead of laughing, they just stared at Faris more menacingly. He sensed movement behind his back and glanced over his shoulder. Two men were now standing behind him.

Someone grabbed him as hands tightened sharply around his upper arms. He didn't even try to free himself. All of a sudden, Hesse's pain-killers stopped working, and a dull pressure started to build inside his skull.

Michi pushed past Golzer. "You want me to punch him?" Without waiting for a nod from Golzer, Michi rammed his fist into Faris's abdomen.

Faris saw the blow coming and had tightened his stomach. However, he would have crumpled to the ground if the two other skinheads hadn't been holding him. The pain rushed from his ribs, still bruised from the explosion, up to his shoulders. He gasped for air.

He blearily watched as Michi pulled his arm back a second time.

"Stop!" Golzer said coolly.

The next blow never came. Still gripped by his two guards, Faris straightened back up. "Was that it?" he asked dully.

Michi raised his fist again, but now Golzer stepped forward and reached for his hand. Then, he brought his face very close to Faris's. "Should I tell you something?" he hissed at him. "I'm in a really bad mood right now because, this morning, my little brother cussed me out. He called me a dirty Nazi. Can you believe that?" He stared antagonistically into Faris's face.

He then snorted crossly. "Let him go!" he commanded the two watchdogs.

His pals hesitated.

"Do what I say!" Golzer's voice sliced through the air. They finally obeyed him, and Faris was relieved to discover that he could stand without swaying.

"Now what?" he asked. "What about the bombing?"

Golzer's eyes reflected authentic indignation. Indignation at being accused of planning a bombing attack that he believed had to have been committed by a foreigner. At that moment, Faris knew with certainty that the neo-Nazi had had nothing to do with the crime.

Golzer jerked his chin toward the motorcycle. "Beat it!"

Faris's eyebrows rose in astonishment. This was the last thing he had expected.

"Beat it!" Golzer repeated. "And don't ever forget that my boys have nothing to do with the cowardly attacks your camel-fucker friends are committing in our homeland."

Camel fucker. A sardonic laugh started to build inside Faris's chest. *Once you've found a useful phrase, stick with it!*

He held back the laugh and stared at the neo-Nazi. Golzer's eyes bore into his, and for several seconds, they struggled silently with each other. Eventually, Faris nodded. "Alright," he declared quietly. "You didn't have anything to do with it." He swallowed the rest of the sentence.

Because you're way too stupid.

That wouldn't have been true anyway. Golzer was anything but stupid.

Faris decided to ask Paul to check up on Golzer. He bobbed his head slightly. "Have a nice day!" he said. And with that, he turned around. As he walked over to the motorcycle, he figured that someone was going to jump him from behind. But nothing happened. Golzer seemed to have his crew well under control.

The young men motionlessly watched Faris climb onto the motorcycle and start the machine.

CHAPTER 14

Once on the other side of the Friedrichshain district border, Faris stopped at the edge of the road and waited for the pain in his ribs to subside. His body felt as if someone had run it through the wringer. As he took several deep breaths, he fished out his phone and dialed Paul's number.

His partner's first words revealed that Paul and the others were following a train of thought similar to his. "We're in the process of looking into people who might have a score to settle with you," Paul informed him.

Faris's ribs throbbed. He tried to find a more comfortable position. A stabbing pain was shooting through his chest, and he inhaled sharply.

Paul didn't miss the sound. "What's going on?"

"Nothing." He knew that Paul suspected he was lying, but he also knew that his partner wouldn't press the point. For a few seconds, Faris found it hard to breathe.

He could hear the concern in Paul's voice when he continued. "We'll check on a few possible candidates. Rainer Golzer, for example."

Faris shook his head. "He's off the list."

For a moment, it was silent on the other end of the line. Faris imagined the thoughts inside his partner's brain tumbling like puzzle pieces into the right spots, gradually building a picture that wouldn't please him at all. "*Off* the list?" Paul repeated slowly.

Faris didn't say anything.

"How can you be so sure?"

"I was just there," Faris said calmly.

"Are you crazy?" his colleague bellowed. "You didn't …"

Faris didn't hear more than that, since he lowered his phone before Paul's furious voice could shatter his ear drum. "Done now?" he asked, once the blue streak firing out of his phone grew quieter.

"I simply don't understand, Faris!" Paul groaned, before taking a deep sigh. "How badly beat up are you?"

"Not at all. Just a small rib bruise that dates from the explosion."

"You're a real asshole, you know, right?"

"Maybe. Just to be sure, have someone check into Golzer, but I'm convinced he isn't our man. Do you have anything else?"

"We still have to figure out if we're dealing with an Islamist attack or not."

"I can't imagine that's what this is," Faris declared.

"We'll keep working on it. At the moment, Ben is pulling together a more detailed analysis of the video."

Faris leaned slightly forward in order to alleviate his pain. Apparently, he made some sound while doing that because Paul responded with alarm again.

"You're feeling shitty, aren't you?"

He didn't deny it. "I think I need a little break. I'll call back as soon as something occurs to me."

Paul didn't reply, and Faris felt a flash of guilt. His colleague was obviously worried about him.

He tried to make his voice sound cheerful. "Stay cool, old man," he said jovially. "Everything's fine!"

When he hung up, he cut off the last part of the curse Paul was in the process of uttering.

Driven by nervous restlessness, Faris drove around aimlessly for a while. Time was inexorably running out, and there was nothing he could do to help his colleagues with their investigation. The words from the museum bomber echoed through his mind.

Wrong answer!

Then, the shrill cry from the woman at the subway station.

What did you do?

And finally, the distorted, mocking voice of the caller.

Somewhere out there, Faris, a man is hanging on a cross … if it stops before you find him …

Faris clenched his fingers around the handlebars and wished he were sitting in his own car. His copy of Metallica's *Kill 'em All* was stuck in his CD player. *Seek and Destroy* would have fit his mood nicely right about now.

He eventually turned off, down a narrow avenue. The motorcycle bumped across the cobblestones, and oak trees lined both sides of the street. A church tower clock, somewhere nearby, struck four-thirty. He rolled to a stop before laying his arms across the handlebars and resting his head against them.

He immediately lifted his head back up as he realized where he was. A car drove past, its tires generating a bright, buzzing sound on the paved road. Faris's gaze fell on a street sign hidden behind a tree branch. He could just barely make it out from where he was sitting.

Ahornstraße.

"Shit!" he cursed. He had been so wrapped up in his gloomy thoughts that his subconscious had led him here unawares.

He reluctantly looked around.

He had parked the motorcycle right in front of a building marked with the number 10, an ultramodern, snowy white box of condos. The precisely clipped front lawn contrasted sharply with the overgrown hedge on the other side of the street, behind which a preschool sat. And if it wasn't bad enough that Faris's emotions had driven him here, this was the very moment that the front door of Number 10 opened, and a woman stepped out.

Laura.

Faris's eyes darted to the faded leather bracelet on his wrist, and his heart constricted.

She was wearing chinos, sneakers and a light blue t-shirt that probably

117

matched her eyes perfectly. On her hip, she was carrying her young daughter, blonde like her mother and a little plump, as toddlers tend to be.

"Lilly," Faris murmured.

He felt like a voyeur. And there was nothing he could do to stop his memories from catapulting him into the past. To that evening, over two and a half years ago …

"Faris?" Laura had shouted that day from her home office.

With a sigh, he had lowered the book he had just picked up. "Yeah, sweetheart?"

"I'd like to show you something in here." Tense excitement vibrated in Laura's voice. It was clear to Faris that he wouldn't get his peace and quiet back until he took a look at what she wanted to show him. He set his book back down. There was no need for a bookmark, since he hadn't even made it past the first page. He stood up and walked into the adjacent room in their small apartment, where Laura had set up a white desk and her white laptop. Some video that she had found on the internet was running on the screen. Faris caught sight of a prominent video platform's logo.

In the video, a small girl with blonde curls and a flowery dress was running behind a large, long-haired dog. She was crowing happily at the top of her lungs, and the dog spun around in a circle, barking joyfully. With this, the clip ended.

"Isn't she sweet?" Laura asked. With a beaming smile, she glanced over her shoulder at Faris.

Faris opted to make a joke. "The girl or the dog?" he asked.

Laura took a swipe at him. "Idiot! The child, of course! You know I meant the girl."

He just smiled, but it felt tedious to be manipulated like this. Laura had a specific goal in mind in sharing this video with him, and he knew this all too well.

She pointed to the title of the video. *Lilly and Tommy playing.*

To Faris's relief, she was no longer paying attention to him, and so she didn't see the smile fade from his face. For the past few months,

Laura had been talking about having a baby. She was a vibrant woman, one who pursued all of her goals with great single-mindedness. In her mind, she was convinced that she would have a girl, and her name would be Lilly. The fact that Faris was quite opposed to starting a family at this point was, for her, just a small stumbling block on the path to her goal.

"I was just googling the name," she explained brightly. "And there were a lot of hits. This video was the best one." She restarted it. The child crowed again, the dog barked again.

Faris's head suddenly started hurting. "How do you know that Lilly is the child's name?" he asked, still trying to make a joke, though his tension was more obvious this time. "It could belong to the dog."

Laura shot him an annoyed look. "Tommy as a girl's name?"

She could be very stubborn when it came to ignoring his jokes.

Faris gave up. "Fine. It's a cute film."

Three months later, Laura was pregnant with another man's child.

This was the scene running through Faris's head as he sat on Hesse's motorcycle and watched Laura strap her child into a jogging stroller. He noticed that he was playing with his leather bracelet and stopped instantly. Laura pushed the stroller through the low garden gate out onto the street. When she caught sight of Faris, a shadow fell across her heart-shaped face.

Faris felt like he had been caught red-handed. He kicked down the motorcycle's stand and took a few steps toward his ex-girlfriend. He managed to utter, "Hi, Laura."

"Hello, Faris."

At least, she wasn't yelling at him right off the bat. Her gaze scanned his face for a few moments before registering the bandage on his forehead and his split lip. Concern swept across her face, but it was quickly replaced by chilly reserve. She finally tore her eyes from him and looked down at the child. "Lilly, say hello to Faris."

The name sliced through him like a knife.

"Hello!" the child chirped. She looked uncertain – obviously she sensed the tension that ran between her mother and the strange, dark-haired man.

Faris nodded at the girl. "Hello, Lilly." He held back all the other words that wanted to come because he didn't want to sound bitter. What could he have said anyway? *You've settled down nicely in your new life. How could you name the child Lilly?*

Come back to me!

He flinched. Had he said that last sentence out loud? Obviously not, since Laura was now smiling. That smile looked timid, but not angry. "What are you doing here?" she asked.

He gazed at Lilly and pressed his lips together to keep from telling Laura about the explosion in the subway. One of the reasons she had left him was because she could no longer stand the constant fear she felt for him.

"Nothing. I just happened to be in the area."

Her pale blue eyes searched his. *Yeah, right!* he read in them, but to his relief, he didn't say anything.

Her t-shirt really did match her eyes perfectly.

"We're doing alright, Faris," she murmured after a few moments, and he understood that she had held back two critical words.

Without you.

He nodded. Started to beat his retreat. "Of course. I didn't mean to bother you."

She smiled at him again, and this time, Faris's knees felt weak.

"You're not." Her eyes shifted to his wrist. "You're still wearing that bracelet," she said.

Faris plunged his hands into his back jeans pockets. "I think I should go."

Laura just nodded.

Faris climbed awkwardly back onto the motorcycle seat. He was aware that the child was gazing at him just as intently as Laura was. With a grin, he nodded at Lilly. "Take care!"

Laura didn't say a word.

Faris started the machine.

Richard Westphal threw an irritated glance at his watch. It was already four-thirty! Once again, the meeting had lasted longer than he had thought it would, and now he had to hurry. He strode quickly around the corner onto Ku'damm in order to reach the closest subway station. The next moment, he ran into a group of men and women, all of whom were wearing the colorful scarves associated with the church conference. They were singing some stupid hymn. He barely managed to avoid running into one of the men.

"God almighty!" he cursed.

The man turned toward him. He was around fifty, and his beard had more gray in it than brown.

"Sing with us!" he urged Westphal cheerfully.

Westphal could hardly believe his ears. "Get out of my way, sir!" he demanded.

The bearded man simply raised his eyebrows quizzically. The eyes of the rest of the group members were now on Westphal, but despite the curiosity that was reflected in their gazes, they stubbornly continued to sing. Westphal swallowed back another expletive. He took a step to the side, but that didn't help. The group was blocking the entire sidewalk.

"For shit's sake!" he exclaimed.

One of the women stopped singing. "You aren't doing yourself any good, running around all the time," she declared.

Westphal stared at her suburban perm. "That's none of your business now, is it?" He tightened his grip on his briefcase, shifted one shoulder to the front, and simply forged his way through the crowd. To the right and left of him, the singing gradually tapered off among the rest of the conference attendees. "Well, I never!" Westphal heard someone murmur indignantly.

Refusing to let that stop him, he lifted his chin and forged on. His mood worsened appreciably when the moronic singing undauntedly resumed behind his back.

If it had been up to him, this dumb church conference would have taken place somewhere on the moon. No, better yet – on Mars! That would have been even a little farther away. But instead, the singing, praying suckers were clogging up Berlin's streets and had been annoying him for days. This morning, one of them even handed him one of those glow sticks. Unbelievable!

As he walked along, Westphal pulled the stick-like object out of his suit pocket. He stared at it grumpily. The moto and logo for the conference were printed in bright letters on the white plastic.

Speaking the Word of God Boldly.

What sentimental nonsense!

Westphal glanced around. He had almost reached the subway station at Adenauerplatz, and just a few meters away from him, a trash can was hanging from a light pole. Naturally, it was spilling over with empty food containers and other garbage from the various fast-food places around the intersection. Typical! The city agreed to host an event like this church conference, and it wasn't even capable of making sure that all the trash these people generated was neatly disposed of!

The glow stick still in hand, Westphal paused beside the overflowing trash can. Several wasps buzzed around his head, but he didn't pay attention to them. He briefly considered snapping the finger-thick plastic rod to see in which color it would glow, and before he could convince himself to abandon this childish impulse, he did it. Nothing happened.

The stupid thing was broken!

Westphal angrily stuffed the glow stick into the trash can, then continued on his way. He had a client waiting for him!

Bobby watched the man in the suit shove something into the overflowing trash can. His interest was immediately aroused. Those snobby types often threw away things that he – Bobby – could use to make a little money. With difficulty, he stood up from his blanket close to the subway station entrance, skirted the bicycles that were chained up there, and shuffled over to the trash can.

He peered curiously between the cardboard boxes and the half-eaten burgers. With his pointer finger, he pushed aside a crumpled newspaper. A wasp grew angry, and buzzing aggressively, it dove at his face. Bobby swatted it away at the same moment his eyes fell on the object the Suit had thrown away.

It was one of those church conference glow sticks, one that had already been kinked. That was obvious from the milky line running across the white plastic surface.

Disappointment spread through Bobby, since he had been hoping for something of value. Nonetheless, he picked up the thin white object with the rainbow-colored band and examined it from all sides. A little catsup was smeared on it, but he cleaned that off with the hem of his shirt. He then hung the stick around his neck. Now, he almost felt like one of the conference visitors! He chuckled softly.

A group of teenagers wrapped in colorful scarves walked past him. Bobby liked the conference-goers. Most of them were generous, and maybe they would be willing to give him more money if they could clearly see that he was one of them. With an eager smile, he returned to his spot and counted up his gains. Almost ten euros. He grinned inwardly. Yes, he was definitely a fan of the conference!

Bobby spontaneously decided that he had worked enough for today. He carefully rolled up his blanket before stowing it in the Aldi bag that served as his suitcase. He would find a spot to unwind in Preußenpark and just enjoy life a little.

Several minutes later, he stretched out in the middle of a circular grassy area. The sun shone down warmly on him, and he gladly held his face up to it. Ten euros in less than two hours! He usually didn't receive that much over the course of an entire day. He played with the glow stick, as he dozed a little. Somewhere, a church bell tolled the top of the hour, but he didn't count the strokes.

He was just about to stand up when the glow stick made a strange sound. It was like a small bang, fairly quiet, but Bobby had good ears. In bewilderment, he gazed down at the white stick.

A second later, he was engulfed by a fireball.

Faris hadn't even crossed two streets when his phone went off in his pocket. He pulled over on the side of the road, hastily fished out the device, and answered it on its sixth ring. "Yes?"

"Faris?" Paul's voice.

Faris only needed to hear his name, the cadence with which Paul spoke it, to know that something had happened. "What is it?" he exclaimed.

"The caller," Paul said. "He contacted us. And was pretty mad that he hadn't reached you. I tried to calm him down, Faris, but ..."

The hairs on Faris's neck started to rise. "But *what*?" he said, hearing his voice grow rougher.

Paul didn't answer immediately, though Faris could hear him breathing.

"He set off another bomb, Faris. Just now. In Preußenpark. Close to Ku'damm."

Faris closed his eyes. "Shit!"

"Where are you now?" Paul asked.

"In Zehlendorf." Faris checked his rearview mirror. For a moment, he thought he saw Laura turn the corner, but when he looked closer, he realized it was a woman he didn't know.

"You need to get back here as quickly as possible," Paul said. "Effective immediately, you're back on the team."

CHAPTER 15

After the second bombing within the space of a few hours, chaos reigned on Keithstraße. In order to enter the building, Faris had to fight his way through a ring of reporters, waving away microphone after microphone that was held up in his face. "No comment," he said at least a dozen times. Right before the heavy door swung shut behind him, he saw the journalists dash over to two patrol cars that were just rolling up to park on the other side of the street. Niklas Hesse was nowhere in sight, but that wasn't surprising, since Faris had his motorcycle.

The interior of the building was no less frenzied. The telephones behind the reception desk rang incessantly. Faris saw that two members of the support staff had been allocated to the porter on duty, to help manage the flood of incoming calls. None of the three glanced up when Faris strode past them toward the staircase. He tried to imagine what the situation must be like in the emergency center. Presumably the staff there were whizzing around at the speed of light.

Things were somewhat calmer on the upper floors, but even here, the tension was palpable everywhere you looked. Faris passed by colleagues in uniform who were accompanying witnesses down the hallway, or who were tending to those who had come in to make their statements. He gazed into tired, stressed faces as he hurried up the last stretch of stairs to reach the War Room.

The room was hardly recognizable from the last time he had been in here. Ben seemed to have transferred half of the FCI team in and the case table was just as jammed full of computers and technical gear as Hesse's heavy oak table at Tempelhof. A pale, wiry guy was in the process of connecting black and gray boxes with a length of cable, the purpose of which was a mystery to Faris.

Somebody had brought in two televisions: an old-fashioned, boxy device on wheels with birchwood veneer, and a contemporary flatscreen TV. The older one was running channel N24, the newer one showed one of the new capital city stations. Someone had activated the split-screen, and in the lower right corner, a different station was showing in a little window. Like both of the others, this station was running content about the second explosion in Preußenpark.

In thick red letters, a countdown had been written at the top of the case wall.

31 hours.

The number had obviously been wiped off and adjusted several times already. The previously clean white surface underneath it was now a reddish smear.

Deep in conversation, Tromsdorff, Gitta and Marc Sommer were standing in front of Gitta's glass office. Ben was busy doing something on his computer, and evidently whatever it was wasn't making him happy, since he threw his arms up in despair. Shannon was nowhere in sight, probably in an interdepartmental meeting.

An officer Faris didn't know was standing at the whiteboard, on which the notes, drawings and, above all, question marks had multiplied significantly. The stranger looked close to retirement age. Faris guessed over sixty, since his hair was gray. He was spinning a thick blue marker in his fingers, but his thoughts seemed to be far away, since his gaze was fixed absently on something out the dormer window.

Paul was on the phone, and based on what he was saying into it, was speaking with Marvin Andersen. His back was to the door, so the first person to see Faris was Tromsdorff. He nodded at the newcomer, but before he could say anything, Ben called out. "Shit!"

All eyes turned toward him. He pointed at the flatscreen on which the coverage of the bombing in the park had been replaced by a different report. "Someone turn it up!" he called as he pushed his keyboard aside.

Gitta took care of the volume, and a reporter's voice filled the War Room.

"… I'm standing here at the Kaiser Wilhelm Memorial Church, where the first clashes have occurred in the aftermath of the bombings."

The camera panned over to a group of forty or fifty people who had gathered at the foot of the church, which had been destroyed during World War II. They were holding up placards, on which a devil figure was holding up a communion chalice.

Paul ended his call. "The hard-core Catholics are gathering," he commented drily.

Faris recognized the image on the posters because, even before the church conference began, there had been isolated demonstrations by conservative Catholics who condemned the joint Eucharist with their Protestant brethren. However, this rally was different in character from the earlier peaceful gatherings that had been exemplified by hymns and prayers. This time, the demonstrators seemed angry and belligerent.

Once more, the camera swept across the enraged crowd, before it zoomed in on a man in a priest's black robes, carrying a microphone. "We are now seeing what happens when we hand Satan the chalice!" he thundered. "Our holy Catholic Church is at risk of going under in a sea of flames, and we …"

Faris was distracted from the diatribe by the opening of the conference room door. Dr. Geiger walked in. The first person she greeted was the older officer whom Faris didn't know.

"Ladies and gentlemen," she said loudly, turning toward the rest of the team. "I see that you are informed about the latest developments in the city. We …" Her gaze fell on Faris, and she stopped mid-sentence. "Mr. Iskander." It was obvious that his presence didn't fit her agenda, but she clenched her jaw and continued reluctantly, "It's good that you're here! The bomber made it very clear to us that he wants us to have you on the team."

Faris held back a sarcastic reply.

"Do you have any idea why that might be?" Geiger asked.

Faris shrugged. "Have there been any new victims?" he inquired instead of answering her.

"A homeless man," the older officer supplied.

"Faris, this is Friedrich Gerlach," Tromsdorff said as introduction. "He is our contact with Andersen and his people."

Gerlach nodded mutely at Faris. Except for these three words, he hadn't said anything else, and he seemed to want to keep it that way.

Geiger sank down on one of the chairs. She looked worn-out – exhausted and also slightly shaken.

Faris recalled his own guilty feelings after the bombing at the museum. "You didn't press the button," he said quietly, without even thinking about it.

From where he was sitting, Paul sent him a long, meaningful look. Faris acted as if he didn't notice anything.

Dr. Geiger stared at him. "Of course not," she said archly. "Why would you even think that?"

Faris swallowed his answer and glanced over at Paul. His partner shrugged.

"Alright, good." Tromsdorff held up his arms, drawing everyone's attention to himself. "The caller called back. Shortly before five. He demanded to speak with you, Faris, and was quite annoyed when we told him that you were no longer on the team." He shot Geiger an emphatic look, but her face was impassive. Given how impenetrable and cool she always seemed, she would have made a good politician. "We tried to calm him down," Tromsdorff continued, "but that didn't work. The only thing he said was that Arabic phrase."

"*As-samu alaikum*," Faris interjected.

Tromsdorff nodded. "Exactly. And then he set off the second bomb. It was pure luck that there were no other victims."

Faris rubbed the back of his neck. It felt as if someone had massaged the muscles there with icy cold fingers.

The door of the War Room swung open again, and Shannon stepped inside. With a nod at Faris, she took her seat without saying a word and reached, as usual, for her tennis ball.

Now Paul stood up from his seat. "He called one more time after that to tell us that he wouldn't have any problem delivering us more bodies."

Faris saw his partner shiver. "Did he tell you what he wants?"

"Just that we needed to get you back on the team." Paul glanced over at Dr. Geiger. "That was it. No demands, no ultimatum. Nothing." Frustration and consternation were written across his face. "He wants you to suffer, Faris. The question is *why*? You must've done something to make him want revenge like this."

"I think you should listen to the conversation that Paul had with him," Shannon suggested. "We have analyzed it thoroughly, but perhaps you'll pick up on something we missed." She stretched her neck and looked over at Ben. "Ben, could you play for us the recording of the last call?"

"*Sievers*," Faris heard Paul say.

For a moment, the caller seemed to be startled. You could hear him gasp. "*Where is Faris?*" he finally asked.

"*He isn't here. I'm …*"

"*You can't be serious!*" Despite the distortion, you could still hear how upset the man on the other end of the line was.

As he listened to his own voice on the recording, Paul rubbed his forehead with his thumb and forefinger. From underneath his hand, he caught Faris's eyes. Faris knew that his partner was blaming himself for having been unable to prevent the second bombing.

You didn't press the button, Faris thought. He could tell from Paul's expression that he knew exactly what was going through Faris's head.

"*Faris is on sick le…*" Paul's voice continued on the recording.

He was again interrupted. "*I demand that he be brought back immediately!*"

"*That won't work.*"

"*Wanna bet?*"

"*Listen …*" Paul exclaimed, but the caller cut him off.

"*As-samu alaikum*," he hissed before hanging up.

It was so quiet in the War Room that you could have heard a

pin drop. Everyone here knew that this was the moment the bomb exploded. The recording continued to play and on it, Paul's phone started ringing again. He answered.

"*So,*" the caller said congenially. "*Hopefully, that kind soul can now take his ease! Make sure that by the next time I call, I can talk to Faris. Otherwise, your body count will keep going up!*" And with that, he hung up for a second time.

Ben stopped the recording. Paul let his arm fall from his head to his lap. He looked gray and years older than he had just moments before.

"*That kind soul can now take his ease!*" Shannon repeated. "That is a biblical reference, a saying my grandmother used years ago. From Luke's gospel, I believe."

"Do you think he's a Christian?" This whole time, Faris had suspected that the caller couldn't be a Muslim.

"I'm sure of that," Shannon confirmed.

Faris glanced over at Dr. Geiger to gauge how she was taking these conclusions and theories. To his surprise, she looked open to them. Her arms were folded, and she was nodding thoughtfully. "Does this call help jog any thoughts about a connection you might have with this man?" she asked Faris.

He rubbed his jaw. "Unfortunately, no."

"And how do all of you want to proceed?" Geiger asked, turning to Tromsdorff.

"He will doubtless call back," he replied. "What other reason could there be to demand that Faris be brought here? Ben?"

During this conversation, Ben had been messing with his laptop and one of the black boxes. He now reached for a cell phone and held it up. Faris recognized his own phone. Ben had obviously cleaned off the dust from the subway explosion.

"We haven't had much success at tracing the calls. We installed a trap and trace program on your phone, but it hasn't delivered the results we'd hoped for. All we've figured out is that the culprit is using an internet link to communicate with us."

"What about the sender of the crucifixion video?" Gerlach interjected.

"We know that the email came from Faris's home computer," Ben explained. "And we're assuming that our mysterious culprit somehow smuggled a trojan onto his hard drive."

Faris nodded.

"We could analyze the source of the trojan," Ben continued. "But that would take too long." His eyes met Faris's, and Faris suspected that Ben was wondering if Hesse had had any luck at all in his search. He imperceptibly shook his head.

He saw Geiger lean over to Gerlach and whisper something in his ear. The older officer nodded and jotted something down in a small tablet he pulled out of his pocket. Faris assumed that Gerlach had just been asked to examine his computer. He briefly wondered if he should simply admit – right here, right now – to having asked Hesse to install an illegal search program on his machine to track down the culprit. But then he glanced at Geiger and remembered that he was only here on probation. Because the caller had demanded this. Not because Geiger thought that he could actually be useful.

For a long moment, no one spoke.

"Good." Geiger straightened up. "Do your colleagues from Department 5 have anything new to share, Gerlach?"

"The bomb squad is on continuous alert," the gray-haired officer reported. "By now, we also have the canine units from Brandenburg, Mecklenburg-West Pomerania and Saxony-Anhalt." He smiled grimly. "I'm already receiving complaints from the dog handlers that we're overworking the poor animals. We have yet to find any indication of bombs at the stadium, and our search also includes the other five largest gathering sites. The Brandenburg Gate, Convention Centers Five and Six, the Memorial Church, and the Cathedral. Andersen is currently briefing all the officers who have contacts with informants inside the terrorist scene. But in the little time we have, they won't be of much help." The look he sent Tromsdorff was open and frank. "If we can be honest here, we're hoping that your team will slice the head off the snake."

Tromsdorff sighed. "Or that we find the crucified man in time. Gitta? What's going on with the tips from the public?"

Gitta consulted a pile of folded pages. "I've checked the DigA A entries from the emergency phone center, as well as the phone banks whose numbers were given out in the press release. Her eyes flitted across the paper. "All in all, there are about three hundred tips that are being followed up on right now, of which about two dozen are promising. But none of them bring us even one step farther."

As she was speaking, Faris's gaze wandered over to his phone, which Ben had set down on the table beside him. Regardless of the efforts their colleagues were making, the only solid lead they had was the man on the other end of the line.

While he mulled over what they could do next, the burner phone in his leather jacket started to ring. He pulled it out and answered. It was Hesse.

"The software's found something," he said without greeting. "But I'm not sure you're going to be happy about it."

"Just tell me," Faris urged him.

"Your email was sent from an internet café somewhere close to Ku'damm …"

In the middle of that word, a chirping sound started, sending a shiver down Faris's back. Gitta clapped both hands over her mouth.

Ben's hand darted over to Faris's phone. "It's him!" he confirmed, superfluously.

CHAPTER 16

Faris asked Hesse to call him back later, and he pocketed his temporary phone. In the meantime, Ben had connected Faris's regular phone to an amplifier, and he handed Faris a headset, which the latter put on. Ben, Tromsdorff and Dr. Geiger did the same thing.

"Iskander," Faris answered when everyone was ready.

"Hi, Faris." The electronically distorted voice hit Faris like a punch. "How nice that you're back. I was practically yearning for you."

"I couldn't help that …" Faris started, but the caller interrupted him.

"I know, I know. I'm no longer annoyed that someone else answered instead of you."

Faris made a surprised sound.

The caller chuckled. "You didn't see that coming, did you? Anyway. Let's just say that the little fire I set has cooled my temper."

Faris forced himself to stay calm, even though the words sent fury surging through him. He suddenly remembered the friendly face of the nun with the pale eyes, and he felt his neck muscles tense. He tried to breathe as quietly as possible, but not quietly enough as it turned out.

"Feeling stressed, Faris?" The caller sounded content. "That's good."

"Why?" Faris asked. He knew that he needed to get the man to talk, to provide him with some detail that could help them figure out where he was.

However, the stranger didn't respond to his question. "Are your colleagues listening in on our little chat?" he asked instead. Despite the voice distortion, Faris thought he could hear how relaxed the man was. "Tell Ben he should feel free to turn on the loudspeaker."

Faris jerked his head up. His eyes first stopped on Ben, whose eyes were huge, before moving on to his supervisor.

Ben's hand rose and hovered for a moment over the amplifier to which the headsets were connected. He shot Tromsdorff a questioning look.

His commanding officer hesitated.

"Don't be so shy," the caller ordered, and Faris involuntarily scanned the corners of the room for cameras. Had the man somehow managed to get surveillance access to the War Room, just as he had in the Bismarckstraße subway station?

Finally, Tromsdorff nodded. Ben lowered his hand and pressed the button. Faris's headset emitted a very quiet crackling sound, which the caller obviously heard as well. "Well then," the distorted voice now sounded from the amplifier's loudspeaker.

Tromsdorff, Ben and Faris removed their headsets, but Dr. Geiger was listening so hard that she didn't do the same.

"With whom do I have the honor of speaking?" the stranger asked. "Superintendent Tromsdorff?

"I'm here," Tromsdorff replied. In the interim, Paul had stood up and walked over to the case wall. He now picked up one of the markers and removed its cap. He thought for a few moments, then wrote several words on the board.

The culprit knows SURV!

He underlined the sentence several times.

Faris nodded at him. Marc Sommer, who had been silently standing beside them the whole time, leaned back against a window frame and crossed his arms.

"How nice!" the caller exclaimed. "Welcome, welcome, ladies and gentlemen!"

Tromsdorff tightened his jaw so much that his muscles protruded visibly. He had shoved his jacket sleeves up to his elbows, but now he yanked them back down. It looked as if he suddenly felt cold.

Faris stood up from his chair. As he considered what to say next, he picked up a pad of paper that was lying on the case table. With a pencil, he wrote down: *Does he have access to cameras here, in this room?*

Ben turned one of the knobs on an elongated gray box and shook his head. "Impossible!" he mouthed soundlessly.

Faris was relieved.

"Cat got your tongue, Faris?" the caller inquired. "You haven't said anything in a while."

"Why is it good if I'm feeling stressed?" Faris repeated his earlier question.

The caller asked again. "Do you really think I'm that stupid? If I tell you that, I'd hand you a clue that you could do something with. Do you already have a guess who I might be?"

"Perhaps."

The caller fell silent for a second, then he said, "Know what? When I think about it, the fact that you seem to think I'm an idiot upsets me a little. I mean, it was really silly of you to give up your phone and head off. That was very inconsiderate of you!"

Faris closed his eyes. He had seen that coming.

"I will grant you absolution, but as penance you have to tell me what all you have discovered about me."

Faris searched for Tromsdorff's gaze. His boss's face was inscrutable, but he shook his head slightly.

"Or would you prefer that I set off another bomb?" the caller asked.

"No!" Faris exclaimed.

"Alright. Then give me a proper report, soldier!"

At this final word, Paul wrinkled his forehead thoughtfully. He started playing with his marker, and Faris could see that his brain had just shifted into high gear. Paul wrote *Soldier* on the case wall.

Faris looked over at Tromsdorff. *Should I?* he mouthed. And when Tromsdorff nodded grimly, he began. "We know that you can't be the museum bomber. We also know that you hacked into the police database, and that's how you accessed the details we never released to the public."

"Good work!" The caller sounded pleased.

"So we're right about that?"

"On both counts, yes."

"Nonetheless, there's still some connection between you and the museum bombing," Faris resumed. Perhaps he could force the man to make a mistake. The room Faris sat in was filled with trained case analysts, including himself. They would register every spike in excitement, every tiny exclamation, that could possibly be a clue.

"Who knows?" the man shot back. "Maybe I just used that nice little phrase to get your full attention."

Still standing next to the case wall, Paul energetically shook his head and pointed at one line.

Link between Faris and culprit.

He then tapped the words *Score to settle* before adding three exclamation marks behind them.

All of a sudden, Faris once again became aware of Dr. Geiger's presence. The Department 1 director had removed her headset by now, but unlike Tromsdorff and Ben, who had set theirs down on the table, she was still holding hers. She kept fiddling with it indecisively, as she exchanged long looks with Gerlach.

"What else have you learned?" the caller's voice rasped through the speaker.

Faris shut his eyes and pinched the bridge of his nose. "We know that you're planning an attack at the papal Mass tomorrow."

"Excellent! But that wasn't too hard to figure out, was it?"

Faris didn't respond to this.

The man on the other end of the line laughed. "Chatting with you is a little tedious, Faris, with all your stops and starts."

"No," Faris squeezed out between clenched teeth. "It wasn't that difficult." And then he remembered something. He glanced back at the case wall on which Paul had written *Two culprits*, and he considered what he could do to entice at least some detail out of the stranger on this topic.

"Good boy!" the caller commended him.

"Where do we go from here?" Faris asked to shift course.

"Well, what do you think? You can try to find me, do all that fancy police stuff that you're all so damned proud of. And I'll wait and see if you're successful."

"You view this as a game, don't you?"

The caller's voice sounded amused. "A game? Of course! Isn't it?"

"What do you want from me?" Faris balled his right hand into a fist. "Why me, of all people? I have no idea what I'm supposed to do."

"You disappoint me, Faris! What do you think this is? A bluff, like back there at the museum? No, perhaps it's about time to give you a little leg up. If you decide to call off the service tomorrow evening, I will know."

"I …"

"Let me finish, Faris! You know that I hacked into the police server once before, but I can do it a second time, trust me. It doesn't matter what your super-smart IT people claim. If I get even a little suspicious that you're about to cancel the service, I will set off another bomb that will make the one in the subway look like a breeze. So, what's going to happen next?"

He paused, and when Faris didn't say anything, continued. "The internet café on Knesebeckstraße, Faris. That's where I was when I sent that trojan to your computer yesterday. You asked me what you should do now. Fine, I'll tell you, though to be honest, I'm rather disappointed that it's necessary. Go to that café. That might help you get a little closer to me."

Faris gritted his teeth.

"That is the condition for my absolution. Got it, Faris?"

"Yes."

"Good. That's the next step. Your very special task is as follows: Find my father before it's too late! Otherwise the people in the city … You know what their fate will be, if you fail." He waited a second before pressing for an answer. "You do know, don't you?"

Faris's stomach plummeted. "Yes," he whispered through dry lips.

"Say it!"

"I …"

"Say it, Faris! Say it so that I know you understand everything. What will happen to all those people out there if you fail one more time?"

Faris closed his eyes. "They will die."

"The man definitely has a score to settle with you."

After the caller had hung up, Marc Sommer was the first person to speak. His voice sounded a little hoarse. He was still leaning against the window frame.

Shannon was busily jotting down notes on a piece of paper. "Did you hear what he said? That the man on the cross is his father, I mean."

"He might be feeding us misinformation," Tromsdorff said. "But check it out anyway."

Shannon nodded and continued scribbling on her notepad.

Faris made a decision. "I'm going to head off right away," he said, and he was already halfway to the door when Tromsdorff called out to him.

"Wait! You aren't going anywhere without your gun and badge!"

With that, he explicitly challenged Geiger's mandate. She shook her head rapidly. "Mr. Iskander isn't officially back on the force yet. I will not permit him to …"

"Anke!" Tromsdorff's voice cut in, sharp and hard. He slowly rose to his feet. "I will NOT allow Faris to go out there without a weapon, and believe you me, I don't fucking care what you do with me after all this shit is over. Kick my butt out the door, for all I care, but you will give him back his badge and weapon immediately, or …"

He didn't finish the sentence. His face was now flushed beet red, and his hands were clenched into fists. He slowly opened them, took a deep breath, and sat back down.

Geiger was speechless. Faris could see the wheels turning inside her mind, but to his relief, she was too smart to escalate the confrontation. "Fine," she agreed. She put her headset back on and reached for her phone; an elegant, ultra-flat device. She flipped it open, dialed, gave a few curt orders, and snapped it shut again. "I have set everything in motion. Someone will be here in a few minutes with the items."

It wasn't difficult to interpret the long malevolent look she gave

Tromsdorff. *We will talk later!*

Faris tried to relax. Hopefully this wouldn't cost them all their heads in the end.

"Okay." At the whiteboard, Paul cleared his throat, bringing everyone's attention back to the case. He clicked the lid back on the marker, set it down, and sat on the edge of the case table. "Maybe we shouldn't limit ourselves to the museum case. We should go through all the old cases in which Faris made the arrest. The guy might be trying to lead us astray with clues that are supposed to point us toward the museum bombing."

Faris let his eyes close again. The responsibility resting on his shoulders felt as heavy as lead. The dead from the museum returned to him. All those people he hadn't been able to save! What if he failed now, too? What if, because of him, not hundreds but thousands of people died?

You didn't push the button. Paul's words echoed through his head. His partner had repeated them to him over and over again as Faris lay in the hospital.

Shannon shook her head and glanced up from her notes. She disagreed with Paul. "I don't think we need to expand our search to other cases. The caller's voice was distorted, but he is clearly tense whenever he talks about the museum bombing. I think he is somehow linked to that case. We should focus on that … and on the thing with his father. We might find some connection there."

"He wouldn't have brought up his father, if there wasn't." Paul sounded fully convinced of this.

Faris tried to imagine what it would take for someone to nail their own father to a cross. He couldn't.

"We'll work on both angles," Tromsdorff decided. "Just to be sure." He waved at Paul, who stood back up and wrote another note on the board.

Check on old cases. Revenge.

This time he drew three question marks after it. After a moment's thought, he added:

Father?

"Don't forget that we are searching for two individuals," Faris murmured. He felt tired and a little sick. Before he could continue, a phone somewhere in the room rang.

"It's mine." Without apologizing for the interruption, Dr. Geiger reached inside her jacket pocket and pulled out her phone. "Dr. Geiger," she said and then listened for a few seconds. "That's okay," she replied before ending the call. Then, "Ladies and gentlemen, I'm afraid I have to go. My presence is required elsewhere." And with that, she stood up and exchanged a long silent look with Gerlach, who almost imperceptibly nodded at her. She turned coolly toward Tromsdorff. "Robert, we have now had two bombings. I don't need to remind you that the politicians, the conference organizers and the press are all breathing down my neck. Just make sure that this … this bastard is caught before there are more fatalities!" She left the rest of the threat unspoken, but everyone in the room knew what she really wanted to say.

Otherwise I'll shut down SURV for good.

She stalked over to the door, and the next moment, she was gone.

"I'm sorry, Robert," Faris murmured, not knowing exactly what he should apologize for.

Tromsdorff waved this off. "Let's get to work!"

The door opened again, and an officer that Faris didn't know stepped inside.

"I'm supposed to deliver something here," the man mumbled by way of greeting. He was carrying a brown paper bag, and his eyes scanned the assembly in front of him.

When Faris waved at him, the man headed over and handed him the bag. Faris looked inside. It held his badge and a Sig Sauer P6 along with a shoulder holster.

"Welcome back on board," the officer said.

"Thanks!" The bag felt heavy in Faris's hands, and he could feel Paul watching him. He met his eyes, saw the concern in them, and lowered his head, because he didn't know how to handle that. The memory from early this morning, when he had stood at his window and yearned for this very gun, played through his mind like a film.

CHAPTER 17

The city tour was on the verge of turning into a complete catastrophe.

The whole time, Pia chatted a blue streak with Dennis, and Jenny had hardly been able to get a word in. She kept glancing sideways at Dennis. He had pulled on his leather jacket as they left the hostel, but on the bus, he had taken it off and pushed his t-shirt sleeves up as high as they would go. His tattoos peeked out from under his collar, and Jenny simply couldn't take her eyes off of them. She saw black wings and something that looked like a triple swirled snail. She caught herself wondering if Dennis's stomach might also be tattooed. She started to feel a little giddy.

As they drove past the Brandenburg Gate, he caught her gaze – and smiled.

Pia tugged at his arm to draw his attention back to her. "Did you know," she asked in a rather shrill voice, "that this used to be the city gate? Can you imagine? Berlin once ended here!"

Dennis nodded politely, but Jenny had the feeling that he wasn't all that interested in the history of the city. This time, he turned toward Jenny, and when she made eye contact with him, he rolled his eyes briefly.

She suppressed a giggle. She might have been wrong. This tour might not be as much of a disaster as she had feared.

Suddenly, she recalled a conversation she had had with Pia a few weeks ago. It had been on the day that Jenny had finally gotten her parents' permission to travel to Berlin alone. The girls had been sitting on Jenny's bed and drinking soft drinks.

"Whew!" Pia had said, blowing up her bangs. "That was like pulling teeth. Are your parents always so stuffy?"

Jenny had smiled into her glass. "Always." She felt light and airy. For the first time ever, she was being allowed to travel on her own! And to Berlin, at that. She thanked the good Lord that he had arranged for the church conference to be held in the capital, of all places. "They act as if some new threat to my maidenhood is lurking on every street corner!"

Pia leaned her head against the wall and closed her eyes. For a while, they were both silent, but then Pia said, "Do you think we'll meet a couple of nice boys?"

Jenny grinned. "They're expecting a hundred thousand people. I'd think our chances are pretty good." She felt a tingling in her stomach. This was so exciting!

The room fell quiet again.

"I intend to make it happen!" Pia eventually murmured, dreamily. Her eyes were still shut.

Jenny turned her head. "What will happen?" she asked.

"Silly!" Pia opened her eyes and looked over at Jenny. "I'll lose my virginity, of course!"

Flabbergasted, Jenny glanced over at the door to make sure it was really shut. "If my parents heard you say *that,*" she scolded, "I could kiss our trip goodbye. They'd never let me go with you to Berlin!"

Pia had just laughed. "Stuffy indeed! *Berlin*, Jenny! If not there, then when else could it happen?"

Now, here on this bus, a smile played around Jenny's lips as her fingers fiddled with the glow stick hanging from her neck.

"Do you like that thing?" Dennis's voice tore her out of her thoughts, and she returned from the past.

"The glow stick?"

"Yeah. Everyone's running around with them." Dennis stretched out his hand and tapped the finger-thick plastic rod. As if coincidentally, he brushed against Jenny's fingers, sending an electric jolt through her body.

"So what?" She could feel her cheeks grow warm. "It's a great idea: tomorrow evening, during the service, everyone will light them at the same time." She unclipped the light from her rainbow neck strap and handed it to Dennis.

He examined it. He read the conference motto aloud, "*Speaking the Word of God Boldly.*"

Jenny snatched the light back from him, and this time she made sure that their hands touched. Dennis smiled radiantly back at her. His gaze made her feel nervous. She was aware that Pia was glaring at her darkly because she had managed to divert the conversation with Dennis to herself. And yet, for some reason, she really didn't care if her friend was annoyed. She gazed into Dennis's eyes, and a fluttering started in her stomach.

Maybe *she* would be the one to lose her virginity during this church conference, not Pia. Who would have ever thought *that*?

Exhilaration spread through her body as Dennis now reached for her hand to reclaim the light. "It'll only work once, right?" he asked.

Jenny nodded, and he promptly acted as if he were going to break it in the middle. She flinched, but noticed instantly that he was just teasing. With a laugh, he pretended to hand it back to her, but instead he snapped it back onto the strap around her neck. His fingers came dangerously close to her breasts …

Her heart pounded so rapidly that she felt like it would explode any minute.

After the officer who had brought Faris's gun and badge left, silence descended momentarily on the conference room.

"Make sure you get out of here now!" Tromsdorff finally said. "The caller wants you to check out the internet café. We shouldn't defy his wishes again." He glanced at Faris's phone. "Ben?"

The FCI tech glanced up from his work. "Yes?"

"What do we need to do with Faris's phone?"

Ben scratched his nose. "He obviously has to take it with him. If the man calls in and someone else picks up, we'll have a huge problem on our hands."

Tromsdorff wanted to add something, but Ben grinned brightly. "We won't miss anything, don't worry!" He pointed at his computer. "I've set up a fake exchange station. When he calls, Faris's phone will ring, but we will be able to listen in from here too."

Tromsdorff nodded. "Good. Faris, hit the road!"

Faris was about to stick his phone, as usual, into the inside pocket of his leather jacket, but that was where his temporary phone was already sitting, so he put his main phone into his jeans pocket.

"Faris is my partner," Paul said. "I'll go with him."

"It's more important that you stay here," Tromsdorff replied, but after a moment's hesitation, he reluctantly agreed. "Fine, go on."

A few minutes later, they were sitting in an unmarked police car, a black BMW M3, and driving toward Kurfürstendamm. On their way to the garage, Faris had called Hesse to ask him if he needed his motorcycle back, but the journalist had said no.

"I'm just fine, pal," he had assured Faris. "I still have my delivery van. Take care of the important stuff!"

As Faris steered through the thick traffic in the capital, Paul stared through the windshield at the street and said nothing. When they had to stop at a red light, the silence grew oppressive.

"Creepy," Paul murmured with a shudder.

"What do you mean?"

"The caller, earlier. Did you feel like he was watching us?"

Faris thought about the cameras in the subway station. "He knows a lot," he agreed. "About me, about SURV." The gun underneath his arm felt unfamiliar and heavy, and this revealed how much the past few months had changed him. This never would have bothered him in the past.

Paul nodded, gazing at a young woman in a miniskirt who had just crossed the street in front of them. "Do you think he knows us personally?" The light changed to green, but they still couldn't drive on because the intersection was full of vehicles. "He knew Tromsdorff's name and rank, but he could've researched that as well."

Faris suddenly recalled something that he hadn't thought of before now. "His first contact with me," he murmured. "The caller forbade me from contacting my colleagues. 'At this point,' he said. It confused me at the time, but I forgot about it in all the chaos that followed."

The woman vanished around a corner. Somebody behind them blew their horn.

Faris glanced in the rearview mirror. "And then, after the first explosion, the man specifically gave me permission to bring SURV into the picture. He didn't want just me. He wanted the entire team to investigate him."

"You think that he has a score to settle but possibly not with you, but with the whole SURV unit?"

Faris sent a sideways look at his partner. "You should pass that along to the others. They should start following up on that."

As Paul called the War Room, Faris drummed his fingers impatiently against the steering wheel. "Are these cars ever going to move?" he grumbled.

Paul hung up. "Gitta's on it." He sighed. "I have a bad feeling about all this." A group of women in long skirts and colorful conference scarves was standing on the sidewalk on his side of the road.

Faris impatiently threw his arms up.

"A really bad feeling!" Paul repeated. A chirping sound underscored his words.

It came from Faris's jeans pocket.

"Well now, Faris," the distorted voice said, as soon as Faris fished the phone out of his pants and accepted the call. "I hope you have a good reason for not being at the café yet."

Through narrowed eyes, Faris stared at the still-blocked intersection. "How do you know that?"

"GPS," was the short answer.

Faris nodded. *Of course.*

"We're stuck in traffic," he explained.

"What am I supposed to think about that?" The distorted voice was skeptical, and it sounded to Faris like the caller's response had been just slightly delayed.

"We ..."

"Are you refusing to follow my instructions?"

"No, listen, I ..."

"Stop it, Faris! Stop fucking around with me! I think I need to teach you a little lesson. I will call you back in five minutes. If you can't hand your phone to the internet chick, that little goth-mouse behind the café counter, then someone will die. Somebody who matters more to you than that poor homeless man from earlier."

"No!" Faris now yelled. "Listen, I ..."

"That's it, Faris! My patience is over! Five minutes!" And with those words, the man hung up.

Faris lowered his phone and struggled to regain his self-control.

"Quick! The flasher!"

Paul reacted instantly. He lowered the BMW window and set the magnetic flasher on the top of the car. At the same moment, Faris activated their siren.

Five minutes!

There was no way he could make it. They had just passed Wittenbergplatz and weren't even across Nürnbergerstraße. And as far as he could see, the entire stretch of Tauentzienstraße was a parking lot.

The cars in front of him reluctantly moved to the side.

"Get out of the way!" Faris bellowed, but it was pointless. What if he got out of the car and ran the rest of the way? Impossible! He had been working out for the past two weeks, but he would need more than seven minutes to cover the two kilometers to the café. This would have been true even if he hadn't slammed his skull into the subway station wall this morning.

He honked.

"They can't just evaporate," Paul murmured. "What's going on now?"

In two sentences, Faris explained. The siren punctuated his words with shrill screeching, and the cars right in front of them finally started moving.

Paul had grown pale. "Someone close to you?"

Faris was focusing so hard on the traffic that he wasn't able to respond. He finally had a little space. He drove up on the sidewalk, then accelerated. But after only a few meters, a new obstacle blocked his path, a delivery truck that had pulled out of a driveway and was sitting in the middle of the sidewalk.

"Shit!"

Something that he couldn't immediately identify started to ring. He honked once more, and the truck rolled back enough so he could squeeze by. After barely scraping past several concrete bollards, he accelerated again. He felt Paul fumbling around in his jacket pocket before pulling out his ringing burner phone.

Paul answered and identified himself. "It's Niklas."

"Not now!" Faris shouted. Relieved that he hadn't hit any pedestrians, he returned to the roadway, but had to quickly hit the brakes because the cars in front of him couldn't move out of the way fast enough. "For the love of God!"

Paul switched on the speaker phone.

"Faris, I have to …"

"Not now, Niklas!" Faris shouted. The BMW's engine howled as they took the turn onto Kurfüstendamm on squealing tires. Paul gave an alarmed cry, which mingled with the new sound of chirping from Faris's regular phone.

"Damn it all!" Faris yanked the phone up to his ear, as he tried to keep the car under control with one hand on the wheel. "The five minutes aren't up yet!"

"I know." The caller laughed softly. "I just wanted to be on hand when you failed, my good sir."

"Who?" Faris snapped, slamming on the brakes, then hitting the gas again. A young man who was about to stride across the crosswalk in front of him, jumped back onto the sidewalk. In his rearview mirror, Faris checked to see if anything had happened to him, but the poor guy was just standing there, looking perplexed. One second later, he disappeared from Faris's view.

Hesse's voice croaked through the burner phone's speaker.

"What do you mean?" the caller asked.

"Who do you want to kill?" Horrible images flashed through Faris's mind. *Somebody who matters more to you.* His sister Anisah? His nieces? *Laura!* The miserable bastard!

"Oh, that!" The caller paused dramatically before he spoke. "I'll give you a description: plaid shirt, biker boots, leather jacket …"

Faris's stomach somersaulted. "Niklas!" he shouted. "A bomb! Wherever you happen to be, get out!"

"What? Faris, what's that …"

Faris's ears were filled with the caller's laughter mixed with the howling of the siren and Hesse's incomprehensible babbling.

Knesebeckstraße loomed before him, but the café was at the opposite end of it. Unreachably far away.

"Ten seconds to go, Faris," the caller remarked, and he began to count down.

When he reached four, Faris slammed on the brakes. There was no point. He couldn't reach the café in time.

"Three."

He lowered the phone and grabbed for the one in Paul's hand.

"Two." Although the caller's voice now came from his lap, it was still loud and clear.

Faris pulled the other phone up to his ear. "Get out, Niklas! You have to …"

But it was too late.

"One!" the caller cried.

The air around Faris froze solid.

"Bye for now!" The caller laughed.

And the emptiness of the broken connection pierced Faris's ear.

CHAPTER 18

Faris sluggishly lowered his phone and bent his head down to the steering wheel. His skull roared, and his heart hammered inside his chest. It took every bit of strength for him to keep from throwing up all over the car.

Beside him, Paul seemed to be completely paralyzed. The regular howling of the siren seemed to be coming from incredibly far away. At some point, Paul turned it off. As the silence spread throughout the car, the traffic rushed past them.

"Niklas!" Faris rasped.

He had failed yet again!

Suddenly he remembered that his regular phone was sitting on his lap. "You fucking bastard!" he screamed as he picked it back up again. But here, too, he heard nothing except the buzzing of the disconnected line.

The caller had hung up.

Faris leaned his head back against the headrest. A noise penetrated through the stuffing that suddenly seemed to be stuck in his ears. A ringing. It took several seconds for him to realize that it was his burner phone. He had to gather every ounce of willpower he had to answer the call.

"Shit, Faris," a voice buzzed in his ear. "What the fuck was that?"

It was Niklas Hesse.

With a jerk, Faris sat upright. "You're alive!"

Hesse coughed. "Yes, damn it! But just barely!"

For a moment, Faris's nausea increased, but then it subsided. "How can that be?"

"There was a bomb in my apartment, holy crap!" Hesse's voice sounded shrill, and it almost cracked.

"How did you surv …?"

"The oak table. It took the brunt of the explosion."

Faris closed his eyes in relief. "Thank God!"

"Hey!" Hesse complained. "I'm touched that you obviously feel close to me, but all my computers are gone, pal!"

A laugh surged through Faris's throat. With effort, he held it back. "Don't flatter yourself! I just didn't want to lose someone else in a bom …" He faltered as another wave of nausea swept over him. He waited until it passed.

Paul's worried eyes were focused on him, but he ignored his partner.

"I'm glad that you escaped," he murmured. Over the receiver, from very far off, he heard the sound of police sirens.

"I need to go," Hesse said. "The cavalry is here."

The phone in Faris's lap started to chirp. With a weary gesture, Faris ended the one call and accepted the other one.

"You did that for nothing!" he couldn't help saying.

"No," the voice of the caller confirmed. "You're right. A shame really, but it doesn't matter. Now you know that I have the ways and means to bring you to heel."

Faris rubbed his burning eyes. "What happens next?"

"Nothing's changed. The internet chick. And Faris …"

"Yes?" Faris felt an unfettered desire to rip the guts out of the stranger.

"You can take your time now."

After they had both processed the shock, Faris resumed their course. Paul called the office, and so that Faris could listen in, he turned it on speaker phone.

Tromsdorff had already heard the news about the explosion at the old Tempelhof terminal building. "Several units are already there," he declared. "Apparently, this time we caught a break. The building was cleared out recently. As far we can tell, there are no casualties."

Faris filled him in on who the target of the attack had been.

"Niklas?" Tromsdorff asked sharply. He also knew the reporter well. "You're friends, aren't you?"

"Good friends." Faris shook his head because he still couldn't believe what had almost happened. "The attacker wanted to show that he has me on a short chain."

He made himself a mental note. As soon as he reached the internet café, he would call Anisah and his parents, and ask them to leave the city. The culprit was obviously well-informed about his connections. If he knew that he was friends with Niklas Hesse, he also knew about his family. *And Laura!* Faris clenched his jaw. He would feel considerably better if all of them were out of this bastard's reach.

"Hmm." Tromsdorff didn't say anything for a moment. "Are you doing alright?" he then asked. "I could relieve you of duty ..."

"No, you can't, or another bomb will go off somewhere else." Faris gazed at the phone sitting in his lap. "No, I'll be okay. What should we do next?"

"The best thing you can do is whatever the psycho demands. We have brought in additional staff to go through the old files, to try to trace the caller's father. If you finish up at the café and he hasn't given you any new orders, the two of you should come back here. We'll see from there."

Faris nodded. "Alright."

The internet café proved a total flop. It was one of the more serious iterations of that business type. The interior was dominated by lots of chrome and red leather, plus an oversized cardboard cutout of game heroine Lara Croft. A giant train station clock hanging on the wall informed them that the time available to them was shrinking, but besides that, they didn't learn anything useful.

Behind the glittering counter, a young woman in slightly Gothic-style clothes was busy making lattes for two female guests. Paul identified himself and asked her if they could take a look at the surveillance footage from the previous evening. She shook her head regretfully.

"We were closed all day yesterday," she explained. "Nobody could've sent anything from here. We were servicing the computers." She pointed over her shoulder at the door marked *Office*. "I'd be glad to fetch my boss to confirm that for you."

"That won't be necessary," Faris murmured. He had already suspected this was the case. If there actually had been some clue to their mysterious caller's identity here, he wouldn't have sent them here in the first place. "We'll send a colleague over to follow up," he said.

"Whatever." The young woman reached for the two lattes that were now ready. She glanced at Faris and Paul one last time, as if she wanted to ask, *Was that everything?*

They thanked her and left the café. "What was that?" Paul asked once they were back out on the sidewalk. "Why did he send us over here?"

Nothing involved with this case made sense. Faris stared at his watch. "He's playing with us," he murmured. The digital numbers on his watch face jumped at that moment from 6:56 to 6:57.

They had a mere twenty-nine hours left.

Alexander

Standing at the base of the cross, he gazed up at his father. How thin he was! The wrinkled skin of his stomach hung in folds over the white linen loincloth. To Alexander, this cloth looked like a diaper. This was the same thing he had thought years ago, when he was a little boy, and he had studied the picture of the crucified Christ in their church. Now, he knew that Christ had been crucified naked, but of course, he never could have been depicted like that. Yet now, as Alexander studied his handiwork, a profane thought crossed his mind. Underneath his loincloth, had Christ been well-endowed?

He hit himself in the forehead with his fist to drive out this heretical impulse. "Bad, bad!" he whispered. "How could anyone be so sinful?" He then glanced up into the face of the man on the cross. "Forgive me," he added softly.

He was sure that God could hear him. Just as before, the angel's light streamed out from one of the corners of the dungeon, casting sharp shadows everywhere. Alexander felt a sudden urge to step into the light. It had been a long time since the angel had said anything. Alexander really wanted to see if he was still there.

But the angel had forbidden him to come any closer, and Alexander was afraid that something terrible would happen to him if he disobeyed. So he stayed in his spot beside the cross and pursued his own thoughts.

The crucified man moved, though he didn't open his eyes. "Alex?" His voice was only a breath.

"I'm doing it right," Alexander whispered to him affectionately. "You'll be happy with me, Father." And he pressed the crown of thorns more firmly onto the man's head.

The man groaned softly.

A smile flitted across Alexander's face as he examined his handiwork. Fresh blood now ran out from beneath the crown, making its way across the white skin toward the floor.

"WHAT ARE YOU DOING?"

The angel's voice was so unexpected that Alexander flinched in astonishment. He feverishly retreated from the cross, then spun around.

The figure had returned to the garish light.

"WHAT ARE YOU DOING?" the voice repeated.

Alexander trembled in the face of the fury in the voice. "The picture," he whimpered. "In the church. This isn't just like that. He should look just like the picture in the church. I made it better … I … HE said …"

"IT'S ALRIGHT," the angel assured him. "YOU MEANT WELL."

"I did." Alexander squeezed his eyes shut. He so badly wanted to see the angel's face, but the light still blinded him.

"THE PICTURE IN THE CHURCH," the voice said. "I WOULD LIKE TO TALK TO YOU ABOUT THAT, BUT I HAVE A FEW THINGS TO TAKE CARE OF FIRST."

Movement inside the light indicated to Alexander that the angel had turned around. One moment later, he sensed that he was once again alone in the dungeon. Alone with the cross and his father.

The picture in the church. Although the angel was gone again, he still remembered.

He goes to church with Father, every Sunday and sometimes also during the week. They always sit in the same spot, on the left side of the nave. And one day, it just appeared. The picture. Someone had hung it up so that the people in the pews could see it clearly. Alexander is amazed at all the details.

For example, the cross is quite short, very different from all the other crucifixion pictures he knows. In those, the crucified Christ hangs far above the heads of the people, but that isn't the case with the picture here, in their church. In this one, the Lord's feet aren't far off the ground. His father explains to him that this was how it truly was. Why would people, even during Christ's lifetime, have set up such tall crosses? They would have required an excessive amount of wood.

Alexander nodded understandingly.

In the painting, the head of the man on the cross is sunk forward. The crown of thorns and the blood fascinate Alexander, but he can't say why.

"What kind of rope is that?" he asks. The painter hasn't just painted the nails that were driven through the Savior's hands and feet, but also a red rope. It is wrapped around the upper arms of the crucified man …

Alexander looked up at the crucified man in front of him. The rope was sitting at the right spot.

Just like in the picture.

Father is silent all the way home from the service, and Alexander doesn't risk disrupting his thoughts. Unlike in the past, Mother isn't waiting for them with dinner. Alexander still misses her, but Father has made it clear to him that his mother was a lost soul and that it isn't worth mourning her absence.

As Alexander prepares the meal, Father delves into his books. Besides the Bible, he also reads an array of other books with complicated titles and tiny letters.

They are no longer fasting. Father has declared that they'd done that long enough. Since then, he has been searching for new ways to wash away their sins.

On this particular Sunday, he seems to have found one. He carries one of the books over to the table, and while Alexander sets the table, he begins to read. "I adore you, and for myself also, I desire the last drop of water from the sacrificial heart of Jesus! I thank you for this and humbly request that you pour over me this source of eternal life. Cleanse and heal me from all my sins and mortal sins, from my deficiencies and insufficiencies, so that I may become more like you." He then looks up from his book. "Hold out your hands!" he commands.

Alexander reluctantly obeys.

Father picks up the water carafe that is sitting at the center of the table. "We will wash ourselves clean from our sins with the water of life," he murmurs.

And he pours the water over his, and Alexander's, hands.

Jesus Christ seemed to be watching her.

Ira Jenssen frequently felt like this whenever she sat in the front pew at her church and desperately tried to pray. Although the crucified man's head hung forward, Ira always felt as though he was looking straight through her. Sometimes, she wondered if that might have been the painter's intention in the first place. Regardless, he had accurately captured the horrifying details of the crucifixion: the gaunt body, the outspread arms, the protruding ribs, and the painfully curling hands through which the nails had been driven. The crown of thorns. Ira's gaze wandered along the long, blade-like thorns that were piercing the skin of the man on the cross. She started to feel nauseous at the sight of the blood that was pouring from his face and down his neck.

This was a new feeling.

She gritted her teeth and tried to swallow down the tightness in her throat. To distract herself, she concentrated on the red rope and the heated debate that had arisen among the members of the congregation when the picture had first been hung up, years ago.

"It's perverse, in fact," she murmured to herself. She was glad that at this moment she was the only person in the church. This way, she could sit here undisturbed, could attempt once more to say a prayer from the bottom of her heart. And above all, she could indulge in rebellious thoughts without being afraid that she might lose her job because of them.

She let a cynical smile spread across her face. What would her parishioners say if they knew that their revered pastor struggled with doubt, day after day? More than that! That she had lost her faith. Old Mrs. Feldbusch on the church council would shoot off a complaint letter to her supervisor's office in no time, demanding a new minister.

With a sigh, Ira lowered her gaze to her hands. She hadn't folded them. The only times she still managed that was when she was standing in front of the congregation and leading a service; it was important for her to keep up appearances then. But now, all alone in the church, this childish gesture struck her as absurd and pointless.

"Well, God," she murmured. "Now what?"

She didn't receive an answer. But then, she didn't expect one. She lifted her head and stared at the painting. *He* had abandoned his only son to such cruel torment. What difference did it make if *He* didn't show her the right path to take? *He* had taken away her Thomas ...

Thomas!

Her heart tightened painfully.

"The Lord your God is a merciful God; he will not abandon or destroy you." The verse from Deuteronomy came to her lips with astonishing ease. She suppressed a bitter laugh.

A clicking sound revealed that someone had opened the door at the back of the church. As the footsteps grew louder, she realized that her secretary was approaching.

Ira heard a soft cough behind her.

She closed her eyes.

Veronika Herzog believed that her boss was praying whenever she retreated alone into the church. Not even once did her secretary, the person with whom Ira had spent by far the most time since losing Thomas, suspect that she had lost her faith a long time ago.

"Ira?" Veronika's voice was uncertain. "I'm so sorry to interrupt you, but it's important …"

However, Ira remained motionless in her seat for a moment longer. Her eyelids felt as if they weighed a ton. She had to force herself to open them again, and as she turned around to face her secretary, her eyes were burning.

"Good Lord!" Veronika exclaimed. "I didn't mean to …"

Ira forced herself to smile and blinked away the gritty feeling. "It's alright! I was done anyway."

Done! She felt dark humor behind this statement. This was the perfect way of expressing her mood.

"If you want my opinion, Ira," Veronika began, "you desperately need something to distract you from Thomas. Preferably a new relation …"

"What is it, Veronika?" Ira interrupted her sharply. She didn't feel the slightest desire to discuss with her secretary, of all people, the longing she felt for the man whom she had believed, until recently, was the love of her life.

"Of course." Veronika swallowed. "I … I think it would be best if you came and saw it for yourself."

Ira followed Veronika outside. The church, designed in the shape of a Greek cross, stood on the edge of a city square that was adorned with a patch of lawn and a handful of flowers. The shadow of the soaring spire fell across Ira as she and her secretary turned the corner down a side street and headed toward the parsonage.

She let Veronika lead the way into the house, down the perpetually musty-smelling hallway, and into the church office. It stank of glue and plaster, since the Sunday School group had been here this morning for a craft project. The long table, which had been specifically set up along the long wall, was covered with papier maché and finger paint.

"Take a look at this!" Veronika pointed at her computer screen.

Ira tore her gaze away from one of the little blue paper monsters, which looked like a cross between an elephant and the little clownfish from *Finding Nemo*. Veronika had opened a website with the URL *hotnewzz.tv*. The garish flame logo shouted at Ira, demanding her attention.

"I was about to head home, but I wanted to check my email one last time before leaving," Veronika explained. "That was when I discovered *this*."

Do you know this man? asked the headline in large letters.

Ira looked more closely at the picture that was featured underneath it. For some reason, the man looked familiar to her.

"The police are requesting assistance in identifying this victim of a violent crime," she read in the caption. "Please send any clues to the identity of the man to the editor or contact the authorities at the following telephone numbers." After these sentences, several ten-digit Berlin numbers were listed.

"Don't you recognize him?" Veronika exclaimed.

Ira blinked, then it came to her. "Of course!" An icy shiver ran down her body. The man was a member of her congregation. He regularly attended her services, but since he wasn't involved in the congregation's life beyond that, Ira hadn't recognized him immediately. This was also why she couldn't instantly come up with his name.

"That's Werner Ellwanger," Veronika said. "Every Sunday, he sits on the left-hand side, in the pew right in front of the crucifixion painting."

Ira nodded. "That's right."

Victim of a violent crime.

She felt a touch of unease, as if evil had suddenly moved closer to her. With a shiver, she wrapped her cardigan more tightly around her.

"We have to contact the police," Veronika declared with excitement. She reached for the phone and dialed one of the indicated numbers, while Ira turned her gaze back to the photo. The picture had obviously been edited. The skin of the man's cheeks and neck looked too uniform to be real, and the hair also seemed to have been altered.

As Veronika's phone started ringing, Ira reached out for it. The secretary handed her the receiver, and Ira held it to her ear.

"*Landeskriminalamt*," a woman's voice announced. Ira gave her name, all the time wondering what kind of wounds the police computer specialists had erased from the photo.

CHAPTER 19

On their way back to the BMW from the internet café, Faris came to a jolting stop as a wave of dizziness washed over him.

Paul misinterpreted his behavior. "What is it? Did you think of something?"

Faris shook his head. He had not a single good idea. His dizziness grew so strong that he had to grab hold of a lamp post.

"Are you alright?" Paul now sounded concerned. "The paramedic said that you could have a concussion."

Faris waited for a moment, until the world stopped turning. "I'm okay now," he murmured through clenched teeth.

"I'm taking you to the hospital." Paul tried to take his arm, but Faris deflected the movement.

"There's no time for that now." He took a deep breath.

The ringing of his phone prevented Paul from replying. Paul answered it for him. "Gitta, what's going on?" He listened to what Gitta was saying and shrugged when Faris shot him a questioning glance. "No. Faris isn't doing so well. I should take him to … What? Where are we?" He looked around, and his eyes fell on a street sign. "Yes, we are still on Knesebeckstraße. We were just at the internet café." He nodded, several times. "Right, we didn't make any progress there. The attacker's obviously jerking us around. The café wasn't even open yesterday evening. Could you please arrange for an officer to be sent over to take the manager's statement for the files?" Paul gave her the man's name and address. "Could you check on that right away?" he asked, then listened for a moment. "Thanks." He looked at Faris. "I don't know. He looks pretty pale."

Without releasing the lamp post, Faris grabbed Paul's phone and held it up to his own ear. "He's exaggerating," he explained. "I'm doing fine, just a little dizzy, that's all."

"You might have a concussion." Even Gitta sounded worried. Good grief, why did they all have to keep pressing the same button? "Anyway, you've survived a bombing, Faris. It would be best if you …"

"Stop it, Gitta! I'll get myself checked out once we catch the bastard and disarm the bombs."

"Yes, but …"

"But nothing!"

She sighed deeply. "You're pig-headed, you know!" she grumbled. In the background, Faris could hear Tromsdorff talking about the man on the cross. "The boss has just been telling us that we finally know who the man on the cross is," Gitta explained.

Progress at last! Faris felt the adrenaline start to pump through his veins. "Who is he?"

"A man by the name of Werner Ellwanger. We received the clue from a woman … wait … her name is Ira Jenssen. She's the pastor over at the Church of the Passion, a Lutheran congregation on Marheinekeplatz. Tromsdorff is wondering if the two of you want to drive over there and take her statement."

Werner Ellwanger.

Faris turned the name over in his mind, but it didn't ring any bells. If he had heard it somewhere, he at least couldn't recall it.

"We've tracked down Mr. Ellwanger's address," Gitta continued. "Marc is on his way to the apartment. We can send other officers to the pastor, Faris, if you …"

"I'm fine," Faris interrupted her. "Like I told you, everything's okay. Did you check to see if the name Ellwanger shows up on the victim list from the Klersch Museum?"

Gitta blew him a kiss across the phone. "Of course, my lord and master. Unfortunately no hits!"

Faris made a face. He cautiously loosened his grip on the lamp post, and to his relief, his dizziness had passed. They didn't have time to spare for dizzy spells. Ellwanger didn't appear in the old files, but perhaps a chat with the pastor would jog some memory. "Marheinekeplatz, you said?"

"Yes. The parsonage is located on a side street next to the church. Ms. Jenssen promised to wait for you there."

"We're on our way."

The phone crackled as Gitta covered the mouthpiece with her hand. "I'm coming!" she called in a muffled voice, but then it was back to sounding clear. "Faris?"

"Yes?"

"Be careful!"

"I will, Gitta." With a faint smile, Faris ended the call.

Two minutes later, he had informed Paul of their new task. Since he still felt a little dizzy, Faris handed the car keys over to his partner. He didn't want to run the risk of crashing. Paul shook his head, concerned and disgruntled, but he sat down in the driver's seat without saying a word.

As they drove, Faris suddenly remembered that he needed to warn his family and Laura. He pulled his temporary phone out of his jacket pocket and dialed Laura's number.

She didn't answer.

He let it ring until her voicemail picked up.

"Laura, it's me. Listen, this isn't a stalker call. It's really important. I'd like …" he stopped to consider how he could neatly put it. He couldn't make any demands without providing her with an explanation, but he also didn't want to make her worried. He cleared his throat. As he searched for the right words, the mailbox recorded him breathing. He finally opted for honesty. "I have reason to believe that the bomber here in Berlin might be out to get you and Lilly. You need to leave the city. Go to the Baltic for a few days or something. Alright? I'll call back when I know more."

I love you.

He hung up before the last sentence could slip out.

From behind the steering wheel, Paul sent him a sideways glance. Faris dialed the next number, listened for it to start ringing, and hoped that his sister would answer.

But he was out of luck. Anisah didn't pick up; her husband did. "Chalid," his deep voice roared.

"Samir, it's me."

"Faris. Tell me, what's going on with all of you?"

Faris had to move the phone away from his ear because Samir's voice was so loud. "What are you talking about?"

"Some of your colleagues were just here, and they asked us a bunch of questions. Are you in some kind of trouble?" His words held annoyance and frustration. Although Samir wasn't a devout Muslim, he still had problems with Faris's adoption of Western ways. He had made it quite clear, on more than one occasion, that he didn't approve of Anisah's regular meetings with Faris. Not that this really bothered Anisah much.

"Trouble?" Faris asked in confusion.

"They interrogated us about …"

"Wait a second!" Faris interrupted him. The wheels in his head began to turn. "Say that one more time! They *interrogated* you? You must be wrong about that. They *asked* you …"

"They seem to think we might've had something to do with the bombings. Faris, that's ridiculous!"

Faris ground his teeth as he realized what had happened. Dr. Geiger had sent her people over to run a background check on him. She still didn't trust him. She really thought he might be somehow involved with the attacks. This was unbelievable!

"Samir, listen to me. That's just routine. They were there because it's possible that the bomber will try to contact you."

Samir sniffed. "Are you or aren't you in trouble?" It sounded as if he already knew the answer.

You have no idea!

Faris nodded but said something else out loud: "Of course not! But could you do me a favor? Take Anisah and the kids out of the city. There's a chance that the bastard might target them. And take Umi and Abu with you."

"Your parents? Faris, you know how to scare a guy!"

Faris didn't take the bait. "Can you also pass the word along to Reza and Hasim?" Reza and Hasim were his brothers. "They need to be careful, or better yet, they should leave town with the rest of you."

"Really, Faris, this is …"

"I have to go, Samir. Please, please do what I've asked. I'll explain everything to you later."

"Okay. You sound tired, so this time I'll refrain from pointing out that this job of yours …"

"It's been a really crappy day," Faris interrupted him before the usual litany could begin. *Why did you become a cop in the first place? Why would you put yourself and your family in danger? Why didn't you go to college like your brothers?* He could feel Paul's eyes on him. "At the moment, my old phone is out of commission. If you want to reach me, use the number I just called you from. I'll be in touch as soon as everything's all clear."

"Okay." Samir hesitated. "Faris?" he started cautiously.

"Yes?"

"I never again want to have to tell Anisah that you were almost blown to pieces."

As Faris hung up, a sardonic laugh caught in his throat. He leaned his head against his headrest and closed his eyes. His skull pounded, and he thought he could hear people crying out in pain from far away.

What will happen to all those people out there if you fail one more time? the caller's distorted voice whispered, and he heard himself answer.

They will die.

The last word echoed through his head.

Die. Die. Die …

Like the people in the museum.

And goodbye …

164

He swallowed hard before opening his eyes once more and dialing Laura's number. His call went to voicemail again. With a curse, Faris hung up, and then pulled his regular phone out of his pocket and stared at it.

Call, you bastard, he thought. *Tell me what your next move is.* The tension inside him grew with each passing minute.

"Is everything okay?" Paul asked.

"Geiger ran a check on my family," Faris murmured. He was so exhausted that he couldn't even feel upset about this.

"That stupid bitch!" Paul bellowed. "How are you feeling?"

Faris looked over at him before he said, "Focus on the road!"

"Bite me!" Paul shot back, but he remained silent for the rest of the drive.

The Church of the Passion's building dated from the early twentieth century. With its powerful brick facade and bulky tower, it looked almost intimidating to Faris. The parsonage on the side street looked similar – dismal, dusty. And cool.

Ira Jenssen was expecting them. She was a tall, somewhat austere-looking woman. She was wrapped in a cardigan that she was holding closed over her stomach as if she were chilly. When Gitta had told Faris on the phone that their witness was a pastor, he had imagined a chubby, middle-aged woman wearing a dark skirt and staring piercingly at him through her glasses. Ira Jenssen didn't correspond with this image in the slightest. She was young, around thirty. She was wearing jeans, not a skirt. And she wasn't pudgy, in fact she was a little too skinny. Her collarbone stuck out underneath her cardigan, and her wrists looked slender. She had medium-length blonde hair and blue eyes, which weren't as eye-catching as Ben Schneider's but which Faris nonetheless found unusually compelling.

After Faris and Paul identified themselves, Ms. Janssen led them into an office filled with old-fashioned furniture and a table covered with children's craft projects. A woman who was a better fit with Faris's mental image of a pastor was sitting at an aging computer and typing away on its keyboard. Ira Jenssen introduced her as Veronika Herzog, the church secretary, and then asked Faris and Paul to follow her into her office. This contained an expansive desk and a small seating area with a single armchair and a comfy-looking couch. Behind the desk hung a bed sheet covered with children's colorful hand- and footprints. At the sight of that, Faris had to think about Laura and her daughter, and he felt suddenly angry. What if the culprit found them? He stifled an urge to call Laura again.

Ira Jenssen invited them to sit down in the seating area, and she rolled her desk chair over.

Paul opted for the couch, sinking deep into the soft cushions. "You called us because you think you recognize the man in the photo?" he asked, coming straight to the point.

Ira Jenssen leaned to the side and pulled a piece of paper from her desk. She carefully set it down in the middle of the coffee table. It was a printout of the still that Dr. Geiger had given to the press. "It's not just that I recognize him. I know him. His name is Werner Ellwanger, and he's a member of our church. On the website where we found this picture, it says that he's the victim of a violent crime. What happened?"

She paused but then forged on. "Is he dead?" She brushed her fingertips across the spots on Werner Ellwanger's face where Ben had erased the blood.

Faris cleared his throat. "No, he isn't dead, but we're afraid he might soon be. He was abducted, and apparently his abductor plans to ..." he checked his watch and estimated the remaining time, "kill him in about twenty-eight hours."

A deep wrinkle appeared between Ira's eyebrows. "And the information you have is really that accurate?"

"A threat has been made, so yes." Paul leaned forward, which looked difficult to do in the soft couch. "What can you tell us about Werner Ellwanger? Anything tied to him and the church conference would be helpful."

"The church conference?" Ira picked up the printout and examined it thoughtfully. Her knuckles looked rough, and her fingernails were trimmed very short. "Does your investigation have anything to do with the two bombings?"

"What would make you think that?" Paul asked. He looked completely relaxed, but Faris had known him long enough to be aware that he was closely monitoring the pastor's every move.

Ira shrugged. "On TV, they're saying that the bombings have something to do with the conference."

Paul hesitated. He shot Faris a questioning look, but when the latter nodded, he decided for honesty. "Yes," he admitted. "We assume that the disappearance of Mr. Ellwanger has something to do with the bombings."

"An abduction," Ira murmured. "And bombings. About twenty-eight hours you said, right?" She ran a mental calculation. "That's when the papal Mass will be happening. You think there's going to be an attack on the Pope?"

She's smart, Faris thought. With the limited information they had just given her, she had come to the same conclusion he and his colleagues had. He struggled against the fascination he felt for her. "That's irrelevant at this point," he replied more harshly than he had intended to.

Turning toward him, she studied him for a long moment. It felt like she could read his thoughts, so intense was her gaze. He nervously rubbed his mouth.

Paul didn't say anything.

She slowly exhaled. "Forgive me," she murmured. "I'm not accustomed to being confronted with things like this. So, what do I know about Werner Ellwanger?" She picked up the printout and placed it across her knees. As she spoke, she studied the picture. The denim on her left knee was almost threadbare, and now Faris noticed that she wasn't wearing socks. Her feet were clad in plain brown moccasins. "He is a very religious person. He comes to church every Sunday, and there are rumors that he's a little ..." she smiled apologetically, "crazy."

"Crazy?" Paul leaned back. "In what way?"

"Well, I think he's a fairly fanatical Christian. I would personally describe him as a biblical literalist."

"That means he's one of those people who takes everything in the Bible very literally," Paul said.

Ira cocked one eyebrow. "There aren't many people who can explain offhand what biblical literalists believe."

"Mr. Iskander and I belong to a special police unit," he explained. "Our specialty is religiously motivated crimes."

Ira nodded slowly. "I understand." Her fingernails dug into her jeans.

Faris remembered that the caller had said *my father* when he had spoken of his victim. "Do you know if Werner Ellwanger has any family?"

"As far as I know, he's a widower."

Paul ran his hand over one of the pillows sitting on the couch beside him. It was embroidered with an image of a red-haired dachshund. From the clumsy execution of the stitching, it looked as though a child had done it. "Are there any relatives?"

"Yes, a son."

"How old is he?"

"He must be about eighteen or nineteen. He comes to every Sunday service."

Faris sent his partner a meaningful glance. They were both thinking the same thing. Was this son their culprit? "Could you give us the son's name?" Faris inquired, struggling to keep his increasing excitement under control.

Ira didn't have to give this much thought. "Of course. His name is Alexander."

Alexander

The angel. He was still gone, but nevertheless, Alexander thought he knew what he wanted from him. He had to remember things, had to talk about the things that had happened in the past. He looked up at the bright light. "At some point, water wasn't enough for Father," he whispered.

"Only Christ's blood can cleanse us of our sins," Father murmurs as

168

he pours the water over Alexander's and his own hands. He seems agitated and nervous. He hasn't been sleeping well lately. Alexander can hear him walking up and down in his room in the middle of the night. He sees the fear in his father's eyes when their gazes meet. The fear of his own sins. The fear of damnation.

The water splashes softly over Alexander's fingers, but Father doesn't seem to be satisfied with it.

"It isn't working," he whispers.

With a jerk, he sets the carafe down and looks at his hands as if he might be able to see there the filth that is soiling his soul.

"Among believers, devotion to Jesus Christ generates the desire to know him intimately and to identify with him," Father says. "To identify with him." His lips are pressed tightly together, and Alexander can guess what thoughts are tumbling through his mind. "Wait here!" Father commands.

He goes into the kitchen, and when he returns, he is carrying the large meat knife.

Alexander turns cold. "What are you going to do?" His voice has become a rasp.

"Hold your hands out!" Fathers stares at him challengingly.

Alexander obeys with a quiet whimper. And with shock-widened eyes, he watches as Father places the knife point on his own palm and slowly drags it across. Father's blood feels warm as it trickles over Alexander's skin.

"But if we walk in the light," Father repeats, "like he does, we will be in community with one another, and the blood of Jesus Christ, his son, will cleanse us of all sins." He seems transfigured. "Sing!" he orders. Pain has engraved several lines around his mouth and eyes, but he holds his bleeding hands perfectly still.

And Alexander sings.

"What can wash away my sin?
Nothing but the blood of Jesus!
What can make me whole again?

Nothing but the blood of Jesus!
Oh! Precious is the flow
That makes me white as snow;
No other fount I know,
Nothing but the blood of Jesus."

The words sounded muffled in the low, tiled room. The man on the cross lifted his head a little. The rhythmic beeping, which Alexander has grown quite used to, to the point that he hardly registered it anymore, sped up for a moment, but when the man on the cross lowered his head again, the sound slowed back down.

"Am I doing it right?" Alexander wanted to know.

"YES," the angel replied. Alexander hadn't heard him return. He was suddenly back.

"AND THEN?" the angel asked.

Alexander didn't know what he was driving at.

"THEN CAME THE GARDEN SHED," the angel declared.

Once Ira had given Alexander's name to the two officers, the younger of them, the one who had introduced himself as Detective Iskander, placed a call to his team.

"Gitta, it's me." He pressed his phone to his ear. "Could you check on the current address of Alexander Ellwanger?"

His conversation with the woman on the other end of the line gave Ira an opportunity to study him more closely and to consider her current feelings. She felt electrified. The first glance she had exchanged with this man had struck her like a punch. She didn't know why, though.

A memory fluttered through her mind, a memory from the time when she had convinced herself that she was still happy with Thomas. Already then, the shadows of things to come had hung over them, and Thomas had taken refuge in macabre jokes to help them bear the pain.

"Why do you love me, of all people?" he had asked her once. They were lying next to each other in bed. It was summer and so broiling hot that they were only covered with a sheet. Through the thin fabric, their naked bodies were clearly visible.

She reached for Thomas's hand, but then turned on her side and gazed into his face. For a brief moment, his eyes didn't look as sad as usual. She decided to respond to his amused tone. "Perhaps because I'm a masochist?" she joked lightly.

A muscle twitched at Thomas's right temple. "I don't think so." He hadn't moved for several minutes but was lying on his back and staring at the ceiling.

"What do you think, then?" She propped herself up on her elbow.

"Honestly?" His eyes now met hers, and her heart gave a leap.

"Yes."

"I think you have a thing for broken men."

She wrinkled her forehead. "You consider yourself a broken man?"

"Just look at me!" He pointed down at his naked body, then over at his clothes which were tossed carelessly on a chair. Black pants, black turtleneck. He rarely wore a clerical collar since he knew it pained Ira to see him in it.

"Nonsense!" she exclaimed defensively.

He chuckled softly. "You suffer from Mother Theresa Syndrome, Ira Jenssen! Believe me, you have a thing for broken men!"

After that, he had leaned over her and kissed her, and all gloomy thoughts and doubts about whether what they were doing was right were submerged in a wave of passion.

Faris's gaze rested thoughtfully on the pastor's face, and he wondered what she was thinking. A deep furrow had appeared on her forehead.

Gitta had set aside her phone to track down the relevant information about Alexander. As Faris waited for her to come back, he watched as Ira pulled several photo albums from a shelf. She set them down on the coffee table and began to flick through them with Paul. When she glanced up and discovered that Faris was observing her, she smiled faintly. She had a crooked smile that created a dimple on only one side of her mouth.

"I'm back," Gitta announced loudly, causing him to wince.

Ira's smile grew wider before she turned back to the photos. Several strands of hair fell into her face, and she automatically brushed them back behind her ears.

"Apparently Alexander Ellwanger still lives with his father," Gitta said. "At least, that's the address on record."

"How old is he?"

"Wait. Eighteen."

Eighteen. Faris recalled Ira's words. She had mentioned that Alexander still attended church with his father every Sunday. Faris's own teenage years came back to him. He had been much younger than that when he stopped going with his family to the mosque for Friday prayers.

An image of Alexander was gradually forming in Faris's mind.

"Good," he said. "Put out an APB on him! And notify the team. We're bringing someone with us who knows him and can tell us more about him." He glanced over at Ira as he said this.

She pointed questioningly at herself.

Faris nodded. He thanked Gitta and then hung up.

Without saying a word, Ira turned her attention back to the photos. "Here." She turned the album so that Faris and Paul could see it right side up. "That's him." She tapped a picture of a young man with a thin face and neatly cut, chin-length black hair. He was staring into the camera with strangely vacant eyes. Ira waited until Paul and Faris had studied him before pointing at the slightly stooped man of around fifty standing next to him. He looked like an ascetic, as if he didn't have a single gram of fat on his body. Faris recognized him immediately. It was Werner Ellwanger, the man on the cross.

He was about to say something, but the chirping sound from his regular phone cut him off. By this point, he was aware that this sound made his stomach hurt.

He heard Paul sigh. "Here we go again," his partner mumbled.

Ira's face reflected both astonishment and curiosity.

Faris answered the call.

"Where are you right now?" the caller asked.

Faris made eye contact with Paul before answering. "With a witness." He hesitated but then added: "Alexander."

For a brief moment, there was silence on the other end of the line. Then the caller whistled admiringly: "You're making progress, I see. But you're not quite right, I'm afraid. I'm not Alexander."

Faris stifled an urge to ask *Who are you then?* The man had treated him like dirt, had ordered him around, humiliated him, and almost blown him up. Faris was fed up with everything. The pain in his stomach now transformed itself into a clump of blazing fury. He decided to take a random shot. "Why are you doing all this, Alex? Did your Papa paddle you once too often?"

He could feel Paul's and Ira's eyes on him. While Ira looked shocked, Paul just looked uneasy. However, he didn't intervene, and this strengthened Faris's resolve. He grimly waited for a reaction.

This time, the silence lasted a small eternity.

The exclamation was completely unexpected. The caller suddenly shouted. "I. Am. Not. Alexander!"

"Really?" Faris shifted the phone to his other ear. "You let your mouth run off a little, Alex, the last time we spoke on the phone. You mentioned your father. We've figured out who the man on the cross is, and now we also know who you are."

He felt sweat start to trickle down his forehead. He was taking a huge risk, he knew that. But he was incapable of keeping himself under control anymore. All he could do was hope that his intuition was now in command of the situation. His intuition and not that miserable feeling of impending doom that was building inside him again.

The caller struggled to breathe, but the distorted voice grew very cold. "Want a fight? Fine, you can have it! Tell me where you are right now!"

Faris's fingers closed around the bridge of his nose. "No." What had Geiger called him? *A ticking time bomb.* He clenched his jaw.

Ira stared at him, her eyes widening with fear. He turned his back on her. He couldn't bear her gaze any longer.

"No?" The caller sounded baffled.

"No!" Faris repeated firmly.

Paul was struggling with himself, that much was evident, but he still didn't intervene.

"You can do whatever you want," Faris said, "but I won't tell you where I got your name." Ira's eyes burned into his neck.

"That …" The caller was gasping for air. "That, Faris, was a mistake! A major mistake!" He paused, waiting to see if Faris would relent, but when he remained silent, the stranger simply hung up.

The emptiness on the line and the void in Faris's mind were one.

Paul inhaled deeply before expelling the air slowly through his nose. "Hopefully Berlin won't have to pay for that," he murmured.

"But I couldn't tell him anything about Ms. Jenssen," Faris replied flatly. In his mind's eye, something was blowing up at that very second. Something big and full of people, perhaps a city tour bus or one of the excursion boats on the Spree River. His stomach tightened, and his nausea and dizziness returned. He slammed his fist against his knee in frustration. A drawn-out cry escaped his throat.

"Pull yourself together," Paul warned. "That won't help anything!"

A ticking time bomb. Faris took a deep breath. "You're right." He glanced at Ira. "Please forgive me." With disgust, he stared at the phone still clutched in his left hand before jamming it back into his pocket. "What now?" he asked. "The guy denies being Alexander."

"Let's assume that he's lying to protect himself. But maybe he's telling the truth. Think back to our two culprits." Paul stood up with difficulty from the soft couch. "In any case, we now have something to help us focus our investigation."

Faris stuffed his unease back down inside. *A ticking time bomb.* Could Geiger actually be right about him? He nodded as calmly as possible.

Paul pointed at the door. "Let's take Ms. Jenssen to Keithstraße. If it turns out that the guy really isn't Alexander, that's where she will be the most help to us." He was already moving toward the door, but Ira didn't instantly react to the gesture he made to indicate that she should follow them.

Instead of standing up, she leaned over the album, pulled out the picture of Alexander, and studied it. A strand of hair fell across her

174

forehead, over her right eye, but she didn't seem to notice it. "What do you mean, that Berlin might have to pay for that?" Her voice trembled a little as she handed Faris the photo. "Is he going to set off another bomb?"

Faris reached for the picture. *Maybe*, he thought. *Or he might abduct someone in my family*. Hopefully Samir had already bundled Anisah and his parents into the car. *Laura!* Faris gritted his teeth. He had to be able to concentrate in order to do his damned job!

And Ira could, potentially, help him with that.

"The conditions of the abduction. They are … well, very unusual."

He thought about the video of Ellwanger's crucifixion. He hadn't planned to show it to Ira, but who was he to say that this woman might not be able to provide some valuable information if she saw it? Seeking help, he glanced over at his colleague. Paul was standing at the door. He seemed to be just as indecisive as Faris, but he eventually nodded slowly and let go of the doorknob.

"Alright," Faris murmured. He stuck Alexander's photo into the chest pocket of his jacket, then pulled out his regular phone and clicked through the menu until he found the video. Before he hit start, he lowered the volume as much as possible so the horrible sounds in it couldn't be heard. At the spot where the camera had caught a close-up of the cross, Faris hit pause.

He then straightened up and showed Ira the picture.

She didn't react instantly. For quite a while she simply gazed at the terrible image in front of her. Faris could see the thoughts churning inside her head. She grew pale, and her lips parted slightly. She shut them again without making a sound.

"Good Lord!" she finally exclaimed.

Faris reached for the car keys in his pocket. "Our attacker sent the video that photo comes from. Do you see the electrodes on Ellwanger's chest?"

Ira nodded. Her eyes had started to glitter, and with fascination, Faris watched as compassion spread across her face. He realized that she must be a very good pastor.

175

"The electrodes are connected to a heart monitor, and we have reason to believe that they are connected with a bomb that will go off during the papal service."

Ira slowly lifted her right hand and covered her mouth. She blinked her tears away. "Who would do something like that?" she whispered.

Faris paused. "Our main suspect is Alexander." The caller's words echoed through his head.

I. Am. Not. Alexander.

And an inner voice whispered to him that this was true. The stranger had been clearly irate when he called him Alexander.

"No, I don't think so." Ira shook her head energetically. "Sometimes, when I've seen them in the church, I've wondered if the old man is abusing his son, but Alexander isn't …" she frowned as if she found what she was going to say next unpleasant, "smart enough to plan anything like a serial bomb attack."

Paul cleared his throat. "Not smart enough?"

"He seems to be a little, well, developmentally challenged. I'm sorry to put it like that." Ira shrugged in apology, then cocked her head thoughtfully. "May I see the phone one more time?" she asked. Her eyes were lowered, and when Faris handed her his phone, her hands were shaking.

"I know this image," she whispered.

"What?" Perplexed, Paul took a step toward her.

Ira nodded quickly. "Come with me! I have to show you something."

CHAPTER 20

The interior of the cross-shaped church into which Faris and Paul followed Ira was shadowy, although the numerous brick elements in the arches and columns felt rather cozy. It wasn't the first time that Faris wondered why Christian churches exuded such gloom when they had been constructed to bring their members closer to God and to praise him.

Passing the uncomfortable-looking, dark wood pews, Ira walked up to the altar, which was also constructed from bricks. She didn't need to point out what she wanted to show them. Faris caught sight of it immediately.

To the left of the altar, in a small niche, hung a painting. It looked modern, at least as far as Faris could tell. It depicted a low wooden cross on which a man was hanging. His fingers curled painfully up into the air, but that wasn't what set off warning bells inside Faris.

"Shit!" he heard Paul exclaim beside him.

This was just what he had been thinking. The crown of thorns on the head of the painted man matched the one on Werner Ellwanger's head, as did the looped knot on the white loincloth. However, one detail in particular looked exactly like it did on their victim. The man in the painting wasn't just affixed with nails but was also bound with two red ropes that had been wrapped around his upper arms and knotted to the cross-beam.

"I can't believe it!" Paul groaned at the sight of it.

Faris scratched his neck. "He's obviously recreated this painting for some reason." He turned toward Ira, but before he could ask a question, she started to speak.

"At some point, around 2000, the church council commissioned this picture. I wasn't here at the time, but from the stories I've heard, there was quite a bit of controversy after its delivery, concerning whether it should be hung up or not."

"Because of the rope, I'd guess." Paul took a picture of the painting as he spoke.

"Exactly." Ira pointed at the rope. "People didn't think that the artist should have taken such liberties. The Bible doesn't mention anything about ropes." She smiled thinly. "The artist won out in the end. Supposedly there was a heated theological discussion, during which the story of Doubting Thomas from John's Gospel was brought up. In that narrative, it is written that Christ's nail marks were *in his hands*. And the artist was of the opinion that, even if the ropes weren't mentioned in the Bible, this was the only way the evangelist John hadn't gotten this detail wrong."

"I understand." Paul examined the photo on his phone's screen, then sent it to Gitta.

"I don't," Faris admitted.

Ira pointed at the rope. "The painter argued this point: In order for Christ's death to fulfill the ancient prophecies from Isaiah, it was critical that the nails be driven through Jesus's hands. After all, the prophet had written: *See, I have engraved you on the palms of my hands.* It was God's desire that the Roman soldiers would drive the nails through Christ's hands. However, anatomically speaking, it isn't possible to crucify someone like that. The holes in the hands would tear out. Since this didn't happen to Christ, at least according to the artist's thinking, it was an indication that he had been tied up with additional ropes." She smiled again, and this time her expression didn't look so sad, rather strangely sarcastic.

Faris understood. "And that convinced the church council to hang up the picture."

Ira's smile faded. "It was more likely to be the sixty thousand marks they had paid for the picture, but that doesn't matter. As far as I know, after all that drama, the painter never accepted another commission from a church."

Faris and Paul looked at each other. "Could the *painter* be our culprit?" Paul asked.

Ira immediately dismissed this theory by shaking her head. "He died the year before last."

Faris thoughtfully furrowed his brow. "We will need to interview his family. And if he really never again accepted a commission from a congregation, there aren't any other pictures like this one out there. This means that we need to search for our culprit among those who attend this church, even if Alexander is out of the question." He nodded at Ira. "That's good. You have helped us a lot."

Ira couldn't get the terrible photo from Detective Iskander's phone out of her head. She kept seeing Werner Ellwanger in her mind, crucified like Jesus Christ. *Good God!* Her stomach wanted to flip over at the mere thought of it.

After the older of the two police officers, Detective Sievers, had taken a picture of the painting in her church and sent it to his colleagues, he called and filled them in on what Ira had just told them. After that, the officers asked Ira to accompany them to their precinct.

She hurried back to her office to grab her purse. "I'm ready now," she informed Detective Sievers afterward.

"Good." He waited for her in front of the office, while Detective Iskander went to get the car.

Ira followed the officers to a dark BMW with flashers on the top. The sight of it made her stomach tingle. She had never been in a police car before, and although she was only a witness, she felt herself growing tense as she approached the vehicle.

Her gaze fell on Detective Iskander, who was opening the passenger door for her.

Thomas had always held the door for her too …

She stumbled slightly as this thought came to her. The moment she caught sight of the young detective, she felt suddenly unsettled. His eyes! They looked so much like those of her ex. Now, in the evening light, this impression intensified, and Ira suddenly realized the reason for this. The two men shared a particular unique expression. In Thomas's case, she hadn't noticed it until she had realized that he was going to leave her. Long before he himself had admitted it, she had known that he would leave. His eyes, the hopelessness they had contained, had betrayed this to her.

And now she once again saw this emotion in Detective Iskander's eyes.

Pull yourself together! she warned herself, smiling at him as she took her seat. He smiled back, but the smile never reached his eyes. The slightly macho way he treated her was equal parts pleasant and unpleasant, and the injuries to his face, the cut on his forehead and his split lip, bothered her as well.

As he climbed into the back seat, she wondered how he had managed to get those wounds. She considered simply asking him, just to jump start a conversation. But she didn't have a chance, since Detective Sievers then slid into the driver's seat. As they drove, he asked her detailed questions about Alexander. To her embarrassment, she didn't know the answer to most of them. "I'm really sorry," she eventually said. "I'm afraid I won't be of much help to you."

"Don't worry about that," Detective Iskander replied from the back seat. "Our colleagues at the precinct are trained to jog your memory."

His tone made it sound as though he was being facetious. She looked over her shoulder at him to see if he was pulling her leg.

Their eyes met. "Oh," he said. "Please pardon me! That didn't come out right. What I meant to say was ..." He abruptly broke off.

Detective Sievers grinned. "What Faris *meant* to say is that we have a couple of good psychologists on the team who will help you to access those memories you might think you've forgotten. No need to worry about that."

Faris.

So that was his first name.

Ira forced herself to smile. "I was thinking …" She left the sentence floating in the air.

"We have files and lists of names that you can look through," Sievers explained. "We have reason to believe that the culprit's motive is connected to a bombing that took place ten months ago. Perhaps you'll think of something when you read through the list of those victims."

"If you think so." Ira pressed her lips together. Was she mistaken, or was Detective Iskander – Faris – breathing more calmly? An awkward silence suffused the car.

"That thing you said the caller …" Ira didn't know exactly how she should put it. She plucked up her courage and turned so that her back was half-leaning against her door. "That thing about his father spanking him too often." She held her cardigan closed across her stomach. "It was pretty disturbing, to be honest." She wondered for a moment which had unsettled her more: what Faris had implied or the hardly contained anger that had sparked from his eyes. The anger that had now vanished behind the smooth facade and the haunted expression.

"I'm sorry," he said. For a few seconds, he held her gaze, but then he glanced back out the side window. "I didn't mean to frighten you."

Heavens, those eyes! she thought. He looked tired.

They were about to turn left, and Detective Sievers changed lanes to prepare for that. The clicking of the turn signal sounded loud in the silence of the vehicle.

"Are you Muslim?" She put this as a question, recalling the bracelet around his wrist she had caught sight of in her office. Arabic letters. While in college, she had taken several semesters of Arabic, just because it interested her. But her knowledge had grown rusty over the years. The dark leather contained two words, that much she could still make out.

"Yes." His answer was very curt, and Ira sensed that this wasn't a good topic. Her curiosity about this man increased. Faris. A nice name. She thought she remembered that this word meant *knight*. And caught herself wondering if the name suited him or not.

181

It was shortly after nine in the evening when they reached the War Room on Keithstraße. The first thing that caught Faris's eyes was the countdown on the white case wall.

27 hours.

Gitta was taking care of them like a mother hen tending to her chicks. Faris and Paul had hardly sat down before she was handing them two mugs of steaming coffee and asking Ira Jenssen if she wanted one too. Before she could set off to fetch the third coffee, Faris asked Gitta to hang Alexander's picture up on the case wall and to show Ira the list of victims from the museum bombing.

While the two women retreated into Gitta's glass office and Faris sipped cautiously on his coffee, he studied the other people in the room. At that moment, it was fairly quiet. Marc was still at the Ellwangers' apartment, and Gerlach, their contact from Department 5, and even Tromsdorff seemed to be off somewhere. Besides Faris, the only people here were Ben, Paul and Shannon. Ben was sitting behind his computer. Faris had no idea what he was doing, but he looked extremely focused.

The sight reminded him of Hesse, and Faris suddenly recalled that he was running a trace on the email. He considered calling the reporter to check on it, but that would presumably just be a waste of time. Hesse's computer had been destroyed in the explosion. They wouldn't get any closer to the culprit down that trail.

Faris stared thoughtfully ahead and observed Shannon as she paced back and forth in front of the case wall. She was studying a color printout of a scene from the crucifixion video. From where he was sitting, Faris recognized the man in the hood who had securely nailed Werner Ellwanger in place. The picture showed him in profile, but the hood was pulled low over his face so nobody could see any part of his face except the tip of his nose.

Following a hunch, Faris stood up and asked Shannon if he could borrow the printout. He then walked up to Gitta's open office door and knocked on the doorframe. "Excuse me, Ms. Jenssen," he said. "Could you please take a look at this and tell me if the man could possibly be Alexander?" He handed the picture.

She gazed at it for a long time, and Faris suspected that she couldn't take her eyes off the hammer that the hooded figure was holding in his hands. After swallowing hard twice, she finally handed the paper back to Faris. She shook her head regretfully. "I'm sorry. There's so little of him visible here, but the stature would be right."

"The hoodie," Faris pressed. "Have you ever seen Alexander wear that to a service?"

Any little clue could help, he thought, but he knew he was grasping at straws.

Ira took the picture back from him. She needed another few seconds before she replied. "It's just black. I'm sorry, Mr.... . Iskander."

"That's okay." He took the paper back from her. "Thank you anyway."

In the meantime, Shannon had turned to one of the lists and was brooding over it. Faris pinned the printout back on the case wall and returned to his coffee. The desk chair groaned as he dropped back into it.

Paul had propped his arms on the tabletop and was sipping his coffee in silence. However, when he noticed that Faris was studying him, he smiled at him wearily. A warm feeling spread through Faris's chest. He realized that these people here were his family, and then he recalled the caller's words.

If you don't do what I say, somebody who matters more to you will die ...

The warmth in his chest evaporated and was replaced with a feeling of oppressive tightness. What would he do if the bastard did something to one of his co-workers? He swallowed, but the pressure pushing down on him remained. Gitta's eyes met his through the glass pane of her office wall. She nodded encouragingly.

Ira's back was turned to him. She looked lost in these unaccustomed surroundings. Faris struggled against a resurgence of his doomsday feelings, which threatened to drag him under again.

He concentrated on the photo of the man on the cross that Ben had printed out and pinned to the case wall. Right underneath it, at the very end of the list titled *culprits*, stood Alexander Ellwanger's name. Someone had underlined it in thick marker and adorned it with an energetic exclamation mark, which Faris thought looked a little too optimistic.

His stomach protested against the bitter coffee with a slight cramp, and he realized that he hadn't had anything decent to eat all day. He wasn't hungry in the slightest. He pointed at the color printout of the man in the hood. "We should assume that this is Alexander."

Instead of replying, Shannon reached for an eraser and wiped away the exclamation point. "I think so, too. But is he our caller as well?"

Paul set down his mug. "The caller said 'my father', which makes me think, yes. We checked: Werner Ellwanger has only one son."

"On the other hand, Ms. Jenssen doesn't think he would be capable of plotting such an attack," Faris interjected.

Gitta heard what he said. "Ms. Jenssen is right," she said over the head of the pastor, who was focused on the list of museum victims and only glanced up briefly. "I just got done talking to one of Alexander's former teachers. She agreed that Alexander was developmentally challenged." She consulted a pad sitting next to her computer. "When he was fifteen, they measured his IQ. He came in at just over ninety."

"But the caller isn't challenged like that," Faris murmured. "Not at all!"

Before they could further discuss these findings, the door to the War Room opened, and Tromsdorff and Gerlach stepped inside. They both looked tired and exasperated, but there was also a look in Tromsdorff's eyes that Faris hadn't seen even once during this case.

It was a faint flash of hope.

"The APB is out for Alexander Ellwanger," Tromsdorff explained. "No results so far, but sooner or later, we'll get him. A dozen officers are out questioning people who know Ellwanger. Hopefully we'll hear something soon about where the damned cross might be." He stopped in the middle of the room. "Good work, people!"

Faris shook his head in disagreement. "The caller *isn't* Alexander."

"That's possible, but let's focus on him. He might lead us to our unknown caller with the distorted voice."

Tromsdorff walked up to the case wall, removed one of the magnets, and tossed it into the air. This was the only sign of nervousness he showed, and yet Faris thought he could feel his tension and the responsibility that rested on his shoulders.

That rested on *all* of their shoulders.

"The canine units have now done two sweeps of every corner of the Olympic Stadium," Gerlach now cut in. "No explosives were found." His expression suggested he didn't think this was good news, and Faris immediately heard why. "According to information from our colleagues in the state police, there are some new types of explosive out there that the dogs can't detect. We can't say with one hundred percent certainty that the stadium is free of explosives."

Faris reached for his mug and drained it in one gulp. His stomach cramped painfully, but by now, the caffeine had hit his bloodstream. The headache that had been plaguing him was now better. "Has the explosives residue from the other bombings been analyzed yet?" he asked.

This seemed to get Ben's attention. He glanced up from his laptop, exhaling noisily like somebody who has worked himself to the verge of collapse. "They're still working on the analysis."

"Good." Gerlach straightened his shoulders. With his gray hair and slightly raised chin, Faris suddenly thought he looked rather like a military man.

In Gitta's office, Ira leaned back and sighed. "I'm sorry," Faris heard her say. She stood up and appeared at the office door.

"Did you discover anything?" Paul inquired.

She shook her head.

Paul offered her Shannon's seat, and she sat down hesitantly.

"Let's put all the facts aside," Paul suggested. "Tell us about Alexander,"

She didn't seem entirely happy at this request. As she blinked, Faris suspected that the image of the crucified man had been seared onto her eyelids.

"Although he's almost eighteen, his father dominates him completely," she began. "At least, that is my impression. His father tells him what

to eat and drink, and he intervenes in every conversation his son has."
She tucked her hair back behind her ears. "Sometimes, he won't let
Alexander finish a single sentence. Like a mother who doesn't think
her toddler can string a sentence together."

Gitta nodded, and even Faris knew that kind of mother all too well.
His sister Anisah tended toward that end of the spectrum.

"I remember, my secretary told me that Ellwanger made his son
fast rigorously." She frowned, as if she found it hard to believe this. "A
boy in the middle of adolescence." Her breathing now grew laborious.

Appearing in the door to her office. Gitta considered the scene briefly
and then walked over to stand beside Ira. Ira turned toward her, and
Gitta smiled at her cheerfully. She frequently used this technique. *I've
got your back*, she implied. *Everything's alright.*

Ira's hands were rigidly intertwined. "I still remember how upset
Veronika was," she continued. "She tried to convince Alexander to
rebel against his father, but he couldn't. He could never bring himself
to contradict his father even once in public."

"He probably never contradicted him at all," Paul surmised. "Do
we know if Werner abused Alexander?"

"You mean physically?"

He nodded.

Ira shrugged. "No. I mean, I don't think so." She thought for a
moment. "Alexander is practically a grown man. Wouldn't he defend
himself?" She uttered the question before fully realizing what she had
said. Her eyes grew large and darted over to the picture of the man
on the cross hanging up on the wall. A frightened "Oh!" escaped her
lips as the color drained from her face.

"He did defend himself," Shannon murmured. "In his own way."
Ira covered her mouth.

"It is quite typical," Paul said. "A person who has been abused since
their childhood reacts in one of three ways." He held up his fingers and
counted them off. "Either he suppresses the bad stuff. Or he becomes
a rigorous pacifist. Or, and this happens with some frequency, he
himself turns violent."

"But … to crucify a person …" Ira's voice was only a wisp.

The next moment, the door was shoved open, and Marc hurried inside. He looked harried and sweaty and was carrying a box packed full of books and objects of all kinds.

"I came right over from Ellwanger's apartment." He pushed aside some of Ben's gadgets and set the box down on the case table. "You wouldn't believe what it looks like in there!" He pulled out a camera and handed it to Ben. Without asking any questions, the technician connected it to his laptop.

Only a few seconds later, the projector beamed the first of the photos Marc had taken in Werner Ellwanger's apartment onto the screen.

"Oh God!" Ira groaned, and as picture after picture flashed up on the screen, she kept repeating, "Oh God!"

Alexander

"THE SUMMER HOUSE," the angel reminded Alexander. Although he had left some time ago, he now resumed their conversation as if he had only been gone for a few seconds.

"TELL ME ABOUT THE SUMMER HOUSE!"

But Alexander couldn't. His head was buzzing with all the horrible memories he had buried down deep inside, the ones the angel was dredging back up again with his persistent, unrelenting questions.

He pressed his hands over his ears and squeezed his eyes shut. "No!" he whimpered. "Please don't!"

"WHAT HAPPENED IN THE SUMMER HOUSE?" the angel pressed pitilessly.

"The …" Alexander struggled to force the words through his throat. "The whippings."

"DID HE BEAT YOU?"

"No!" The idea was so absurd that Alexander opened his eyes in astonishment. "He never beat me."

The angel was silent. Alexander had the feeling that what he had just said surprised the angel.

"WHAT DID HE DO?"

Alexander swallowed. "He whipped *himself*. As penance for his sins." The images now flooded his mind. He saw all the blood – on the leather cords, on his father's back, on the walls. The ceiling.

He felt sick, gagged. And he felt ashamed.

"IT'S OKAY," the angel said. "YOU DON'T NEED TO FEEL ASHAMED."

But he still felt ashamed. For his own weakness.

"WHAT HAPPENED AFTER THAT?" the angel asked.

"After that?" Alexander's knees trembled, but his nausea had disappeared, making room for something else. Cold horror that squeezed his heart like a hand. "After that, everything was much worse," he whispered.

CHAPTER 21

Ellwanger's apartment resembled a museum.

A museum for Christian art.

Oil paintings hung on all the walls, all of them depicting crucifixion scenes. There were crucifixion icons, crucifixions in oil, etchings, and modern crayon sketches that almost looked more brutal than the more objective representations, because of their stark color contrasts.

While Ben scrolled through one photo after the other of this macabre private collection, Ira kept her hand pressed over her mouth. "I knew he was a little *off*," she murmured as the slide show came to an end. "But that he was …" She broke off in a mixture of bewilderment and horror. "That's horrifying!" she whispered.

"Those were all the pictures from the living room," Marc explained. "Now comes Alexander's bedroom."

The pictures shifted, no longer showing the gloomy room with the dark furniture and the awful paintings but a chamber with a plain pinewood bed, bare walls, and an unusually neat desk, which held nothing except a paper desk pad, a very thin silver laptop, and a small bronze crucifix. The subsequent pictures showed the room from all possible angles. Its bleakness was almost creepier than the clutter in the living room. To Faris, it looked like a silent scream.

"In that apartment, you couldn't help going insane eventually," Ira mumbled.

"The computer," Ben said. He clicked back several pictures before pointing at the silver laptop on Alexander's desk. "It might hold some-thing we could use. Did you bring it with you?"

Marc pulled the thin device out of his box. "Here it is."

Ben took it from him, opened it, and plugged it into a power cord. As he started to search through the hard drive, Shannon began to go through the books that were also in the box. "A bunch of fundamentalist stuff," she said. She pulled out a book that was adorned with hundreds of yellow and green sticky notes. "This looks promising." Without another word to the rest of the team, she carried it over to her own, disorganized, desk. Ira relinquished Shannon's desk chair to her. After picking her tennis ball up, Shannon opened the book at the first of the marked pages.

"There was nothing else of interest in the apartment," Marc explained. "The cellar was extremely neat, and all that was down there were two bikes. However, we found one other thing. A rental contract for an allotment garden."

An electric shock went through Faris. "Ellwanger has a garden plot?"

March pulled a notebook out of his pocket, flipped through it, and found the page he was looking for. "Yes. At the Garden Colony at the Airport. That's the name of the organization. It must be somewhere close to Tempelhof."

Faris and Paul exchanged a look.

"If we're lucky," Paul said with deliberate calm, "we might find the cross out there."

"Exactly." Faris stood up. "I suggest we go take a look!"

Alexander

"WHAT WAS WORSE?" The voice of the angel was very soft, and yet Alexander was trembling under the relentless pressure he was under to relive all the horrible things that had happened.

"Why are you doing this?" he asked.

He didn't understand the answer he received. "SO THAT THE WORLD CAN FINALLY UNDERSTAND. NOW TALK. WHAT WAS WORSE?"

"He didn't beat me," Alexander reiterated. "That would've been easier to take. But he wouldn't do that even when I begged him."

"No!" Father gasps. "I can't do it anymore. You have to do it for me!" The whip dangles from his hand, the blood on it long dried because it has been many days since it was last used.

Alexander falls back a step. "No, Papa. Please, not that!"

But Father presses on. His face is gray and haggard. Alexander can see the devil lurking behind his eyes. He reluctantly holds out his hand, takes the whip.

It weighs heavily in his grip.

"Don't ask me to do this!" he begs. Tears run down his cheeks, wetting his entire face.

"Do it!" His father gazes at him so imploringly that he finally gives in.

And raises the whip over his head …

"HE HOPED TO FIND RELIEF FROM HIS SINS THROUGH THE SCOURGING." The angel's voice was very quiet. Mournful.

Alexander nodded. "But it didn't work. His burden *didn't* grow lighter. And he knew why." He hesitated, waiting for the angel to speak on his behalf.

But the angel remained silent.

"He said that the burden he felt was the burden of the entire world."

"HE BELIEVED THAT HE WAS JESUS CHRIST."

Alexander shook his head. "No. He tried to explain it to me, but I didn't understand. *Complete identification with Christ*, he called it. It was the only way for him to get rid of his sins."

"THAT WAS THE MOMENT HE STARTED DEMANDING THAT YOU CRUCIFY HIM?"

Alexander lowered his head. "Yes," he whispered.

Gustav Dellinghaus enjoyed spending his evenings patrolling the gardens of the Garden Colony at the Airport, for which he was chair of the executive board.

For about half an hour, he simply strolled cheerfully through the darkness down the pebbled paths. "His" gardens sat to the right and left of him – all of them organically cultivated and organized neatly. This was how he liked it! He passed old Mrs. Reiß' rustic fence. In the light of his flashlight, his gaze fell on the lawn, which was overrun with dandelions. The majority of the yellow flowers were past their peak and had already transformed into white puffballs.

Dellinghaus stopped moving and leaned down to one of the plants that he could reach through the fence slats. As he pulled it up, the little umbrellas took flight with a lurch. With a disgruntled look on his face, Dellinghaus straightened back up again and made himself a mental note. Tomorrow, he would call Mrs. Reiß and tell her that this was unacceptable. Regardless of the eco-friendly gardening rules, she was obliged to make sure no invasive weeds grew on her parcel. The executive board had just added this stipulation to its rules because the increase in air-borne seeds was a growing problem. Dellinghaus pulled out a handkerchief and blew his nose. It was true that Mrs. Reiß was quite frail, but they couldn't take that into consideration. If the old woman was now unable to tend to her plot, then her adult daughter should take care of it!

With a sigh, Dellinghaus continued on his way.

Over the past few weeks, he had received several complaint calls. The Ellwangers' garden had long been a thorn in the eyes of their adjacent lessees. Of course, the beds were nicely tended, but something didn't seem quite right with the summer house. It gave them a weird feeling, one of the neighboring gardeners had tried to explain, and now Dellinghaus was on his way to take a closer look at the situation. He reached one of the path intersections and looked around. The Ellwangers' plot was located on Cherry Lane.

Dellinghaus turned left and quickly reached his destination. He aimed his flashlight beam at the allotment.

At first glance, everything looked completely normal. The grass needed to be mowed again soon, but there were no dandelions or other weeds in sight, and even the summer house was neatly painted.

There was no bulk waste on the small terrace, no trash bags lying around to attract pests.

What could have bothered the neighbors?

Dellinghaus was about to leave, when something caught his eye.

One of the summer house's windowpanes was broken.

This immediately awoke his sense of duty. He would have to inform Ellwanger. They couldn't have any homeless riffraff taking up residence here. It would be best for him to simply check to make sure that hadn't already happened. He swiftly unclipped from his belt the ring holding the spare keys to all garden gates in the colony. But before he could find the right key, his eyes fell on the thick padlock that had been mounted right above the garden gate's lock.

"What the devil?" he mumbled.

It was forbidden to secure any of the allotments in such a way that members of the executive board could not enter. Dellinghaus's eyes wandered over to the summer house with the broken window. He suddenly understood what the neighbors had meant when they described having a bad feeling about things over here.

He felt cold.

He assiduously pushed his feelings of discomfort aside. *We'll see about that!* He wasn't the kind of man who let himself be put off by a little barbed wire and a stupid garden gate. He glanced to the right and the left to see if anyone was watching him, before quickly climbing over the fence. He then strode down the narrow path between the beds and onto the small terrace made of washed concrete slabs. The broken window was now right in front of him.

Again he felt cold, and again he suppressed the feeling. He leaned forward to risk a look through the shattered pane. It was pitch black inside.

He hesitated.

But then he shined the flashlight through the hole. For one moment, all he saw were dust particles floating in the sharply defined beam of light. It took only a second though, for the light to illuminate the details hidden in the darkness.

Dellinghaus dropped his flashlight. It clattered to the ground and rolled across the terrace without going out.

Dellinghaus couldn't have cared less.

His eyes wide with horror, he whirled around.

And ran as fast as his feet could carry him.

Since Marc had already been to Werner Ellwanger's apartment, Tromsdorff ordered him to drive along with Faris to check out the allotment gardens at Tempelhof. However Faris protested and insisted that Paul be allowed to come along as his partner, so ultimately all three of them climbed into the BMW and drove off. Thanks to their flashers and siren, it only took them thirty minutes to cover the distance. When they arrived, they found themselves standing uncertainly in front of the locked barbed wire gate that apparently protected the gardens from undesirable visitors.

From the path inside the gardens, a flashlight beam struck them. Before they could figure out what was going on, a man in rubber boots and overalls hurried toward them. He opened the gate, then walked past them with a curt nod and a mumbled "Good evening!" Paul caught the gate before it swung shut.

The three of them had just stepped through the gate when a second man ran toward them. He was short, hardly 5'3", and about Paul's age, but while Faris's partner looked fit despite his slight paunch, this man looked very out of shape. A much-too-short, obviously hand knitted sweater hung over pants that he was holding up with some kind of toolbelt. Tools of various kinds dangled from several loops.

"Goodness, you're fast!" he called from several steps away. "I just called you." As Paul studied him in bewilderment, the man added: "You're not from the police?"

"We are." Paul held out his ID and badge. "The homicide division." He introduced himself, Faris and Marc.

The man nodded admiringly. "Murder squad! I knew what I discovered had to be important. Good work!"

"Wait a second!" Faris raised his hand. "What are you talking about?"

He felt the man's eyes scan him from top to bottom and steeled himself for the wall of prejudice he was about to hit. However, this man seemed to have more important things on his mind.

He hurriedly gulped several times. "Well, the summer house!" He waved his right hand in the darkness, somewhere behind him. "The Ellwangers'. That's why I called you! Are you …"

"Stop!" Faris's voice was suddenly very sharp. "You mean that you called us … the police … because something's wrong with the Ellwangers' summer house?" Adrenaline immediately started surging through his veins.

"Yes!" The man nodded energetically. "That's why you're here, right?"

"Yes." Paul now took charge. "First things first, please tell us your name."

"Dellinghaus," the man sputtered. "Gustav Dellinghaus. I'm the chairman of the executive board for this garden colony."

"Good. So, what did you discover?" Paul inquired.

"You have to see it yourself! It is … shocking!" Dellinghaus spun around and hurried back in the direction from which he had come. They followed the dancing beam of his flashlight. At Dellinghaus's heels, they strode down various paths until they came to an allotment that Faris thought looked just as boring as all the others.

The summer house walls were white plaster, and the structure was so tiny that Faris could tell instantly the cross couldn't be in there. So what was the cause of Dellinghaus's agitation?

"I had to cut the padlock," the short man confessed. "Ellwanger won't be happy about that, but after what I saw in there, I thought …" He broke off as he pushed open the gate. "The lock is the least of our worries." And with that, he hastened straight across the grass to the massive summer house door, which looked strangely out of place in the small structure. To the right of the door was a window.

Dellinghaus pointed at it with his flashlight. "There!" he exclaimed. "You can look inside!"

There was no cross inside the summer house. They saw that right away when they peered through the broken window. The single room inside the small building was much too small for that.

Faris and Paul looked at each other, and without further ado, Paul reached through the shattered pane and opened the window. He immediately climbed through it, followed by Faris and then Marc.

"Holy shit!" Marc murmured as he located the light switch and a dim light brightened the room. "What next?"

They were facing the back wall of the tiny structure. A workbench was in front of them and extending above it was one of those metal tool walls covered with holes, into which you could insert hooks and storage holders. But unlike other typical tool walls, no hammers or wrenches were hanging here. Instead, a dozen different whips were mounted on it. Faris saw several multi-corded leather whips, two of which had metal hooks braided into the fine laces. One of the whips was made of arm-length hemp ropes with little balls on their ends. There were also several thick braided leather bull whips, as well as some whose cords weren't made of leather or rope but a handful of thin chains instead. All of these instruments of torture had one thing in common.

They were soaked with blood.

For most of them, the blood was older and had already turned black. Only one of the leather whips seemed to have been used recently. A swarm of flies took off into the air as Paul pulled on gloves and reached for this whip.

"The man is sick!" Marc murmured. His face had taken on a greenish hue, and he tried to frantically swat away the flies. "I …" He swallowed. "I'll go out and question Dellinghaus about all this." He was visibly relieved to be escaping the sight of these instruments of pain, and as he climbed back out through the open window, he almost tripped over his own feet.

Paul had hung the whip back up on its hook by now and turned his attention to the trunk sitting underneath the workbench. He carefully pulled it out. It was one of those metal boxes people took along with them on desert expeditions and secured with massive spring locks. The eyes that were meant to hold the locks' hangers were empty. Apparently, Ellwanger hadn't thought it necessary to lock the trunk.

"Should I?" Paul asked, his voice sounding tense.

Faris shook his head. He felt a prickling at the back of his neck. "Better not to. Let's have a canine unit sent over."

Paul took a step back in relief. As he did so, he discovered a box that had obviously been standing behind the trunk. "Look at this!" He leaned down again and pulled the box out. It was a moving box from a well-known Berlin company, and someone had closed it without sealing it well. One of the cardboard flaps was pointing up in the air so that Faris could take a quick look at the box's contents.

"What is all this?" Paul muttered.

Faris shook his head.

The box was two-thirds full.

Of glow sticks, printed with the church conference motto.

"Thanks a lot." At Ku'damm, Jenny accepted her change as she smiled at the young woman with the vendor's tray from whom she had just bought her second glow stick.

"Thank you!" the woman replied, before turning to the next customer. The slender white objects still seemed to be selling like hot cakes, even this far into the conference.

"Happy now?" Pia asked. Her arms were folded across her chest, and she was grinning widely.

Jenny weighed the new glow stick in her hand. Something about it was different from the one she had bought right after her arrival, but she couldn't have said what it was.

"Why did you get another one?" Pia wanted to know.

Because I would like to give it to Dennis, Jenny thought, but she was reluctant to say that. After the two girls and Dennis had finished their city tour, the three of them had gone out for burgers. From that moment on, Dennis made no secret that he preferred chatting with Jenny than with Pia. Pia's tone had initially turned rather frosty, but then she had pulled herself together and made the most of it. At some point, Dennis's phone went off, and he had rather sullenly answered it. He said "yeah" several times, and then, "Forget it, Rainer!" With that, he hung up. "My brother," he explained with a roll of his eyes. He left shortly after that, but before he walked off, he gave both of them a quick kiss on the cheek. Jenny convinced herself that her kiss was slightly longer than Pia's.

She quietly smiled to herself.

Pia guffawed loudly. "You're in love!" she cried out. And with that, she seemed to overcome her last bit of jealousy.

Jenny felt herself flush.

"Hey, our little Jen has discovered the opposite sex! That's great!" Pia linked her arm through Jenny's and pulled her on.

Still uncertain, Jenny blew a strand of hair off her face. "Are you sure you're not mad?"

"No way!" Pia waved this off. "There are enough sweet guys out there." As if to prove that she was right, two young men walked toward them, their carefully gelled hair making them look like models. They were talking excitedly to each other and didn't pay any attention to the girls.

Once they had passed by, Pia shrugged. "You'll never know what you just missed out on, boys!" She then grinned again and swiped the glow stick from Jenny, who hadn't tucked the object in her pocket yet. "Hey!" she exclaimed as she weighed it in her own hand. "That's funny!"

"Give that back!" Jenny tried to get her stick back.

Pia avoided her grasp, but then she handed it back to Jenny anyway. "You should get it back from him after the service tomorrow. When he dumps you, you can clone him from the skin cells on it."

Jenny didn't miss the barb that lay hidden in those words. Pia seemed quite certain that Dennis would eventually ditch her. Jenny pressed her lips together and searched for a suitable retort. However, nothing came to her. Nothing that was simultaneously ambiguous and joking enough to not poison the atmosphere. So she didn't say anything.

"What should we do now?" Pia asked.

Jenny hung the new glow stick around her neck. "Suggest something," she said a little apathetically. Since she couldn't spend the rest of the evening with Dennis, there wasn't much that interested her.

"Faris!" Marc called from outside. "Come over here!" He sounded startled.

Faris glanced one last time at the milky white glow sticks, then shrugged. With a nod at Paul, he climbed out the window. Marc was nowhere in sight.

"I'm over here!" his voice shouted from behind the summer house.

"Faris?" Paul's voice came through the window. "Do you know what just occurred to me?" He sounded excited, and for a moment, Faris didn't know which of his two colleagues he should attend to first.

"Faris, get over here!" Marc yelled. "We found something."

Faris stuck his head back through the summer house window. "I'll be right back, Paul," he said before striding off the terrace in search of a path between the beds. As he walked around the little building, he found Marc standing next to Dellinghaus in front of a compost pile in the back corner of the garden. He looked very pale. In the light of Dellinghaus's flashlight, he saw several lathes that someone had stacked up on top of the mound of compost. They were nailed together. Like crosses.

"That's ..." Faris leaned over to take a closer look at the object, but at that moment, his phone chirped.

He pulled it out of his pocket. "Yeah?" he answered.

The caller uttered only one single sentence. "You still haven't turned off your phone's GPS!"

The blood in Faris's veins turned to ice. In the aftermath of the adrenaline rush from the internet café incident, he hadn't thought to do that. He spun around, but it was too late.

Before his eyes, the summer house exploded into a glowing fireball that illuminated the night.

PART TWO
HOUR 15 TO HOUR 28

My God, my God,
Why have you forsaken me?
(Mark 15:34)

PART TWO

HOUR 15 TO HOUR 28

CHAPTER 22

It is difficult for him to breathe. He has to work hard to fill his lungs. His arms are spread wide, and the nails driven through his hands and feet are glinting with blood. But strangely enough, he still doesn't feel any pain. Is this a sign that God is looking down on him benevolently?

How many hours have already passed?

He has no idea.

He has forbidden Alexander to take him down too early, and the boy seems to be obeying. Good boy!

The beeping is now receding into the background, drowned out by the gradually increasing pounding in his ears. His heart is pumping laboriously; he can feel it. His fingers are growing numb and cold, while in contrast his legs feel hot and prickly.

He swallows. His mouth is dry, just like the Bible said.

"I'm thirsty," he whispers, although nobody is holding up to his mouth a sponge saturated in vinegar. So he begins to sing. A hymn his mother had taught him and which he still knows by heart.

A hymn that they sometimes – much too rarely – sing in church.

"Oh sacred head now wounded …" The words are garbled as they cross his lips, so he lapses into humming. He hums verses, but it is the seventh he likes the best.

He sings it loudly, and it doesn't matter to him that the lines sound like he is babbling.

"My lord of life, desiring
Thy glory now to see,
Beside the cross expiring,
I'd breathe my soul to Thee."

Someone is next to him. His eyes are blurry. His head is so heavy.

A hand touches his side. Is it the Lord who has finally come to him? He tries to blink his eyes clear several times, and finally he can see the figure standing in front of him.

"Who are you?" he gasps.

He thinks he sees the figure shake his head, and red-hot horror begins to flood his body. Does this mean that the Lord doesn't approve of what he is doing here, to His honor?

"What do you require of me?" he tries to ask, but all he can do at this point is gurgle. This time his words sound like a drawn-out groan.

The figure seems to understand, nonetheless. Breath gusts across his shoulders and ear as the figure leans close to him.

"You know what I require of you," a voice says softly.

It isn't Alexander's voice.

He wants to lift his head, but he can no longer do that.

A sob lodges itself in his throat.

"Who are you?" he whimpers.

But he doesn't receive an answer. The figure has disappeared. He blinks rapidly, has to somehow clear the veil that has descended before his eyes. He hears footsteps moving away. And all of a sudden, he is alone.

He struggles to lift his head and finally leans it against the wood behind him. And screams.

The blast wave from the explosion surged over him as it passed, slammed into him with full force and threw him backwards. Then, the flames came. They enveloped him, ate into his skin. Burned the flesh from his bones so that pain shot down every nerve in his body until his brain felt as though it had started to cook inside his skull …

"Mr. Iskander?" The voice penetrated through the cotton wrapped around him, and Faris struggled to pull himself out of his memory. Blinking, he stared into the dark face that was floating above him. It took him a few moments to realize that he wasn't back in the Klersch Museum. This time, the fire wave from the explosion hadn't caught him directly like it had back then, but rather it had just knocked him off his feet and into a bush.

He found himself in the ER unit at St. Josef's Hospital. He was sitting on a narrow cot in one of the treatment rooms. His feet couldn't touch the floor, which intensified the feeling of helplessness that had taken root in his chest.

Although this explosion hadn't caught him, he felt as if the flames had cauterized his insides.

Paul!

Faris groaned aloud.

The Afro-German ER doctor who was just in the process of binding his right wrist glanced at him in concern. "Are you feeling alright?"

Faris lifted his left hand and rubbed his thumb across his forehead. "Yes," he murmured. "Just a little flashback."

And the fact that my best friend and partner was trapped inside that hell …

He felt a need to double over.

"A flashback?" The doctor had a deep, rather melodious voice, which indicated that he hadn't grown up in Germany. *Dr. Makame* was printed on the small plastic name tag he wore on the lapel of his blue scrubs.

Faris nodded. "I was in a different explosion, several months ago. I couldn't help remembering that."

An expression of professional sympathy flashed across the doctor's ebony face. "That's understandable. But this time, you were lucky."

Lucky! Faris didn't know if he should laugh or scream. He would have preferred to punch someone in the face, but he didn't know if that someone should be the doctor or himself.

Dr. Makame finished his task and took a step back. "Except for your sprained wrist, there doesn't seem to be much wrong with you.

Just to be certain, we're waiting for the x-rays we took to come back."

Faris cleared his voice. "What about my partner?" His voice sounded like parchment.

After the explosion had died down, he had picked himself up and stared in bewilderment at the ruins that had been the summer house. He recalled rushing over to his partner, who was lying in the middle of the rubble. The image of Paul's blackened skin had seared itself into his retina, as if it had been painted on with acid. The minutes that followed were missing from Faris's memory. The next thing he remembered were the sirens of several emergency vehicles coming to a screeching stop right in front of the garden fence. Strong hands had ripped him away from Paul, and while the paramedics had tended to his partner, Faris had simply stood there. Stunned. Numb. Eventually, the paramedics had bundled Paul into one of the ambulances, and it sped off to the hospital. After that, Faris had picked up his phone which had been torn out of his hands by the blast. For several minutes, he had stared at it, incapable of feeling anything, unable to even blink. And then, following an impulse catalyzed by either defiance or cowardice, he turned off his phone.

"How is my partner doing?" he now repeated.

Dr. Makame's face was blank. "He's in surgery now." He shrugged regretfully. "You will be notified about his status once they know more." He held his hand out to Faris. "I wish you all the best! Thank your god for your survival today."

In this cold, clinical environment, the last sentence felt out of place, but despite the fact that Faris had stopped believing in Allah years ago, the doctor's words made him feel surprisingly good. He nodded in astonishment. He then watched the doctor walk out of the small treatment room, leaving the door open behind him.

A nurse in black nun's garb and totally incongruous hot pink Crocs hurried past the door. She sent him a quick distracted look.

He remained sitting on the cot for a moment longer, as he tried to recall what he needed to do to stand up.

Paul's burnt face flashed across his mind every time he blinked. He forced his eyes to stay open, but eventually his eyeballs hurt so much that he gave up and lowered his lids. With his head hanging, he defied the onslaught of images that rushed at him. The red finger-nail pointing at him accusingly. The fire wave rolling toward him in slow motion. The terrified face of the girl at the subway station, the sound of a defibrillator, Paul's blackened skin. Always that. Burnt, foul-smelling, blistered flesh.

He opened his eyes and leaned his head back. With both hands, he reached for his hair and pulled at it as if he could tear the memories out of his skull along with strands of hair.

The nun with the garish shoes strode past his door again. This time, she stopped and said something to him.

Faris stared at her. Her words didn't make even the slightest sense to him.

"Are you feeling alright?" the nun repeated taking a step toward him.

Faris jumped down off the cot, at which his knees threatened to buckle under him. But then he suddenly had himself under control. His eyes were still burning. "Thank you," he said huskily. "I'm okay." He stumbled toward the door. "I think I'll head out and free up your room." At the threshold, he had to grab hold of the doorframe.

The nurse studied him skeptically. "Are you sure you don't want to rest here for a few minutes?"

But Faris wanted anything but that. He wanted, no, he *had* to get out of here! Out of this cool building that was filled with the sound of squealing wheeled stretchers and the medical personnel's squeaking orthopedic shoes. Filled with the beeping of various devices, the sound of which reminded him of the cardiac monitor hooked up to the man on the cross. "Thank you, I'm alright." He stepped out into the corridor.

A pale mother carrying an apathetic toddler walked by. Faris nodded at her mechanically.

He then turned toward the nurse who was still standing there, looking uncertain about whether or not she should let him go. "Honestly, I don't need anything. Dr. Makame is off checking my x-rays. If he needs me, I'll be outside. I have to make a phone call." And with those words, he simply walked off.

The fresh night air wrapped around him like a piece of silk that settled across his face. He now noticed that his entire body was bathed in a cold sweat. In a windowpane, he searched for his reflection, and then understood immediately why the nun had watched him so doubtfully. The bandage on his forehead was dirty, and a new bloody scratch now ran across his cheek. He looked pale and haggard. His hair was standing up all over his head, and the rings under his eyes were dark purple. But these weren't what made him look more dead than alive. It was the expression in his eyes.

The nurse with the pink shoes appeared on the other side of the door to the ER area to scrutinize him. She reminded Faris of the old nun with the pale eyes on the subway. He sensed that he hardly had the energy to keep going. It was as if he had been running on fumes forever.

An ambulance drove through the hospital gate. It wasn't using its flashers, and it was driving very slowly. As chaos broke out in the ER, Faris became aware that the world was still turning. The people in Berlin were still living their lives. They were having heart attacks and babies. They were laughing, they were arguing, and they were expecting him and his colleagues to protect them from the insanity of this unknown bomber. Faris's thoughts flashed to Laura. Anger started to burn in his stomach, and he stoked it until it grew, and he could grab onto it. He knew that over the next few hours, this alone would give him the strength to keep going.

With a shake of his head, he fished out the burner phone he had purchased on Kurfürstenstraße. He gazed at it for several seconds, trying to screw up the courage to call Gitta. When he found the strength, he listened to her report about what had happened, which she gave as best she could through soft intermittent sobs. As she spoke, the slowly approaching ambulance reached the ER entrance. An older man on a stretcher was unloaded and carried into the ER in the company of several paramedics. Faris turned his attention back to the conversation.

"... called Christa and informed her about what happened," Gitta said. The ER's automatic doors closed behind the old man and his rescuers. "She must be on her way to the hospital by now."

Christa. Paul's wife.

Faris shut his eyes. This time he didn't see any horrible images, just the slender, expressive face of Christa Sievers. What could he say to her?

"I'll wait here for her," he murmured, knowing that this would cost him too much. "What are the rest of you doing?"

"After you were taken back by the doctor, Tromsdorff ordered Marc to return here." Marc hadn't sustained any injuries from the explosion. "He is preparing his report and giving us a description of the inside of the summer house, and then we'll decide what happens next. Ben says that it's unusual for an explosion to create such a fireball. Maybe that'll help us a little. And then all of us are supposed to try to get a little sleep. You, first and foremost."

Faris ignored her last sentence. The fireball had transformed all the clues that they might have found inside the summer house into ashes. All they had now were Faris's and Marc's memories of the small structure's interior.

"At some point, Marc stepped outside," he said. "I'm not sure if he knows that we found a metal box that probably contained the bomb. Besides that, the summer house also held an entire box of those glow sticks that are being sold to the conference goers."

"Mmhmm." Gitta was probably jotting down a note. "I'll pass that along. Good. Anything else?"

Faris's skull felt as if it were being inflated with a balloon filling with flammable gas that was about to burst into flames. "Not that I can think of, but I'll call you as soon as I remember anything."

"Oh, by the way, we sent the pastor back home. She didn't have anything else that could help us."

"Thanks, Gitta."

"She knows what happened, Faris. I wouldn't be surprised if she shows up at the hospital."

Faris nodded silently and tried to decide if this was good news or bad. Ira Jenssen was a witness. Someone external. Her presence might help him keep from going to pieces. Anything that could keep him from breaking down was presumably a good thing.

"Thanks, Gitta," he murmured again. "Bye."

"Goodbye, Faris."

The hospital's operating rooms were right next to the ER. With their yellow ingrain wallpaper, the passages in front of them probably looked just as dismal as the hundreds of others across the country. There were few seating options. One of them was located underneath a modernist bronze relief of a figure, which to Faris's eyes looked like an exhausted guardian angel.

An elderly couple was sitting underneath it, holding hands. Faris nodded at them mutely, then noticed the woman sitting within a niche, who was kneading a handkerchief.

"Faris!" The woman jumped up and rushed to him like a drowning person. He had to catch her. With a sob, she leaned against his chest, and he wrapped his arms around her thin shoulders.

"Christa." His lips were numb, and his feelings of guilt washed over him like a swell that might drown him. After all, he was the one who had insisted that Tromsdorff let Paul drive along to the summer house with him. And besides that, the caller had discovered where they were from his phone, and then blown up the summer house. "I should've been with him. I should be the one in there …"

"Shh!" She pushed her way out of his hug. "Don't be ridiculous!" Her eyes were very large and very red, but she was no longer crying. Trembling, she took a deep breath.

"Do you know any details …" he began.

She shook her head and cut off his question. "No. They're still operating. One doctor came by and told me that he had third- and fourth-degree burns." Her voice faltered. "It doesn't look good, Faris."

Faris wrapped his arm around her shoulders and guided her back to the seat in the niche. He perched next to her on the edge of an uncomfortable piece of furniture made from steel mesh.

"I've always known that this could happen," Christa whispered. "I knew it when I married Paul, but I didn't want to accept it." She blinked, then turned her head to look at Faris. She was so pale that he could see the fine network of blue veins across her cheeks. "Why do we ever feel invincible? Do you know what the last thing was, that I said to him this morning?"

"He isn't dead, Christa," Faris said very quietly. She didn't seem to even register his presence.

"I complained! Because once again, I had to help him find his keys." She stopped talking to listen to something that only she could hear.

"Have you told anyone about this?" he asked. "Someone who could stay with you?"

She nodded mechanically. "My sister will be here any minute."

"Good." Faris concentrated on the throbbing in his ears.

"We postponed our vacation," Christa resumed, and suddenly tears started to trickle down her cheeks. "Did you know that? I was mad, but Paul said that we could go just as easily next month." She made a sound that reminded Faris of the whimpering of a small child. "He said that we will have many opportunities to travel."

Faris closed his eyes. He didn't know if it was only minutes or hours that passed until the door to the operating rooms swung open. A doctor in green scrubs approached them.

"Mrs. Sievers?" he asked.

"Yes?" Christa stood up, a fearful look on her face.

The doctor fixed his eyes on her, and at that moment, Faris knew. He pushed himself onto his feet as well.

Christa, however, gazed at the doctor full of desperate hope. "How is he?" she whispered.

"He had extensive third- and fourth-degree burns," the doctor said, adding a long medical explanation to this. Numerous incomprehensible words obscuring what he obviously didn't want to say. He eventually fell quiet and looked sad.

Christa stared at him in bewilderment. "And that means?"

Faris stepped closer, preparing to catch her. Out of the corner of his eye, he noticed the door to the corridor swing open and Tromsdorff enter.

The doctor took a deep breath. "That means that there was nothing more we could do for him."

"But when will he get better?" Christa cried out.

At that moment, what Faris wanted to do more than anything was to scream at the top of his lungs, but he refused to give in. "He's dead, Christa," he said softly. The realization of what his words meant hit him at full blast.

"No!" All at once, Christa spun around and stared at him out of wild eyes. "Don't say that!" Suddenly her voice was no longer quiet and whimpering, but aggressive. "He can't be dead!"

Faris wished he could agree, wished he could hold her tight and tell her that everything would be alright again. But he couldn't. He couldn't lie to her. He gazed pleadingly into the doctor's eyes. *Help me!* he demanded silently from him, and finally the man pulled himself together.

"I am very sorry," he said unhappily. "We couldn't do anything else for your husband. The injuries were too severe."

Christa's reaction was worse this time. Faris watched, as the words she heard reached her brain. Watched as she realized that she would never see Paul again, as she struggled against this truth and eventually lost that fight. Her body buckled with almost uncanny speed. Her skin was practically gray, her lips pale. "No!" she whispered. "Say it isn't true, Faris!"

He was silent. There was nothing that could alleviate her anguish.

"You were supposed to watch out for him!" she suddenly screamed. Her words struck him all the harder because he knew that his guilt was much greater than this. The bomb had been planted for him. Paul had died in his place.

Faris tried to swallow the pain in his throat. "Christa, I ..." He fell into hopeless silence.

"It would be best for me to leave you on your own," the doctor mumbled. He hurried back to the operating rooms, and the sound of the swinging door as it closed cut off the sound of his rapid steps.

Christa's fists were clenched, and Faris hoped that she would punch him. But she didn't. All she did was stare at him, her eyes now welling as she whispered: "Why are you still alive, and he ..." She broke off as Tromsdorff reached for her elbow.

"Come with me," was all he said. Nothing more. His voice was as thin as paper. He led Christa to the metal chairs and she slowly sank onto one of them. On the other side of the room, the door swung open, and a man and woman rushed inside and headed straight toward them.

Her sister and brother-in-law, Faris assumed. As he watched them tend to Christa, sitting down to the right and left of her, wrapping her in their arms and attempting to console her, his feeling of loneliness returned; the one that he had felt for the first time earlier that day at Niklas's apartment.

He took a step back, and then another.

And finally he turned around and left. Tromsdorff followed him.

CHAPTER 23

Wrapped in the night's darkness, Ira sat outside the hospital entrance in her car. After taking a taxi home from the police precinct, she had climbed into her own car and driven over here.

For a long time, she stared uncertainly through her lowered window at the hospital's illuminated glass entrance door, but then it opened, and Detective Iskander appeared. His walk no longer exhibited any of the strength that she had previously perceived in it. He seemed on the verge of collapse.

His boss was beside him. Superintendent Tromsdorff.

Neither of them noticed her. They came to a stop underneath a tree that grew in a circular bed in front of the hospital entrance. It looked like some supernatural power had frozen Faris mid-stride. For several minutes, he simply stood there, motionless; his eyes fixed on the sidewalk in front of him, his fists balled tightly. At his side, Tromsdorff looked helpless.

"Faris," he said. "Talk to me."

With an excruciatingly slow motion, Detective Iskander lifted his head, but said nothing. The light from the streetlights fell wan and cold across them both.

Ira became aware that she was eavesdropping. She rolled up her window. Detective Iskander – Faris, she corrected herself in her thoughts – said something. Tromsdorff nodded soberly.

For a while, the two men faced each other, until Faris finally sank down wearily onto the small bench under the tree. He propped his elbows on his knees and buried his face in his hands.

Tromsdorff continued to talk to him. Without looking up, Faris shook his head.

Tromsdorff said something else, and again Faris shook his head, energetically this time. When he looked up, his eyes flashed angrily. He lifted one side of his jacket under which the grip of his gun flashed.

His boss held his hand out expectantly, and as he did that, Ira rolled her window back down. She simply had to know what was going on.

For a third time, Faris shook his head. "You gave it back to me," Ira heard him declare. "You knew what that meant."

"Hell, Faris!" Tromsdorff threw his hands up helplessly. "I'm just worried about you!"

"You don't need to be. Focus on the case instead."

"Are you okay?"

Faris lowered his head between his knees as if he suddenly felt nauseous. Ira could see the tension stiffening his neck and jawline. *He's about to explode*, she thought, horrified at what she saw. But Faris didn't explode. Quite the opposite.

In an increasingly quiet and completely expressionless voice, he said: "I just can't, Robert. The rest of you will have to catch this bastard. I'm finished."

The final sentence sent a surprisingly sharp jolt through Ira's chest.

"If he calls and you've sent a bullet through …" Tromsdorff didn't complete the sentence as Faris furiously jerked his hand into the air. "Alright," Tromsdorff said, more placatingly.

"He won't call me again," Faris said. "He blew up the summer house after tracking me down through my phone. He thinks I'm dead." He reached into his jacket pocket and pulled out his regular phone. With an extremely weary gesture, he handed it to Tromsdorff. "I turned it off after Paul …"

Something crossed Tromsdorff's face. He was about to say something but decided against it. He accepted the phone with a glance – and turned it back on. He then handed it back to Faris. "Call a taxi, go home, and try to get a little sleep. It's been a damned long day! But please leave your phone on. The guy might not call back, but I don't want to take that risk."

Faris drew one more deep breath. His lips grew pale as he did, as if the movement of his ribs pained him. "Sure." He looked up at his boss. "Catch the bastard!" he whispered hoarsely.

Tromsdorff reached out to lay a hand on his shoulder, but then hesitated and lowered his arm.

Ira thought she could see Faris's loneliness, like a gloomy aura that surrounded him.

"Will you be alright?" Tromsdorff asked. "I can call Anisah."

"No, I'm fine." Faris stood up. He met Tromsdorff's eyes. His boss studied him for a long moment before nodding.

"Call me if anything happens!"

Faris didn't respond.

"Faris! Did you hear me?"

"Yes." Faris rubbed his face with both hands.

Tromsdorff was about to turn away when Faris pulled his gun out of his holster and held it out to his boss on an open palm. "Just in case," he said.

Tromsdorff glanced swiftly around to see if anyone was watching them. Ira noticed that he looked extremely relieved. "Thank you." He was almost whispering. Taking the gun from Faris, he stuck it into his suit pocket.

After Tromsdorff disappeared, Faris stood under the tree for a while without moving. A low-hanging branch brushed against his cheek, but he didn't seem to feel it. After a small eternity, he gave himself a shake. He was about to walk off, when four young men appeared, walking toward him. They were wearing baggy pants and baseball caps, and they looked like they recognized Faris.

Faris paused.

For a moment, he looked unsure about what to do next. But then he straightened his shoulders and marched right at the gang.

In the light of the street lamps, Ira saw the delighted grins that spread across the faces of the teenagers. They spread out a little and walked toward Faris in a wide line.

"Idiot!" Ira didn't spend much time considering her options. She shoved the key into her ignition and started the engine. She flipped her car around as quickly as she could and reached Faris when he was about ten paces away from the teens.

She hurriedly leaned over and opened the passenger window. "Mr. Iskander!"

He looked over at her. There was something dark in his eyes that gave Ira a chill. But then he recognized her. "Ms. Jenssen."

She gazed out of the windshield at the teens. "Would you like a lift somewhere?"

Faris turned back toward the gang. "No thanks!"

Ira glanced from him back to the young men. "That won't bring your partner back!" she said softly.

He blinked. The darkness in his eyes vanished. "No. You're right." His hands were stuffed in the pockets of his leather jacket.

The teens said something among themselves and decided to go back the way they had come. Once they vanished around the corner, Ira breathed in relief. "I can take you home if you like," she offered.

He shook his head. "No need." And he just walked off.

Feeling a little insulted, she watched him walk down a row of residential yards and then turn down a narrow path that led into a small park. She was making a fool of herself. She hardly knew this man, so why did she feel like she needed to take care of him? It couldn't just be because he had sad eyes, could it?

You and your Mother Theresa Syndrome, she could still hear Thomas say with a laugh. *You've always had a thing for broken men.*

"Dammit!" she exclaimed as she pulled out her car key and followed Faris into the darkness.

She found him on a bridge that spanned an artificial duck pond. He was resting his arms on the wrought iron railing and staring unseeingly into the murky water, which was illuminated by several old-fashioned lamp posts scattered around the pond's edge.

She hesitantly approached him.

He didn't turn to face her, but she could tell he had noticed her by the stiffening of his shoulders.

"Does your profession require you to get on people's nerves?" he asked.

She flinched and suddenly felt like a stalker. "No," she replied as nonchalantly as possible as she joined him on the bridge. The water below their feet smelled brackish. One lonely duck was swimming around, and it didn't look particularly happy to be there.

"Why are you following me?" Faris still hadn't looked at her.

She rubbed her nose. "Maybe I had a feeling that I needed to prevent something stupid from happening."

He finally shot her a sideways glance. Even in the dim light from the lanterns, she could see that his eyes were reddened. "Did you know that this was the first day they gave me back my gun? I've been suspended from service for a while now."

Shit, Ira thought. He had caught sight of her at the hospital entrance. He must think terrible things about her!

She nodded sympathetically. She had enough experience talking to people in mourning to know that it was helpful to stick to topics they brought up themselves. "Why were you suspended?" she asked cautiously.

"Because I beat up a neo-Nazi."

"Oh." The sound slipped out of her mouth before she could hold it back. She thought about the young gang from earlier.

Faris's gaze was inscrutable. She could hardly bear the expression in his eyes. "He called me a bomber."

"I understand."

He turned away from her to watch the duck that now swam underneath their bridge. "No," he contradicted her quietly. "You don't."

"You might be right." She fell silent, searching for some point of connection for her next words. "What happens now with the culprit you're looking for?"

He laughed. It was a strained, angry sound, but it was obviously a laugh. It sounded so wrong that Ira had to gulp. "You mean now that I'm incapable of chasing him?" he asked.

"You are too hard on yourself. You just lost your partner. I don't think anyone is asking that you fire on all pistons right now."

He turned his head and gazed at her. Despite all the sadness, his gaze was questioning. She suppressed the turmoil that he generated within her. "Everyone else in the unit is searching for the man. They don't need me."

"You don't really believe that!" Ira studied him intensely, then altered her tack. "Or if you believe it, part of you doesn't want to."

His eyes flashed in surprise. Good grief, they really did look a lot like Thomas'!

"You should be a police officer," he said. "You have good observational skills."

"I'm a minister."

"Hmm." Faris stared once more at the water. A light breeze swept through the trees, and Ira felt cold.

"Why do you think that your colleagues suddenly don't need you anymore?" she pressed.

At first, she was afraid that he wouldn't answer, but he eventually sighed. "He tracked me down, and then he deliberately set off the bomb that killed my partner. After that, I just turned off my phone. Before that, he always called after he blew something up. If he did that this time too, then he must think that I'm dead."

He pulled his phone out of his pocket and held it out to her. She took it, unsure what she was supposed to do with it.

"Click on the message I received this morning."

Cautiously, she did as he asked. She was aware that he was watching her as she did this, and she wondered what he was thinking at this very moment.

Faris didn't know exactly why he wanted to show this pushy pastor the crucifixion video. Perhaps he just wanted to shock her enough to make her go away. But somewhere in his heart, he was glad that she was there. Of course, he had given his gun to Tromsdorff out of fear that he might blow his brains out during the night, but who knew what the future might hold?

He watched with mixed feelings as Ira clicked on the video link and then watched the video of the crucifixion. By the end of it, she looked so pale and transparent that he felt like a jerk.

"The bomber sent me that this morning," he explained, taking the phone back from her. "And since then, he's been hounding me from place to place, and each time I get there too late, a bomb goes off somewhere."

"He's playing games with you?" Faris didn't reply to this.

"But since the bombing at the garden colony, he hasn't contacted you," she continued. "That means he can't be sure if you're dead or not."

He looked at her in surprise.

"Your phone would show if he'd tried to call," she added. "So."

He stuck the phone back in his pocket. It felt as if it were burning a hole in in it, and he didn't know which was worse: the fact that the bastard could call any minute, or the waiting to see if that would happen.

"You said yourself that your colleagues care." Ira carefully laid a hand on his arm, which rested on the railing. She seemed puzzled when he didn't pull it away, but he simply felt as if he would never be able to move again, for as long as he lived. "You should try to sleep a little. You said that the attack will take place during the papal Mass tomorrow evening. There are still a few hours until then."

She pulled back her hand, and Faris sensed a totally irrational flash of regret.

He thought about Werner Ellwanger. Somewhere out there, he was hanging on a cross. The man who had nailed him to it now had Paul on his conscience too. And he, Faris, was just standing here, stewing in self-pity! He felt disgusted with himself.

He wanted to move his arms off of the raining, wanted to straighten up, to keep going. None of these things happened. He felt as if he were locked inside a lead suit that enclosed every bit of him. Even breathing seemed difficult.

Ira reached for his elbow. "Come on," she said. "If you tell me where you live, I will take you home."

Faris had just sat down in Ira's compact car when his new phone rang. Glad that for at least the first part of the trip there wouldn't be any uncomfortable silences, he answered it.

It was his father. "Are you doing alright, my boy?"

"Yes, Abu," Faris replied. Although he had only been four years old when they arrived in Germany and his family spoke fluent German, he had never stopped calling his father by the Arabic word for Papa. "Did Samir get all of you out of Berlin?"

"Me and Umi and all of your siblings, and even your nephews and nieces," his father answered. "We are …"

"Stop!" Faris hastily interrupted him. "Don't tell me. I'm not sure if my phone is being tapped."

This made his father fall silent for a moment. "You mother wasn't particularly thrilled that you were the only one who wasn't leaving the city," he finally grumbled. Something else was echoing in his words.

It's all your own fault. If you hadn't become a police officer …

To Faris's relief, his father refrained from his usual accusation, and he ran his fingers through his hair, feeling Ira's eyes on him.

"I need to go now, Abu. It's getting really late," he said.

"Of course. Take care of yourself. I will pray for Allah to do just that!"

The unexpected warmth and concern that echoed in his father's words added to the guilt that Faris already felt. "Thank you, Abu. Please tell Umi and Anisah hello for me."

"I will do that. *As-salamu alaikum.*"

The well-meaning phrase felt like a blow. Faris had to tighten his jaw and take a deep breath before he could reply. "*Wa-alaikumu s-salām*, Abu."

"Mr. Iskander?" Ira's voice.

He didn't react to it.

"Faris?" she asked. At this, he realized that they had arrived at his home. He couldn't remember the rest of the drive.

221

He forced himself to nod at Ira.

"Everything alright?" She looked a little pale.

"I'm okay." He sounded weak. Breathless.

And that was how he felt as well.

"A Japanese bookshop." Ira gazed curiously into the shop window. Although it was by now a few minutes after midnight, the shop owner still had the light on.

Midnight! In less than twenty-four hours, the bomb in the Olympic Stadium would go off. Faris froze mid-movement at this thought, but then realized that he couldn't feel anything at this point.

He couldn't care less.

He opened the apartment building door and gazed at Ira questioningly.

She shifted slightly. "Is there anyone who can stay with you?" she asked. "A family member or someone?"

Laura! shot through his mind.

He slowly shook his head. He thought about Anisah, his big sister. She was the only one he could perhaps bear right now, but something prevented him from mentioning her. She and the rest of his family were now far away from Berlin. Oppressive feelings of doom enveloped him like a blanket.

Ira hesitated. "To be honest, I'm not sure if it would be wise to leave you alone."

He wasn't sure either. The thought of closing the door behind him and feeling the crush of the walls around him felt so unbearable that he mutely held the door open for Ira. As she passed by, she looked into his eyes.

He glanced away.

"Are Christian ministers always so concerned about people they hardly know?" he asked after they had entered his apartment and he had hung up his jacket.

Her gaze was caught by the dark red burn scar that protruded from under his t-shirt sleeve. She smiled slightly. "Always!"

He gazed at her skeptically, then invited her into his living room. He wasn't the neatest of housekeepers, but his apartment was relatively clean. Several magazines were sitting around, in addition to an empty glass from the previous evening, which he rapidly cleared away.

Ira sat down on his leather couch, and before he could weigh the odds of another uncomfortable silence, she pointed at the leather bracelet on his arm. "That's pretty. Where did you get it?"

Faris stared at it as if he were seeing it for the first time. He didn't feel capable of talking about Laura even a little right now, so all he said was: "On a trip."

Ira peered at the faded letters. "That's Arabic, isn't it?"

He nodded.

"What does it say?"

"*I will support you with a thousand angels, one after the other.*" That was the first Quran quotation he could think of.

If Ira doubted the claim that the two short words translated into such a long sentence, she concealed that fact well. "Nice," she remarked. She apparently wanted to add something to that, but she didn't seem to know quite what that was.

Faris glanced down at his clothes. "I'll be right back. I need to change." One look in the hallway mirror had revealed that his clothes were torn up, thanks to his flight into the bushes. At this rate, his closet would be empty by tomorrow morning.

He stumbled into his room, removed his holster, and pulled off his dirty t-shirt. He leaned down to take off his shoes when he suddenly felt so dizzy, he staggered. He banged his hip into his bed, and the bed legs scraped across the smooth floorboards with a loud screech.

"Is everything okay?" Ira called from the living room.

Faris couldn't answer. He felt so sick he had to double over. Although he reached for something to grab onto, he found nothing within reach, and a moment later, he found himself kneeling on the floor.

"Oh no!"

Ira was there, but he hadn't heard her come in. He felt her hands on his bare torso, sensed her attempts to pull him up. He helped her as much as he could. His dizziness evaporated, and only the weakness in his knees remained.

He shook off Ira's hands and stood up. "Sorry about that," he murmured.

"Lay down," she ordered.

"You aren't my mother," he protested sluggishly, but Ira didn't soften. She steered him over to his bed.

"Lay down, or I'll have to force you down."

"I'd like to see you try!"

She gave an ironic chuckle. "All I would have to do is give a good puff. Now do it!"

And with that, he gave up. He collapsed onto his bed, and as he pulled off his shoes, he watched as Ira closed his curtains.

"Are you also going to help me get my pants off?" he asked. Everything in his head was spinning.

"You can manage that yourself." She walked over to the door. "I'll be right here. Just call if you need anything!"

"Okay, Umi," he mumbled and was already asleep by the time Ira left the room.

He instantly found himself back in a nightmare.

He was walking along a corridor, and he knew that it was a passage in the Klersch Museum. The fact that this building no longer existed felt irrational even in this dream state, and he felt profoundly disoriented.

His feet carried him toward an ornamented door, and he knew exactly what was waiting for him behind it. He tried to stop walking, but he couldn't. Step by step, he drew closer to the door.

The terror punctured his body like burning fingers. He felt his ribs, his shoulders, his head injuries. Everything seemed to be surrounded by dazzling flames, and as he glanced down at his body, he expected to see fire flickering through his skin.

But there was nothing to see.

Even the burn scar on his chest was gone. With the clarity of his own dream, he knew this despite the fact he was wearing a long-sleeved fleece shirt. The shirt he had been wearing the day of the explosion at the Klersch Museum.

He doubled his efforts to stop his feet from moving. But it was in vain.

He had now reached the door, and as if by an enchanted hand, it opened before him.

"No!" he whispered.

The people behind the door gazed at him through empty eyes. He saw Laura and Anisah. Lilly. His parents. And Paul. Paul's face was charred black, and the heat of the explosion had solidified his eyeballs into glassy white marbles.

Faris whimpered.

"You should've been there!" Paul declared accusingly. He spoke with the caller's distorted voice. And then he lifted his shirt which hung untucked over his waistband.

He was wearing a suicide vest. A smile appeared on his face, the same smile that had always appeared whenever he had teased Faris about something.

"Paul," Faris breathed. "No!"

Paul slowly raised his arm. He was holding the trigger, a small square box with a red button on it.

"You can't do that." Faris knew he needed to speak louder if he was going to prevent Paul from pressing the button, but he simply couldn't. All he was able to get across his lips was a toneless whisper.

"You didn't push the button, Faris," Paul said. He was now speaking in his own voice. "I did!" He laughed.

And then he pushed the red button.

A fireball rolled toward Faris, engulfed him, and melted his skin off his bones although he felt no pain. He saw his parents burn up, Anisah. Laura. And with a tortured scream, he collapsed.

"Faris!"

Someone was shaking him. He groped around him, because he felt like he was falling. Was he shouting? He didn't know. With effort, he was trying to work his way back to reality. "Oh, Allah!" he groaned.

"You were dreaming!"

Ira was next to him. She was sitting on the edge of his bed, cradling him in her arms like a child. "Shh, calm down. It was just a dream!"

When everything was over, she couldn't have said how it happened. She had been holding on to Faris as he flailed around in his sleep. She shook him and tried to free him from his nightmare, and her efforts were successful. But it took him a long time to find his way back to the real world. He clung to her like a drowning man, and she held him back.

She inhaled his scent deeply, a combination of soap and sweat.

And then it happened.

Her mind divided itself. One part of her felt Faris's lips on her neck, his breath brushing across her skin, and his hands under her blouse. She enjoyed the shiver that shot through both of them. Her other half observed all this from a distance and wondered what in the world she was doing here. This second half watched as Faris kissed her as he gasped and clung to her. The distant part of her psyche knew that he simply felt lust for her because he needed to forget so badly. He was damaged in the deepest part of his soul and was seeking a means to heal that wound. She knew that she was being used, but she couldn't help enjoying what he was doing. And when he peeled off his jeans, when he stretched on top of her and penetrated her, she moaned in pleasure while also wishing to curl up in shame.

Neither of them needed long. They climaxed at the same time, and drenched in sweat and breathing heavily, they remained lying next to each other.

Ira turned on her side and studied Faris, who was staring at the ceiling into empty space. She wanted to say something, but for a moment, the words failed her. And so she raised her hand and ran her fingers softly across the horrible red scar that covered his right rib cage and the upper part of his bicep. "That looks pretty bad."

He didn't react. He pulled an arm over his eyes and was silent. His chest rose and fell intermittently. Ira could see his abdominal muscles. She was filled with feelings of warmth and contentment, and to her own surprise, the things her distant self had just been whispering to her didn't matter anymore. She didn't feel bad, just calm and fulfilled.

She wished she knew what was going on inside his head, but she didn't risk asking the relevant questions. At some point, he sat up with a jerk.

"I'm sorry," he said roughly. His gaze wandered away from her half-naked body. "I ..." He swung his leg off the bed. "I think ..."

She didn't move right away, but when he remained seated and made no move to actually stand up, she touched a spot between his shoulder blades. Compared with his skin, hers was quite pale. Faris cringed under her touch as if he had been struck.

He slowly sank back down. "Now what?"

She looked at him. "What are you thinking?"

He glanced at the alarm clock on his nightstand. It was past three o'clock. Despite his nightmare, he had still slept a couple of hours.

He closed his eyes again. "I'm tired," he mumbled wearily.

"Then sleep!" Ira said softly, with a smile. "I'll keep a watch on your phone."

Alexander

"WHY DIDN'T YOU DO IT?" The angel asked. "CRUCIFY HIM, I MEAN."

Alexander struggled against the feelings that raged inside him. Was this the right thing for him to do? He didn't know. He was so incredibly tired. "I wasn't strong enough," he admitted. "None of the crosses I was able to build with my limited abilities were good enough. But then you came."

"THEN I CAME. ONE DAY, I WAS STANDING AT YOUR DOOR."

"Were you looking for me?"

"YOU COULD SAY THAT."

Alexander felt himself smile, which made his body feel much lighter.

"When I saw you, I knew that my father had been right the whole time. The Lord wanted this to happen. That was why He sent you to me. You're His angel, right?"

The voice in the dazzling light started to laugh, and in that laugh rang the sadness of all eternity.

CHAPTER 24

It was already midnight by the time Laura Zöller finally got her daughter Lilly to sleep. Exhausted and annoyed, she pulled the bedroom door shut behind her and cursed her husband, Christian. He had a knack for getting called in whenever Lilly was being especially demanding.

Barefoot to keep from waking up the child, Laura glided across the oak parquet hallways to the living room. There she opened a bottle of red wine and poured herself a glass. With a sigh, she dropped into the leather couch and switched on the television.

Several stations were running coverage about today's bombings in Berlin. She didn't want to hear about them, so she clicked through the channels until she found a program about a medieval manuscript someone had found several years ago. But she couldn't concentrate on the narrator's warm, sonorous voice.

She suddenly found herself thinking about Faris.

Why had he showed up here, today of all days?

He hadn't been around since she had told him she was pregnant, and she was basically happy about that. However, seeing him standing there today with all those terrible injuries to his face had been painful.

With a shake of her head, she took a big sip of wine as the historian flipped through one page after the other.

It was hard for her to admit that she had been glad to see him. When she left, she had told him that it was because he didn't want to have children. He had no idea there was a totally different reason behind her flight to the arms of another man. She could no longer bear living in a constant state of fear – for him. His appearance today had made it more than clear how wise she had been to leave.

With a sigh, she reached for her cell phone. After coming home, she had simply deposited it on the coffee table and not picked it up since then. Someone had called and left her a message.

She hesitated, then dialed her mailbox.

The sound of Faris's voice struck her like a blow. "Laura, it's me. Listen, this isn't a stalker call. It's really important. I'd like …" And then he broke off. She could hear him breathing.

Her stomach plummeted as if she were riding a roller coaster.

"Mama!" Lilly's fussy voice called from her bedroom.

Laura sighed. "Mama's coming right away, sweetie!" she shouted. She then listened to see if Faris had anything else to say.

Wasn't a stalker call, he had claimed.

But then what was it?

She could still hear him breathing, struggling for words, and this sound alone was so painful that she lowered the phone into her lap.

"Mama!" Lilly practically screeched. The neighbors had already complained once about her waking up frequently during the middle of the night and making a noise. She had recently started sleeping poorly, often having nightmares, and Laura wondered why that was.

With quiet regret and an equally soft curse on her lips, she deleted Faris's message. Regardless of what he had said to her, she didn't have the nerves to deal with it right now. He definitely wasn't good for her.

She set her wine glass down on the table. Hesitating for a moment, she turned off her phone and walked over to her daughter's room.

"Mama is here, sweetie. You don't need to be afraid."

"Look who's here!" Pia jabbed Jenny in the side, causing her to spill her drink.

They were standing in a disco on a side street off of Ku'damm that they had been told was especially popular. Although Jenny hadn't felt like painting the town red that night, she at least found this place interesting.

The people were edgy without being *too* edgy, and you didn't need to feel worried about getting hit on here. The clientele was made up of normal-looking people and slightly gothic emos. The music was alright, as were the drink prices – at least, for a city like Berlin.

Jenny licked drops from her sloshed cocktail off her fingers. "Be careful!" she growled at her friend before looking at where she was pointing.

With that, butterflies began to flutter in her stomach. At the bar, less than ten meters away, Dennis was standing and chatting with a small blonde woman – so small that she looked as if was twelve. He had swapped out the t-shirt he had been wearing earlier that day for a muscle shirt. In the flashing lights from the dance floor, Jenny could now see his tattoos more clearly.

On his right arm was a life-sized black wing. It looked as if feathers spread and flexed whenever Dennis moved. Jenny was fascinated. In contrast to this artwork, the crucifix Dennis had on his other arm looked almost boring.

"Hi, Dennis!" Pia shouted over the music as she waved so enthusiastically that a number of people glanced her way.

Jenny wished she could sink into the floor, but Pia managed to attract Dennis's attention. When he recognized them, a smile spread across his face. He said something to the petite blonde woman, who responded by sticking out her tongue at him and turning away.

He then walked over to Pia and Jenny. "Hi! What are you doing here?" He looked around. "This doesn't look like quite your thing!"

"What do you mean?" Jenny shot back. She had drunk two cocktails and felt airy and overconfident. "What kind of person do you have to be, to come to this place?"

He picked up on her playful reference to what he had said at lunch and chuckled. "Touché! It's good to see you both!" He was only looking at Jenny as he said this, and the butterflies in her stomach started fluttering faster.

"I think I'll go to the restroom!" Pia had to yell this, since at just that moment the DJ put on a new track that was somewhat louder than the last one.

Jenny nodded at her, and she pushed her way through the crowd.

"Want something to drink?" Dennis asked.

Jenny shook her head. "Better not. I had two, oh, what are they called? Swimming pools? If I drank one more, you'd probably have to carry me out of here."

Dennis studied her with amusement. "That's not such a bad idea," he grinned. "Prefer a coke?"

"Yes!"

Jenny watched him work his way back to the bar. The short blonde tried to draw him back, but he put her off a second time, and at this point, she seemed to finally give up. She shot Jenny an envious glance. Jenny could hardly believe her own good luck.

"Here." Dennis was smiling as he returned and handed her a glass of coke.

He was drinking a beer, which wasn't really a surprise. *It suits him*, Jenny thought.

"Do you have any other plans for today?" he asked. He, too, had to shout against the music, and as he did this, he leaned very close to Jenny's ear. As his breath brushed her skin, she shivered a little.

"No clue!"

"It's getting late. We need to head back to the hostel." Pia was suddenly back. "Otherwise we'll be so tired we won't be able to stay awake tomorrow."

Jenny rolled her eyes. "Killjoy!" she grumbled in the same tone of voice that Pia had used earlier that day.

She laughed. "Come on!" She shot Dennis a sideways glance. His wing tattoo seemed to fascinate her as well. "Even the nicest of nights has to come to an end!"

"Yes," Dennis replied. "But not yet!" To Jenny, his gaze felt like lead weights on her, and she could imagine what it would feel like if he actually touched her. *Really* touched her. The butterflies were chasing each other like crazy.

"Do you know somewhere else we could go?" she asked him.

"Of course." He jerked his head toward the door. "If you want to come, I'll show you."

Jenny was about to agree.

"Jenn!" Pia exclaimed uneasily. "I don't think that's a good idea!"

"Why not?" Dennis now turned on her. "You're acting like I'm the bomber who's blowing up the city." He made the sound of an explosion, then laughed loudly before taking one last swig from his beer bottle.

"I'll come with you," Jenny decided.

Pia looked annoyed. "That's your call," she said. "I'm going back to the hostel. Don't wake me up when you get back." She gave Dennis a terse goodbye, then strode off angrily.

Jenny had to giggle. "She's a little jealous," she said.

"Jealous?" Dennis's eyes flashed with amusement.

She linked her arm through his. "And? Where do you want to take me now?"

She felt amazing.

Faris wasn't sleeping. He had fallen into some kind of unconsciousness, deep and dark and dreamless. It wasn't until his mind had overcome his profound exhaustion that he transitioned into a sleep state filled with confusing dreams. He once again saw Paul's charred body, but this time Faris was holding him in his arms. Paul's eyes were closed, his eyelids glinting black, but suddenly they flew open. His eyeballs were still milky white, like marbles, and yet Faris knew that his partner was looking at him. "You didn't push the trigger," he said, and Faris shoved him away as if Paul had burned him. He stumbled backwards. "I'll watch your phone," a female voice said. But it wasn't Ira standing next to him, but Laura. He doubled over, and the fire from the explosion rushed toward them, enveloping first her, then him. However, he couldn't feel the flames. All he could feel was horror as Laura fell to dust before his eyes ...

With a gasp, he woke up. The room was almost completely dark.

Only a thin strip of light fell through a gap in the curtains.

"You were dreaming again," he heard a quiet voice say, out of the darkness. He had no idea how late it was. He felt totally disoriented.

"You're still here," was all he could think of to say. He regretted the space that lay between the two of them.

"Yes," was her only answer. She was sitting in the chair at the foot of his bed, and he could still smell her scent.

"I'm sorry," he said, not quite sure what he was apologizing for.

"Who is Laura?"

He propped himself up on his elbows. Had he murmured her name in his sleep? He bit his tongue before another apology slipped out. "My ex-girlfriend." His body felt as if it had been through the wringer. "How late is it?"

"A few minutes after six."

Wow, he had actually managed to sleep for several hours back-to-back, something he hadn't been able to do even once over the past ten months. He automatically estimated how much time they had left to prevent the explosion at the Olympic Stadium and came up with eighteen hours. With a jerk, he sat upright. The cut on his forehead throbbed dully, as did his shoulders and all the bruises he had received the day before. But to his relief, he was no longer dizzy. Clearly, the sleep really had done him good.

"Don't worry, the caller didn't call," Ira said. "And none of your colleagues did either. I plugged your phone in, just in case. I couldn't find a cord for your other phone, but the battery is still full."

Faris had to think about where the cable that had come with his burner phone was. He then remembered that he had left it in his sweatshirt jacket.

He swung his legs off the bed and set his feet on the floor. He was still half-naked. Who else would have dressed him? Glancing back over his shoulder, his eyes wandered to Ira, who looked like a silhouette against the weak light.

As far as he could see, she was once again wearing her jeans, blouse and cardigan. Her hair even looked as neat as it had done the night before. If the memory of what had taken place between them hadn't been so crystal clear, he would have thought he had imagined everything. "You really were here, the whole time." He said this as an observation, not a question.

She nodded. "I promised to watch your phone."

He lowered his head. "You're a strange woman, you know, right?"

"Thank you for the compliment."

He felt a need to escape this situation. Besides that, he needed to know if there was anything new in the case, so he stood up, pulled on his boxers, and picked up his burner phone from the nightstand where Ira had left it. Despite the early hour, he dialed Laura's number. He didn't know if she had heard his message and was now safe somewhere. His wondering didn't change. Laura had turned off her phone, and he gritted his teeth. He then dialed the number for the FCI and waited several seconds until someone answered.

"Schneider." Ben's sullen, exhausted voice spoke.

"Ben?"

"Faris!" Ben immediately sounded more awake. "How are you doing?" His question indicated that he knew about Paul's death.

"So far, okay."

"Hey, what happened to Paul …"

Faris swiftly interrupted him. "Later. Any news?"

He heard Ben yawn and felt ashamed that he had slept while his colleagues had put in overtime. "Some. For example, we now know that our culprit has put nanothermite in his bombs."

Thermite. Faris saw Paul's charred face in his mind's eye. He felt sick again. His gaze fell on Ira's outline. She hadn't moved a millimeter. He couldn't make out her eyes, but he was certain that she was still watching him.

"And we found several interesting things on the computer Marc confiscated from Ellwanger's apartment. One of them looks like a schematic for a heart monitor."

"I'll be right there," Faris said.

But to his amazement, Ben dismissed his exclamation. "You don't need to. We have things under control here, everything is running smoothly. As long as the caller isn't contacting you again, we're doing alright without you. Tromsdorff ordered all of us to chase you back home the instant you showed up." He hesitated for a moment. "Good grief, Faris, he's really worried about you."

Faris rubbed his forehead. His gut reaction was to protest at his exclusion from the team, but he let things be. His stomach cramped painfully, and he became aware that he hadn't eaten anything during the past twenty-four hours. "Tell me," he said. "You can locate a cell phone's position, right?"

"No problem, if it's turned on."

Faris bit his lower lip. "And if it isn't?"

"Then no way. What I can do is try to find out where it was last dialed before it was turned off."

That would at least give him a clue as to whether or not Laura had actually left Berlin. "Could you do that for me?" Faris asked.

"You don't think I have enough to do right now, do you, Detective?"

"It's about Laura."

"Oh." Ben cleared his throat. "Okay. Give me the number."

Faris gave it to him.

"Good. Wait a second." Ben set his phone down, and several minutes passed before he returned.

"The phone was turned off around twelve-thirty. Right before that, it was dialed in the Steglitz neighborhood."

Faris massaged his forehead. Steglitz was the location of Laura's apartment and of the clinic where she worked as a pediatrician. Laura was probably still in Berlin. He attempted to release the tension that this news caused him. "Thanks, Ben," he murmured before hanging up.

For a few moments, he gazed at the phone in his hand. He eventually tossed it on the bed and started to get dressed.

Without rising from her chair, Ira turned on the floor lamp. The pale yellow glow blinded Faris and submerged everything in a new, unpleasant light.

"Yeah," he said quietly. "A dumb situation?"

She slowly shook her head. "Why?"

At that moment, he would have paid a fortune to know what was going on behind those blue eyes. Did Ira feel just as lousy as he did? He had used her, after all. He remembered how he had clung to her, as if there were no other anchor for him in the world. In the darkness, he hadn't given any thought about whether what he was doing was right, but now in the light, he was disgusted with himself. He picked up his pants and pulled them on.

"You're a pastor," he said flatly.

At that, she laughed. "Yes. But there's no celibacy clause in *my* faith." Her voice sounded a little jittery.

He didn't comment on that. Instead, he pulled a clean t-shirt out of his closet. It was his last one. His bruises protested dully as he tugged it over them. Every muscle in his body ached. How in the world he had managed to have sex last night was a mystery to him.

He reached for his jacket and slipped it on. He would pick up a breakfast roll somewhere along the way. "I have to go," he said. The quintessential cowardly excuse. He practically started laughing at himself. "If you would like to take a shower before you ..." It was impossible to finish that sentence. He broke off, clearing his throat.

She still didn't move. In the light of the lamp, her eyes looked like x-ray machines. With a nod, she pointed at the door. "I made breakfast," she said.

Alexander

He woke up with a jerk and realized that he must have fallen asleep due to the exhaustion brought on by all the memories, by all the images that had burned through him. The hard floor on which he was lying was cold and damp. Alexander shivered. His whole body felt frozen. How long had he slept? He suddenly found himself thinking about how the angel had appeared to him the first time, what he had said. He had told him then everything that he was supposed to say now. He also recalled that the angel had had a face. A very human face. And no wings. Did he have wings now? Alexander couldn't see much because of the dazzling light, but he thought he had seen a wing.

The memories were now bright and crystal clear, and all on his own, he began to recount what had happened.

He enters the garden very early that morning. The sun still hasn't risen. His father is kneeling on the dew-damp grass and praying. As Alexander comes to a stop behind him, his neck tenses.

"You're here," he whispers. "That's good."

Everything inside Alexander wants to resist what he is supposed to do now, but he also knows that he has no choice. Somewhere nearby, concealed in the shadows of the night, stands the Angel of God, watching to see if he does his task well.

He sets a trembling hand on Father's shoulder. "Come," he says. "It's time!"

Father stands up. He looks weak, fearful. But there is also a glint in his eye, a certainty that they are doing the right thing.

Alexander leads his father here through the darkness, into the depths of the cell, and at the sight of the cross stretched out on the floor, they both turn pale. Alexander hasn't built the cross. The angel has done it. And it is practically perfect.

The angel is now with them, and he gives them the time they need. Alexander's eyes skim the tools spread out on the floor. The hammer. The nails. The coiled rope. Everything is here. Everything is ready. So perfect.

Tears spring to his father's eyes.

"You may begin," the angel says in his human voice. A moment later, the glaring light flashes on, illuminating the scene in pale blue.

With a heavy heart, Alexander watches as his father lies down on the cross. He then reaches for the hammer . . . .

Alexander interrupted his story. "Angel?" he asked cautiously.

He received no answer.

"Angel?" he asked again.

Still only silence.

The stone into which his heart had turned so long ago now softened back into flesh and blood. It suddenly hurt him so badly that he doubled over, gasping.

"Angel?" he screamed.

And then, he finally decided to take the risk. He stepped forward. Into the garish light that surrounded him like an aura. His eyes burned, but he didn't turn away. He took another step forward.

And all at once, he could see.

The light. It wasn't coming from an angel. It was just a plain flood lamp mounted on a stand that someone had shone into his eyes. He had been blinded. The angel ... Was there a chance he wasn't even real?

The question was so horrible that it tore apart his heart of flesh and blood. He spun around.

And finally he fled.

Constable Walter Assauer struggled against his weariness. His eyelids kept threatening to close.

How he hated these night shifts!

He stared through the windshield of his parked patrol vehicle out into the breaking day and thought about Jutta, his wife. She was probably still sleeping comfortably in their bed, snoring quietly. He was jealous of her ability to sleep – not just right now, but in general. She didn't know that his doctor had recently told him that something was growing on his prostate. Walter hadn't told Jutta yet, because he had no idea what to say. How do you tell your wife of forty years that you might have cancer? An especially aggressive form at that, which might only leave you six months to live.

There were no words for that.

And so he said nothing, had convinced himself that it was better if she didn't have to worry about him. He didn't want to spoil for her the final days left to them.

"Hey!" From the passenger seat, Lukas Jellinghaus, his partner, punched him lightly on the thigh. "What's worrying you so much again?"

Walter shrugged. "Nothing!"

"You aren't having problems with Jutta, are you?" Lukas teased. "Only two more years until your fortieth anniversary!"

Two more years!

Walter felt suddenly wistful. He longed to tell Lukas that he most likely wouldn't be around for even his thirty-ninth anniversary. However, just as he was opening his mouth, someone dashed right across the street in front of them without looking right or left.

Walter reached for his key and started the engine. "Back to work!" he sighed.

They caught up with the man who was now running toward Victoria Park. Coming to a stop a few meters away, they climbed out of their vehicle.

"Please stop!" Lukas called to the man.

He obeyed and stopped, trembling all over, his head lowered.

Another fucking junkie! Walter thought. Each of them had their own demons that were hounding them. The man's face was smooth and very pale. His hair fell, tangled and long, across his cheeks. They looked oddly rigid, as if some liquid had dried on them.

"Oh shit!" Walter heard Lukas mumble, and at that moment, he realized what he was seeing.

The man was spattered with blood. His pants, his shirt. Everything was plastered darkly to his gaunt body.

But that wasn't what shocked Walter the most about this young man. It was his expression. It looked vacant, panic-stricken and so manic that Walter felt his stomach drop. The pupils looked like giant black holes that wanted to suck him in.

"Isn't this ... "

Lukas didn't need to finish the sentence because Walter recognized the young man. It was the guy the police were scouring the city for.

It was Alexander Ellwanger.

CHAPTER 25

Ira had worked hard to craft a breakfast from the few items she found in Faris's cupboards. She had set the table with plates, utensils and cups. A few pieces of toast and an almost empty jar of jelly completed the meal. A bowl of fresh fruit, the only thing Faris refused to do without, stood in the middle of the table.

Ira now demanded that he sit down as she switched on the coffee maker. As the water began to drip, her gaze fell on a dusty bottle of wine that Faris had left standing on top of his refrigerator.

"You must be keeping that for a special day."

"Actually I'm not." Faris shook his head. A co-worker had given him that bottle, and when he looked into it, he had realized that it was an expensive wine. That was the only reason he had kept it.

Ira looked at him quizzically.

"I don't drink alcohol," he said.

"You ..." she broke off as a pale flush spread across her cheeks. "Of course! You're Muslim."

He leaned back. "Right."

She threw up her arms angrily. "God, Faris! If I have to drag every word out of you, this breakfast won't be pleasant for either of us."

I didn't ask you to come here.

The retort sat on his tongue, but he swallowed it down. He gazed out the window at the sky that was beginning to brighten, and then he thought about the previous night. He was very glad that Ira had been with him. If she hadn't been, he wasn't sure what he might have done to himself.

He forced a weak smile. "Please forgive me. You're right. I'm Muslim, but that's not the reason. At least, it's not the main reason. I was raised Muslim, and my father avoided alcohol for religious reasons. When I was a teenager, I started this practice too, even though his piety always annoyed me." He propped his arms on the tabletop. "I think I did it more for health and fitness reasons. But over the past few months, I have been glad of this habit."

Ira sat down. "Why?"

The coffee maker gurgled.

"Because after all that has happened, I probably would've become an alcoholic."

She nodded sympathetically. "In my faith, wine represents belonging." She dropped the topic now and pointed at the plates. "This isn't a grand meal, but I didn't want to go out shopping and leave you here alone."

Faris slowly reached for a piece of toast and began to spread jelly on it. "Why are you doing this?" he asked, making a gesture that incorporated her, him, the food, the kitchen.

She picked up her knife and twisted it between her fingers as she studied Faris. "Taking care of you?" She glanced at the phone that was sitting next to him on the table, and she looked uncomfortable, as if it weren't an electronic device but a fat tarantula she was a little frightened of. Faris pushed it slightly aside. She hadn't said a word about the brutal video.

He nodded and bit into his toast. His mouth started watering. That was how hungry he was, all of a sudden.

She shrugged. "Perhaps because I have a feeling that it's necessary."

He chewed. Swallowed. "Your profession," he remarked curtly.

She raised an eyebrow in confusion.

"You're a pastor," he explained. "You have to take care of people, save them."

"This isn't the way I usually do it." A faint flush spread across her cheeks. He knew she was thinking about sleeping with him.

"I believe you."

A weak smile appeared on her face. "You're the one more used to saving people."

A platitude was sitting on his tongue, something like *There are different ways to save people*, but he kept that to himself. "What's going on with you?" he heard himself ask.

She looked astonished. "What's *supposed* to be going on with me?"

"Do you have a family?"

She shook her head. Her face reflected a calm professional demeanor toward the topic he had just broached, and he knew that she would now watch him once more with the eyes of a minister. Didn't Christian pastors like to call their congregational members their little lambs? He didn't like the idea of her viewing him as a sheep, and he tried to escape this feeling. The memory of the previous night suddenly felt more confusing than it had before.

"A husband?" He hesitated, considering. "Are you even allowed to have a husband? As a pastor, I mean?"

She nodded. Suddenly she seemed distant.

"I'm sorry," he murmured, deciding to jump back to safer terrain. His cheeks also felt suspiciously hot. "Thanks to SURV, I know quite a bit about your faith, but not much about your profession."

"What is SURV?" She seemed relieved to change the subject.

"SURV is the acronym for Special Unit for Religious Violence. It's a fairly new department, and it falls under the murder commission.

"You work with terrorist attacks?" The coffee was now brewed. Ira stood up and brought the glass carafe to the table.

Faris picked it up and poured them both a cup. "No. My colleagues from Department 5 are responsible for those; SURV investigates all sorts of religiously motivated crimes. Honor killings. Threats at abortion clinics, and so on. My colleagues and I specialize in the distinctive characteristics of the world's major religions. Moral codes and stuff like that."

"Then you're the specialist for Islam." In the meantime, Ira had made herself a piece of toast and eaten it. She was a quick and efficient eater, a woman who didn't place much stock in counting calories.

"Yes," he replied. "We have specialists for Christian fundamentalists, as well as Islamic and Jewish ones. You have met them already."

"Fundamentalism." She shook her head as if she had trouble understanding how this phenomenon could have come into being. "They're the ones who value the laws their religion proscribes more than humanity." She suddenly became thoughtful. "Jesus Christ once said that the laws were made for people, not people for the laws."

"Wise words," Faris said.

She smiled wanly. "Aren't they?" With that, she changed the subject. "I read somewhere that most of the religiously motivated murders are done by Muslims." She said it very matter-of-factly, and Faris was surprised that this didn't annoy him, especially considering how the statements by Rainer Golzer had had the opposite effect. "Is that true?" she asked.

"Unfortunately, it is."

"That has to be hard for you."

"What do you mean?" Faris took a sip of his coffee, studying Ira over the rim of his mug.

She shrugged. "If it were Christians doing things like that, I think I'd feel guilty somehow."

Things like that. Like the burning towers of the World Trade Center. That was what most people meant when they said *things like that.* But in his case, the past ten months had been filled with visions of the explosion at the Klersch Museum.

"Why? You wouldn't be the one who had pressed the button." As he said this, an unexpected pain shot through him. It wasn't until it started to subside that Faris realized that he had just uttered Paul's words.

Paul!

Faris struggled to keep from gazing down the black hole that his partner's death had left within him.

Ira stared straight ahead as she considered this. She looked serious. She probably took everything she did seriously.

"No," she said quietly. "I wouldn't have. But I would have to question my God if there were people who actually thought that he demanded the deaths of thousands of people."

The events of the past day raced through Faris's mind. The bomb in the subway. The bomb at Hesse's office. The bomb at the summer house. None of them had been set off by an Islamist culprit. Nor had the bomb at the Klersch Museum been.

Ira seemed to somehow know what he was thinking about. "The explosion that made that …" She pointed at the burn scar on his upper arm.

"From the Klersch Museum."

Ira nodded. "I remember that. The officer that was so seriously hurt during it. That was you."

"Yes." Faris swallowed.

"This can't be easy for you." She didn't explain exactly what she meant, but he assumed that she was talking about the recent bombings.

He didn't say anything, just studied her. "Did you know that the museum bomber wasn't an Islamist?"

She picked up her cup and twirled it between her palms. It looked as if she were trying to warm herself up with it. "No. But I have to admit that I didn't give all that much thought to the culprit's motives."

Her words made Faris strangely sad. "He was Syrian, and had married a German woman," he explained. "He wanted shared custody of their son, but the authorities had their doubts about him for some reason. They thought he might've been in contact with Islamist groups. They decided not to grant him custody, since they thought he might be a terrorist."

"Because he looked Middle Eastern," Ira added. Her eyes were filled with sympathy, but he wasn't sure for whom it was meant. For the Syrian or for himself. He swallowed.

"Because he looked Middle Eastern. He was faced with prejudice wherever he turned, and eventually that drove him to do the very thing that people had been thinking he would do all along."

He thought about how he had stood there at the museum.

I'm a Muslim like you, he had said

And with that, he had added the drop that caused the barrel to overflow. Like the others, he had believed that an Islamist motive was behind this hostage situation. Although he himself was Middle Eastern, although he worked for SURV and experienced on a daily basis how many crimes had religious motives but had absolutely nothing to do with terrorist backgrounds, he had made this fatal mistake.

And that mistake had driven the hostage-taker to press the button.

As he thought about this, he rubbed his forehead.

The topic was too overwhelming for him, so he tried to change it. He glanced up. "You didn't answer my question. Are you married?"

She shook her head slowly. "There was someone, once." Her face hardened so abruptly that Faris was startled.

"He's dead," he guessed, but to his surprise, Ira shook her head again. This time she smiled as she did so.

"No, he isn't. My life isn't as dramatic as yours, I'm afraid. Thomas …" A wistful look flitted across her face as she uttered the name. "He's a Catholic priest."

Faris didn't understand what that was supposed to mean.

"Catholic priests aren't allowed to marry. Thomas and I … we were in a relationship until a few weeks ago. We had to keep it a secret, otherwise he would have lost his job." She shrugged. "At the end, he chose his job over me."

"I understand." Faris forced a mouthful of coffee down his constricted throat.

Ira also took a sip. "You look like him."

Faris glanced over at his reflection in the windowpane. It was almost light outside, so he couldn't see himself very clearly. Long, messy hair. Reddened eyes. "I look like your German Catholic priest?"

"It's your eyes." She shivered. This topic seemed to bother her.

For a few moments, neither of them said anything.

"Where do you go, when you can't be alone?" Faris finally asked.

If the question surprised her, she didn't let it show. "I have a friend. Jasmin. An Italian. Her father runs a trattoria in Charlottenburg called *Da Rossi*. When I feel like my ceiling might fall in on me, I go over there, and after that, I usually feel be ..."

Faris's phone interrupted her sentence, and he quickly reached for it. Ira watched as he grew pale. "The bomber?" she whispered.

Faris nodded gloomily, then answered.

He didn't say anything, just waited.

"Who is this?" the caller's distorted voice inquired.

"Who do you think?" Faris replied through clenched teeth.

"Faris?" A short hesitation. "You're alive?"

The shock was audible, and there was something else mixed in the question. Faris wasn't sure, but to his ears, it almost sounded like relief. The caller's next words confirmed his suspicion.

"How lovely! We can now continue our little dance."

It wasn't just relief. It was delight. Delight that this sadistic little game wasn't over yet. Fury flooded Faris's heart, and the numbness that had settled over him since Paul's death instantly evaporated. "I'm alive!" he hissed. "But my partner went up in that explosion at the summer house, and you know ..."

"Paul Sievers is dead?" For several seconds, the other end of the line was silent.

And then the stranger hung up.

Over the course of the night, Dennis and Jenny tried out various clubs, and the last one they visited close to dawn was so full that they only lasted there for fifteen minutes.

Jenny giggled as they stepped out of the stuffy, ear-splitting atmosphere into the open air. The horizon to the East was already growing lighter, and she felt heady knowing they had stayed out all night.

The effect of the cocktails that Jenny had drunk earlier was slowly abating, but she still felt carefree and wonderful, and she knew this was the result of being with Dennis. She would never need to drink again if he would just stay with her.

At this point in the early morning, the air was considerably cooler, and Jenny was happy about that. She nestled close to Dennis and acted as if she were freezing.

"Are you cold?" He gazed into her eyes.

"A little," she lied. The truth was that his gaze made her feel more hot than cold.

He took off his jacket, draped it around her shoulders, and pulled her tighter against him. Just as she had wanted him to. She tried to hide a satisfied grin.

"Where should we go now?" she asked.

He didn't reply but steered her toward one of the city's numerous parks. He came to a stop in front of a bench that was secluded by a row of tall bushes.

"Let's just sit here," he suggested. Was she mistaken or did his voice suddenly sound a little rawer?

Her heart pounded like crazy.

They sat down, and Jenny let Dennis pull her against his chest. He smelled of fairly pricey aftershave. She had noticed earlier, but now it was making her dizzy.

"Mmmm!" She inhaled his scent appreciatively and closed her eyes. "You smell so good!"

He chuckled softly before leaning down and kissing her.

She felt like she was in seventh heaven.

Something hard now pushed painfully into Jenny's thigh. For one sweet breathless moment, she thought it was Dennis's erection, but she then realized that it was one of the two glow sticks that she had taken off her neck in one of the clubs and stuck into her jeans pocket. With an embarrassed laugh, she readjusted it.

"What is that?" Dennis studied her quizzically.

"Nothing. Just this!" She fished the two glow sticks out of her pocket. One of them actually was much heavier than the other, she thought incidentally, feeling a little uneasy at this discovery. But this was totally irrelevant at the moment. She held the glow sticks under Dennis's nose.

"They were poking me." She giggled as overconfidence sparkled like champagne in her veins. "And I thought you were just so happy to see me!" she exclaimed, quoting something she had heard in some stupid TV show.

Startled by her lewdness, Dennis just looked at her. He then started laughing. "Maybe I am," he teased. He took the glow sticks away from her. He ran one of them along her jawline, then down her neck to the neckline of her blouse.

She trembled. Everything inside of her felt as soft as wax, and when Dennis set the glow sticks aside and finally began to slide his hands underneath her clothes, she closed her eyes and savored the moment.

CHAPTER 26

The conversation with the caller had mobilized Faris's reserves. He was suddenly back in fighting mode, and the desire to stop the bastard flamed up inside him with a new intensity. He felt a tingling in his veins that he hadn't experienced in hours, and he knew that his adrenaline was back in full force.

"I have to go," he told Ira.

She was still sitting at the kitchen table. Her left fingers were resting lightly on the edge of her mug, and her eyes wandered searchingly across his face.

"Yes," she finally said. "I think you're better now."

He listened to his inner voices. It was possible that this strength was coming from one last flash of rebellion before his ultimate collapse, but he was determined to use it to finally bring this matter to an end. He would catch the bomber if it was the last thing he did!

Ira seemed to catch sight of something in his eyes that bothered her, and she shivered. She quickly dropped her eyes to her hand. "Go!" she declared. "I'll figure out my way home."

He paused, sensing that he should say something about last night. But he didn't have any idea what that something should be. The embarrassment he felt at the thought of Ira's bare skin under his hands made him dizzy.

"Thanks," he mumbled.

She smiled a melancholy smile. "Glad to be of assistance."

He drove his own car to Keithstraße, and shortly before seven o'clock, he stepped into the War Room. He paused briefly at the door and soaked up the scene. Almost all of his co-workers were there already: Gitta, Ben, Marc, and Shannon. Marc and Gitta were wearing different clothes from yesterday, which slightly soothed Faris's guilty conscience. At least they had made it home as well. On the other hand, Shannon was still wearing the same outfit as the day before, and Ben didn't look as if he had changed his clothes either, although this was harder to guess. He always wore the same beige shirts and pants.

The red countdown number had dropped to seventeen hours now.

On the once white surface of the case wall, dozens of photos were now taped up. Photos of the completely destroyed subway station, of computer fragments from Hesse's abode, of the charred summer house. Photos of the victims who had been identified so far. Faris recognized the face of a famous Berlin actress who had been on the subway. And he saw pictures of several teenagers whose IDs had been photographed. The elderly nun with the pale eyes was also among the dead. Her body looked strangely undamaged, almost as if, even in death, God had held his hands over her. Faris studied the old woman's slender, pale face for a few moments before letting his eyes continue to wander. At the sight of a blackened corpse, his stomach lurched. *Paul!* his mind screamed, and it took a second glance for him to read the name that stood above the photo. *Bobby.* He realized that this was the homeless man. The spot where a photo of Paul should have hung was empty. The vacant area in the otherwise cluttered wall struck Faris as a reflection of his own mental space.

Gitta was the first to notice him.

"Faris!" She was on her feet and in his arms before he could even take a breath. "Oh, Faris!" She clung to him, though only for a brief moment. She then pushed him away from her and examined him. Tears ran in broad rivers down her cheeks, before dripping from her jaw and onto the floor.

"Gitta." Even this single word had difficulty leaving his throat. His t-shirt was wet where her cheek had pressed.

Gitta's outburst had alerted the others that he was there. Shannon interrupted her reading of Werner Ellwanger's books and looked up. She stood up at the same moment as Marc, but unlike the latter, who just stood helplessly at his desk looking as if he wished he were miles away, she walked over to Faris. She shyly held out her hand. "So sorry, dear," she said huskily. Although her head was lowered, Faris could still tell that her eyelids were red. She never cried around her colleagues, and on one other occasion when she couldn't help it, she had disappeared into the women's restroom.

When she turned around and went back to her desk, her movements were jerky.

Marc still hadn't moved. He gulped, then sat back down. Faris let him. There wasn't anything to say.

As Faris stepped into the room, Ben had been on the phone, listening hard to whatever the other person had been saying. He now leaned over his computer screen. "Thanks," he said. "That helps us a lot." He then hung up without saying goodbye, stood up, and strode over to Faris.

Like Shannon, he couldn't look right at Faris. "I ... shit! What is there to say?" He lifted his head. His eyes swept quickly across Faris's face, and Faris wished he knew what he had seen there. It must have been alarming, since Ben took a quick step back in response. "My condolences," he exclaimed before beating a retreat.

Faris looked around. Paul's desk chair was the only unoccupied chair in the War Room, and something inside him rebelled against the thought of using it. So he crossed his arms and leaned against the case table. It was very obvious that Paul's death had changed something in this room. A grim energy now emanated from the people that he knew so well. It washed over Faris like a heat wave, engulfing him. *Emotional radioactivity*, he thought. It felt as if everything in here would vanish in an extraordinarily blinding flash of light.

"Let's concentrate on catching this pig," he said.

He could almost physically feel the others' relief. With grim, silent faces, they all returned to their work.

"Where's Tromsdorff?" Faris asked.

"He had to appear in front of the Senator of the Interior," Marc explained. "Along with Geiger and the other departmental chiefs."

Faris nodded before turning toward the case wall.

A mind map of sorts was dedicated to the summer house explosion. All the details that were known had been written down inside hurriedly drawn circles. For a while, Faris couldn't take his eyes off of it, but then he turned to some words that Paul had jotted down the day before. The handwriting was jaunty, so typically Paul, that for a minute, Faris couldn't move. Images and memories swept through his mind.

"Hey." Someone touched his shoulder, and he yanked himself out of the past. Gitta was standing next to him. She had traded her colorful garments for ones in a subdued dark blue. Faris surmised that this was probably the most somber color she had in her closet.

He automatically glanced down at his black t-shirt.

"Everything alright?" Gitta asked softly.

Nothing's alright!

Faris held back this reply. "Yeah." He was about to add something when Ben uttered a satisfied "There you go!" at his desk.

All eyes turned toward him. "What have you got?" Shannon asked.

He pointed at his monitor. "This is the schematic we found on Alexander's computer. I think it might be a diagram of the heart monitor that's attached to Ellwanger. We don't see much of it on the video. I was able to zoom in on one clip and print it." He held up a color printout that had been lying next to his keyboard. It was fairly blurry, but a company logo was still recognizable on it. *MedicCare*, Faris read.

"*MedicCare* has its headquarters in Eastern Europe," Ben continued. "To be more exact, in Ukraine. They're an hour ahead of us, and this morning, I reached someone who works there. I spoke to one of the developers." He looked down the line of his co-workers. "Did you know that almost all of them there speak German?" When nobody replied, he cleared his throat. "Anyway, I sent them the diagram, and they have just responded. It is actually an original schematic from one of their devices." He fell silent and grinned widely.

"And?" Faris wasn't quite clear about what they were supposed to do with this information. He could tell from the others' puzzled faces that they felt the same as he did.

"I described our little problem to the technicians there," Ben continued. He seemed a little annoyed at having to provide an explanation. "They studied the diagram and told me how the culprit will make the bombs go off. It's a ton of technical jargon, which I'll spare you, but there's one important thing. The *MedicCare* team is certain that all we have to do is shut off the monitor, to prevent him from sending the detonation impulse." He looked around triumphantly.

"Nice," Shannon grunted drily. "All we have to do now is find it."

Ben ducked his head, but then shrugged indifferently. "That's your job," he grumbled. He retreated to his computer and buried himself once more in his data and programs. As usual, whenever he felt like he had done good work that the others didn't respect enough, he acted as though he had been insulted.

Before any of them could say anything, Gitta's office phone rang. She hurried to her desk.

"Are you serious?" she exclaimed immediately. "That's amazing!" As she hung up, an expression of grim satisfaction flashed across her face. "That was Tromsdorff." She pressed her hands flatly against each other and tapped her lips with her pointer fingers. "It looks like some officers in the Kreuzberg area have picked up a young man who might be Alexander. They're bringing him over here."

As they waited for the suspect to be delivered, Faris used the time to read through the newest file entries in the DigA A. He still couldn't bring himself to sit at Paul's desk, so he had asked Marc if he could have his old spot back. Marc nodded without saying a word. Taking his black cup with him, he set off to brew a fresh pot of coffee.

The list of entries for their case had by now grown to a practically unmanageable scale. Faris knew that the DigA A was powered by algorithms that structured and organized the bulk of information and then searched for connections that the investigators might have missed. He couldn't recall, however, that SURV had ever solved a case as a result of these algorithms. Nor did he ever inquire if other departments had similar experiences. He wanted to remain convinced that human reason protected Berlin from villains, not some series of zeroes and ones on a computer somewhere.

He opened several memos at random, skimmed them, and then closed them because they didn't help him any. As he stared at the long list of entries, trying to determine the best way to handle the data, a new entry appeared at the bottom of the list, bearing a current timestamp. When Faris clicked on it, he saw that the file contained the transcript from the interview with a Norbert Langner, the husband of one of the Klersch Museum victims. The man had alibis that covered all four bombings, so he wasn't a suspect.

Following a hunch, Faris opened the list of museum victims. He skimmed the names until he found the woman in question. At the time of her death, Nina Langner had been twenty-seven years old. The lines swam in front of Faris's eyes for a moment. He blinked and continued to read down the list.

> *Langner, Nina.*
> *Mayer, Hiltrud.*
> *Mechow, Ludmilla.*

There were no files on Ludmilla Mechow. With a quick check, Faris determined that the interviews with her relatives were the only ones missing from the system.

Suddenly, Tromsdorff's voice interrupted Faris's thoughts.

"... and take him to the interrogation room!"

Faris now noticed that someone must have left the War Room, because the door was standing wide open. He could see a section of the corridor and the landing at the top of the stairs, as well as the group of men about to reach it. Tromsdorff was ahead, followed by two officers in uniform who were leading a young man with shaggy black hair whose hands were cuffed in front of him. As they walked past the door to the conference room, the prisoner lifted his head. His chin-length hair slipped to the side, and his narrow, pale face emerged.

"Good Lord!" Gitta gasped, as her eyes flew to the photo from Ira's album hanging on the case wall.

A cold stone settled into Faris's chest.

The man *was* Alexander Ellwanger.

And it was startling how young he looked.

Faris asked Tromsdorff if he could be the first to interview Alexander. Tromsdorff was reluctant to agree, since Faris was still officially suspended, but Dr. Geiger wasn't in the office yet and they needed fast results. So Tromsdorff finally agreed, though with a visibly heavy heart.

Before he joined Alexander, Faris removed several photos from the case wall and placed them in a folder. At the door to the interrogation room, he paused to steel himself for what was coming, and it took several seconds before he had the strength to enter the room.

The air in the small, bare room was cool and smelled a little stale. There was no furniture in the room except for a table with a mounted microphone and two plain plastic chairs.

Alexander was sitting on one of the chairs. Someone had removed his handcuffs. He sat there like a pile of misery, his head lowered, and his hands folded as if in prayer. A strong stench emanated from him, one that Faris knew all too well. Sweat and blood. Alexander's clothes were covered with dried blood splatter. His black hoodie was stuck to his skin, and his ribs were visible through the fabric.

Faris glanced at the one-way mirror to his right. He knew that his fellow officers were in the adjacent room. One of them was ready to rush in to take over the interview as soon as anything unforeseen happened or Faris reached a dead end.

Earlier, Paul had been the one who did that …

Faris was instantly overcome by a gnawing, forlorn feeling. The awareness that he couldn't fall back on his partner's support, that he never would be able to do that again, was gut-wrenching. He took a deep breath, and then strode over to the table and deposited his folder on it. Faris ignored the recorder positioned between himself and the young man. "Alexander Ellwanger?" he asked.

Alexander didn't react immediately. Faris could hear him mumble inarticulately, and he assumed that the boy was praying. After two or three minutes that Faris let pass without interruption, Alexander raised his head. "Yes." His voice was hoarse.

He was practically a child. His facial features looked soft, and a soft down covered his upper lip and chin. The blood spattered across his body had reached his face. He had tried to scrub it off, but not thoroughly enough. Residue remained on his cheekbone and beside his left nostril. The undersides of his fingernails were black.

Faris kept his eyes fixed on Alexander's hands as he pulled his chair out from the table and sat down.

"You got yourself pretty dirty," he started.

The young man studied his hands as if they didn't belong to him. "That's blood," he whispered almost inaudibly.

Faris waited a moment to see if he wanted to say anything else, but he didn't. "Your father's blood?" Faris asked.

Alexander nodded.

Faris looked up in surprise as he stifled a rush of excitement. Was it really going to be this easy to get a confession? "Did you ... crucify your father, Mr. Ellwanger?" he asked gently.

"Mr. Ellwanger is my father. Please call me Alexander. Everyone else does."

"Fine. Alexander. Did you crucify your father?" This time the question made him less uncomfortable.

Alexander pressed his palms together. It looked as if he had to hold onto himself. After a small eternity, he looked up. "Yes."

"Where is he?"

But Alexander just shook his head and pressed his lips together.

Faris leaned forward slightly. "You'd rather not tell me?"

Alexander shook his head again.

"Why not?

"Because I'm not allowed to."

The neon bulb on the ceiling buzzed softly. In Faris's ears, the noise turned into a faint beeping. "Who has forbidden you to?"

"My father."

Faris inhaled through his teeth. "What did you say?"

Alexander looked skyward. In his eyes shimmered with something that looked like madness.

"Your father forbade you to tell anyone where you set up his cross." Faris expressed this as a statement.

Alexander nodded.

"You're talking about your heavenly father – about God, right?"

"No."

"Why did your father forbid it, Alexander?"

Alexander didn't know the answer to this, or he was reluctant to give it. He simply lowered his head. His black hair fell in front of his eyes and strengthened Faris's impression of having a stubborn teenager in front of him.

"Why did your father forbid it?" he repeated.

"Because Christ hasn't appeared to him yet."

Faris leaned back. "You're going to have to explain that to me."

And to his amazement, Alexander actually did start to talk. He talked about spiritual experiences, about the forgiveness of sins through washing with blood, from the boundless fear of eternal damnation. And he talked about encountering God in Jesus Christ and about rising in the suffering of Christ.

Faris didn't understand a single word he said.

He shot a quick glance at the mirror and wished that he could see his colleagues. Hopefully, Shannon had some idea of what to do with all this babbling.

He then turned back to the young man who sat slumped over on his chair. A profound horror penetrated his chest. "Correct me if I'm wrong, but you nailed your father to a cross so that he could have some kind of spiritual experience?"

Alexander nodded.

"But what do the bombs mean, then?" The question came sharp and hard.

Alexander's head snapped up in astonishment. "What bombs?" His face was frankly astounded.

"The bombs you set off yesterday, Alexander!"

The young man instantly looked as if he wanted to jump up and run away. His hands began to tremble, as did his chin. He didn't look as cool and clever as the caller had seemed all along, and more than that, he didn't look anything like a bomber. Faris found himself staring at Alexander's hoodie. It looked like the top worn by the man in the video. Faris took this as proof that Alexander's claims were true. He *had* nailed his father to the cross, and he was filmed while doing it. But the caller – their mysterious second culprit – was still unknown.

"I don't know anything about any bombs," Alexander murmured, wrenching Faris out of his thoughts.

"Who helped you do this?" Faris countered.

Alexander understood that he was talking about the crucifixion, not about the bombs. "I ... nobody ..." The lie was written across his face. Someone had helped him, and he knew who it was.

Faris hesitated. He considered what his next steps should be and decided to increase the pressure on Alexander. He would continue to act as if he thought the young man was the bomber. Normally, suspects were more willing to name their accomplices if they knew the consequences of what they had done.

With a jerk, Faris jumped to his feet. "Do you think I'm an idiot? You crucified your father, as you have admitted yourself. You attached electrodes to him that are linked to a bomb at the Olympic Stadium. You blew up the subway at the Bismarckstraße station, my friend's office, and your father's summer house ..."

As he said these last words, he ran out of air. He saw Paul's blackened face and braced himself against the table to keep from staggering.

Alexander tried to pull away from him as far as possible. "I didn't do those things," he whispered, tears pooling in his eyes.

Faris reached for the file holding the photos. He pulled them out, one after the other, and slammed them down in front of Alexander. Pictures of the old nun, the blackened corpse of the homeless man, the ruins of the summer house. Faris's heart was pounding.

"Look at what your bombs did!" he said to Alexander, tapping the picture of the nun. "This was a nun, Alexander. Your bomb killed her as she was heading to a service of worship. Do you want to know her name? Her name was Sister Xaveria." He had read her name up on the case wall and had memorized it. "What do you think? Was this woman looking forward to seeing the Pope this evening? And she was traveling with children. *Children*, Alexander!"

He had to stop again. His heart was about to crack his already injured ribs. Taking his seat once more, he forced himself to breathe evenly and felt the eyes of his colleagues boring into the back of his head.

"I … had … nothing … to do … with … the bombs," Alexander stammered. The tears that had been glittering in his eyes were now streaming down his cheeks. He reached for the picture of the nun and brushed his fingertips across it. "The angel! He has to be the one!"

"Which angel?" Faris's voice sounded breathless and flat. He stood up. The whistling in his ears masked the sound of the door opening.

"Take a break," Marc suggested. "I'll take over for a while."

Faris nodded at him gratefully. Out in the hallway, he leaned against the wall and tipped his head back so that he could feel the rough plaster. Images flashed through his mind, one after the other for only a fraction of a second. The old nun with the pale eyes. The remains of the homeless man. Paul's disfigured face. He heard the child at the Klersch Museum sobbing. It cried and cried until Faris didn't think he could take it anymore. Until he almost lost his mind, until he turned around. He balled his hand up and punched the plastered wall – once, twice.

"Let it be!" Tromsdorff was beside him, grasping his arm. "Come on."

As Faris followed him into the observation room next to the interview space, Marc was just in the process of asking: "Where are the bombs, Alexander?"

CHAPTER 27

"I had nothing to do with the bombs."

Alexander's hoarse voice almost cracked as Marc fired over and over again at him the same question about the bombs.

Marc had activated the recorder Faris had ignored and was sitting on the edge of the table. This posture, which at first glance looked relaxed and casual, actually made the interviewee feel threatened because the detective was two heads taller than him.

"Don't lie to me!" Marc said quietly but resolutely.

"I ... I didn't ..."

Without missing a beat, Marc changed tactics. "Who did then, Alexander?" The question struck like a shot from a pistol.

The young man was no longer crying, but his words contained a sob. "I told you already – the angel!"

"What kind of angel?"

Alexander's eyes darted over to the mirror. Faris read despair and fear in his wide eyes. He instantly felt a connection with the young man, whose loneliness was palpable, even through the glass pane.

"The angel of the Lord," Alexander whispered. "He came." His words ended in a trembling breath.

Marc waited for a moment. "Where did he come *from*?" he asked.

Alexander closed his eyes. His chest rose and fell violently, as if he was under extreme duress. "I haven't been able to remember. The angel kept blinding me with this bright light. Bright angelic light, you know."

Marc shook his head gently.

"You forget everything when it's so bright and hot. Heavenly light, and the angel always stood inside it. I wondered why he didn't have any wings. But that was after my father …" He fell silent.

Marc waited patiently. When Alexander showed no indication of picking up where he had stopped, Marc finished the sentence. "After you crucified your father."

"Yes. He ordered me to do that."

"Who? The angel or your father?"

"The angel. After Father admitted to him that he wanted to be crucified, I mean. The angel told me that it was a good thing."

"Let's go back to the day the angel first appeared. Can you describe him for me?"

"He looked human. I'm sure you know that angels can take human form. That was why he didn't have any wings."

Marc nodded thoughtfully. "Describe him."

At this, Alexander abruptly put on the brakes. "No!"

Marc didn't make the mistake of putting too much pressure on him. Seemingly relaxed, he simply changed the subject. "But can you tell me what happened when he came?"

Alexander lifted his chin. "He rang the doorbell. I remember that because I thought it was strange. Angels don't have to knock when they enter a room, do they?"

"No, Alexander, they don't have to." Without moving, Marc gazed down at Alexander. "Keep talking. What happened next?"

"The angel sat down in the living room with my father. They talked for a long time, and I listened in. But that was a sin."

"Did you understand anything they were talking about?"

"Just that they were talking about a woman."

"A woman. Did you catch her name?"

Alexander shook his head.

"That angel he was talking about." Faris leaned forward to get a better look at Alexander. "Do you think he's imagining him, or is this angel

262

our culprit?"

Shannon tilted her head thoughtfully. "Whenever somebody talks about hearing voices, the first thing you think of is schizophrenia, but in this case, that doesn't fit. Alexander isn't showing any signs of losing touch with reality. He lacks the madness element." Through the pane, she studied Alexander, who had lowered his head again. "No, I'm positive that he hasn't just imagined this angel. That is definitely our second culprit."

Faris was about to ask something when the door swung open and Gitta rushed in. She looked agitated and was holding a single piece of paper that looked like a printout from a DigA A file. "This just came in!" she exclaimed, waving the paper in the air.

Tromsdorff took the page from her and skimmed it. "This is …" The color drained from his face, and he handed the sheet to Faris and Shannon.

The memo came from an officer in the explosives unit.

In the meantime, Marc had decided to change tactics in the interrogation room. "Alexander, I am sure that you would agree with me that murder is a grave sin." He didn't wait for Alexander to say anything. "We *have* to find out where the next bomb is located, the one that is supposed to go off in the Olympic Stadium tonight. The angel you saw might be able to help us to save the lives of many, many people."

Alexander gave a horrified scream and shouted: "I don't know where it is!"

As he said this, Faris finished reading the memo.

And knew where the bomb was located.

"Shit!" he said, tonelessly.

At that moment, his phone started to chirp. Fishing it rapidly out of his pocket, he answered the call.

"Now do you believe me, that I'm not Alexander?"

How Faris loathed this distorted, cool voice. A veil slipped down over his eyes, and the world around him turned blood red. Nonetheless, he had enough presence of mind to push his speaker phone button. Shannon and Tromsdorff could now listen in. And in the War Room, he knew that Ben was recording every word.

"You're not saying anything, Faris," the caller remarked. "Tell me, are you tired already?"

"Just fuck off!" The words were out before Faris could even try to hold them back. Shannon, who was standing right next to him at the mirror, stared at him in shock.

But the caller just laughed. "You're upset, I get that. Want to tell me what you've been asking Alexander about?"

"How do you know that he's here?" Faris fired back and realized the answer to that himself. "You hacked the DigA A again."

"Right. Your computer experts thought they plugged that little hole I made in your firewall. They managed to do that, but they stupidly missed the back entrance that I used this time. It looks like I might be just a little better than they are."

"What do you want?" Faris asked through clenched teeth.

"I answered your question," the caller replied sweetly. "Now, please be so kind as to answer mine."

"What were you asking about?"

"Don't jerk me around, Faris!" the stranger hissed. "Remember that I'm the one who has the trigger."

Faris closed his eyes. "We asked Alexander where the cross is."

"You want to take my father down, don't you?"

My father. There it was again!

"We looked into it," Faris said. "Werner Ellwanger has only one son, Alexander."

"There's a chance you weren't thorough enough, you know."

Faris's eyes fell on the printout he was still holding, and then he glanced through the glass to where Marc was just in the process of leaning over Alexander and whispering something in his ear. They now knew why the bomb dogs hadn't found anything at the stadium.

"The bomb isn't in the stadium, is it?" he asked.

The caller said, "That's right."

Faris once again skimmed the lines in the memo. A local man had brought one of the church conference glow sticks to the police, because his son had taken it apart out of curiosity and found something odd inside. Officers from the explosives unit had examined the stick and immediately posted their findings.

Detonator cap was written on the sheet. *Nanothermite. Radio detonator.*

All at once, everything made horrifying sense.

"You now know where the bombs are, right, Faris?" the caller asked softly.

"In the conference glow sticks."

The glow sticks were intended for use at tonight's worship service. The people would pour into the stadium, bringing with them the very bombs that would kill them there.

"How many of them are there?"

The caller didn't respond.

"You've taken a huge risk!" Faris rubbed his eyes. He had to somehow convince the bomber to share information that would help them catch him.

"How is that?"

"What if someone snaps the glow stick before the service begins?"

"Oh, that!" The caller chuckled. "People do that so often that of course I took that into consideration. If someone snaps one of them beforehand, nothing will happen. The stick won't glow, but that's all."

"It won't explode if it's snapped?"

"No, if I'd done that, you would've figured everything out too early, and I wanted to keep the game going a bit longer. By the way, whatever you're thinking, I didn't connect all the glow sticks with the heart monitor."

"Oh?"

"I can set some of them off directly by remote signal. Separately. As with that homeless man."

Faris pressed his thumb and forefinger against his eyelids. The red veil in front of his eyes unraveled into a shower of sparks but returned as soon as he lowered his hand. "And on the subway."

"Ah." The caller hesitated. "I hid a larger charge down there. A glow stick bomb wouldn't have caused as much damage." His tone was relaxed; it was as if he were chatting about a Sunday drive or a child's birthday party, completely unemotional.

"And the summer house?" Faris's voice cracked on the last word.

"Yeah, the summer house …"

Was Faris mistaken or was there a twinge of regret in the caller's words? He had already sensed earlier that the caller was shaken by Paul's death. This impression was now reinforced.

A long, unpleasant silence extended between them.

"How much damage are you going to cause?" Faris finally asked when it was clear to him that the caller wouldn't continue.

"Imagine a hand grenade enhanced with nanothermite. Immediately fatal for a radius of ten to twelve meters, and extreme burns up to forty meters – burns which will also lead swiftly to death. Beyond that point … You have enough imagination to figure out the rest."

Faris was already imagining what it would be like if several such bombs blew up in the packed stadium. "How many of these things have you distributed around Berlin?"

"About five hundred."

In Faris's mind, a gigantic fireball appeared and engulfed the stadium completely.

"How many of those can you set off individually?"

"A few. I gave one of those to a businessman, but he obviously handed it off to someone else. Bobby wasn't my target, but what would you think about a sweet blonde girl over on Ahornstraße …"

"You bastard!" Faris didn't realize that he had shouted until he caught sight of Shannon's and Tromsdorff's startled faces. He had balled his hand into a fist and raised it as if he could somehow stop whatever was coming next. "Don't you dare do anything to Lilly …"

But it was too late. The caller had hung up.

Laura was in a hurry. She had to get to the hospital. Her shift started in less than half an hour, and before that, she had to drop her daughter off at day care. Lilly wasn't making any of this easy. The goodbye ritual always took at least ten minutes, and if Laura added that to the amount of time it took her to reach the hospital, she was already late.

She set the little girl down outside the front door, and the child dashed off toward the street.

"Be careful, Lilly!" Laura cried. "Not out on the street!" But as she watched, she noticed what had attracted her daughter's attention.

On the path, right in front of the gate, an object was lying on the ground. Lilly leaned over and picked it up.

"What do you have there?" Laura walked over, curious. "Show me." It was one of those glow sticks from the conference. Laura picked it up, and Lilly stuck out her hands. "Have it!" she demanded. She held out her chubby hands expectantly.

"You want to have it back, right?" Laura considered this. The thing was totally clean and looked brand new. One of their fellow apartment dwellers had probably lost it out here recently. If she was lucky, Lilly would remain interested in the glow stick long enough for Laura to make a hasty departure without any theatrics and get to work on time. She weighed the stick in her hand. She wondered fleetingly why it felt so heavy, but her thoughts moved on.

"Why not?" She handed the glow stick to the girl. "But don't put it in your mouth, alright?"

For a moment, Faris listened to the emptiness on the line, then leaned back against the wall. It felt as if the last bit of strength was trickling out of him. He watched as Shannon joined Marc and Alexander in the interview room, and he knew that she was about to apply all of her psychological skills to getting something out of the boy.

"Come with me." Tromsdorff took Faris's elbow and steered him back to the War Room, where he maneuvered him to one of the chairs. Within Faris's mind circled a single, horrible thought.

Lilly with one of those glow sticks. And wherever Lilly was, Laura wouldn't be far away. In his mind's eye, he saw an explosion and heard a child weeping, but this time it wasn't the boy from the Klersch Museum. It was Lilly. The child who should have been his. Laura's child.

He became aware that he was still holding his phone, and with flying fingers, he dialed Laura's number. Hopefully she would actually pick up this time.

It rang three times, and she did indeed pick up this time. "This is Laura." She seemed to be in her car. He could hear engine sounds.

"Laura!" he cried. "Thanks for picking up! I …"

"Faris." She interrupted him impatiently. "Can't you just leave me alone?"

"No, Laura, listen. It's important. You …"

She hung up. He stared at his phone, stunned with incomprehension. He dialed again, but this time she rejected his call.

"Dammit all!" he cursed.

"Faris?" The voice penetrated the cotton that seemed to surround him. Something came to rest heavily on his shoulder. He blinked and saw that Tromsdorff was standing in front of him. "Everything okay?"

Faris nodded. "Yes. No." He leaned his head back, and his muscles ached. "Sorry about that."

Tromsdorff removed his hand from Faris's shoulder. "It's okay. I ordered a patrol car to go to Laura's hospital and warn her. Calm down now. The boys will make sure that nothing happens to her or the child."

Faris took a deep breath. "Thanks."

"Hey!" Ben called. He had just been chatting with Gitta about the DigA A's firewall. "Look at that!" He pointed at the television, which was showing channel N24.

A reporter with medium-length, hennaed hair was explaining that the Berlin bomber had apparently contacted the press and made a statement.

"This video," she said," was sent to us a few minutes ago." On the lower part of the screen, words streamed by.

The Berlin bomber's confession video +++ Still no demands +++ Another bomb has gone off

The video began, opening with footage from the papal visit to Berlin in 2011. Faris saw the former Pope holding a Mass in the Olympic Stadium, followed by a short video of him saying goodbye to various church dignitaries at the Tegel Airport runway and then flying off. The pictures from the video dissolved into the first few words from the motto for the current conference, which appeared in blood red letters against a black background.

SPEAKING THE WORD OF GOD

These were followed by images of medieval crusaders conquering the city of Jerusalem and slaughtering their enemies. After that came a long-distant shot of the Kaaba in Mecca. Thousands of pilgrims surrounded the holy site, which was the destination of their Hajj, the pilgrimage prescribed for every Muslim. Right after that, the twin towers of the World Trade Center collapsed. The picture then shifted to a video of Orthodox Jews at the Wailing Wall in Jerusalem, each making the same rocking movement as they prayed, and after that, the footage switched to the tall Israeli wall, at the foot of which people were standing and crying.

Finally, in conclusion, the rest of the conference motto, red on black.

BOLDLY.

The screen went black for a moment, before more text appeared.

WHY ARE YOUR GODS LETTING *THIS HAPPEN?*

For a couple of seconds, these words remained on the screen before disappearing as the video ended. The reporter reappeared.

"This video was made by the bomber," she said. She turned toward a gray-haired man with a prominent overbite who was standing beside her. "We have here our expert, Horst Reichenau. Mr. Reichenau, what do you think the attacker is trying to tell us with these images?"

The gray man began his tedious analysis, but before he reached the end of his first word, Tromsdorff muted the report. "We need to discuss this among ourselves," he muttered.

CHAPTER 28

The bell of the Church of the Passion struck nine as Ira left the parsonage to run the previous night out of her bones. She ran through the morning-chilled air, wrapped in her thoughts. When Faris had left, she had sat for a while longer at the kitchen table, just staring into space. Out of her wallet, she pulled out the business card for the *Da Rossi* restaurant. She flipped it over and jotted down a few words on the back of it.

I enjoyed it. Call me when you are on the other side of all this.

As soon as she wrote this, the two sentences struck her as silly and adolescent. She crumpled up the card and tossed it in the garbage can. With that, she left Faris's apartment.

Once she got home, she went to bed, but wasn't surprised when she couldn't fall asleep. By the light of day, she found the words on the back of the card embarrassing, and she wished that she could return to Faris's apartment and fish the card out of the trash can.

It pained her that Faris had called out the name Laura in his dream, but she warned herself to remain reasonable. She encountered Faris in a moment of weakness and grief. That had been very obvious from the way he had clung to her last night.

She increased her pace. She usually ran the first kilometers at a modest tempo, but today she felt a need to run flat out, to run for all she was worth, so she took long, loping strides through the park until she was wheezing, and her sides hurt.

After an hour, she was drenched in sweat, so she set off for the parsonage. With weak knees, she walked into her office.

"Good morning, Veronika." Ira reached for a towel that was hanging close to a small sink in a corner.

"Good morning." Veronika studied her skeptically. "Is everything alright?"

At that moment, Ira was glad her face was overheated, since she had the feeling that the events of the previous night were written across her face. If she weren't beet red already, she would have flushed at this question. "Just needed to get away from the world for a little while," she replied with a smile, hoping that Veronika would believe her.

To her relief, the secretary's thoughts seemed to be somewhere else. "Hmm. Okay. That police detective called, by the way. What was his name again?"

Faris! Ira almost declared, but she caught herself. "Iskander?"

Veronika nodded. "Exactly. He asked if we knew anything about Werner Ellwanger having an illegitimate son."

"And? Do we?" Ira poured coffee into a cup from a discount shop. It was decorated with a kitsch picture of a puppy. As she added a shot of milk to it, she listened to what Veronika was saying.

"At first, I wasn't sure, but the question started me thinking. I asked around a little, among the old women of the congregation, you know. There were some rumors. Ellwanger supposedly had a cleaning lady once, a young thing from the East – Poland or Russia or wherever. No idea what she was doing here in the first place, considering the Iron Curtain and all. But anyway, there was a rumor that Ellwanger got this woman pregnant. That must've been at some point in the mid-seventies. She upped and vanished all of a sudden. Probably went back home to have her baby."

An illegitimate child. Ira had to forcibly banish all the images of Ellwanger hanging on the cross. She took a deep breath. Her heart rate, which had been elevated because of her run, was now calming

271

down, and the sweat on her body had started to dry.

"I then decided to dig a little more." Veronika smiled like a cat who had just eaten a canary. "One of the old ladies remembered the cleaning woman. Even her name."

Less than a minute later, Ira was sitting at her office desk as she reached for her phone. Paul Sievers had given her his business card, and she hoped that someone would answer if she dialed this number. Her fingers trembled slightly as she punched it in. The thought of hearing Faris's voice at any moment set her nerves on edge. She felt the same way she had that day when she thought that Thomas was leaving her.

It only rang twice before a man picked up the phone. "Marc Sommer here."

It wasn't Faris.

Disappointment sat in her stomach like a stone.

"Ira Jenssen," she replied. "Is Detective Iskander there?"

He was on the phone so quickly that he must have been standing right next to his colleague. "Ira?"

"Faris, hi." She glanced over at the door. Good, she had closed it! Veronika wouldn't be able to listen in. Her cheeks grew warm, and she didn't know if that was due to her memory of the previous night or the sound of his voice. She pulled herself together. "My secretary found out the name of the mother of Ellwanger's illegitimate son."

Did her voice really sound that raw?

"What is it?" He sounded electrified.

Only because of the information, she warned herself.

She consulted the piece of paper she had jotted the name down on. "Ludmilla," she said. "Ludmilla Mechow."

The name lit a fire under Faris. "Thanks, Ira!" he exclaimed, before hanging up without saying goodbye.

"Gitta!" he shouted as he strode across the War Room. "Show me the list of museum victims!"

She had already opened the file in question by the time he reached her office. His head was buzzing, and he had to blink several times in order to see clearly. He quickly skimmed down the list until he found the right entry.

Mechow, Ludmilla.

He had been right.

Triumph spread through his chest. Finally a breakthrough!

"The bomber's mother," he murmured. "She was killed in the museum."

After Faris had hung up without saying a word, Ira sat for a while at her desk, staring at the sheet with the children's handprints. She had given him a major clue, she consoled herself. That was the only reason he had hung up so rudely. It had nothing, absolutely nothing, to do with her personally.

And also nothing to do with last night.

She suppressed the feeling of warmth that spread through her stomach whenever she thought about that. Deep melancholy washed over her, and she felt like a naive teenager.

"It was just sex, Ira Jenssen!" she said, under her breath. She reached for her coffee cup and stared at the puppy. Maybe she should get herself a dog.

With a sigh, she set down the mug and pushed herself up to her feet.

Veronika glanced up questioningly as she opened the office door.

"I'm going to the graveyard for a moment. The sexton asked me to decide if he should take down two trees there."

Veronika didn't seem to believe her. "Are you sure everything's okay?"

Ira nodded. "Of course! Why wouldn't it be? In case you need to reach me, I'm taking my phone along."

She reached for her jacket and left the office without any additional explanation. Of course, she had simply used the meeting with the sexton as a pretext. She just needed a little fresh air to clear her head of all the disturbing memories from the night before. At this time of day the graveyard was usually empty. She would be able to think through things clearly there.

She zipped up her jacket even though it wasn't cool, and she set off toward the graveyard entrance. A delivery van she had never seen before was parked in front of the small nursery located right inside the gate. She toyed with the idea of asking the owner of the nursery if he was expanding his motor pool, but this van was painted in such an eye-catching violet that it didn't fit even slightly with the company's other vehicles. The garish thing probably belonged to someone who was visiting the grave of a deceased relative. It was an odd time to do that, but then again, she was here too.

She strode down the path that ran between the graves. The constant noise that the metropolis made seemed quieter to her now that she was on the other side of the tall walls. She loved the peaceful atmosphere of this place. This was where she did her best thinking.

Past a row of birdhouses that had been mounted to the wall in the shape of a pine tree, she walked aimlessly for a few minutes. She passed mausoleums and simple graves with marble gravestones.

A squirrel scampered across her path.

In the distance, she heard the iron gate screech. Someone must have entered the graveyard behind her. She didn't pay any further attention to the quick, energetic footsteps, but concentrated on one of the old grave inscriptions. A quote from Corinthians was carved above a bas relief of Christ's head.

By His power, God raised the Lord from the dead, and He will raise us also.

Ira had to think about Detective Sievers and about how she wished she could convince Faris of the truth of this Bible verse. But she had a hard time believing it herself. She shook her head.

"What good are you as a pastor!" she chided herself.

The rapid footsteps faded away.

All of a sudden, Ira felt silly for having crept over here to lick the wounds that Faris had inflicted.

Annoyed at herself, she decided it was time to return to the office.

Laura woke up to a pounding headache and the unpleasant sensation of being on a rocking ship. The air around her smelled like old vomit. A regular, nerve-wracking beeping penetrated her consciousness. Her stomach lurched, but she didn't need to throw up. She lucked out on that, considering that her mouth was stuffed with a thick gag. There was a metallic taste in her mouth.

What had happened?

She remembered stepping out of her car at the hospital parking lot. Despite the glow stick which she had been allowed to keep as a toy, Lilly had thrown a fit as she was leaving, and Laura was running late for work. That was why the only parking space she was able to find was in the far rear corner of the doctors' parking lot, where tall bushes shielded it from the street.

The last thing she recalled were the footsteps. Steps that seemed to be right behind her. Before she could turn around, someone had placed something over her mouth and nose. She had registered the scent of something sharp and medicinal, and that was all …

Now, her hands and feet were bound, and whoever overpowered her had done a good job of it. She was tied up like a Christmas present. Slowly, her mind began functioning again. She had been abducted. A memory flickered in her mind: Faris! He had tried to reach her on the phone to tell her something. Had he been trying to warn her?

She groaned, because her skull felt like it was about to explode.

Where was that beeping coming from?

A bomb?

Fear shot through her body, and she tried to sit up. She reached the halfway point, but then couldn't stop herself from tipping backwards and banging her head – hard. Stars danced in front of her eyes as the nausea intensified. She inhaled as deeply as she could. Her nostrils constricted. Panic tightened her throat, but then she realized that she could still breathe freely and easily. This helped to calm her down. If only that annoying beeping would stop!

She rolled over awkwardly. She was surrounded by dim light and a chill that emanated from the surface on which she was lying. With her fingertips, she felt along that surface. Tiles, apparently. She could feel the grooves between them. The swaying motion subsided, and she realized that she wasn't on a ship. But where was she?

As she tried to focus on the direction from which the beeping came, veils rolled across her eyes. She had to blink to clear her vision.

The sound was driving her crazy. She wrenched herself back and forth and caught sight of the outline of some device. She saw a blue surface – and white lines that were flitting across that surface from left to right. This looked familiar to her for some reason, but the veils over her eyes were too thick for her to really see what it was.

The chemical taste in her mouth gradually faded.

She closed her eyes for a moment, then opened them again. The blue surface was now in perfect focus. The lines running across it formed little sine waves.

A cardiac monitor!

With a jerk, she sat upright. In front of her, a huge shadow rose into the air. Her eyes widened. A scream welled inside her, but the gag prevented her from making more than a toneless groan.

Like a stone outcropping that might fall on her at any moment, a wooden cross loomed over her head. And on the cross – her mind was reluctant to accept this fact – hung a man.

"Faris?"

Gitta's voice was so flat that Faris knew, instantly, that she had learned something bad. Tromsdorff had sent two officers to the TV station that had received the confession video from the bomber, but the clues dried up there. Several computer techs were now busy analyzing the video file. In the meantime, Faris had returned to the case wall where he was considering who their unknown caller could be. Along with Tromsdorff and Shannon, he had developed several theories that he had then discarded. Marc had joined them and given them his two cents before going back to Alexander in the interview room. And throughout, they had waited for a response to the request for assistance that Gitta had sent off to Ukraine.

By this point, it was noon. Just twelve hours remained.

"What is it, Gitta?" he asked, setting down the marker he had been twirling for several minutes and walking toward her. He came to a stop at her doorway. She was staring up at him with huge eyes.

"I know who Ellwanger's illegitimate son is," she gasped.

The name was up on her computer screen, and it seared itself into his retinas.

It couldn't be! Never!

As if it were far away, he heard his phone start chirping, but he was incapable of answering it. All at once, the puzzle pieces fell neatly into place. All at once, he understood all the bizarre, illogical things that the stranger had done. All at once, everything made horrible sense.

With trembling hands, he picked up the phone, but his voice failed him.

"Faris," the caller said in the now familiar distorted voice. The tingling in Faris's stomach turned into sheer ice.

How could he have been so damned blind?

His voice sounded flat and hoarse as he said: "You fucking bastard!"

PART THREE
HOUR 29 TO HOUR 40

It is finished.
(John 19:30)

CHAPTER 29

He is exhausted. His last reserves are rapidly decreasing, and even the IV drip that Alexander had put in – the one that was supposed to help him make it until the Lord appeared to him – can no longer keep his strength up.

He has to make his peace with the thought that his plan has failed.

Devotion to Jesus Christ instills in believers the desire to know Him intimately and to identify with Him.

He recalls these words from one of his books. Could he really have been wrong about this?

"Alexander," he whispers, hoping that the boy can hear him. "You have to take me down."

There is movement close by. Someone is there. He can feel it, even though his eyes keep failing him and all he can see is darkness.

He hears a muffled sound. Almost as if someone has a gag in their mouth.

Werner tries to inhale. He can barely do that anymore.

"Take me down!" he begs.

And then he feels a hand, warm and comforting, on his thigh. He tears his eyes open.

"Lord?" he groans.

The warm hand is quickly snatched back. "You miserable asshole!" a voice hisses, one that sounds vaguely familiar.

Alexander? He isn't sure.

"Help me," he implores.

"No," the voice says close to his ear. He can feel breathing against his neck.

"Take me down!" He wants to scream, but he is past that point. "My God!"

The voice at his ear starts to laugh. It is a hate-filled, triumphant laugh.

"It is time," the voice says.

He doesn't understand. "For what?"

"Time for you to die," the voice says.

A door rattles shut.

He feels alone. Completely alone.

This time he doesn't laugh, and he doesn't scream.

He starts to weep.

The caller chuckled. "I take it you've finally figured out who I am."

The eyes of everyone else in the room rested heavily on Faris. He pinched his nose and tried to pull himself together. It took a moment before he was able to utter the name. "Niklas." His knees were trembling.

"Very good." The distorter was turned off, and Hesse's familiar voice was suddenly speaking into Faris's ear. "How did you figure it out?"

"Why, Niklas?" Faris could only whisper. Out of the corner of his eye, he watched as the other team members clustered around him. It looked as if they wanted to build a protective wall around him, and he was grateful for that.

"We're about to get to that," Hesse demurred calmly. "First, tell me how you discovered who I was."

Faris met Gitta's eyes. "I didn't. Gitta learned that your mother was one of the museum victims. Listen, Niklas, I understand that you blame me for her de …"

"You never change," Hesse cut him off. "Always ready to bear the guilt of the world on your own shoulders, aren't you?" He chuckled, a sound that sent goosebumps down Faris's back. It made Hesse feel like a stranger, like someone that Faris had never met. The person on the other end of the line was no longer the friend he had known for so long. At some point in the previous months – during that time he had refused to tell Faris about – Niklas Hesse must have turned into someone else. And talking to this other person felt to Faris like gazing into an unending chasm. To keep himself from plunging into it, he kept his eyes on Gitta.

"Why have you done all this, Niklas?" he asked again.

"Oh! We'll have plenty of time to chat about that, old friend. But for now, I just want you to do what I tell you."

Faris glanced up at Tromsdorff. His lips were now a very thin line, and with his head tilted, he was listening to Hesse's words which weren't just coming out of Faris's phone, but also out of the speaker attached to Ben's devices. And as Faris looked into Tromsdorff's eyes, he discovered a steeliness there that he had never seen before.

"You know where the cross is by now, don't you?" Hesse asked.

Faris envisioned the spacious terminal in the old airport and, in a flash, realized why he had felt a sense of impending doom there. Even now, hours later, the thought of it gave him chills. "Tempelhof," he murmured.

"Good." Hesse sounded satisfied. "I want you here in one hour."

"Why in an hour?" Faris asked. The drive to the airport would only take him twenty minutes, thirty max.

Hesse didn't answer the question. "In one hour," he repeated. "Or else."

Ben shivered. "What does that mean? A duel or what?"

Faris once again caught Tromsdorff's eyes. *What should I do?*

Tromsdorff looked uncertain.

"Come alone, Faris." Hesse's voice broke through the silence. "And when you get here, enter the airport the same way we did together. If you don't do as I ask, I'll set off the next bomb."

"What are your plans?" Faris felt a need to sit down, but he struggled against it. He was afraid that if he did that, he would never find the strength to stand up again. He stared at Tromsdorff, pleading silently.

Let me go! he mouthed silently.

Tromsdorff still hesitated. Faris could guess what was going on in his mind. It would go against all of the protocols to allow a detective to go by himself into such a situation. If he agreed, it could cost them all their jobs. The entire SURV team would be at risk.

As would be the lives of hundreds, even thousands, of people.

Impatience prickled through Faris's veins. He wished he could rush out of the room and speed off in his car. But he stood there and waited for Tromsdorff's decision.

Hesse seemed to notice the hesitation. "I'm weighing up my options for the next bomb. What do you think of the banking district? There aren't all that many working there today, but a small attack on Deutsche Bank would have some kind of impact on the stock market, don't you think?" He paused thoughtfully. "Or what about the glow stick that Lilly …"

"Don't you dare!" Faris shouted so hoarsely that the words hurt his throat. "If anything happens to her …" he tried to imply a threat, all the while hoping that the officers Tromsdorff had sent had already reached Laura and taken her to safety.

Hesse simply laughed, then hung up.

In the meantime, Tromsdorff had made his mind up. Turning around, he marched over to his office and returned a few minutes later with Faris's gun. He held it out to Faris. "Just in case."

Faris stuck the gun into his waistband. He hadn't thought to put his holster on this morning. With that, he turned to leave.

"Wait!" Ben threw up his arm to stop Faris. "If you find Ellwanger and that cross, you can just disarm the bombs."

"I know, by turning off the monitor." Faris recalled Ben's instructions.

"Yes, but we won't be able to take out the bombs that the bastard can directly control that way." Ben let the sentence hang in the air for a moment before he added: "If you come face-to-face with Hesse, shoot him."

Faris could feel a black hole open up within him. "We'll see," he murmured.

A few minutes later, he was behind the wheel of the BMW and turning off of Keithstraße onto Kurfürstenstraße when Hesse called back. Ben had activated a phone link so that Faris's colleagues in the War Room could also talk to Hesse, and he had provided Faris with a headset so that he could keep both hands on the wheel and talk on the phone at the same time. This was critical, because Faris was trembling so much that he could hardly insert the key into the ignition.

"Explain to me now why you're doing all this," he said as struggled to keep from swerving out of his lane. The last thing he needed was to draw the attention of a traffic officer.

"You know the answer to that already," Hesse replied. Faris recalled how the reporter's office had been blown up. That had prevented Hesse's name from making it onto a list of suspects. "My mother was killed in the …"

"That's bullshit!" Faris interrupted him angrily. If he listened closely, he could hear noises from the War Room. "I know you well, don't forget that!" He controlled himself before continuing. "Your relationship with your mother was anything but close."

He remembered one evening at the police academy when he and Hesse had eaten supper together and chatted about their families. And he still hadn't forgotten the day when Hesse admitted to him that his mother had given him away when he was five years old. Because she "simply wasn't in the mood to keep me around" as Hesse had put it. Faris had extrapolated from this declaration that she could no longer handle the raising of her son, and he had been taken away from her because of that. But he hadn't contradicted Hesse, because he knew how important rage could be, to keep oneself from coming apart at the seams over a particular situation. Because of her, Hesse had spent his childhood in an orphanage. Thus, there was no reason at all for him to have reacted violently to her death at the museum.

"You know me?" Hesse hissed. Although the voice distorter was turned off, his voice now sounded even stranger than before. *Full of madness. And hate.* "You think you know me? Whatever made you think that? You might have known the Niklas who went to the police academy with you."

Faris switched on his turn signal and turned right onto Potsdamer Straße. Hesse's burst of anger intensified the feeling that he was talking to a total stranger. He drove underneath a bridge.

"Did you know that I didn't work in Wiesbaden long?"

"No. You never wanted …"

"Just let him talk, Faris," Tromsdorff urged over the phone link, and Faris could guess what his supervisor wanted to achieve from this.

As long as he's talking, he's not pressing the trigger.

Hesse chuckled in amusement, since he had also heard Tromsdorff's voice.

And he resumed his story. "I spent a couple of months at the academy, and then they asked me if I might be interested in working as an instructor for police officers in Afghanistan."

"And you agreed." Faris came to a stop at a red light. A flashy, dark blue Mercedes was sitting in front of him. A sticker announcing *No brats on board* was stuck to the back window.

"I did," Hesse confirmed. "I went to Afghanistan, to the Balch Province, and I helped to train the students there." He took a deep breath that sounded like a sigh. He was then silent for a while.

The noises from the War Room grew louder than before. Faris's co-workers were talking among themselves about something, but he couldn't make out what they were saying.

In the meantime, he had driven down Potsdamer Straße. Hesse still hadn't said anything by the time he turned onto Hauptstraße, so he asked cautiously: "And?"

Hesse sighed again. "After I had been there for a few months, I met a woman."

A premonition sent a shudder through Faris, like a cool draft. "The picture on your desk." He recalled the young, dark-haired woman with the golden star earrings in the photo he had seen in Hesse's office.

"Faridah," Hesse said softly. "That was her name."

"A lovely name." Faris struggled with a sudden flash of sympathy. He suspected that something bad had happened to Faridah. He had to force himself to focus on the fact that Hesse's fingers were on the trigger.

"She is dead." The three words sounded like a sob.

Faris could feel the edge of the abyss they were standing next to. "What happened?" he asked carefully.

"I fell in love with her. And she felt the same for me." For a long moment, the only sound on the phone was Hesse's heavy breathing. "That cost her her life."

As Faris drove past the Old Schöneberger Cemetery and the two churches that stood right next to each other there, he listened to the reporter's belabored breathing.

"They condemned her for that," he finally said slowly.

Another long pause followed this.

"And then stoned her."

Over his headset, Faris heard Shannon swear under her breath.

Although he was in traffic and shouldn't have done it, Faris closed his eyes. It took a long beep from another car to jolt him back to reality. His eyes flew open, and he swerved back into his lane. A sports car sped past him angrily, and he saw the driver shouting at him.

"She was married," he said quietly. He didn't need to ask. He just knew.

Hesse made a noise that sounded like a whimper. "I was forced to watch." He was now talking quietly too. Very quietly. And yet the words seared themselves into Faris's brain. "They made me watch, Faris! I watched the stones fly, every single one of them. Do you know what sound a stone makes when it hits a skull? Do you know what it feels like to hope that the next rock will be the one that finally kills someone because you can't take it anymore?"

Faris could hear the trembling in Hesse's voice, followed by a cough.

The reporter suddenly sounded cool and composed again. The transformation was so abrupt that it filled Faris with horror.

"I left Afghanistan after that and returned to Berlin. Believe me, it took me quite a while to work through all that."

Faris had to stop at another light. A small group of conference-goers walked down the crosswalk. Demonstrators holding printed devil posters were standing on the other side of the street. The light switched to green, and Faris accelerated. At this point, he was glad that Hesse had given him an hour to reach the airport. The traffic was awful.

"And you established *hotnewzz*," Faris said. "You had started writing already back in your teens whenever something was bothering you."

"Sometimes I can't go to sleep at night, because I can't get those pictures out of my head. And then I write stuff. It helps."

Faris had always envied Hesse for this. He didn't have any effective mechanism for getting rid of the often-horrifying images that his job left him with. He hesitated.

"Or you build bombs and blow them up."

Hesse ignored him. "I had just gotten about halfway back up on my feet, when what do you think happened?" He didn't give Faris a chance to respond but provided the answer himself. "That bastard in the museum blew up my mother."

"The catalyst," Faris heard Shannon say in the War Room, and he felt a twinge at this because it had always been Paul who had said those words in the past. All at once, every bit of sympathy he felt for Hesse vanished. This man on the other end of the line – he was no longer his friend. He wasn't some pathetic victim, but the asshole who had his partner's death on his conscience!

"Despite the fact my mother gave me away like an old hat when I was five," Hesse continued, "I kept in touch with her. And when she died, I took care of her estate. It was from some of the papers she left behind that I learned who my biological father was. My mom spent her whole life refusing to tell me who he was. And you know what else she failed to tell me? That I had a half-brother."

"Alexander."

"Alexander." Hesse chuckled softly, and Faris couldn't deny the impression that he was slowly drifting into insanity. "But you know what? We can chat about all this later. Where are you now?"

Faris looked through the windshield. "I'm at the Stadtring, right at the underpass."

"Wh ..." The line crackled as Faris drove through the short tunnel. For a moment, the connection was quite bad. "... tell you!"

Faris considered his next move. "What happens if I don't come alone?"

"If you don't, your sweetheart dies!" The threat had a derisive edge and sounded completely insane.

Faris's fingers tightened around the steering wheel, and his foot pressed harder on the gas pedal. "Which sweetheart?" he asked carefully, although he felt like he already knew the answer.

"Don't act so naive!" Hesse snarled.

Faris gulped in horror. "Laura?" The word hurt his throat.

"Wait a sec." More crackling in the line. "Say hello to Faris, my dear!" There was a snap, then a voice said: "Faris?"

"Laura!" He could hardly breathe.

"He overpowered me," she murmured. She sounded sleepy. "You have to …"

He didn't hear the rest because Hesse was back on the line now. "That makes everything a little more interesting, doesn't it?" The connection was poor. "In any case, it shows that you had better do what I say!"

Hot fury shot through Faris's veins, and he was glad of it, because it made him feel stronger. Nonetheless, he needed to keep a clear head. He knew that Tromsdorff and the others were listening. Tromsdorff would do everything he could to help him bring Hesse in. But as long as the bastard had his fingers on the trigger, there wasn't much they could do.

Except obey the orders they were given.

"What do you want from me?" Faris asked through dry lips. "What do you hope to achieve with this little game?"

Hesse didn't answer.

"Why don't you just blow up the stadium and be done with it?"

"The stadium? Oh, right. That's going to be the crowning glory of my little play. My crown of thorns, so to speak." The journalist chuckled again. "The entire world will begin to understand, then."

"Understand what? That their gods weren't able to protect them from you?"

Hesse made a puzzled sound, then fell silent for a moment. "You saw the video I sent to N24, right?"

"Of course. Just tell me, what do you hope to achieve with all this?"

"I'm going to play it on the big screen right before the bombs explode. Someone's always filming stuff when a disaster like that happens. And this video will land on the internet. My question to the world will be out there in huge letters, Faris. *Why are your gods letting this happen?* Right after that, the explosion that will pulverize the stadium. People will finally start telling their gods to go to hell! Excuse the pun."

A frantic mumbling broke out in the War Room.

Faris blinked. His head ached, and whenever he blinked, he saw dark red dots zoom around him. "It's still ..." he glanced at the clock, "... eleven hours until the Pope's Mass. What's going to happen until then, Niklas?"

Hesse didn't reply. Instead he said, "Do you know what's going on in the stadium right now? A Taizé service. They're singing, Faris. I'm afraid I might need to rework my schedule a little. I've been planning to use the papal Mass for my fiery finale, but God has other plans." He giggled. "I would guess that the stands are about two-thirds full. Do you know how many people that is? Just think!"

Faris wanted to respond, but wasn't fast enough.

Hesse had hung up.

"That's insane!" Shannon said, now closer to the microphone so that Faris could hear her clearly. Deep inside, Faris felt regret. Regret that the Niklas Hesse he had once known no longer existed. He tried to imagine what had happened in Afghanistan. To be made to watch the stoning of a woman that you loved ... He had a hard time imagining what that must be like. Laura's face suddenly flashed through his mind. She was in the hands of this mad man. He had to focus if he wanted to save her.

"He's crazy," he mumbled. "Totally crazy."

"He's definitely showing signs of being delusional," Tromsdorff agreed. "He thinks he's on a mission."

And Marc added: "He really thinks he can make the human race give up their religions, doesn't he?"

"People have tried for centuries to answer the question of theodicy,"

Shannon said. "No catastrophe – whether caused by humans or by nature – has ever compelled them to fundamentally question or give up their faith."

For a moment, they were all silent, in shock.

Agitated beeping from behind Faris reminded him that he needed to concentrate on the road. He now realized that he had been driving slower and slower, and now he accelerated again. The driver who had almost plowed into his bumper shot him the middle finger as he passed him. Faris decided against making an apologetic gesture. "You heard that he has Laura, right?"

Tromsdorff's voice was flat. "We did. I informed Andersen. The GSG 9 has been on standby for hours already. He is deploying them as we speak. Where are you?"

Faris could guess at the actual meaning behind those words.

Don't go in alone.

He gritted his teeth. He had just exited the city freeway and was turning right onto Tempelhofer Damm. An older woman merged into his lane, right in front of his bumper. He had to slam on the brakes to keep from hitting her, and in his thoughts, he shot the most scathing profanity he could think of in her direction. Out loud he said: "Almost there. Hesse isn't stupid. He's set up cameras or something like that all over the place. The officers won't stand a chance of storming the airport before he pushes the trigger."

"Still!" Tromsdorff didn't say anything for several seconds. "We'll only survive this as a team, Faris! Did you hear me? As a team!"

Faris was silent.

"Notify them before you go in," Tromsdorff ordered.

The mood in the Olympic Stadium was amazing, and Jenny felt equally amazing. She was here, at this conference, at the side of the coolest guy she had ever known.

She shot a sideways look at Dennis.

After last night – this morning, she corrected herself, since it had been almost dawn – when he had kissed her to the point of sheer unconsciousness on the park bench, he had pulled back from her. Breathing heavily, he had gasped: "Not here. Not like this!"

At first, Jenny had been disappointed, but then she realized that he was right.

Tonight! Today would finally be the day. Dennis had booked a hotel room. Her body was filled with a tingling sensation as she thought about having sex for the first time with *him*.

Her fingers clutched at the glow stick that was hanging from her neck.

Dennis noticed her gaze. He smiled at her and wrapped his hand around hers. His skin was warm and a little rough.

On the stage up front, the one on which the Pope would step a few hours later, a huge gospel choir was singing Taizé songs. They were currently singing in French.

"C'est toi, ma lampe, Seigneur ... "

Jenny hummed along to the familiar tune.

But the only thing she could think about was what was going to happen tonight.

The officers from the 632 and the GSG 9 had set up a mobile deployment base within a short distance of the airport, and as ordered, Faris checked in with them. There were several discussions about why they shouldn't allow him to enter the building alone, but Hesse managed to reach Marvin Andersen and to make it clear that he was the one calling these shots. So, as Hesse instructed, Faris entered the terminal on his own, using the same entrance that he and the reporter had used the day before. He immediately found himself back in the gigantic terminal hall. His gun was in his hand. This time, the feeling of impending doom was so palpable that his pistol felt as heavy as lead.

"So nice to see you." Hesse's voice echoed through the cavernous space. He was standing at the other end of the hall, on the steps that led up the former main entrance. His hands were hanging loose at his sides, and – Faris could hardly believe his eyes – they were empty. No trace of a gun or of the trigger Faris had expected to see.

Duel, he heard Ben's words again.

What was going on here?

Faris pointed his pistol at Hesse. The distance between them seemed to stretch into eternity, and then, like a rubber band stretched to its fullest extent and then released, everything snapped back to its appropriate position. It took a moment for Faris to realize that he had suffered a dizzy spell, which had caused that perception.

"I'm here, Niklas," he said. "Now what?"

"Come with me!" Hesse strode down the steps and turned left to where another staircase led down to the basement level.

Through his scope, Faris watched his former friend cross the hall. *Shoot him!*

The demand rang so clearly through his mind that he almost looked around to see if someone was standing behind him. The black hole that he had sensed inside of him earlier grew larger, and Faris tightened his jaw. He wouldn't look into this abyss! He tried as forcefully as he could to command the cold voice in his head to shut up.

"Your trigger finger is twitching," Hesse remarked with a smile. "I hope you have yourself under control."

Faris ignored it. "Where are you taking me, Niklas?" he asked as they descended the lower staircase. "To the basement restrooms?"

Hesse's smile turned into a wide grin. "I don't care if you want to leave a trail of breadcrumbs for your fellow officers. But don't play me for a fool. Yes, the cross is in the old restrooms in the basement, people! You'll need to use the stairs on the left."

Faris took one of his hands off the gun and pressed his earpiece more firmly into his ear. "Did you get that, Robert?"

"Loud and clear," Tromsdorff confirmed.

"Hesse is unarmed," Faris reported.

The reporter laughed. By now, he had reached the door to the former men's restroom. With a mocking gesture, he shoved it open and invited Faris to enter. A regular, slow beeping sound could now be heard in the corridor.

The heart monitor.

Faris stepped into the low space, and on the other side of the door, he took a step to the side in order to keep Hesse in sight. For a moment, his gun was pointing at the floor.

The sight of the cross struck him like a whip. The upper beam almost touched the ceiling, and Werner Ellwanger's feet cleared the dirty floor tiles by only a few centimeters. The pungent smell of blood and other bodily fluids forged an unpleasant and bitter path through Faris's consciousness. The electrodes on Ellwanger's chest were practically flush with his pale, waxy skin. Faris could see the cables that ran from them to a receiver attached to Ellwanger's hip. He assumed that this was the receiver that conveyed the recorded data to the monitor, which would then send the signal for the bombs across the city to …

Faris's thoughts came to a stumbling halt as he caught sight of Laura. Tied up and gagged, she was lying in a corner. She stared at him fearfully with large blue eyes and looked so forlorn that it almost destroyed him.

"I'm here," he said to her.

Hesse laughed loudly. "Yes, your knight in shining armor is here. Did you know, Laura Darling, that in German, *Faris* means *knight*. That's true, isn't it? How about we see if he is a white or a black knight."

As he was talking, Faris glanced over at the heart monitor, which was standing a little to the side. The screen attached to the front of it indicated a regular sine curve. A strong spotlight and a camera on a tripod were positioned right next to the entry door. The spotlight illuminated every centimeter of the entire scene. In its light, the blood on Ellwanger's white body stood out garish and bright.

Faris turned his attention back to Laura. Her silky hairy was tousled, her face was pale. He could see several dark red spots on her neck that looked like bruises. What had the bastard done to her?

"I'm here now," he said to Hesse. "Let her go!"

"Why would I do that?" Loathing and madness flashed across the reporter's face. "No, Faris," he added slowly. "Laura will die, and you will watch, just as I had to watch Faridah's death."

Out of the corner of his eye, Faris saw Laura start to frantically shake her head.

I won't let that happen! he thought as forcefully as he could, hoping that she would be able to see the determination in his body language. He didn't understand what he and Laura had to do with Faridah's death, but he was convinced that he had passed the point of being able to argue rationally with Hesse. *Delusional*, he could hear Shannon saying. In Hesse's reality, Faris was guilty of everything that had happened, and there was nothing he could do to change that.

"What happened to you?" he murmured. "Why do you hate me so much?"

Something crackled in Faris's earpiece. The reception down here was bad. He pointed his gun at Hesse's abdomen. "And what makes you so sure that I won't just shoot you right here and now?"

The chasm within Faris was now wide and bottomless.

Hesse shrugged. "Probably the fact that you aren't sure if I have an ace up my sleeve."

That was true. Hesse's demeanor projected confidence and self-assuredness. It was likely that everything playing itself out here was part of his plan.

But what was the plan? What did Hesse plan to do?

Faris racked his brain, but he simply couldn't connect the dots.

Impending doom ...

He struggled against the overwhelming urge to close his eyes. He longed for peace and quiet. For sleep.

"You know that my superiors consider me a ticking time bomb," he said softly. "What makes you so sure that I won't just give it a gamble?"

Hesse took a step back. Uncertainty suddenly flared in his eyes, and Faris was surprised at himself. This wasn't the first time that someone had been able to see in his eyes the black abyss lurking inside him.

Without taking his eyes from Hesse, Faris moved backwards, closer to the heart monitor. Under other circumstances, the constant beeping would have had a calming effect on him. But right now, the regular, quiet rhythm pierced him.

CHAPTER 30

"Something's not right here." Ben Schneider was tapping the top of his pen rhythmically against his teeth as he gazed at the heart monitor on Alexander's computer. In the background, he could hear the dueling words flying between Faris and Hesse. Ben's stomach felt uneasy.

They were missing something. *But what?*

The situation seemed so utterly unreal. Hesse's actions were completely illogical. Could that be explained away by his madness?

Why didn't the reporter have a gun to use against Faris? Why had they found the diagram for the heart monitor on Alexander Ellwanger's computer? As things looked right now, Alexander was a victim – so how had the diagram gotten onto his computer? It was this last question that was the primary cause of Ben's stomachache.

As he considered this, his eyes moved restlessly across the screen. The Wi-Fi indicator in the upper right corner was gray. The computer was offline, just as it was supposed to be. Ben himself had disconnected the machine from the internet, as soon as Marc Sommer had handed it to him. Ben clicked aimlessly through the various windows on the desktop. And suddenly he found himself staring at the diagram's creation date.

"Shit!" he exclaimed. His stomachache intensified tenfold.

He once again glanced at the Wi-Fi indicator. With flying fingers, Ben now opened one of the utility programs and inputted a command order.

His eyes widened as he caught sight of an IP address that appeared where the word *inactive* should have been. He suddenly leaped to his feet so quickly that his chair rolled backward and slammed against the wall.

"Faris!" he shouted. "Faris, can you hear me? Do NOT turn off the monitor under any circumstances! Did you hear me?" He glanced over at his fellow officers' shocked faces, but he didn't pay the slightest attention to their puzzled looks. "The bombs will explode as soon as you turn off the monitor!"

A loud crackling in his earpiece caused a dull pain to spread through Faris's head. The connection down here was almost completely nonexistent. He only heard fragments of what the others were saying from the War Room.

"Fa … me … turn off …"

With the hand with which he had just been reaching for the monitor switch, he reached for his ear. "Ben? Is that you?" He shot a sideways glance at Hesse who was now back to being calm and relaxed. "Ben? What did you say? I didn't get it." Unsettled, Faris once again reached for the switch.

Laura's gaze rested on him like a great weight. He forced himself to not be distracted from what he needed to do.

Focus!

Had Ben wanted to tell him something; or had that simply been part of the conversation that his colleagues were having back on Keithstraße? He had no idea. Ben's voice had sounded excited, but that could have been caused by the problems with the connection. The beeping of the monitor had become even, nerve-frazzling background noise.

Faris glanced up at Ellwanger, whose face resembled that of a man who had already been dead for a long time. The streaks of blood that ran down his cheeks, chin and neck looked like gaping wounds in the garish glare of the spotlight. As Faris argued with himself about what to do next, Ellwanger suddenly opened his eyes.

Faris flinched.

Ellwanger's eyes were bleary. His lips moved without making a sound.

Then a long, drawn-out sound issued from his mouth. Half groan, half word.

"Looor…?"

Faris clenched his teeth. It was obvious that the man was in anguish. He had to finally make up his mind! He looked over at Hesse irresolutely, and slowly stretched his hand out toward the switch for a third time.

Jenny leaned against Dennis's chest and swayed with the rhythm of the music. The glow stick she had given him hung from a rainbow-patterned strap around his neck. She was holding her own glow stick and swinging it back and forth, despite the fact it wasn't glowing yet. Some of the other worshippers had already lit theirs, but Jenny wanted to wait until tonight.

She closed her eyes and imagined how beautiful it would look when thousands of people lit their glow sticks and held them into the night sky. It would be a sign, a sign of ecumenicism and mutual understanding.

But after that … After the Pope had come out on stage and held the first truly ecumenical Mass, she would go with Dennis to the hotel and …

She shook off her heated thoughts and held back a grin.

Pia, who was standing next to her, studied Jenny. The two girls winked at each other conspiratorially.

"Hey!" Dennis said suddenly with a jerk.

Jenny pulled out of his arms. "What is it?"

He pointed at the large screen behind the gospel choir. Until just now, bright geometric shapes had been flickering there in time with the music, but now they had disappeared, and a film had started to play.

Images of the papal visit in 2011 flashed into view.

"What's going on?" Jenny heard Pia murmur.

Alexander

Alexander looked at his hands.

The hands that had nailed his father to a cross.

He shook his head in utter disbelief.

The angel was gone. He hadn't come along to this bare room, and Alexander felt so extraordinarily lonely that he gave a hiccupping sob.

Had he done the right thing or not? The two men who had interviewed him – the dark-haired one with the burning look in his eyes, and the prim and proper officer in the polo shirt – they had seemed horrified by what he had done.

Something stirred in him, and he thought about how his father had preached over and over again about how he needed to fight against the devil in his own body.

Icy horror washed over him. What if he had lost that battle a long time ago?

He whimpered.

What if the angel hadn't been an angel at all, but a demon? An emissary from Satan?

This thought came to him all of a sudden, and it was so horrible that Alexander slowly pushed himself upright. His eyes flashed around the sparse room.

And then he noticed the pipe hanging from the ceiling.

Faris felt like an insect skewered under a microscope. Laura stared at him, panic-stricken, as Hesse smiled at him gently. And Ellwanger gazed down at him through clouded eyes.

The beeping of the monitor briefly accelerated, but then sank back down to its old rhythm. Hesse took a step closer, and Faris raised his gun in his direction in order to send him back to his spot. At that moment, he detected triumph in the reporter's eyes.

"You bastard!" he exclaimed. "You want me to turn off the monitor, don't you? The bombs will go off when I do that!" He stepped away from the machine.

Ellwanger groaned. This time he formed an actual word out of his anguished sounds: "Lord?"

Faris wrapped both hands around his gun. "Is that true?" he yelled at Hesse, who smiled grimly.

"Yes."

All of a sudden, the last puzzle pieces fell into the right slots. "You planned all of this!" Faris wheezed. "That's why you're playing these games with me! You wanted to keep your hands clean! You wanted to use me to trigger the last bombs."

You didn't push the trigger. He heard Paul's words echo through his mind. Shit, he almost had, this time! He had been so close to stepping into Hesse's twisted plan.

"Why?" he bellowed. To his right, Laura tried to sit up.

Without breaking his smile, Hesse shrugged. "Let's call it my version of divine judgement. *If I succeed at getting you to do it, then my cause is just.* Something like that."

Faris's stomach did a somersault. He shook his head. "All of this is so personal, Niklas," he said quietly.

"Personal? Oh! True. Know what, when I think about it, I resent you for having SURV. All of you and your fucking self-righteousness, which makes you think that you're some kind of experts on religious matters! You and her." He stared down at Laura. "Look at her! She still loves you, did you know that? And that just isn't fair! Faridah …" He fell silent, taking a breath that sounded like a sob.

Faris couldn't believe it. "You resent me for …"

"You have a team, friends, a family! You always land on your feet, regardless of what happens to you!" He seemed to really believe that! Faris almost started laughing. Hesse stretched his hands out to him. They were trembling. "I thought you'd be the perfect candidate for all this." His smile turned diabolical. "Maybe I just wanted to punish you for the fact that you have my mother's blood on your hands! You do, you know."

You have my mother's blood on your hands.

Faris felt his knees go weak. He felt an irrepressible urge to pull the trigger, and he was aware that the darkness inside of him would swallow him up if he gave in to this desire.

He took a deep breath. By this point, Laura had managed to get up onto her knees. Bent forward, she was kneeling diagonally beside the cross. It looked as if she was praying. Faris tightened his grip on the gun. He used the barrel to point at the door. "Upstairs!" he ordered.

Hesse just looked at him in bewilderment.

"Upstairs!" Faris now bellowed. Every single nerve in his body was vibrating tautly.

The journalist obeyed him without a word. They climbed the stairs, one after the other, and when they reached the halfway point, the crackling in Faris's earpiece finally stopped. He took his left hand off the gun and pressed it farther into his ear. "Ben?"

"Faris! Thank God! Under no circumstance should you …"

"Thank God?" Faris interrupted.

"Listen, under no circumstance should you turn off the monitor!" Ben said sharply. "Do you hear me? Do not turn off the monitor."

"It's okay, Ben. I didn't touch the monitor. What's up with it?"

Ben's words tumbled over each other as he now explained. "I had a funny feeling the whole time. I kept wondering why the diagram was on Alexander's computer. After all, he obviously wasn't involved with the planning of the bomb attacks. And do you know why the diagram was there? Because Hesse put it there, Faris! I thought I had disconnected the laptop from the internet when Marc brought it to me. But the bastard had built himself a back door. The file creation date revealed that the diagram wasn't installed on the hard drive until *after* we had already secured the laptop. He wanted …"

"Thanks, Ben," Faris cut him off. "You can fill me in on the rest of it later, okay?"

"Faris," Tromsdorff now joined the conversation. "Where is Hesse?"

Faris listened deep inside himself. The queasy feeling wasn't gone yet. "He's here with me. Right in front of my muzzle." The situation still felt as strangely unsettled as it had before, and Tromsdorff seemed to be entertaining the same thoughts. He didn't say anything.

"Ben." Faris ran his tongue across his lips. "How am I supposed to disarm the damned thing?"

His colleague didn't reply immediately. "Shit, I don't know, but the bomb squad is on its way to you."

In less than five minutes, the restrooms were swarming with police officers. While Hesse was arrested and Werner Ellwanger received attention, two experts from the bomb squad began their investigation of the heart monitor, in order to prevent the fatal trigger impulse that would set off the glow stick explosions across the city. One of the uniformed officers wanted to assist Laura, but Faris insisted on taking care of her himself.

"Everything's okay now," he said as he walked over to her. "I'm here."

She stood in front of him, swaying slightly. Her hands were still bound, and with the gag in her mouth and her huge eyes, the panic on her face felt like a punch.

The first thing he did was remove the gag.

"Thank you," she gasped as he loosened the ties around her wrists. Her knees then gave way, and she would have fallen if Faris hadn't caught her. For a moment, he held her as tightly as he could without hurting her. She rested her head against his chest and inhaled deeply before exhaling with a muffled groan. Just fleetingly, he indulged in the illusion that everything between them could be fixed and that they would find a way back to each other through their shared experience. But with a forceful jerk, Laura pulled away from him, and the look she shot him vaporized any hopes he might have had. He instantly knew that what had just happened would become yet another obstacle between them. He could already see the subtle accusation lurking in her eyes.

None of this would have happened if you weren't a police officer!

He braced himself against the pain that would inevitably follow this awareness.

"I'll get someone who can take care of you," he promised softly. He took a step back and motioned for the uniformed officer from earlier. As his colleague knelt down before Laura and untied the rope around her ankles, Faris returned to the airport's terminal building.

Since he had last been in here, someone had opened a large gate. Several emergency vehicles and two ambulances were standing there. They looked miniscule in this huge hall.

Faris watched as the officer led Laura out of the basement and over to one of the ambulances. The paramedic, a man wearing the bright-red gear of the fire department, reached for her arm and guided her over to a luggage carousel in the center of the space. He gently nudged her to sit down.

"She was probably sedated," Faris said. And in his mind, he added: *Take good care of her.*

Laura persistently avoided his eyes. She kept her head lowered, and her hair covered her face. Slowly, step by step, he retreated as he struggled against the overwhelming emptiness he felt inside. In order to escape it, he concentrated on the throbbing uneasiness at the back of his mind. It hadn't abated at all, and he couldn't figure out why that was. Dozens of unanswered questions were gnawing at him.

He reached for his earpiece, but there were so many loud, excited voices coming from the War Room that he suspected he wouldn't be able to get anyone's attention. So he took out the earpiece and stuck it into his pocket before pulling out his phone and calling Gitta.

"It's me," he announced as soon as she picked up.

"Faris." She almost sounded intoxicated. Elated, happy. Euphoric even. "You did it, hot shot! I could …"

Faris interrupted her. "Later, Gitta! Then you can kiss and cuddle me all you want. But right now I need you to go tell Alexander that we saved his father."

"Are you sure that he'll be happy about that?" Gitta suddenly sounded somber and skeptical.

"No clue, but he should know, don't you think?"

"Yeah, you're right." Faris heard the rapid click of her heels on the linoleum flooring outside of the War Room. "I'm on my way."

Right before Gitta unlocked the door to the interview room, she heard a strange gurgling sound.

With fingers flying, she fumbled for the key and stuck it in the lock. Her hands were trembling, and it took her a couple of tries to insert it correctly. However, she finally succeeded and turned the key. She hastily pushed open the door, and as it swung open, she caught sight of two legs dangling in the air.

"Oh, God!" Gitta whispered in horror.

After he sent Gitta off to inform Alexander Ellwanger, Faris hung up. He didn't know what he should do next. Laura had been taken off in an ambulance without glancing his way even once. Faris suddenly felt exhausted, completely and eternally exhausted. He decided to head down to the restrooms where the bomb squad was still at work examining the complicated wiring on the heart monitor.

Werner Ellwanger was still nailed to the cross, but someone had laid it on the floor, which meant that he wasn't in as much pain as before. Faris knew that a cardiac monitor would sound an alarm if even one of the electrodes was detached. They wouldn't be able to disconnect Ellwanger from the electrodes until the experts had managed to deactivate the transmission pulse.

"Why aren't you taking him off the cross?" Faris asked the paramedic. The nails that had been driven through Ellwanger's flesh looked huge. The sight of them alone turned Faris's stomach.

"We're having a hard time gauging how stable he is," was the explanation he got. The paramedic, a short, gaunt man with protruding ears pointed at the curve on the monitor. "That looks remarkably good considering how much time he has been hanging on the cross, but we don't want to run any risks. If we pull out the nails and he goes into shock, then that won't help anyone."

No one except Niklas Hesse, Faris thought grimly. In this condition, the shock could instantly kill Ellwanger, and Hesse would achieve his goal after all.

Since he didn't have anything better to do at the moment, Faris stepped closer to the camera that was still standing close to the door. He removed it from the tripod and flipped open the hinged viewscreen. A video file was open on it, and Faris hit play. It was some kind of interview. An interview with Alexander who, a picture of misery – blood-smeared and half-mad with fear –, was talking with someone he kept calling *angel*. A quiet voice off-screen provided answers to his questions, and Faris grew cold as he recognized Hesse's voice.

He heard Alexander moan: *"Are you an angel?"*

And Hesse laughed softly. *"Maybe. An emissary."*

"An emissary from God?" Alexander whispered. *"What should I do now?"*

And Hesse commanded: *"Tell me about him. Tell me everything!"*

Alexander's face winced in sheer horror.

"You monster," Faris murmured. He forwarded the video and came to a spot in which Alexander was babbling on and on about a flowerbed in the allotment garden. He cut off the camera. He no longer felt sick to his stomach. He was long past that.

With long strides, he marched back up to the terminal hall, where a couple of officers had taken Niklas Hesse into one of the former airline offices and were now guarding him with guns out. Faris angrily slammed the camera against the reporter's chest.

"Why this, on top of everything else?" he barked. "Why did you make Alexander jump through all your hoops?"

Hesse just laughed. He was sitting in a rickety plastic chair, and the camera had fallen into his lap. "I think you should take a closer look at the flower beds in Daddy's little garden."

"What will we find there?" Stars danced behind Faris's eyelids whenever he blinked.

"Didn't you watch the whole video?" With his cuffed hands, Hesse reached for the camera and held it out to Faris.

He accepted it. "Tell me!"

Hesse ignored the demand, but didn't shift his gaze from Faris's eyes. "Who's the monster here?" Hesse asked, now speaking quite softly. "Justice, Faris. That's what this is about." With a shrug, he continued: "We didn't finish our conversation earlier."

Faris didn't feel the least need to do that, but he nonetheless exclaimed: "Talk!"

"I learned that Werner Ellwanger was my father from my mother's papers. I visited him." He chuckled, but this time it sounded sad.

Resigned. "I honestly thought I was finally getting a family. That was just a few months after Faridah had died in that miserable barrage of stones." He took a breath, trembling. "Two days after my mother had been bombed out of existence by that religious fanatic."

Faris decided not to bring up the fact that the museum attacker had detonated his bomb for reasons other than religious zeal. That was just another of the absurdities in this case, he thought. It had been a non-religiously motivated attack that had driven Hesse off the deep end and inspired him to take up his crusade against all the world's religions.

"But I sadly realized that my father was a religious maniac, a man who had psychologically abused his son for years. Alexander was just as mad as he was." Hesse sniffed. "Did you know that he thought I was an angel, that first time I showed up at their door? At first, it was a test. I just wanted to find out how crazy Alexander was. When I realized that his fanaticism was full blown enough for him to actually crucify his father, my plan for all this fell into place."

His gesture encompassed the entire airport. All at once, he no longer looked merely calm. He straightened his shoulders, and his face radiated a feeling that annoyed Faris. He suddenly looked ... satisfied.

For some reason, the video up on the screen gave Jenny goosebumps. The first words of the conference motto stood in blood-red letters up on the large screen.

The Word of God

Suddenly chaos broke out in the crowd, and police officers stormed through the stadium's entrances.

"What's going on?" Dennis mumbled. He now removed the arm he had slipped around Jenny's waist earlier.

"Ladies and gentlemen," a voice announced over the stadium's loudspeaker, "due to an unforeseen turn of events, we are asking you to promptly make your way to one of the exits. Please remain calm. You are not in danger."

Jenny's hand flew up to her mouth. She watched as the crowd began to move toward the exits. There was pushing and shoving in some spots, but the event organizers and the police had the situation under control. Working in coordination, they prevented panic from breaking out. When Jenny was only a few steps away from the exit, she noticed that the glow sticks were being collected from all of the worshippers.

Her blood turned to ice. She immediately sensed that something bad was about to happen.

The image up on the big screen started to flicker. The red letters faded.

For a moment, the picture was black.

And then the video started up again.

Hesse's self-satisfied expression pushed Faris over the edge. He was suddenly no longer able to keep himself under control.

He rushed forward, grabbed Hesse's collar, and yanked him up onto his feet.

"Come with me!" he snarled, and before the other officers could intervene, he dragged Hesse out the door and toward the top of the stairs. "You're going to tell the men downstairs how they can cut off the transmission signal!"

As they stepped into the restroom, they found the two medics working frantically. The beeping on the heart monitor had accelerated drastically and was now a shrill staccato.

"Shit!" one of the medics exclaimed. "He's crashing!" Feverishly pulling out a syringe, he inserted it into Ellwanger's arm.

The explosives experts looked as if they had all the time in the world. They didn't lift their heads but remained focused on their efforts to disable the transmitter. Their heads were leaning over the opened guts of the monitor, and they were whispering to each other.

"Right or left?" one of them asked the other. He was holding a small pair of wire cutters and moving it back and forth between two thin wires. "The odds are fifty–fifty."

"Just stay calm," the other replied. His words and unruffled voice stood in such stark contrast to the medic's flurry of activity that Faris had to shake his head.

"Something here isn't right," he heard the medic say. The beeping slowed down for a moment, then sped up again.

Faris wrenched his concentration back onto Hesse. The unease he had felt before now returned. He slowly reached a hand under his jacket and felt for the gun that he had stuck there after the reporter's arrest.

Hesse saw him, and his eyebrows rose slightly. Faris suddenly registered the heightened tension between him and Hesse, and he tightened his grip on his gun. A chirping sound broke the silence, and Faris winced in surprise. He pulled his hand back out from under his jacket, and without taking his eyes off Hesse, he answered his phone.

It was Gitta.

"Alexander is dead," she said. She sounded as guilty as if she herself had been the cause.

"What happened?" Regret flooded Faris's body, and for a moment, he was so distressed that the paramedics' flurry of activity and the sudden excited murmuring of the explosives officers retreated into the background. He had wished something different for Alexander, had hoped that the young man would someday successfully work through everything that had happened here and possibly lead a relatively normal life.

"He hanged himself," Gitta reported. "With his shoelaces." He could hear the tears in her voice.

"There's nothing you can do about it," Faris declared.

"Damn it!" a paramedic exclaimed. "This heartbeat ..."

Faris turned his back on the group.

Gitta sighed. "I know. But still ..." She told him goodbye and hung up.

The paramedic's eyes darted in bewilderment from Werner Ellwanger to the heart monitor. Faris pocketed his phone. "Your brother hung himself in his cell," he informed Hesse.

The reporter didn't respond immediately, but then began to laugh. "Judas!" he wheezed. "Just like Judas!"

He stopped laughing just as abruptly as he had started. His eyes showed amusement. "Say it yourself. It's totally absurd!" For several seconds, he giggled unstably, and then his expression turned to one of cunning. "Alexander was the last victim but one," he said.

After that, everything happened at the speed of lightning.

The beeping on the monitor accelerated again, becoming a swirling, panicked staccato. Hesse swiftly shook his shoulders, which momentarily puzzled Faris. But then the blood in his veins turned to ice. A small black box slid out of Hesse's sleeve into his hand. The reporter fumbled with it, and Faris aimed his gun.

The shot echoed through the tiled room.

A red spot bloomed at the center of Hesse's chest. The beeping of the heart monitor sped up.

Hesse looked down at his chest in astonishment, then lifted his head. Triumph glittered in his eyes. The black box slipped through his fingers and clattered to the floor. As the reporter staggered, Faris realized that the box was actually a remote transmitter.

Lilly! a voice screeched in his mind.

"Shit!" shouted one of the two bomb experts.

With both hands, Hesse tore open his shirt, and at first, Faris didn't understand what the pale dots on his chest meant. But then the realization spread through his veins like ice water, and as Hesse collapsed, Faris understood.

They were electrodes.

The beeping on the medical device went crazy.

"Fifty–fifty!" the bomb tech yelled.

Faris couldn't take his eyes off of Hesse's face as his life ebbed away.

And then, Hesse was dead.

And as the beeping turned into a long, prolonged screech, Faris Iskander dropped his gun and sank to his knees.

EPILOGUE

A ticking time bomb.

That was the accusation Faris saw in Dr. Geiger's face that evening, when he was sitting across from her in an interview room at Keithstraße.

"You almost screwed everything up," she said. She was standing in the center of the room, and the way she had crossed her arms didn't completely conceal the pressure she seemed to be under. "If Officer Kellner from the bomb squad had picked the wrong wire to cut right before Hesse died, we'd all be outside right now, sweeping up a ton of rubble."

All Faris could do was shrug. Over the past few hours of questioning, he had had to bear up under the same accusations, and he no longer had it in him to resist. How could he have guessed that the heart monitor was linked to Hesse and not Werner Ellwanger? He simply hadn't known – and could not have. He honestly didn't care if Geiger kicked him out to the curb. He closed his eyes and gazed into the chasm inside himself, to see if Hesse's death had made it any deeper.

He couldn't tell.

"Cases like this take a team effort," he said placidly, recalling that Tromsdorff had said the same thing to him. If they were lucky, the powers upstairs would view it the same way, and SURV would be protected for at least a while from Geiger's meddling.

Geiger untangled her arms. She held her hand out expectantly.

"Your weapon."

"I handed it in hours ago," he mumbled. "I assume there's no point in asking when I might get it back again?"

Geiger shrugged. Her normally perfectly styled hair looked slightly tousled.

Faris stood up. "Are we done now?" He was suddenly sick and tired of all this!

She blinked several times rapidly. "For now," she said coolly.

Before Faris set off for home, he decided to make a quick stop at the War Room. For some reason, he felt a need to sit for a few minutes at his old desk and to say farewell to Paul.

Several hours had passed since the deployment, and he actually didn't expect to find anyone around, but to his amazement, the team was all there. Tromsdorff and Gitta. Shannon, Ben and Marc. As if they couldn't actually believe that they had managed to avert the catastrophe, the team – his team – was still sitting together and talking.

"Good grief," he exclaimed. "Don't you all have homes to go to?"

Gitta jumped up and rushed at him, bracelets jangling. Making good on his promise on the phone, she hugged him so tightly that all of the bruises and injuries he had sustained over the past day and a half protested with dull pain.

"Ouch!" he said, and Gitta took a concerned step back. He smiled at her. "Gotcha!"

She laughed and took a playful swing at him. "Idiot!"

"I love you too!" With a groan, he sank into a chair that Shannon pushed toward him. His eyes came to rest on Paul's empty spot. "Why are all of you still here?"

"Believe me, I sent them all home to sleep," Tromsdorff declared. "But none of us wanted to go quite yet. We wanted to first find out how you were doing. Besides, we thought you might like to hear what we found out."

Faris's eyes traveled along the row of tired faces. Each of them had achieved the impossible over the previous hours. A warm feeling of belonging started to glow inside him, lessening the blow of Paul's death just a little. He gave a half smile. "Okay. Out with it!"

It was Shannon who started. "I don't think we need to spend much more time talking about Hesse, do we?" And yet she did so anyway. "I looked into his mother, Ludmilla Mechow. She was a conservative Catholic, a religious bigot of sorts. She could never make her peace with Hesse's existence. When he was five, he was taken into a children's home. Over the course of his childhood, his greatest wish was to have a real family. When his lover was killed in Afghanistan, he lost his grip on reality. However the catalyst for his actions was Ludmilla's death in the bombing at the Klersch Museum. As a result of her death, he learned about his father, contacted him, and, tragically, found in him a much worse fanatic than his mother had been." She paused and silently studied Faris for a moment. "Hesse was a highly manipulative character. The video he made of Alexander underneath the cross indicated that. He took pleasure in having his half-brother under his complete control. And hey! He stuck the electrodes onto himself so that you would blame yourself for setting off the bombs."

"Why did he make the video?" Faris asked.

"He obviously wanted to make a statement to the tune of 'Look at all the bad things religions do!'"

"Did Ellwanger really murder his wife? Hesse hinted at that."

Tromsdorff nodded. "They've found her body. She was buried under a flower bed in his allotment garden. We are looking into the motive, but she had probably threatened to take Alexander away from him at some point. At least, that's what Alexander said on the video."

"Jesus Christ!" Shannon murmured. "When I think about how Alexander must have felt to be caught in that harsh spotlight that Hesse pointed at him. He seems to have thought that it was some kind of angelic aura."

For a moment, the team members were wrapped in their own thoughts. "I'd be interested to know if he gave Alexander any kind of narcotics, to make him easier to manipulate."

It was possible, Faris thought. He had seen Alexander in the video, and the young man had definitely not been right in the head. But right now there was something else that interested Faris more than the question about drugs.

"How is Werner Ellwanger doing?" he asked.

"He's alive, and he will be tried for the murder of his wife, as well as his abuse of Alexander." Shannon sounded satisfied.

Faris nodded. "Good!" And then something totally different crossed his mind. Laura. He pulled out his phone. During the long hours of his interviews, he had turned it off. He turned it back on now and waited for a moment to see if he had missed any calls.

Several had come in, but none from Laura. His sister Anisah had called him, though. His fellow officers had contacted his family to assure them that Faris was safe. He would discuss everything else with Anisah and the others later on.

Laura, on the other hand …

"The transmitter that Hesse was holding …" he began, but he couldn't finish the question that was burning in his mind.

However Tromsdorff understood. He nodded. "The officers told me that it would have detonated the glow stick he had left for Lilly to find."

Faris lowered his head. "Okay," he whispered. If he hadn't fired, Lilly would now be dead. And yet, he wasn't sure that this knowledge would make it easier for him to work through everything that had happened. He simply couldn't get the image of Niklas dying out of his mind. That, and one other image. His memory of the earlier Niklas – the Niklas who had been full of vigor and idealism.

Faris tried to rub the weariness out of his burning eyes. When he had been taken to Keithstraße for questioning, his colleagues assured him that Laura was doing well. That was all he needed to do. When she felt a need to talk to him about what had happened, she would reach out to him. And yet, he was certain that this would never happen. He held back a sigh and stuck his phone back into his pocket.

For a moment, his thoughts flashed to Ira Jensen. "How could Hesse talk to me simultaneously on two different lines?" he asked. He was thinking about how he had driven to the internet café. He had been talking with the caller, while on his burner phone he had warned Hesse about his own bomb. For the first time, he realized how brilliant the reporter's gambit had been.

Ben cleared his throat. "Technically, that wasn't difficult. For example, there are programs that can imitate your voice when you input words via a keyboard. Hesse was a journalist. He could easily type and chat with you at the same time."

"We have now finished analyzing the recordings of the various calls," Tromsdorff interjected. "When you were en route to the café, Hesse's replies were all delayed, just slightly. We would've picked up on that, if we'd known what we were looking for."

"We should've realized it was him earlier than we did," Faris said quietly. He was steeling himself against the impending onset of guilt. Today he hadn't pressed the button, but he had come awfully close to it.

For a long time, nobody in the room said anything, but then the others started to discuss Hesse's psyche. Shannon was still full of vim and vigor and looked as though she wanted to start writing a book about the case right away.

Faris envied her strength.

He could hardly follow the others' conversation, and at some point, their voices faded into the distance, sounding as if they were coming out of a tin bucket.

Finally, Tromsdorff ordered him to get his sorry ass over to the hospital.

He protested. "If I have to see or hear even one more heart monitor today, I'll …" He didn't finish the sentence … *blow my brains out* was what he has been about to say, but this seemed inappropriate in the circumstances.

Tromsdorff sighed. "You old jackass!" he bellowed, but cheerfully. "Then at least go home and rest up!"

The sheets in the hotel room were the color of lilacs, as was the carpet. But Jenny didn't care about that. She sank back into the clean pillow and listened to the pattering of the shower behind the bathroom door.

Her entire body felt tingly with excitement and anticipation, and she savored that feeling, which was all the stronger because she had just – barely – escaped a terrible catastrophe

After the video had restarted up on the large screen, the police officers had been very upset. Absolute panic had appeared in the eyes of the young officer standing next to Jenny.

But then … nothing happened. The young officer had looked unbelievably relieved, and after a few minutes, returned to his task of shooing people out of the stadium and relieving them of their glow sticks.

Rumors had spread rapidly through the stadium. Everyone suspected that a bomb attack had just been prevented.

The late-night service and ecumenical Eucharist had been canceled. As an alternative, Dennis took the girls to a really cool restaurant on Ku'damm. After a little while, Pia had discreetly left, and they had finally made their way to the hotel room that Dennis had reserved.

A smile flashed across Jenny's face. Dennis turned off the water in the bathroom, and he stepped into the room with only a towel wrapped around his waist. The black winged tattoo on his arm looked mysterious. With a smile, Jenny rolled over onto her side and propped her head up on her hand.

It had been an exciting day.

And it would be an even more exciting night.

The contrast between the tension of the previous hours and the unbearable silence in his small apartment was too much for him. Faris showered, then paced back and forth in his living room like a prisoner for half an hour. He called Anisah and listened for several minutes to her worried, yet relieved, barrage of words, before he managed to assure her that everything was fine with him. It took him quite a bit of effort to prevent her from immediately coming over to his apartment to take care of him.

A few minutes after hanging up, he suspected that he had made a wrong call on that. The desire to beat his fists to a bloody pulp against his walls grew and grew, and he finally couldn't take it anymore. He grabbed his jacket and rushed out of his apartment.

For some time, he wandered aimlessly through Berlin, and he eventually came to a stop in the middle of the sidewalk. A pedestrian, who almost ran into him, gave him a wide berth and shot him a disgruntled look, though he kept all thoughts to himself after catching sight of the look on Faris's face. Faris watched him round the next building, and he imagined that this man was returning home to his wife and kids. Trying not to sigh, he glanced at his watch.

The service at the Olympic Stadium had been scheduled to start right about now. Had all this negatively impacted the ecumenical effort? He had no idea, nor did he really care. Not at the moment.

He resumed his walk but stopped again before too long. His eyes fell on a small Italian restaurant that was still fairly full despite the lateness of the hour.

I have a friend. He could hear Ira's voice in his head. *Her father owns a trattoria in Charlottenburg.*

Da Rossi was printed on the sign over the door.

Faris had to smile. Had his subconscious brought him here? He studied the cozy taproom through the window. About half of the red-checkered tables were occupied. He smelled pizza and garlic, and Faris suddenly noticed that he was hungry. Ira's toast this morning was the only thing he had eaten during the past forty hours.

He patted his inside jacket pocket. He had his wallet with him.

After brief deliberation, he stepped inside the small restaurant. A young woman with a side ponytail greeted him cheerfully. "Table for two?" she asked. Jasmin, he assumed. He shook his head. "I'm alone."

She looked around, thinking. A short flight of steps to the left of the entrance led up to another level. There were four tables up there, and no one was sitting at them. Faris felt a little stab of disappointment. Had he actually hoped to run into Ira here?

He followed the young woman up the steps to one of the tables. "I'll bring you a menu right away," she said. "Would you like to order something to drink?" A waist-high wall separated this part of the restaurant from the rest of it and gave this section a cozy, secluded feeling. A woman's jacket was draped over one of the chairs at the adjacent table, but no purse was in sight. Obviously, the woman who was sitting up here had stepped into the restroom. A half-drunk glass of red wine was on the table.

Faris stared at it for a moment, thinking quickly. "Bring me a glass of wine please," he said.

"Dry?"

He had no idea if he liked dry wines. He didn't know if he even liked wine at all, but he nodded.

The young woman vanished. A server appeared shortly afterwards, bringing him his order. He took the glass and stared into the dark red, shimmering liquid, hesitant to try it.

"I thought you didn't drink alcohol," a familiar voice suddenly said.

Faris looked up from his glass. Ira was standing next to him. She looked fresh and calm, like someone you could lean on. He resisted the urge to jump up and wrap his arms around her.

"A pastor once told me that in her faith wine represented belonging," he replied.

"Sounds like a smart woman." She didn't ask if he minded her joining him, but simply moved her glass over from the adjacent table. She then pulled out the second chair at his table and sat down. She toasted Faris, but didn't drink. "What brought you here?" A rosy flush spread across her cheeks. "Oh God!" she exclaimed. "Don't tell me you found the business card!"

Faris looked at her in bewilderment. "Which business card?" He didn't know anything about a business card.

"I left you a ..." She quickly waved this off. "It's okay!" She raised her glass slightly. Relief was written across her face, and the flush on her cheeks slowly faded.

He clinked his glass against hers and took a sip. The wine trickled, warm and strangely soothing, down his throat. He felt as if he needed to say something smart.

"Maybe it was your God who brought me here," he murmured.

She gazed at him for a long moment before shaking her head. "Or fate."

"Isn't that the same thing?"

She shrugged and set her glass carefully onto the checkered tablecloth. "God. Fate. Maybe we no longer need constructs like these, after what we went through today."

He didn't know what to say to this. He considered his options. "I'm glad you're here," he admitted.

Ira was quiet for a moment. "Shouldn't you be at home, resting from your concussion?" She started to spin her glass on the table and suddenly looked self-conscious.

"I tried."

"For how long?"

A smile was making its way up to his face. He could feel it. It felt as warm as the wine in his stomach. "An eternity! Half an hour."

She laughed, and it was good to see her do it. He took another sip.

"You saved the city from a terrible catastrophe today," she said. "Will you be publicly thanked for this?"

He shrugged. "Maybe, maybe not. My boss wants to close the unit I work for."

"You aren't serious!" Ira's eyes widened. She had very expressive eyes.

"Could we talk about something else?" he asked. "I actually came in here to forget about all that for a while."

Ira gave this some thought, and he felt like she was on the verge of pointing out to him how destructive it was to suppress things. But she didn't, and he was grateful for that.

Instead she pointed at his wrist with a smile. "You took off the bracelet."

Surprised, he followed her gaze. He had. Reaching into his jacket pocket, he felt the worn leather on the bracelet. At some point during his aimless walk through the city, he must have removed it. His thoughts flew briefly to Laura.

"That's a shame!" Ira said. "I liked it."

He shrugged. *Someday*, he thought, *I might tell her the truth about what's printed on it.*

Lightning Source UK Ltd.
Milton Keynes UK
UKHW040856280921
391315UK00003B/380